"Keith Brooke's *Genetopia* is a biotech fever dream... Masterfully written, this is a parable of difference that demands to be read, and read again"
**Stephen Baxter**

"I am so here! *Genetopia* is a meditation on identity — what it means to be human and what it means to be you — and the necessity of change. It's also one heck of an adventure story. Snatch it up!"

**Michael Swanwick**

"*Genetopia* is beyond any facile summary, a minor masterpiece that should usher Brooke at last into the recognized front ranks of SF writers."

*Locus*

"[*Genetopia*] is a marvelously rich book about what it means to be human and where we'll go in the future ... It's a book that makes you think and that makes it a book worth reading."

*SFRevu*

# KEITH BROOKE

# THE ACCORD

SOLARIS

First published 2009 by Solaris
an imprint of BL Publishing
Games Workshop Ltd
Willow Road
Nottingham
NG7 2WS
UK

*www.solarisbooks.com*

ISBN-13: 978 1 84416 710 4
ISBN-10: 1 84416 710 0

10 9 8 7 6 5 4 3 2 1

A CIP catalogue record for this book is available from the
British Library.

Designed & typeset by BL Publishing

Printed and bound in the UK.

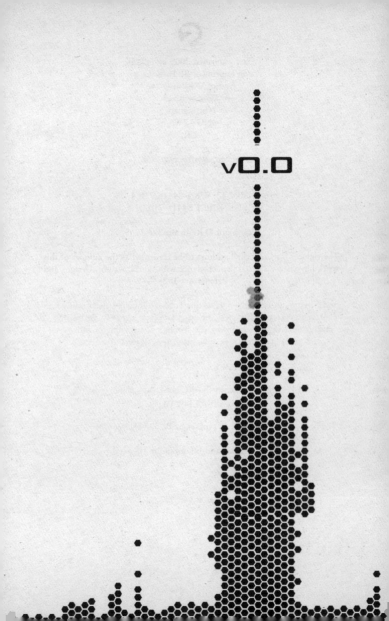

v0.0

# 0.01

LAST NIGHT I dreamed. The same old dream. The same old dream, and different every single time.

You... laughing, fooling around. To see you so liberated, so *you*, is a blessing in itself. I hardly need more, although... I always need more. You take my hand, lead me down to the river. Long sleek cruisers line up like toys along the far shore. A rank of needle towers, each sixty storeys high, scrapes the sky beyond them.

We walk. And talk, of childhood, of writing in chalk on the pavement outside your house, of tying skipping ropes between gate and lamp post to snare passers-by. Of the local beach, childhood playground, childhood escape, shaggy dunes alternating with craggy chalk extrusions, a row of white coastguards' cottages facing the sea. That childhood, long before you were elected, long before you married the man who controls us both.

You will take me there one day. You tell me that, in the dream, the same old, different old dream.

NOAH BARAKH TUCKED his head low against the drizzle and walked. The river loured, flat and grey to his left, a scattering of tour boats lining the far shore, a single, half-constructed needle tower clawing a vertical, dark slot out of the city skyline. All around, people pressed, hurried, coats slick, breath steaming.

Noah didn't like to come to the city. As one of the pre-eminent v-space architects of the time, Noah, if anyone, should be adept at remote working, and his studio out in the wild Essex flood-marshes was normally his chosen place to pursue his labours.

But some days there was still no substitute for an old-fashioned flesh-meet, and this was one of those days.

The fact that Electee Priscilla would be at the Complex was irrelevant. Noah ducked lower against the rain, kept walking, dodging puddles and pedestrians and spray from passing traffic. And smiling, smiling at the pain and longing that loomed large over every aspect of his miserable, world-changing, epoch-making little life.

The doors slid open for him, greeted him cheerily; there was always a welcome for Professor Barakh. He walked into the lift and closed his eyes to deal with mail while he was whisked up to the fifth floor.

She was there already, talking intensely with Warrener, but as the door opened she looked up. Her eyes met Noah's briefly, a smile pulled at her mouth, and then she was talking again, her sentence barely interrupted. Noah and Priscilla were colleagues, she the electee overseeing the project, he the advisor, the consultant, the architect. There was nothing more to it than that. There could not be – she had made that much clear already.


"WE ARE BUILDING it," Noah reiterated. "It is an incremental process. With all the computational power in the world, we could not push the process much faster than we do currently."

"We run and re-run realities all the time," said Priscilla, leaning towards him across the wide meeting table. He had explained that to her months ago: so many realities needed in order to build consensus!

Noah's attention was caught by the charms hanging from a delicate silver chain around her neck. He had kissed that neck, he knew its taste, knew the soft gasp she gave in response to the touch of his lips, his teeth, his tongue. But he did not, had not. Could not.

"We do," said Noah. "It is the process. Consensual reality, however, is of a different order of magnitude. It will come when consensus has been reached, a critical mass of realities, an accord, if you will." He smiled, realising that it was the first time he had spoken the name aloud, the label the media were applying to the project: the Accord, the consensual reality that would leave all other VRs behind, a reality built from the mass of human experience, a super-city of the mind, a reality where humankind could live on after death.

Noah was its principal architect; he and his team were building the Accord. Noah Barakh knew that he would go down in history as the man who built heaven.

And every night he ran and re-ran realities, private realities, a consensus of one.

Priscilla nodded. "I'm not pushing you, Professor Barakh," she said softly, her blue eyes locked on his. "I am being pushed."

In his head she pinged him, one to one, a warm hug, a friendly embrace. She didn't mean to come down on him like this, he knew.

She did not need to mention the trillions of euros that had been sunk into this, but she mentioned them still. She did not even need to push him. Noah Barakh would deliver the Accord: they all knew that. But still, they had to jump through the political hoops, and minuted records of these meetings helped tick boxes in Brussels and Shanghai.

WE SIT IN a Seventeenth-century pub by the water. This time, this dream, we are out on the coast, a broad Essex creek laid out before us through the windows. Yachts stand higgledy-piggledy on the exposed mud, wading birds scuttle and probe, dogs walk their owners in an age-old routine.

We have just kissed across the table. We have spent the morning making love, sunlight streaming into our room above the bar.

Your hand is on the table. I cover it with mine.

"You were so shocked!" you say, chuckling. "Even though we had always flirted like that."

"Not like that," I say.

That day, the day we are laughing about, was the day we had crossed the line. Fleetingly. For the shortest of times we had been more than electee and consultant.

"You asked and I answered!" you say, mock-indignant.

"I asked what was on your mind, you seemed distracted."

"I was. It was a revelation to me, a paradigm shift: that moment when you changed from Professor Barakh to *oh my!* Something about the look in your eye just then, the way you held my gaze a moment too long..." You smile, reliving that moment, as we do so often.

"You didn't put it quite like that."

Your smile broadens. "So I was more succinct."

"You said you were imagining fucking me like there was no tomorrow."

You look down. "I shouldn't have said that."

"You should."

I dream of you. I always dream of you. I make sure that I do. I am the architect of Accord: I can run reality. I can run realities.

NOAH HAD BEEN hooked into pre-consensus Accord for most of the day. Emerging was a disorientating experience. He had been walking the streets of a consensual Manhattan, downing bourbon with a faux-Dylan Thomas in the White Horse, unconvinced as ever by the quality of the reconstruct. That was not what consensual reality was all about in any case: it was a consensus of the living, of the yet-to-die. Already, the Accord was being built from the consensus of over a million souls, and the project teams were adding more every day, batched up and re-batched into assorted realities, fractal fragments of what would become consensus. Poor

Dylan was a gimmick, a toy to amuse the electees and the media, and all he had was virtual whiskey and a way with words with which to defend himself.

Noah rose from his chaise longue and walked slowly to the window. Marie was down at the end of the garden, hacking at a rambling rose.

Noah swallowed, turned his gaze away, stared unfocused at the distant marshes; ribbons of silver water snaked through hard mud matted with samphire and purslane.

He should not feel this way. He had done nothing wrong. He had not betrayed Marie, had not once laid a finger on another woman. On *the* other woman. Priscilla. Not once.

He turned his back on the window.

He had betrayed Marie many times. He had the guilt many times over. He was betraying her now, always, repeatedly.

He closed his eyes: mail from Elector Burnham. Priscilla must have reported back to him by now, even though Noah had given her little to report. The elector would want hard dates, commitments, a precise measure put on the unquantifiable... When do you know that heaven has been built? When do you know it is time to open the gates? Noah knew they were close, but the gut feeling of an artist of the uber-real was not adequate for Burnham's needs.

He opened his eyes, left the mail unviewed. Let them think he was lost in his work.

He sank back onto the chaise, and was immediately back in the data-shell of the Accord. It was time to reload. Those who chose to live on in the Accord after death would only do so as the last-recorded instance of themselves – the final minutes, hours, days would be lost forever, all the way back to their last upload... always working from the last snapshot of the soul. Noah had not uploaded for most of a month, preferring to let instances of himself continue to play out their existence in the Accord realities in which he had placed them. But now it really was time to reload, before anyone spotted what he had been doing.

He drifted, allowed himself to be read for change, development, difference, so that the new him would overlay any previous instances.

Outside the window, Marie sang an old pop song, something about love, always something about love.

THAT TIME... WEEKS before. She should never have said what she did, her words the gentle flutter of the butterfly's wings.

"You look distracted... What's in your thoughts?" he had asked Priscilla.

They were in the research unit in Bethnal Green, leaning close, drinking tea, peering into multiple overlays of data on the widescreen display. Noah had been trying to explain the concept of fractal realities, how they would ultimately combine to form a super-reality, an over-reality, an entire virtual universe in which the dead could live again. She understood, he knew. She was just playing dumb, teasing him, toying with him. But then... then she had paused, her eyes locked with his. Something had changed. He had thought for a moment that she was struggling with the pressure again, the expectations, but then... no, there was something else in her look, something new.

"You really want to know?"

He nodded.

"You sure?"

Noah sensed boundaries being pushed, lines being redrawn. He nodded again.

"I'm thinking, well fuck, I'm thinking, Christ, I'd like to screw that man like there's no fucking tomorrow."

Noah stared. He felt his skin prickling with unexpected heat. He felt his throat suddenly dry, his heart racing. He stared. *I love you*, he thought. He had always loved her, from the very first day.

"And now you're thinking, Christ, how do I get out of this awkward, embarrassing situation with the woman who is ten years my senior and controls my budget, aren't you?" She looked away now, down, into her steaming tea.

"No," he said softly. "I'm thinking how much I would like to kiss you right now, even though there are people in the room. I'm thinking how beautiful your eyes are – how here I am, a man trying to create perfection but who has perfection sitting right at his side. And finally, I'm thinking, Christ, yes, yes, please do fuck me like there's no tomorrow."

Warrener strode across from his console just then. "The Shanghai question?" he asked Noah.

"Hnh? Oh... Shanghai. They can wait, can't they?"

Warrener gave him a funny look and then turned away. But by then the moment was lost and Priscilla was staring into the distance, dealing with mail, moving on.


THAT BUTTERFLY FLUTTER, the grit in the oyster shell, the spark before the forest fire...

Noah tried to carry on as normal, but his normal had been abruptly redefined by that brief exchange. It didn't help that his had become largely a monitoring and waiting role, the architecture in place, the information infrastructure built. Teams around the world were coordinating the effort of uploading humankind en masse into the countless fragments of virtual reality that would, one day soon, coalesce into a single consensus.

But Noah's role was little more than overseer for now: watching for signs that consensus had emerged. When it did, so the theory went, a super-reality would be formed, one strictly bound by the algorithms and protocols of consensus, of what *is*. Everyday reality is a collective-conscious interpretation of physical phenomena – colour isn't colour, it's just a shared set of rules for how we interpret different wavelengths of electromagnetic radiation. Consensual reality is a collective interpretation of *non*-physical phenomena, a synergy of the perception and recall of massed humankind.

Noah and his teams had built those fragments of reality where the protocols were emerging. They built and rebuilt realities all the time.

And now... the butterfly flutter, the mote, the spark...

Noah Barakh could build realities. He was the architect of Accord.

He could build his own private realities...

WE MEET ON the South Bank, by the Dali sculptures – the elephant with multiple-jointed, stilt-like legs, the split torso with the embedded spider.

"Noah?" Your voice tilts up, quizzical. You're curious, unsure why I've asked you here. "What is it? What's the big secret that we can't meet at the Unit, or at my office?" You glance upriver as you say that, towards Parliament.

"May we walk?" I ask, and set off towards the London Eye, the refurbished Ferris wheel rotating almost imperceptibly.

It is sunny, a gentle breeze from across the water, a babble of people all around, jugglers and human statues plying their arts across the wide walkway by the Thames.

You take my arm, a thing you would do with anyone and yet intimate still. The pressure of your hand on my arm, the rhythm of your walk, give me heart.

"This is not real," I tell you. "We are in a fragment of pre-consensus simulated reality. You and I are the most recently warehoused snapshots of our selves."

You look away. It jars to be told such things: it is an affront to consensus – if we do not believe this is real, then Accord will never emerge.

"I can tell you another truth, too."

You look at me again.

"You want to fuck me like there's no tomorrow."

Your mouth opens. You make as if to speak, then stop, then laugh. Finally, you say, "I can't remember the last time I have been so lost for words, Noah."

"You do not remember," I explain. "A week after the copy of you that is instanced in this reality was made and warehoused, you and I spoke... of this. You told me that you felt this way, and I told you that I felt the same way about you. That I *feel* the same way."

You're watching me closely. "You're telling me we're lovers, Noah?"

I shake my head. "We cannot," I tell you. "You are married to Elector Burnham. I am married to Marie. We cannot."

"No..." you say. "We could never..."

"But here," I say. "Here it is all so different. Here it is as different as we choose it to be."

"No... Noah, I'm sorry, but... this isn't a game." You put a hand on your chest. "I feel real. I *am* real. And I am married, Noah. And so are you. What about Marie? You love her, don't you? You told me you love her. Noah, I'm sorry, but this isn't going to happen."

I AM NOAH Barakh. I am the architect of Accord. I build realities. I run them. I rerun them.

"YOU'RE TELLING ME we're lovers, Noah? That we actually crossed that line?"

I shake my head. "Not out there," I tell you. "Not in the world. But here – here we can live out our dreams. We can explore, Priscilla. We can cross the line from friendly flirtation to lovers to wherever that may lead us. Here we can *be*."

You lower your head. "No... Noah, I'm sorry..."

YOU LOWER YOUR head and look up at me.

"I..." You stop. You start again: "I... I guess..."

\* \* \*

IT WAS NEARLY two weeks before their next encounter. Noah had mailed Priscilla, gently reminding her of their conversation, prompting her but not pressing. Priscilla had not replied.

He walked into the crowded boardroom and seated himself at one of the few remaining places.

Electee Priscilla was already there. She caught his look immediately, held it.

Noah swallowed, looked away.

A short time later, Elector Burnham entered the room and the meeting could begin. Afterwards, there was coffee and Noah mixed with the attendees until finally his path crossed that of Priscilla.

"You know that we can't," she told him, cutting straight to the point. "It's impossible."

"Can't?"

"Like there's no tomorrow," she said. "Or like anything."

"You have changed your mind? You have decided that there is nothing between us, after all?"

She locked his gaze. "Not one bit," she said.

"So...?"

"Darling!" A smile broke out across her features and she turned and kissed Elector Burnham on the cheek, one hand resting lightly, briefly, on his chest.

"Elector," said Noah, bowing his head.

Burnham studied him with narrowed eyes for a moment and then smiled, and said, "Noah, you old code monkey! When're you going to be finished, eh? Heaven can't wait forever."

Later, as the crowded room started to thin, Noah got Priscilla alone again. "So tell me," he said, "why is it impossible?" He did not know why he asked, why he pushed – he had never done anything like this before, had never been so compelled.

She raised her eyebrows. "Because I am a respected electee and you a high-profile v-space architect, and if it ever got out we would both be ruined. Because I am married to a man who is not only one of our state's five electors, but an utterly ruthless bastard into the bargain. He would destroy you. He would destroy us both. And not least, Noah, because you are married too – had you forgotten that?"

"I have never done anything like this before. I have never wanted to…"

"And you won't. Not with me. I'm sorry, Noah. I should never have said what I did. It simply is not possible."

Noah smiled then… "But it is," he said. "It is."

I TAKE YOU to New York, make you walk half the length of Manhattan – the only way to see it properly. We take the ferry from Battery Park out to the Statue of Liberty and climb up inside to look back upon the city. I kiss you there. Kiss you while you look back upon the city of my birth. We cross Brooklyn Bridge on foot, heading ultimately for the Heights. We both marvel and laugh at the aches and pains and fatigue we are suffering from all the walking. "This is a reality," I remind you. "It is *meant* to feel real!"

I am showing you my childhood haunts, distant memories as they are for me. You want to know it all, everything about me. You want to get inside my head, find the real person that I am. I have never known anything like this, an all-consuming passion to share. You know me so well already. It is a continuing cause of wonder to me that since we started this thing, we each of us have discovered a person, a lover, hidden inside the public person we already knew, and that the private you, the private me – we really are two halves of a single whole.

How could we ever have known that it would be like this? How could we ever have known what we might have been missing if we had turned away, accepting the impossibility of our relationship?

You stop me halfway across Brooklyn Bridge. I think it is to do the tourist thing and stare back at the view of the Manhattan skyline, but no: you take my face in your hands and kiss me long and hard.

"Thank you," you say, in such a quiet voice, your head now resting sideways on my shoulder, your eyes distant.

I raise an eyebrow. "Why?"

"Just... thank you."

You take my hand and we resume our walk. Almost at the far side, you smile at me and say, "Will you come and see where I grew up one day? I'll take you, show you everything."

I smile. We will do that.

EVERYTHING IS NEW, fresh. I have been reborn, but reborn whole, adult, myself. I have been reloaded.

I am in my studio, rising from the chaise longue. I am in a reality, I know, one of the fractal realities that will contribute to consensus. Out in the garden, you are there. Priscilla. My love. The other half of me.

I remember you telling me that it wasn't to be – that "we" could never be. That it was simply not possible.

I create realities. I run and rerun realities until one day they will come together into a whole, a consensus.

In my realities we can be free; we can be us. We can be.

In my realities we can explore the selves that we hide from the world, plot the course of our love, find out what "we" really is, and can be.

I am in my studio, rising from the chaise longue. Walking towards the French windows, pushing one open, going to greet you in the garden, in our garden, in a world where all the complications, all the responsibilities and risks and assumptions – a world where all of that is as nothing.

I have been reloaded.

I go to greet you.

* * *

"OKAY, THEN..." SHE said. She wouldn't meet his eyes and it was not simply that she was not looking directly into the cam. She would not meet his look. "Okay – come. Now. He's going back to the city for the weekend. Come to me, Noah. Prove that what you say about us is true."

Noah cut the link.

He had told her. Told her how it was, how in realities other than this, where they were able to be together, they had fallen so deeply, madly in love... gone way beyond the mutual attraction they felt now.

Finally, he had told her that he loved her – that the Priscilla he knew from meetings and consultations and social events for the project was a woman who fascinated and beguiled him.

And she had said, "Okay then..."

He pushed open the French windows of his studio, called across the garden to his wife. "Darling?" She looked. "I've been called away. London. I may be late."

She rolled her eyes and shooed him on his way. He loved her, and was surprised at his own surprise: he had always loved her. This was not about him loving or not loving Marie, it was about Priscilla, always about Priscilla.

SHE HAD TOLD him to enter by the side door, that it would be open, and so he did. He had never been to this house before – a weekend home in the heart of the North Downs granted to Elector Burnham by the state.

The house gave every impression of being unoccupied. She had told him that she and her husband had planned to be here for a quiet weekend, and that Burnham had taken his bodyguard and two assistants with him when he was called away.

Hesitantly, Noah called out, "Priscilla?" Then more loudly, "Priscilla, are you here?"

There was no response.

He almost turned away then. He could just get back into his car, slot it into auto and let it drive him home.

But he stopped. Was he scared? Scared to take that one more step, to cross the line once and for all? But that was stupid. He had crossed that line long ago, crossed it again and again in multiple fractal realities.

There was no sign of Priscilla in any of the ground-floor rooms, so he came to the stairs and, after another momentary hesitation, started to climb.

He found her in one of the bedrooms. She lay slumped on the floor, her body twisted. Blood pooled around her, staining the cream carpet almost black. Red spatters punctuated the wall and a nearby chair.

Her face was white, so deathly white, one strand of long damp hair trailing across her cheek, her eyes staring, unmoving.

The blood came from a gaping wound in her chest.

But she was breathing...

Noah rushed to her, kneeled, hot stickiness seeping through the knees of his trousers. He reached out a hand, tentatively touched knuckles to her cheek.

Her eyes moved, locked on him.

"N... Noah?" she gasped.

"My love..." He leaned close; her voice so faint.

"He found out..."

"Who found out?" But he did not need to ask. Burnham. The elector had done this.

"He was suspicious. He read my mail..."

His face was almost touching hers. His tears started to fall onto her cheek.

He kissed her. Softly, briefly, on the lips. They had never kissed before now, had barely even touched, and yet he knew her so well, knew her responses, the way she moved. He knew what they could have had, what they could have been together...

I FIND YOU out in the marshes, walking along the sea-wall, arms wrapped around yourself against the stiff easterly. You have been crying; I think you still are, although you smile when you see me.

"Noah?"

I meet your look and wait.

"Why can't we be like this in reality?"

I take you in my arms now, bury my face in your hair.

"This *is* reality," I tell you. "It is now."

You sense something. You have always been so perceptive to subtle changes in intonation, in body language.

"What's happened, Noah?"

I tell you straight. "You are dead," I say. "Burnham became suspicious, so he read your mail, found the things we had said. He killed you. He will probably get away with it – he is an elector, after all."

You understand immediately.

"Oh, Noah," you say, stroking my cheek. "You must hurt so badly."

Out in the real world: the grieving, the loss, the pain of holding the woman I love in my arms as she dies.

But there is more than that, the part you leave unspoken.

Out in the real world, I would grieve, but then I would come to terms with loss, with a love that never really was. I would move on.

With every day that passed I would move further from you.

I hold you away from me, so that you must look into my eyes. "I could not carry on without you," I tell you now. "How could I?"

Back in my studio… the drugs, they would have been quick. I took them after I had reloaded for the last time.

This is it now. This, our reality. A fractal reality, a component of the consensus that must happen very soon now, a critical mass of consensual realities that will take on a permanence of their own, a new reality. A new heaven. A new heaven for you, Priscilla, and me.

I smile. We are together. What more could we possibly want?

"You said you were going to show me," I say now.

You look briefly puzzled.

"You said you would take me there, to the place where you grew up."

Now, at last, you manage a smile. You pull away, lead me by the hand back towards the cottage, the car. Together, electee and architect await the coming of consensus, of Accord.

# 0.02

ELECTOR JACK BURNHAM emerged from the Council of Electors, aware that he had sampled a tiny fragment of heaven itself, or at least, the heaven that was being constructed under his authority.

He opened his eyes, and the first thing he saw was the back of Tate's square, shaved head. His bodyguard was looking out of the window of the sixth-floor apartment in Aldgate. Beyond him, Burnham could see the half-built needle tower he had approved the year before.

Tate turned, nodded, went to pour a cup of white tea for the elector.

Burnham closed his eyes. Elector al-Naqawi was still there, in the meetspace, a fragmental reality constructed just for today's meeting.

Burnham was curious...

AL-NAQAWI, OF ALL electors, is the most fervently sceptical. And yet he waits in the meetspace, as if he had known Burnham would return. He dips his black-turbaned head in acknowledgement as Burnham steps through the sideways-scrolling doorway and reappears before him.

"My condolences," he says.

Burnham nods. "My thanks, Sayyid," he says.

"They have found the man who did this thing?"

Burnham doesn't allow his expression even to flicker. He looks evenly at al-Naqawi. "Barakh killed himself," he says. "He shot my wife and then he killed himself with an overdose."

"Forgive me," says al-Naqawi, "but they live on. Or at least their recorded images live on in the abomination they call the Accord."

"We do not know that," says Burnham. "The Accord had not yet reached consensus two weeks ago. There is nothing to say that they successfully transferred to a reality shard that is now part of the Accord."

"There is nothing to say that they did not."

There is silence between them for a while.

"It would be entirely understandable if you wished to pursue an investigation," says al-Naqawi. "This unhappy incident has raised concerns about the nature of the Accord: that it was created by a criminal who may, for all we know, currently be using it for refuge, is a significant concern. If you desire backing in pushing for such an investigation then I would be honoured to assist in coordinating the campaign."

Burnham nods. "Thank you, my honourable friend," he says, although al-Naqawi, while an honourable man as far as Burnham knows, is not a friend, and his motives for pledging support are nothing to do with those he has stated. "Support from you and the Front is always welcome."

Al-Naqawi and his followers have opposed the Accord project from the outset, arguing that it is an abomination, that man has no right to try to build his own heaven; that on the one hand there can only be one true heaven, and on the other it is blasphemous to even try to build an alternative.

Al-Naqawi is on shaky ground, and he knows it: he cannot argue that Barakh is fleeing justice by hiding in the Accord if he also argues for the unreality of the Accord – that it is a blasphemous shadow world, occupied by simulacra and soulless echoes. But al-Naqawi will take any opportunity to challenge the Accord, and so he could be a useful ally if Burnham chooses to pursue Barakh, or the ghost-Barakh.

Burnham bows his head. "I am still grieving," he says, and this is true. There is a cavernous hole at the heart of his existence that was once occupied by Priscilla. He loves her with a startling intensity, despite her betrayal. "I am still grieving, but I appreciate your support. We will talk again?"

Because now al-Naqawi has planted the seed, Burnham is hooked, and he knows he is hooked. Barakh is out there, somewhere. In the Accord. Whether the true Barakh really does live on in virtual heaven or it's a mere fragment of the man, an echo, he is there.

With Priscilla.

Burnham feels the ache with renewed intensity, a chill in his gut that spreads up his body, his neck, tightens his scalp. He is quite disturbed by the physicality of his emotions.

Elector al-Naqawi nods, and places a hand softly on Burnham's arm. "We will talk again, my friend."

WE DON'T MAKE it as far as your childhood home in Deanmere Gap, or even nearby Eastbourne. Reality intervenes. Or rather, *un*-reality intervenes...

We have an electric car, and there are so few other vehicles on the road that I can almost drive manually down the A22 without looking. There are many millions of personae in the pre-consensus Accord, but they are distributed right across its many fractal shards. The place is deserted. We have our own private world. Our own private worlds, for there are other instances of us uploaded, other Noahs, other Priscillas; I am the man who built heaven, who built heavens; the duplication was an inevitable result of us taking over an experimental phase to pursue our personal agenda. I ran us in parallel. All contradictions will be resolved when consensus is reached.

We find the first anomaly a few miles past Forest Row.

"What is it? What is it?" you ask me, as I pause in mid-sentence.

I stare across to the left, hands off the wheel as I let the car cruise in automatic.

"See?" I point. "The trees?"

We pass through woodland, but the trees… the detail is gone… at a glance all is fine, but stare hard at one spot and they won't resolve themselves into branches, leaves, trunks. Blocks of dark green and brown shift under scrutiny, resisting the eye's attempts to distinguish form, detail. We pass a cottage set back from the road among the trees. It is little more than a few blocks the colour of red bricks, no features visible.

"Consensus is incomplete," I say. "The warp and weft of its fabric are showing. But not to worry: it is not so much failing as unfinished. We are still in a coherent reality shard. Consensus is close, my love."

Ahead, the A22 is a smooth, featureless grey band, rough at the edges, cutting through blocks of forest colours that shift and flow. The road looks as if it has been daubed on with a palette knife. My pulse races. I understand what we are encountering, but still it is hard to control basic animal reactions to the unknowable.

We continue, and by the time we reach Wych Cross reality has returned in glorious technicolour.

A short time later, we turn off the main road, looking for a pub for lunch.

"Will there be anywhere open?" you ask, leaning forward in your seat like a little girl.

"Who knows? We might have to end up cooking for ourselves."

The Old Bull is open. We stop the car at the back in a high-walled parking area. Once out in the open we pause, embrace, your face against my shoulder. Your scent is almost overpowering, the smell of your hair, your skin.

I want the moment to last.

Instead… the trees… the limestone wall… blocks of colour, shifting, reorganising.

You gasp as I hold you tighter.

"It's okay," I tell you. "Just another anomaly. Consensus settling around us." I hope my uncertainty isn't explicit in the tone of my voice.

We enter the Old Bull through the beer garden door. We order drinks and baguettes from the barman who otherwise sits on a stool, watching the stories on a tabloid news-sheet; we find seats by the window, looking out over the empty village high street. A black and white cat prowls; a dove looks, ponders, rises in a flurry of wing-beats.

"Noah?"

You take my hand and kiss it, tenderly, slowly. We have kissed in these reality shards before; many of us have kissed many times. But this is different. This is new. We are here. We are here waiting for consensus to happen around us.

I look down. I don't know what to say at this moment. I am unaccustomed to this kind of intensity, even now.

We eat. We talk. We laugh. We hold hands across the table.

We pass through the beer garden, clinging onto each other. We pause in the car park, pull each other close, bodies pressing hard, suddenly urgent. I press you against the car, my hands exploring... hips... breasts... nipple... the curve of your waist. You pull me tight against you.

A lull, cheeks pressed together, breathing ragged.

"Noah... I love you. I love that you have done this for me, for us. I... I struggle to find the words for what you've done."

"I love you," I say. "Just those words."

We step back from the car, kiss again, softly, barely touching.

"Tell me you'll always be mine, Noah."

And then I feel the ground shift, a deep slow movement like an earthquake.

The tremor passes right through my body, resonating with my bones, making me feel as if my skeleton is about to be shaken to dust.

You clutch my arm.

"It's okay," I say. "It'll be all right."

"But *what* will be all right?" you ask. "What in fuck's name was that?"

"I think…"

Another heaving beneath.

I stumble, your hand snatched from my arm.

"I think… Priscilla? Priscilla?"

But you have gone.

I turn around and I am in a wasteland, heaps of rubble all about, great gouges in the ground, dust thick in the air.

I am alone.

Priscilla?

Priscilla? Where have you gone, my love?

BURNHAM EMERGED FROM meetspace again, opened his eyes, saw a pot of tea and a filled cup sitting on the walnut dresser to his right. He reached out. The tea was barely lukewarm to the touch.

"Tate?" he called.

While his bodyguard refreshed the tea, Burnham wandered out onto the small roof terrace. To his right, the gherkin-shaped Swiss Re building towered over the surrounding cityscape, to his left, Tower Bridge peeked through a gap between buildings.

Tate appeared with the fresh tea.

Burnham smiled. "Don't you just love this city?" he asked. "The contrast! Shabby back streets, a bridge out of Walt Disney, and that," – he waved towards the Gherkin – "an enormous sex-toy of a building! I fucking *love* it."

Tate nodded. "Shall I pour, JB?" he asked.

"Someone has to," said Burnham, "and it sure as fuck ain't going to be me."

He sat on a lounger, stretched back, hands on either arm of the seat. As soon as he closed his eyes, messages scrolled, but he blinked them away. He realised he was gripping the seat tightly, so he forced his muscles to relax and then put his hands behind his head.

So up and down! These last two weeks… his mood could swing second by second. The anger and grief he could understand – he had just lost his wife of close to twenty years, for fuck's sake – but the manic side, the amplified lust for life, it disturbed him, it seemed inappropriate, indecent. It was him, but it was a magnified version of him, almost a different *instance* of him, in Barakh's parlance, and he didn't like it.

Priscilla… why had she betrayed him? He loved her still. He missed her with every breath that he took.

He hadn't planned it. Hadn't gone there to kill her. He believed that, even though he could not explain why he had taken her gun from the dresser instead of simply snatching his own from the shoulder holster he always wore. There was nothing premeditated about that; he had not done it in order to avoid detection; it was simply the irrational act of a mind deranged by passion and rage.


BACK THEN…

The car, rolling backwards out of the driveway, Tate at the wheel, Burnham in the back more furious with himself than he had ever been in his life – for having kept control, said nothing, behaved as if all was dandy when he knew it was not. He had evidence, damn it!

He was a master of control – anyone in his position had to be – but in private… Priscilla had always said she loved the spark, the fire, the private passion that only she saw. But this time he had remained in control, desperately in control, not let anything slip.

"Stop."

The car came to a halt in the drive.

Burnham stepped out, crunched through the gravel back to the front door, let himself in, climbed the stairs, pushed at the bedroom door, suddenly tentative…

She was wearing a white robe, towelling her hair, fresh from the shower, getting herself ready, washing her husband off her hair, her body. They had screwed only an hour earlier, and she had been convincing. If he had not known otherwise he would never have guessed it was just a performance, an act. He had been performing too. He had shown passion where passion was demanded, said the right words, carried out the act... with manic control over his every action, every response.

Afterwards, they had lain in each other's arms, said nothing, as they had so often lain in each other's arms and said nothing in the past.

He looked at her now. She was still a striking woman, one who might be unkindly termed handsome rather than pretty. Slim and strong, with a firm jaw, piercing blue eyes, a sheen of copper in her dark brown hair, a sinuous, almost indecent, grace to the way she moved. As a young woman her manner had been less confident, her vitality constrained, her looks awkward and mismatched; now, she was beautiful. She really was beautiful. For a moment, Burnham forgot why he was here.

She turned, opened her mouth as if to speak, then stopped, then said, "Jack... I thought...?"

"You thought I was someone else?"

She knew. Straight away she knew. It was in her eyes. They had always communicated so well, had always seen through to the one no one else saw.

"No. I just thought you had gone. What do you mean, Jackie?"

"You thought it was Barakh. How long have you been screwing him?"

How long? The mails implied it was a recent thing, weeks at most, but the words had been ambiguous, implying far more... Months? Longer?

"He has never laid a finger on me, nor I on him."

"That's a lie. Don't take the piss, Priscilla. I've read the mails..."

"Jackie... I'm telling the truth."

Just for a moment – an instant – he believed her, wanted to believe her. They had always communicated so well. They had never lied about anything that mattered.

One time, years earlier, she had asked him if he was having an affair with one of his researchers – Kelly or Shelley or something – a nobody, a kid he could barely picture now, let alone remember her name. It had been nonsense and they had talked it through, analysed the hints and signs that had led Priscilla to suspect, demonstrated that it was coincidence, trivia, happenstance.

He wanted that to be so now. He wanted Priscilla to gently explain how he had misinterpreted the signs, the evidence, the unspoken truths.

But no.

*Jackie... I'm telling the truth.*

It was a tired defence, a defence heavy with omission.

"Jackie?"

He didn't know how it happened, but suddenly she was on the floor, lying awkwardly, and he was pulling at the top-left drawer of her dressing table, fumbling for her small handgun.

And then she was dead.

He had seen people die violent deaths before. He had worked with aid agencies after the Mexico City 'quake and the dirty bombs in Paris. Before that he had served with the pacifying forces in Algeria, Libya, Turkey. He had killed six men and one woman in the line of duty. The flashbacks would haunt him for the rest of his life.

But this was different. So different.

Priscilla's chest looked as if it had exploded. There was blood everywhere, soaking her robe, the carpet. Wet flecks had spattered Burnham's face.

She looked surprised, and it was when he saw this that he slumped to his knees and started to sob, and it was moments later that Tate appeared in the doorway, gun braced, ready to shoot.

Burnham straightened, shook off Tate's helping hands, gave his bodyguard the gun.

Outside, a sliver of sun had broken through the heavy clouds, and Burnham saw that Tate had turned the car and reversed it back into the drive, ready to depart.

Now…

"Fucking boat people!"

Elector Burnham blinked out of the message, a low-res newsfeed showing another overloaded tub crowded with people. It could have been any boat, anyplace. They were all the same. This one was a small fishing smack, straw-thin people lining its flanks, peering out at the promised land. The *refused* land. At this moment there were forty-six vessels classed as large enough to carry fifty or more passengers scattered along the south coast, and God knows how many more smaller boats. The Navy was keeping them at sea, but how long could that last? Most of Europe's border integrity forces were concentrated around the Mediterranean rim, where the problem was on a far greater scale than this.

Tate stood impassively by the windows as Burnham sat on his lounger, sipping at a cup of tea and feeling powerless. The sun soothed him, a break from the relentless rain of the past month. Burnham remembered when this kind of day had been the norm, when Britain didn't have a regular rainy season in early summer.

Days like today, he felt the burden.

How was he to stop the flood of humankind flowing around the planet in search of somewhere to eke out an existence? How could a mere politician feed the world?

"They're all going to die, aren't they?"

Tate raised an eyebrow.

"The boat people. Most of Africa. Most of the *Med*, for fuck's sake. We've gone past the point where we could stop any of this." His fellow electors had been arguing over this for years: they were living through a time when humankind was being forced to scale back. Large losses were inevitable. "It's all about survival now, isn't it?"

"I'd say it always has been, JB."

The rain started, and for long minutes Burnham sat back, eyes closed, enjoying its delicate touch on his skin, relief from the muggy London air.

"Tate?"

"Sir?"

"I want to find Barakh. I want to find out if he's hiding in the Accord. I want to find out how to get my hands on him."

Silence.

Burnham looked at Tate.

"It's okay," he said. "I'm not expecting you to hack into the system yourself. Find someone on the project team, someone who could be leaned on. I want answers. I don't care how you get them."

"Sir."


IT IS A wasteland. I walk through the rubble, staggering as aftershocks tug at the ground beneath my feet. The plain appears to go on forever. There is no variation, no distant hills, no trees or buildings, no vegetation at all. Just rock, dust, great chasms in the ground.

"Priscilla?"

My throat is sore, dry, raw from calling.

The sky is a thin grey, stained ochre by the dust, the sun veiled, harsh.

Consensus is asserting itself. The countless shards of ur-reality are drawing together, becoming integrated, becoming one.

But I am an anomaly. We are anomalies. We have multiple instances, something the protocols cannot allow. I have anticipated this though: consensus should draw my shards together, integrate me, make me one, just as it should do for Priscilla.

But…

*Priscilla?*

I am alone.

And I am lost.

I do not know where this is. Will all shards be integrated, or will some be cast adrift, abandoned? In the mathematics of complexity and chaos it is not possible to pin down the specifics of such an event. I do not know.

I fear, though. I fear that I am in a virtual cul-de-sac. That I am in lost space. Or that you are.

*Priscilla?*

THE GROUND HEAVES again. My legs go from under me and I clutch at the rocky ground, face in the dust... in the grass.

I turn, sit, and dizziness cartwheels my brain.

The sun is bright, the sky blue drifted with white.

Still dizzy... Falling through space, even though I am sitting here, not moving.

Falling.

Falling.

Falling.

PRISCILLA?

I climb to my feet. I am home again, in the garden, looking down the grassy slope towards the seawall. The tide is high; it looks like a spring tide, topping the saltings, silvering the great mats of vegetation.

I am alone.

I breathe deep.

Alone.

I remember the tender touch of your lips on mine, the urgent pressing of our bodies.

Alone.

I close my eyes, reach out, feel netspace around me. *Find her.*

I wait, patient. I walk along the seawall, my regular haunt. Redshanks fly up ahead of me, shrilling their sentinel cry.

She is gone. She is dead. She was not consolidated when consensus struck. She was an anomaly. She is no more.

Priscilla is dead.

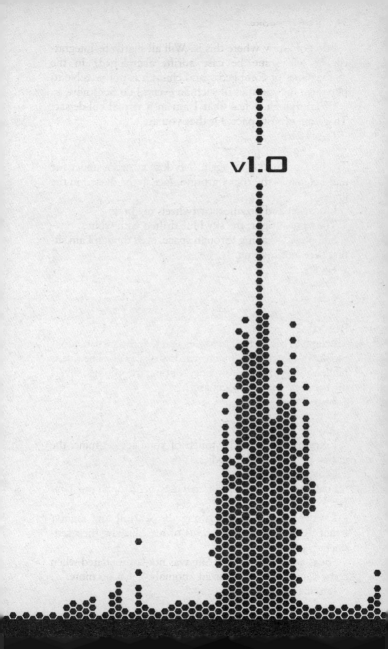

# 1.01

THE ACCORD WAS still big news two weeks after hitting consensus – two weeks after it became real, as people were saying.

"But what's going on in there?"

Burnham gave his easy smile, took a breath, the studio lights hot on his skin. He had the confidence to not rush in, knew that a well-handled pause could do wonders to give the impression of someone in control, calm, confident.

"People are living their lives," he said. "Or rather, their *after*-lives."

Shawna Brakes flashed perfect white teeth at him. When she nodded her hair and head moved as one. On screen she looked, well, pretty much perfect, but in the flesh so much of her was clearly fake. In the flesh she looked Photoshopped. "When can we speak to someone inside the Accord, elector? When can we see it?"

"You need to talk to one of the technical team for a precise answer on that one, Shawna, but my understanding is that such a thing is just not possible. We can monitor activity in the Accord, but that's a technical process, a study of data-flows and processing activity. We cannot look in, just as they cannot look out: the Accord is a self-contained entity. As soon as consensus was reached it coalesced into an independent *thing* – a world, if you like – governed by its own protocols of what is real and what is not."

"Isn't that just a bit scary?"

Burnham smiled again. "Not at all. As I say, we are monitoring it closely, and everything is functioning as expected. The Accord is there, waiting for us all if we choose to enter it when our time in this world draws to a close. It is perhaps the highest achievement of our species."

He kept the smile on his face as he spoke. He was in control. He would not let his guard slip. This should have been his greatest triumph, but now the success of the project he had guided was laced with bitterness.

"What would you say to those who argue that it's social engineering on a scale unprecedented and unjustified?"

"Electee Nesbitt is entitled to his views," said Burnham. "And it's a valid position to take, in some respects: the Accord is a human construct, an artificial environment designed to sustain our continued existence after death, so of course it's a form of social engineering. But since consensus it has defined itself in its own terms, established its own protocols for what is real and what is not. That's not social engineering in the old socialist paradigm – it's an evolutionary thing, an organic process.

"In any case, much as I respect Electee Nesbitt – I did elect him, after all! – I do find some of his public statements a little contradictory, to say the least. On the one hand he campaigns against the Accord because he says it is social engineering, but on the other he strongly proclaims our right to defend our coasts and our assets against – what was the term he used the other day? – 'that plague of African locusts'… Although I would dispute his use of language, he supports the State's position on border integrity, but surely *that* is a form of social engineering? I must ask him to clarify his arguments for me the next time our paths cross…"

As he spoke these words, making the connection between the Accord and the migration question,

Burnham realised he had opened himself up to an obvious line of questioning.

"What do you say to the growing campaign to use the Accord to, if you like, give mankind another chance?"

"The Soul Harvesters?" Burnham asked, buying time because he did not have an answer he could comfortably give in public. He couldn't just admit that a large proportion of the human population had, quite literally, missed the boat – the scale of loss was just too huge...

Shawna nodded, her hair looking as if it had been carved from soap.

The Soul Harvesters... Even the most optimistic extrapolations produced horrific figures for the loss of human life over the coming decades. Climate shift was destroying agriculture, replacing previously rich land with desert and dustbowl; rising sea levels were flooding densely populated and food-producing areas. Shortages of fossil fuels were making inroads into industrial agriculture, transport, and all kinds of manufacturing industries. Resource drain and mass migration were fuelling conflicts so that for the last fifteen years more of the world had been at war than at peace. And then there were the epidemics. AIDS had killed millions and was now in abrupt decline, but in its place malaria, drug-resistant tuberculosis, influenza, and a relentless onslaught of new haemorrhagic fevers were chasing each other around the globe on the backs of the migrating masses. Little wonder that Nesbitt and his retro-fascist followers found such a receptive audience.

But the Soul Harvesters took a different tack, one of acceptance. In the coming decades billions would die – but everyone had a chance of renewal in the Accord! Even now, there were armies of volunteers travelling the most devastated regions of the world, collecting personality dumps of everyone who wanted to be reborn upon their death.

"The Soul Harvesters?" Burnham repeated. "I am full of admiration for them. But at present it's a mere drop in the ocean. I have personally ensured that the campaign receives state sponsorship, but it is simply not possible to keep pace with the tragedy that is upon us."

Shawna smiled, bobbed her head, and Burnham realised that in front of a projected audience of nine and a half million he had effectively admitted that a large proportion of the human race was well and truly fucked.

"Moving on…"

MR WARRENER. THANK you for making the time to meet me." Elector Burnham smiles, indicates a reclining seat made from slats of bamboo, and sits on a similar seat, both on a wooden deck that extends over the perfect clear water of the lagoon. Flatfish cruise over the coarse sand, and the air around the two of them is punctuated by the slashing flight and dives of white seabirds.

Burnham is wearing black Speedos and wraparound shades. The cane seat is just on the pleasurable side of uncomfortable against his skin. A jug of sangria sits on a low table between the two seats, two glasses waiting to be filled.

"Fuck me, but this is *real*!" says Burnham. Sometimes a meetspace is little more than a blank canvas – a greyscreen backdrop with seats for the participants and no further effort to lend verisimilitude. But this… this meetspace belongs to the project, and they've taken a lot of trouble over its construction. "Is this what heaven's like?" asks Burnham, filling the two glasses.

Warrener pulls at his pencil moustache. "It uses the same algorithms," he says. For some reason Burnham hadn't expected the gentle Edinburgh accent. "But it would be misleading to say that this is the Accord. Consensus would not allow this kind of intrusion."

"Come now, Mr Warrener. There are always loopholes, aren't there?"

"There are no loopholes with consensus, elector."

Burnham chooses not to pursue the point. There is always a way, though.

"I'm very impressed," he says, instead. "If this is anything close to what the Accord is like, then it's very convincing."

"Believe me, elector, it is more than convincing. The whole point about consensus is that when the point of accordance was reached, it became *real*. At the moment of consensus, the 'very convincing' became the real. The dead came alive."

"I've watched the PR."

Warrener looks away. Through the gaps in the deck Burnham sees a school of bright blue fish, basking in the shade. So fucking convincing!

"Did Barakh come alive?"

For a moment, Burnham thinks Warrener is going to refuse to cooperate. "Feel free to terminate this meeting whenever you choose," he says gently. He has read that some Yakuza gangs use v-space in this way when they wish to interrogate someone. The separation of mental from physical is a powerful tool. Right now, Warrener sits back on his cane lounger, in his own little subset of a very convincing heaven, while back in the real world... Back in the real world he is with Tate.

"We cannot tell if Noah successfully transferred to the Accord, elector. The protocols lock us out of that kind of data. Also, we know that Noah is a special case. We know that he was running several instances of himself in various fractal realities pre-consensus. The protocols would have to regularise that. They might have allowed only one instance to persist; they might have tried a merge; they might have erased his presence altogether. The protocols are the most fundamental rules of consensus – they are the laws of the universe in the Accord, they decree what is and they decree what cannot be."

"Did he survive?"

"It is more probable than not that there is an instance of Noah Barakh in the Accord," says Warrener.

"And Elector Burnham?"

"The same conditions apply..." Warrener is clearly struggling. "Where there were instances of Noah, there were also instances of the electee. It appears that Noah was running some kind of private... experiment. He was running multiple reality fragments for... for private purposes."

"So what you're telling me is that if Barakh is in there then my wife almost certainly is too?"

"The probabilities are the same, yes."

"Then we need to find them."

"But that's not possible. It's simply not possible, elector."

This time, Burnham chooses to pursue the point. "You don't understand me," he tells Warrener. "I said, we need to find them."

"But... the protocols prevent it."

"Then if I were you, Mr Warrener, I would be very concerned."


PRIVATE EXPERIMENTS...

Private experiments that always featured instances of both Barakh and Priscilla. How many affairs had they been having, for fuck's sake? What kind of thing was this Accord, that it could be used for one man's sex games? For the first time, Jack Burnham started to understand some of the fears the tabs were propagating about the Accord: where were the controls? What was going on in there? Was it heaven or had he financed the construction of hell?

Burnham was in the back of his car, Tate driving.

They slowed, approaching a placard-waving crowd. Middle-aged women, children – Jesus, a small boy with *African't* felt-tipped across his forehead, couldn't be older than four or five. The look of hatred in the kid's eyes!

Something struck the windscreen with a loud thud. A brick, it had looked like.

"Should we really try to get through this?" asked Lucy Chang, sitting beside Burnham.

The elector was lost in thought. Civil society – it was a myth. In truth, we were all like this, each one of us pushing up against the envelope of acceptable behaviour. The angry child, the baying mob, the betrayed husband… Every last one of us could turn into a monster. Even sweet, efficient Lucy Chang.

He smiled in what he hoped was a reassuring manner. "No worries, Lucy," he said. "This car is impact-proof to the nth degree. If worst came to worst, we'd just put the handbrake on and wait for the riot squad to clear the mob, but it won't come to that – look, they're falling back even now."

Sure enough, a double line of police with riot shields was pushing the crowd back, clearing a path for Burnham's car.

Soon, they passed through a gate in a fence, three metres high and topped with coiled razor wire. A couple of metres on, there was another fence, another gate, and then they were in the compound.

They got out of the car as a small group of officials approached from a temporary cabin. Looking round, Burnham couldn't see much of the camp – they had entered in one corner, and most of it was laid out beyond the office cabin, and the parked vans and jeeps.

They paused to greet the officials, anonymous suits every one of them, nobodies. Lucy made the introductions, but Burnham's mind just wasn't on it…

They started to walk through the parked vehicles, and now Burnham saw the makeshift shelters – temporary cabins like the office unit, tents, a handful of battered old caravans. Thin, black faces turned to watch the approaching group with its trail of camera crews. Overhead, a swarm of mini-copters trailed them, filming their every move – some for the news agencies, others for security.

"Between two and three o'clock this morning," said Lucy, her eyes looking distant from that double-vision thing, looking out at the real world while simultaneously viewing a data-stream fed via the chip embedded in the stem of the sunglasses pushed high on her head. "That was when they landed."

"How many?"

"It was clearly a coordinated landing. Two hundred and sixteen made it alive. A further thirty-seven bodies have been found at last count."

Burnham had watched the footage in the car. Small boats had landed in the early hours along the south coast, from Brighton to Rye. Some were known to have launched from the larger vessels, but some... could they really have voyaged from North Africa in those tiny boats?

"How did they die?"

"Most drowned either trying to swim ashore or in capsized boats. Nine were shot by vigilantes."

Burnham kept his face straight, trying not to show any shock to the cameras. Nesbitt and his followers had proposed a bill only a few days earlier promoting the right of Britons to defend their borders by whatever means necessary – collective self-defence, he called it. It wasn't law yet, but it was only a matter of time.

They stopped at the first cabin, where a group of women and children sat, doe-eyed, unresponsive. They looked to be in shock. Or maybe sick, according to the common prejudice, inbound carriers of every deadly disease known to humankind. Most looked to be on the edge of death. A small boy with a grossly distended belly lay sobbing softly in his mother's arms, the arms little more than sticks of bone clothed in lax, lifeless skin. A man with only one leg bore heavy scarring over his exposed torso; Burnham guessed he had survived a haemorrhagic virus, somehow managing not to bleed to death. Scenes like this were familiar from southern Europe, but... well... in *Bexhill-on-Sea*, for fuck's sake?

These people had endured so much. If they thought anything, they probably thought they had made it, they had landed, they had broken through the cordons.

But if, indeed, they harboured such thoughts, then they were wrong.

They would be shipped out within fourteen days. Looking at them, Burnham felt sick at his knowledge of their fate, but he knew that was the law, and he knew that it had to be the law. It was all about survival now. It always had been, but now, looking at these empty people who had given so much and gained nothing, he finally believed it to be true.


HE DIDN'T KNOW what he had expected a Soul Harvester to look like, but it would not have been the weedy, jeans-clad kid just stepping out of a patched-together caravan, followed by a group of boat-children. The van stood on piles of bricks and didn't look as if it had moved in years; maybe this had been some kind of travellers' camp before the migrants' compound was established; internal migration was a big issue, too, with the east coast losses over the last few years.

The Harvester looked happy for no apparent reason and that was when Burnham twigged that this was what the kid was doing: he had that kind of evangelical look in his eye, a puppy-dog eagerness, an utter conviction. Barakh really had built heaven with all the God bits expunged, a humanist heaven, and here was one of his apostles.

"Sir. Mr Burnham. *Elector* Burnham." The kid shuffled forward, proffering a hand which Burnham avoided touching while simultaneously smiling and dipping his head so that his ignoring of the hand did not seem like a rebuff.

Burnham blinked, and the instant was long enough for a subliminal data stab to inform him that the kid was no kid: he was actually the other side of thirty years old, and one of the region's main coordinators of soul harvesting. He had mailed Burnham twenty-three times over the past six months, and doorstepped him twice.

"Charlie," said Burnham. "We meet again."

Charlie Bonnetti grinned, and Burnham wondered if he was genuinely a bit goofy, or if it was just a disingenuous act he affected. The latter, probably, Burnham thought.

"So what brings you here? I thought you people were out travelling the world?" Gathering up as many of the lost as they could before it was all too late.

"I'm just back from Mozambique," said Bonnetti. "I gathered somewhere close to eleven hundred souls."

"That's some going."

"But these people are just as much in need of our mission as any others," said Bonnetti. "They've travelled all this way – the least we can do is gather them up before..."

It always amused Burnham. Was he really that daunting that people should be so wary about arguing with him, or confronting him with their views?

"Before every last one of them is shipped back to Rabat or Safi or Nouadhibou? It's the legal requirement, Charlie. You know it is. And you know that I don't have the powers to make exceptions just like that. It's heartbreaking, it really is. But what viable alternative do we have?"

"Return to the quota system," said Bonnetti, made confident now by Burnham's warm, embracing, infront-of-the-cameras manner. "We could take more of the displaced in."

Burnham, clapped Bonnetti on the shoulder and said, "Walk with me, Charlie."

They headed past the caravan and through a cluster of tarpaulin-clad shelters.

"We're on the same side, Charlie," he said. "When it comes down to it we're both drawing a line in the dirt.

Our only difference is where to draw the line. Sure, we could let more migrants in, but as you say, we'd have to have a quota system. And when we hit the quota, we're back in exactly the same position: defending border integrity, dealing with illegal entrants with camps like this. It really is heartbreaking."

Word had circulated that the visit was taking place, and soon the illegals were swarming around them like flies.

At first, Burnham was perturbed by it, assuming they would try to hound him for clemency. But then he realised that it was not him that they wanted to see, it was Charlie Fucking Bonnetti.

Burnham drew back, and stood with Lucy as hands clutched at Bonnetti, tugging at his clothes. For a moment, Burnham thought it might turn ugly, but Bonnetti handled it skilfully, suddenly transformed from awkward young man to someone with natural authority.

"Fuck me," Burnham muttered into Lucy's ear. "They all want to be *saved*."

Bonnetti plugged a cable into the pod attached to his belt – the kid probably had enough data storage on his body to hold the brain dumps of an entire nation.

The cable led to a kind of skullcap. Burnham watched as Bonnetti stretched it over a young girl's head and it moulded itself to the contours of her skull. This was the device Bonnetti's technical people had developed from an open-sourced block of Accord coding – these caps were being used in the field all around the world.

Beyond, the chain-link fence topped with razor wire loomed, a permanent reminder of the status of this camp's occupants. Security guards looked on, eyes screened by mirrored visors, hands resting casually on machine guns.

Bonnetti was in his element, playing a clapping game with the girl, having her in fits of giggles as he repeatedly lost count. Burnham guessed the girl was about six or seven, but he knew her small frame could be the result of malnutrition and she could easily be several years older.

Burnham realised he was waiting for something to happen and that that was a mistake, for the recording had probably started the moment the cap had moulded itself to the girl's skull.

Sure enough, soon Bonnetti did something to the cap that made it lose its shape and he peeled it from the girl's head, the brain dump apparently complete. Just then, a woman – the girl's mother, Burnham presumed – stepped forward, bent over Bonnetti where he sat in the dirt, and smothered him in a long embrace, talking to him in French, words Burnham could not quite catch.

Maybe these people had achieved something after all, he realised. They had come all this way, managed to land against all the odds, and would be sent packing within days, but... there was a place reserved for that child in heaven.

Now, Bonnetti attached the cap to the girl's mother. While his recording device did its work, he engaged the woman in conversation. She seemed happy, a happiness bordering on hysteria, Burnham thought uncomfortably.

When they had finished, she took Bonnetti in her arms again and sobbed violently into his shoulder, rocking back and forth, manhandling him so roughly that Burnham wondered why no one intervened.

Finally, Bonnetti stood, and turned to face Burnham. "You see what it means to these people?" he said, as much for the cameras as for Burnham. "It's probably the first time they've ever known real hope."

The first time since landing on Brighton beach and thinking they'd reached the promised land, Burnham thought, but he said nothing.

Just then, the woman yelled something in a piercing half-shriek. Was it French, or some other language? Burnham wasn't sure any more.

The woman had her daughter by the hand, and the girl was in that limbo between puzzlement and terror.

In her other hand, the woman held a kitchen knife, its blade about ten centimetres long.

In a single movement, she swung her hand, the knife, slashed it across her daughter's throat. Blood geysered out of severed arteries, and the girl made an awful gasping sound – from her mouth or from the new opening in her throat, Burnham couldn't tell, didn't like to even *think*.

The girl slumped, and her mother released her hand.

Everyone stood motionless, stunned.

Overhead, news and security copters dropped lower, closer to the action.

The woman wailed, dropped the knife, ran through the crowd towards the fence.

She would never get over it, but she threw herself at it nonetheless, tried to pull herself up. Gunfire rang out, either from one of the guards or from a security copter.

The woman's body jerked. For a moment she looked as if she was going to hang there, somehow lodged into the chain-link, and then she slid down, toppled back into the dirt, lay motionless.

A child started to wail. A man shouted. Another man snapped an order. People started to move about.

Burnham was transfixed, though, transfixed by the look on the woman's face. Lying on her back in the dirt, her torso ripped through by four bullets, her right hand crimson with her daughter's blood, she was smiling, at peace, triumphant even. She bore the look of a woman who knew with utter conviction that she would soon join her daughter in heaven.

# 1.02

ELECTEE PRISCILLA BURNHAM wakes in greyness. She is standing. She feels... a sense of vitality. She runs a hand over her body, looks down. She is wearing jeans and a T-shirt bearing a swirling pattern across the front, a bunch of silver bangles around her left wrist. She has lost about ten kilos, is firm where she should not be firm, pert where pertness had long-since departed. Her body looks and feels about twenty years younger.

"Fucking *result*," she says softly.

She is dead.

She realises that.

This is no meetspace. This is the real thing. She is dead and just waiting to enter heaven.

She remembers cocktails at the Savoy. She remembers sipping a cosmo and focusing inwardly to read mail, most of them dull, repetitive, but a really sweet one from Noah Barakh, pressing to make sure she was okay with notes he had sent her for the next meeting. Next day: the project meeting, the routine brain dump, and nothing more after that.

That must have been the last time then, the last time she had warehoused a copy of herself before she had died.

Before she had died... what a curious phrase to have in your head. The Accord leaves people thinking thoughts they had never evolved to handle... *Before she had died.*

The outline of a door appears, lines of light. She steps forward, the door scrolls up and she steps out into her old bedroom in Deanmere Gap. She had lived here for seven years, after she and her mother had moved out from Eastbourne. The sash window is half-open, net curtains partly obscuring the view to the trees. The room has been redecorated several times since she last came here, but it is still her room.

She goes out to the landing.

"Mum?"

There is no response.

Her mother is dead. *Dead* dead. Before the technology for brain dumping had been developed. And even then, her last years had been spent lost in some mental limbo. She had missed heaven by many years.

Priscilla sits on the top step, where she had often sat as a girl.

A tear swells in the corner of an eye, brims over, trails down her left cheek. *Must be coming on*, she thinks. *So fucking emotional.*

She rubs the tears away with the inside of a wrist, stands.

Priscilla is dead. Long live Priscilla!


ELECTEE CLIVE NESBITT: sitting alone at a table in a Starbucks that could have been anywhere, sipping at his macchiato, chatting into the feed grafted into his jaw. His chestnut hair somehow managed to look simultaneously neat but tousled – either ruffled by his gran or raked through in long-fingernailed passion, depending on the target demographic of the moment. Clive Nesbitt was a politician carefully tailored to tick lots of often-contradictory boxes.

He stood, adjusting the hang of his stone chinos as he did so. His open-necked, windowpane-checked shirt revealed a collarbone tattoo, something interwoven and Celtic, so very retro-modern.

"Jack," he said, holding out his hand.

Burnham shook, sat, smiled. "Good to see you, Clive," he said. "Shawna sends her best." They'd already exchanged about Burnham's comments on the Shawna Brakes show, no ground given on either side. Nesbitt was riding a popular wave, and they both knew it.

"She's one of the best," said Nesbitt, grinning easily. "Ten million people a week can't be wrong, can they?"

Burnham chose not to rise to that one. This coffee-shop chat would be running live on all the newsfeeds, directional mikes picking up every word. There were almost certainly bugs on the table too if the waiting staff had anything about them. Nesbitt was probably even providing a syndicated feed direct himself; Burnham's feed only went to Lucy in the office.

"Ninety-four more last night, Jack."

"And thirty-six dead," Burnham replied. "Your vigilantes are pre-empting your bill."

"They're not mine, Jack. They're the vanguard of a popular movement."

Burnham pinged Nesbitt, the third time he'd tried since entering the coffee shop, and this time an answering ping bounced back, the secure connection established.

*Okay, Clive*, Burnham sent. *Let's cut the bullshit. What's this all about?*

Nesbitt <smiled>, <shrugged>, sent: *I like you, Jackie. You're one of the good guys. I'll always be grateful for what you've done for me.*

"We have to take a tougher line with these people, Jack. We can't keep letting them land. The whole south coast will be littered with transit camps – for no purpose!"

*I said let's cut the bullshit, okay?*

"And how do you propose to do that? Blow them out of the water as soon as they enter European territory?" They were both keeping their voices calm, amenable.

"The language of deterrence can be very effective, Jack. You know that."

*Sure, Jack. Sure. Okay: I know you've been digging around the Accord project, and for good reason. I thought you might appreciate a bit of a steer.*

*??*

*Ask about Shanghai, Jack. Ask about Shanghai.*

"You're really proposing that we take offensive action against these boat people? They're helpless, defence-less... You want us to blow them out of the water, or what?"

"There are ways to deter, Jack. We have a fine Navy, with a lot of experience. I wouldn't wish to instruct them on their own areas of expertise, but I'm sure they could offer effective ways to implement a policy of hardened self-defence. It's what the people are demanding, Jack."

*Why are you doing this?* At least part of the price was this public encounter: there was far more spin in it for Nesbitt than there was for Burnham. But there was more than that...

*The Accord was a corrupt project from the outset. How can we engineer our own paradise? Barakh's whole ideology harks back to defeated socialist ideas of a managed culture – now he's trying to take heaven into social control, or at least, some perverted simulacrum of heaven. He's a new Stalin, Jack, and like we did with Stalin we're now learning about the true Barakh: a murderer, a liar and cheat, and corrupt to the heart – just ask about Shanghai, Jack; Barakh has been running rings around us for years, misappropriating funds on a staggering scale. There are valuable lessons to be learnt from the Accord – enormous technical advances. But the Accord itself... it's wrong, Jack. It's one man's control-freak vision of a world that can never be. I'm going to help you pull the plug on it, Jack. I'm going to help you get Barakh and destroy his egomaniacal paradise.*

"More coffee, Jack...?"

Burnham shook his head. He hadn't even touched his cappuccino.

HE HAD MET her on a handful of occasions – formal receptions, project social events at Christmas and various landmark stages. She looked no different to his recollection: a small woman, stick thin, with big dyed-red hair and eyes too large and plate-like for her delicate face, so much so that she looked like a middle-aged anime character.

"Marie," said Burnham. "Thank you for agreeing to see me."

Marie Barakh stepped back from the door so that Burnham could enter. He followed her through to a large conservatory that looked down a grassy slope to the salt marshes, a dark grey-green mat of vegetation cut through with twisting silver ribbons of tidal creek.

"Noah loves the marshes," Marie said, easing herself into a cane bucket seat. "When he was here he always had to walk out along the seawall at least once a day, whatever the weather. He probably doesn't strike you as an outdoor man, does he, Elector Burnham?"

She talked about her late husband as if he had just popped out to visit a friend, or to pick up a few things from the local market. Lucy Chang had commented on this phenomenon only yesterday: how the Accord was turning death into a temporary parting of the ways; the bereaved no longer speaking of the departed in the past tense – they are merely *somewhere else*...

Burnham sat across from Marie and looked out over the well-tended garden. "It's very quiet here," he said, wondering how she coped with such a lonely existence. Living like this, miles from the nearest town, just yourself and the marshes, was a way of life he could never really imagine himself accepting.

"We like it this way," said Marie.

This morning Burnham had been up before five so that he could spend an hour going through subcommittee papers – why so much paper, for Christ's sake? – before Tate had called for him, Lucy Chang already in the back of the car to brief him on the day's schedule. Later, sitting at his desk, every time he looked up there had been a different combination of people in the office, talking to each other, or to him, staring into the middle distance as they viewed datafeeds or mails, sub-voking into jaw-mikes, walking purposefully in or out or across the room... And somehow... this had been normal, comforting, the way things operate, the way things should be.

Out in the garden, a black and white cat stalked flies dancing over the wet grass.

He'd pissed everyone off when he made a spur of the moment decision to head out into the wilds of Essex to visit the widow of the man who had killed his wife. He caught himself... The man everyone *thought* had killed his wife. Even now, Lucy was out in the back of the car, rearranging and rescheduling, placating lobbyists and bullshitters in meetspaces where she was able to deputise for her errant elector.

"We have a lot in common, don't we?"

She fixed his look then. "No, Elector, I don't think so. We have only one thing in common, and that... nothing happened between them. It's been investigated and they were not having an affair."

"In this world..."

"They never did anything. My husband was never unfaithful."

"But in their heads, Marie... In the Accord..."

"That was before consensus, Elector Burnham. That was before the Accord became real."

"And now...?"

Finally, she looked away. The cat was lying on its back now, paws in the air, twisting like a puppy in a muck heap.

"We have no way of knowing what is happening in the Accord," she said.

"Except that it is functioning as modelled, it has become real to all its inhabitants. In the Accord, your husband, my wife... the best projections say that they probably survive, and that they survive together."

"He killed her."

"You think that will stop them?"

"My husband is a good man, Elector Burnham. Despite everything that people have said in the last few weeks. He gave us heaven. He gave us a future when... when the politicians can only offer us varying degrees of survival."

She peered up at him, a fierce glint in her eye, but Burnham met her look.

"We politicians," he said, "gave your husband the resources and the protection to build the Accord. And yes, we offer survival – would you have us do otherwise?"

Outside, the cat looked up as a press drone drifted over the trees and positioned itself above the garden. Word must have got around about the elector's visit. Almost immediately the drone started pinging Burnham with requests for a feed, for interview responses, for confirmation that he was going to sue the Barakh estate for damages or that he was having an affair with Marie, or any number of equally ludicrous propositions. After a few seconds, the barrage was being safely filtered out by his firewall.

"Tell me," said Burnham, turning his face away from the window so no one could lip-read his words from the drone's camerazzi coverage, "did your husband ever talk about our Shanghai operation?"

She looked genuinely puzzled by this change of conversational direction, but she gathered herself quickly – she was clearly smart enough to realise that this was important to Burnham, despite his efforts at nonchalance.

"Shanghai?" she asked. "My husband mentioned it in conversation, yes. There's a branch of the project there.

He's visited a few times over the last couple of years or so."

"What did he tell you about it?"

Marie Barakh shrugged. "I really don't remember, Elector Burnham," she said. "Nothing memorable. He never talked much about his travels, or his work, for that matter. I don't think he thought I understood what he was doing, other than the superficial level of explanation he reserved for politicians and the press, and he had enough of talking at that level during office hours..."

Burnham ignored the slight, and waited, silently, until she filled the gap.

"There are branches of the project all over the world, aren't there, Elector Burnham? Shanghai, Brussels, New York, San Francisco, Warsaw, São Paolo, Sydney, Madrid... I'm sure I've missed some from the list, haven't I? Noah travels to them all. There was nothing special about Shanghai, as far as I can recall. And I don't suppose you're going to tell me why you're asking in such a casual manner, even as you make sure your face is shielded from the press drones?"

Burnham stared at her, realising that she, too, had been careful to discreetly turn away from the cameras so that her words could not be lip-read.

"Don't you think you should leave these investigations to the appropriate agencies?" she asked him. "You have a world to save. Or, at least, some survival to ration out..."

MARIE BARAKH'S WORDS echoed in his ears as he walked back to the car. She came across as demure and very proper, but beneath that façade there lay a complex and surprisingly bitter woman. The surprise was not so much the bitterness – after what had so recently been revealed about her husband she had plenty of reason to be bitter – but that it was directed at the world with such passion, rather than at her lying, cheating partner.

He straightened, bones in his spine cracking audibly. Why was he wasting his time on this vengeful pursuit of ghosts, when he did indeed have survival to dole out? He thought again, as he often did, of the camp he had visited at Bexhill-on-Sea, of the boats scattered along the south coast, such a graphic illustration of the quest for human survival as all around them the world was well and truly fucked. He shouldn't be thinking like this. He needed to keep a grip on things, look for the positive, and pursue it relentlessly. That was all that was left.

He looked up. There were five press drones now, one of them only a few metres over his head. A pinged interview request slipped through his firewall filters, just then, but he blocked the new encrypt immediately.

Let them make what they wanted of this visit.

YOU ARE DEAD. Forever. Lost because I brought you with me into pre-consensus Accord and was unable to ensure that you would be consolidated when consensus struck.

Or you have been consolidated elsewhere in the Accord, somewhere where your presence had been stronger. I can find you, then.

Or you are dead, but you will return. Your instances in the pre-consensus Accord had failed to consolidate, the anomaly that you were had been smoothed out of existence... but you were warehoused, you were dead, the normal protocols of drawing the dead into the Accord would find you, wake you.

I recline in my chaise longue, looking out across the lawn to the salt marshes.

You are gone from me, and all I have are thought experiments to help me decide if you will return, or not.

I reach out to netspace again, feel the flows of data, the currents on which the Accord is built. My search routines have found nothing yet. The population of the Accord grows steadily, at a rate of more than 2,000 a day, but not one of these lost souls is my beloved.

I try to get a grasp of what the Accord is like now consensus has been achieved, what it *is*.

It is our world.

It is defined by the consensus of those who contributed to its construction, those who inhabit it.

But where are the limits? What is beyond the known, the shared? Is that tree really falling in the forest?

Countless shards of pre-reality have not been assimilated, as was always likely. They were anomalies, false starts, side branches.

Priscilla?

I turn from the window. I have a skullcap here, synched to my house net. I have taken brain dumps here many times over recent years. I slip the cap into place, fire up the routines, but there is no response. There is no Accord, no project. The Accord will not allow me to twist it in tangles of its own logic.

I sit back again, close my eyes, feel the data-flows. Wait.


"BUT NESBITT AND his fascist friends are popular! They really are the voice of the people."

Lucy Chang shook her head. "The electorate is both stratified and segmented in complex ways, Jack," she said. "It has never been as simple as a representative having the wholehearted backing of the people, although Electee Nesbitt likes to portray it so."

The car sped through the narrow lanes away from the Barakh house, Tate at the wheel, a police bike out front, press lost, unable to keep up. They had probably stayed behind, hoping to pin Marie down in an interview, but Burnham had learnt that she was far more savvy than he had previously assumed. He somehow doubted she would be giving quotes on anything but her own terms.

"Explain?"

"Some of the people support him on some of his chosen themes, split by demographics, geography and subject," explained Lucy. "Southern England, right across the social classes, more in the under-forty-fives than the liberal wrinklies, back him strong to very strongly on migration and repatriation. Across the country, a slim majority in the lowest thirty percentile on the income range back him on the Accord – they see it as a middle class thing, something they might be excluded from on financial grounds, even though there are nothing more than tabloid scare stories and Nesbitt's misinformation campaign to back them on that. But it's wrong to think that just because he has mass support on migration he has the same kind of backing on the Accord – apart from a few segments, the people *want* the Accord. They want the hope it gives them."

"You don't want me to go after the Accord?"

She didn't answer. It wasn't a case of what she wanted or not. Burnham sat back in his seat, looking out at the warehouses they were passing. Half of them were abandoned, in varying states of disrepair. Several had been taken over by travellers, internal migrants from coastal towns now vulnerable to the tide.

"You find anything about Shanghai?"

Businesslike, Lucy nodded, said, "A little. Enough to suggest we should pursue enquiries."

Burnham returned his look to his assistant. Her expression gave nothing away.

He raised an eyebrow, and she continued: "The model used for project management is a deliberate echo of the informational and organisational infrastructure of the Accord itself. Pre-consensus, the Accord consisted of numerous reality shards: fragments of virtual reality where consensus was becoming manifest – full consensus was reached when the reality shards converged into a single, unified reality. The project is distributed around the world: project teams in twenty-seven major cities. Each project centre is a fragment of the whole, just as each reality shard was a fragment of the pre-consensus Accord. Rather than have centres of excellence, each team worked across the range of project activities. In the current political climate this is a resilient model – lose one centre to civil war or political wrangling and the project will continue apace, viz Tunis and Manila; lose a specialist centre and everything might grind to a halt. With netspace and VR architecture at its disposal, virtual teams can collaborate across the globe just as if they were side by side, so the model is very powerful."

Burnham nodded. "The point?" he prompted.

"Shanghai is different," said Lucy. "On the surface Shanghai appears like any other project centre, but check out the personnel profiles and it's clearly a specialist centre."

"Specialist? In what?"

"Theoretical physics. There are more theoretical physicists working at, or collaborating with, the Shanghai centre than at any single university in the world. Cosmology, quantum theory, dimensional mathematics."

"What the fuck has that got to do with the Accord?"

"I don't know, Jack. But physicists and their toys don't come cheap – there appears to have been a degree of innovative accounting practices associated with Shanghai. In the last fiscal year, the centre has absorbed something like twelve percent of project funding."

Burnham stared at his assistant. That was one fuckload of creative accounting... He remembered Nesbitt's accusations about malpractice. "Was that legitimate spend, or has someone been tapping the funds?"

"It appears to be legitimate, in that it was paying for research personnel and activities under the remit of the project. There is no indication of embezzlement."

"But what were they doing? What *are* they doing?"

"I don't know, Jack."

Burnham sat back in his seat and closed his eyes. Barakh was a cheat, and there was plenty of evidence that he had manipulated the project to his own private ends – that in itself was a form of embezzlement. But it staggered Burnham to think that his lead developer could have been manipulating things on the scale suggested by Lucy's investigation. And why?

He sighed, and gave in to the mail and scheduling reminders blinking away in the corner of his field of vision. He would find out: Barakh was undone, it was just a matter of unravelling the threads now.

BURNHAM SITS IN a featureless grey meetspace, body hugged by a chair he can feel but can't see. Malcolm Warrener sits opposite, his seat visible only as a slight change in the light and shadows of the grey backdrop.

Burnham gestures and a screen appears in the air to one side of them, positioned so that they can both see. It shows Warrener – the real flesh-and-blood Warrener – sitting naked in a leather seat, arms strapped to his side. A wad of some kind of fabric is stuffed into his mouth, drool trailing down his chin, sweat glinting on his forehead, running in tracks down his cheeks and body. His eyes bulge like eggs and the tendons in his neck are taut, standing out as he strains against his bonds.

Tate has his back to the observers in meetspace. He is kneeling at Warrener's feet. Doing something Burnham and Warrener can't see on-screen.

"The principle," says Burnham in a conversational tone, "is like a wire stripper. You know what I mean? Cutting off a toe is crude, old-hat. My friend has an adjustable tool which clamps two semi-circular blades around any appendage. When drawn back it strips that appendage of the outer layers of flesh. In the case of a toe, it strips it to the bone. It is much more painful and disfiguring than amputation." This was another trick borrowed from the Yakuza. Tate had not wasted the three years he had spent as a corporate minder in Kyoto.

"Please," gasps Warrener, leaning forward in his seat in meetspace. "You don't need to do this!"

"Find Barakh for me. Find my wife."

"But... I've explained... The Accord doesn't allow that kind of intrusion. The protocols deny all external access, other than the transfer of the dead, and then they cannot communicate back to the outside world. I've looked for any possible way to help you, elector, but there are none."

"That's a great shame for you."

"Please, elector."

On screen, Warrener's body bucks against its bindings, head thrown back, eyes rolling so that they're mostly white.

Here in meetspace, Warrener swallows, looks away, looks at Burnham.

On screen, Tate turns, leans back on his heels, revealing more of his captive. Warrener's right foot is a crimson mess.

"The device is not only used on toes," Burnham says softly, pausing for long seconds to allow that point to sink home. "So... how do I find Barakh and Priscilla?"

"You *can't*... Unless you die and get uploaded."

"Oh, I've considered that. Or sending someone else in there to go after them. But it seems so... final..." And, with no communication possible, it was still so uncertain. Burnham wanted to *know* that Barakh and Priscilla had been found. He wanted to see for himself. So he couldn't simply send Tate or someone else into the Accord after them. How would he know when they had accomplished their mission? And he wasn't ready to die himself...

"The only way you can get them is if you destroy the Accord itself."

Burnham nods. It's looking like the best option. But could he be the man who destroys heaven? Could he kill Priscilla again...?

"How do I do that?" he asks.

Warrener hesitates. "Noah was always prepared to use unconventional approaches," he says finally. "He always argued that some of the best v-space minds were the mavericks, the outsiders..."

"He hired *hackers*?"

Warrener nods. "Sometimes, yes. There's a guy called Chuckboy Lee – best of them all. Lives in a warehouse in Jakarta. The Accord is embedded right across netspace; it'd be almost impossible to unravel. If anyone can pull the plug, Chuckboy Lee's the man."

"How do I track him down?"

"I don't know. He's very elusive. He only ever contacted Noah direct, or Noah went there to see him. And even then he only ever found Lee when he wanted to be found."

Burnham glances at the screen. Tate is leaning close to Warrener, saying something into his ear.

"Please, Elector Burnham. I've told you everything!"

Burnham pauses, then stands, turns, steps through the door that scrolls open before him.

IN THE CAR, just Burnham in the back, Tate driving, sitting in a traffic snarl somewhere just off the Strand.

"So what did you do with him?" asked Burnham.

"We drank tea, talked about the Arsenal game. He's a Hearts man. I like him."

Burnham nodded. By now Warrener would have realised that the whole thing had been a sham: the screen just a window into another meetspace where a virtual Tate went to work on a virtual Warrener. Burnham was not as brutal as Warrener clearly believed he was capable of being.

"Do you enjoy your work?"

Tate glanced back over his shoulder. His expression gave nothing away. "My work is important, JB," he said. "I take pride in it. So that makes me feel good. Good about myself and my place in the world. Is fulfilment the same as enjoyment? I don't know. I'm not looking to move on, if that's what you're worried about."

"I'm envious of you sometimes, you know that?"

Tate looked back again, the car crawling through the gridlock.

"You get to do things. You're *involved*. You know how much of my day I spend just talking to people? Reading papers and talking to people. That's pretty much my life."

"You'd rather be out there, stripping the virtual flesh off some geeky Hearts fan's athlete's foot-infested toes?"

Burnham sighed. "I just want to *do* something. It's so frustrating always sitting back and being told what's happening..."

Tate reached down and yanked at the handbrake. The car had only been edging forward but still it juddered to an abrupt halt. Horns blew behind them.

Tate opened his door and stepped out into the middle of the road. He gestured and cursed at the cars behind him in jovial, couldn't-give-a-flying-fuck manner, and then opened Burnham's door.

Before the elector knew what was happening, he was out in the street and Tate was climbing into his vacated seat.

Burnham looked around, saw the angry faces of drivers stuck behind his car. He looked down at Tate, whose window was now sliding down.

"Get in, then," said Tate. "Drive the fucking car if you want to do something, man."

Burnham stared at him, his mouth half open, then he straightened, tipped his head back and laughed, the most hearty, deep belly laugh he had emitted for as long as he could remember.

He climbed in, slammed the door, reached down to release the handbrake and edged the car forward. "You cheeky fucking bugger," he said to Tate, and laughed again.

# 1.03

THE PROTOCOLS OF Accord are rigid. They are watertight. There is no way around them. That is the way it must be. That is how I seeded them, the direction in which I guided their development. I am their architect.

But... But... I am the man who also planted certain *trapdoors*. I still have work to do. I still have unfinished business.

A door appears before me. It slides up, revealing greyness beyond. I step through, close my eyes, preparing myself for the rush, for the...

... I MADE MYSELF lie there, breathing steadily, deeply, fighting back the surge of adrenaline, the physicality of return. Still, my heart raced, an unfamiliar heart.

After a time, I opened my eyes, sat, swung my legs away from the bunk as steadying hands took my arms.

Zhang Xiaoling. I had ridden her body before, many times, riding her like a sweat, her in Shanghai, me in London or elsewhere. A routine thing, and yet it could never be routine. Now I shifted, familiarising myself with the responses of her body again, intensely aware of my breasts, tight against the fabric of my jacket, the pressure of the seam of my jeans at my crotch.

I thought then of you, of loss.

I stopped myself. I had business here. I had to keep going. There was so much at stake.

Zhang Xiaoling was a good choice – one she had suggested herself. Young and breathtakingly intelligent, she had risen to assume real influence over the Shanghai branch of the project. Her access to people and resources were what I needed on the occasions when I chose to return: no one must know when I am back, other than a select few, so I needed someone on the inside, someone high up.

There were other advantages too: riding a sweat made you deeply aware of all the subtleties and nuances of body, of expression and mannerism. Riding a sweat of another gender, and from another culture, reinforced this, making it harder to lapse into the mode of being me, less likely to betray my true identity. It kept me on my toes.

The office. Picture windows overlooking the park where a huddle of old men stooped over shared game boards, gesturing in the air to control their pieces.

"Deedee."

"Professor Barakh." Rudi de Groot leaned with his back against the window, as if suspended in mid-air. The bright sunlight had prompted his conjunctival grafts to shade themselves almost as black as his skin. "They are waiting."

He led me through into the meeting room, a space much like the office, the same view over the park, the same glass and black iron furniture. Sammy Zhang sat deep in a black leather armchair. Three other young Shanghainese stood nearby, watching me.

"Sammy," I said, taking the seat opposite him.

He looked at me, an expression of distaste on his face.

"You are not Zhang Xiaoling again," he said. He liked to make it clear that he could read me, read Zhang Xiaoling.

I shook my head. "I am Professor Barakh," I said. "We need your help."

Sammy had three dots tattooed into the webbing between finger and thumb of his right hand, just as Zhang Xiaoling – I – had on hers/mine.

"You need more real estate, right?" he said. No messing: this was his meeting; he was the man with the good cards.

I nodded. Virtual territory. The Accord was getting hungry.

"You have the funds?"

I nodded again, allowed myself a brief smile. I was his sister, after all, or at least, I was riding his sister's body.

His expression didn't change, the only hint of feeling that look of slight distaste. He appeared so young, the barely pubescent look all the rage in the more cosmopolitan Chinese cities at present. He had a few wisps of moustache, a long thin face, square glasses worn purely for chic value. I had to remind myself that this kid was older than me, that he was probably the most powerful man in eastern Asia, running or at least controlling pretty much any cybergang of any significance from Sapporo to Port Moresby.

Just then, Deedee pinged me through the latest figures on Sammy Zhang: top of the Hang Seng Index; stock in SZ seen as one of the top ten safest investments for global pension funds according to the latest report in the *Financial Times*; the most recent contract on his head was worth almost $60 million, up three points at latest close of trading. Things were certainly going well for Sammy Zhang.

"We can get you all the capacity you need for now," said Sammy. "But pretty soon you're going to be bringing the whole thing down. We can carve you real estate on all the server farms in the world, we can build virtual space for you in all the null network space in between, but you're still going to be bringing it down, you go on like this."

"The Accord is hungry."

"The Accord is not sustainable in more than the near term. But until you hit that point you need me, Professor Noah Barakh. I am the only man who can supply."

I smiled again. One day in the not too far future Sammy Zhang would be redundant. The Accord would need him no more. But until that day... I nodded, kept my head dipped in deference. "My colleague, Rudi de Groot has the details," I told Sammy. "We are ready to proceed with the transaction."

JACK BURNHAM JUST wanted to get into a hotel, strip out of his damp clothes and wallow in the air con. Nobody had told him Shanghai was so hot and oppressive, the air so humid it was like you were trying to breathe soup...

He left Lucy Chang to deal with the taxi driver. She was talking to him in the Shanghainese dialect, rather than universal business Mandarin, he knew. He had yet to find a language she couldn't just slide into automatically. Grammar and vocabulary feeds direct from the net helped, but it was still pretty damned impressive.

The lobby was heaven. Whatever Barakh had invented, it could only be a dim echo of heaven set against this: air conditioning, driving down from ducts in the ceiling, air with an icy chill, a dryness that you could breathe deep and feel tingle in the depths of your lungs. Quiet, too. Not absolute silence, but just a polite hum of background noise, not the din of petrol cars and electric cars and horns and voices and radios and music and low-flying jets.

Burnham was suddenly very aware of the clothes sticking damply to his body. He put a hand on Tate's arm. "Deal with the bags, would you? I'll wait here. I want to go straight out to the centre." No point showering and drying off: as soon as they set foot outside again the humidity and heat would take its toll.

Fifteen minutes and a glass of ice tea later, they were back outside, Lucy flagging down another cab. Soon they were driving along the Bund, a haphazard jumble of skyscrapers and old colonial buildings to their right, the Huangpu River to their left, and beyond it the Flash Gordon rocket-like Oriental Pearl TV Tower reaching for the sky.

The car dropped down a slip road into a tunnel that passed under the river, the road eventually emerging in the Pudong district, where the skyscrapers dominated. Burnham had always thought of New York as a city where you just had to keep looking up to take it all in, but Shanghai was at least the Big Apple's match. The skyscrapers were staggering, the tops of many of them seemingly lost in the clouds, others bearing flying saucer-like discs at their summits. Soon the car pulled up outside one of the towers, and Lucy started haggling with the driver once again.

"So," said Tate as they waited on the pavement, two islands amid a steady flow of people. "What's the plan? Do I need to know anything?"

Burnham chuckled. Plan? "We just walk in, sponsors' visit. They have to show us around, impress us. And we try to spot anything fishy." And then he added, "And if they don't give us something today, we get heavy with them: full audit, call in the IFA to go through every file on every last workstation. We'll lock the bastards down for six months just asking questions, and all legitimate."

Looking around now, he saw that all of the buildings took security seriously, with heavy metal grilles over the ground-floor windows, armed guards on the doors, security cams watching every angle, drones hanging in the air. Even more like New York than he had first realised, then.

PRISCILLA WALKS. AND walks. And walks.

She wants to know how this place works. Where the limits are.

She wants to explore heaven.

Deanmere Gap is a ghost village, the shop and pub boarded up, not a soul in sight. Not enough people have died yet. But still everything appears to function. There is food in the house, fuel in the car; TV and netspace working as normal. The shop may be shut, but she can order online; there don't appear to be any supply problems, even though there can hardly be enough dead farmers to work the land...

This is what consensus is, what consensus decrees. The Accord must function.

She wants to find the limits, though. Can you die in heaven? What would happen if you just walked? And walked? Beyond the point of exhaustion? Beyond the point of hunger, of thirst?

She walks, out east from the village along the cliff path, eventually finding the South Downs Way, the route well worn through the short grass despite the lack of walkers. She pauses some time later, breathing deep from the incline. White cliffs wrap left and right along the water's edge, and below, the red and white finger of Beachy Head lighthouse stands in shallow water, a narrow walkway connecting it to the beach.

PRISCILLA IS TIRED. She is thirsty and hungry, and she has a blister the size of a plum on her left heel.

It is dark now, and she is just entering Eastbourne, along King Edward's Parade.

She heads down onto the beach, smells the sea on the inshore breeze. Ahead, she can see the lights of the pier.

Priscilla is tired and sore and thirsty and… *alive*!

And fuck, but it feels good!

I LEFT SAMMY Zhang content with the deal he had struck. He was milking us, sucking cash out of our backers like a leech. But… I really didn't care.

I rode a glass-sided lift to the twenty-fourth floor, the streets of Pudong district shrinking to toytown dimensions below. Between the scrapers I see the Oriental Pearl Tower piercing the sky, a needle penetrating one sphere and then another. I always love the Shanghai skyline, and wonder how much of that is me and how much a residual part of Zhang Xiaoling, a gut thing, a cellular connection.

I emerged from the lift, followed a corridor, entered a room that was a single wide-open space, scattered with beanbags, easy chairs, low coffee tables. A screwed up screen had been discarded on the floor near the doorway, its visible surface still showing scrolling numbers, a felt-tip pen slash scrawled across it.

"Sums not adding up again, Huey?" I asked the grey-haired wire of a man hunched up in a nearby sling chair.

He raised his chin from his drawn-up knees. "You Xiaoling or he?"

"Me," I told him.

"He," he said. He pressed the heel of his right hand against his temple. "It works, He. I can see it. Just can't make the language work for it."

Huey Kashvili meant the language of numbers. He had been working on his proof for more than six years.

"We need to move, Huey," I told him. "There's only so long that we can keep going in netspace before we bring the whole infrastructure down." I didn't need to spell out the implications of that: power failures, communications blackout, transport shutdown... the chaos and panic, the knee-jerk reactions in countries already at war with each other. Bring down the net and usher in Armageddon. And that was just in this world. No one knew what the implications might be for the Accord if it ran out of resources...

Huey was staring at the floor.

"You getting on okay with the team now, Huey?" Last I'd heard, three of the team weren't even talking to him.

Silence.

"Huey?"

He pressed the side of his head again. "I'm talking to them now, He. Trying to keep them in line, yes?"

Huey had a team of sixteen snapshot-Hueys, running off an almost-reality shard in one of the project's experimental realms. He was parallel-processing himself. I sat in on one of their meetings once. Only once. They had rigged the RS so that they could bootstrap its processing capacity, running things at twice, three, maybe four times normal speed. Their voices had sounded like speeded-up children's toys, all seventeen of them; at first, I'd thought they were arguing, because of the frantic shrilling of their voices; then I had decided that, no, this was just an effect of their jacked up RS; and finally I had realised that they were indeed arguing – violently, passionately. Five subjective minutes of this had been enough to drive me away. No wonder Huey always looked so shell-shocked, living as he did in constant interior dialogue with the reality shard. What I had seen for mere minutes was inside his head twenty-four seven.

They were our star team. What they had been allowed to publish was still causing ripples in the mathematical sciences several years on, but we had soon classified their output.

Right now, Huey and his sixteen inner twins were trying to find the language to describe Kant-space, trying to delineate a realm that was beyond our ability to experience. But it was there nonetheless, although the Hueys still had to pin down the there of it, too.

Just then, Deedee pinged me. Unexpected visitors, one hour's notice.

He should have known better than to bother me with this, when I get to visit the Shanghai centre so infrequently. But then I saw who the visitor was to be, and understood why I had been warned.


BURNHAM, LUCY, AND Tate received a polite welcome; they were taken to the eighteenth floor and given a white tea in a room that looked out across a park where old men played chess in the pouring rain.

"You seem heavy on the theoretical side here," Burnham said casually at one point, to the skinny young woman in a quaintly retro dove-grey Mao suit, who had been introduced as Zhang Xiaoling and was now showing them round.

"That is a strength, yes," she said, in a voice so soft Burnham had to strain to make out her words.

Burnham stopped in the corridor. "Why?" he asked her.

Zhang Xiaoling was more than just a guide. He had spotted that from the off: she was too well informed, too measured and carefully judged in her responses.

She glanced back, stopped, turned.

"Theory underpins all that we do, elector," she said. There was an edge to her words, he realised. Was it fear? Anger at his unannounced intrusion? He didn't know, but he did know that he had her on edge. He could handle being patronised if he knew he had the advantage.

"So will you tell me why you need not one cosmologist but a whole fucking football team of cosmologists?" said Burnham, keeping his voice light and even.

"To play against the football team of quantum physicists?"

Burnham stared at her, then allowed himself to laugh, allowed her to turn the mood from cagey, hostile, to relaxed, nothing to hide.

Tate had continued past them and was now standing by a window at the far end of the corridor. He beckoned and Burnham went to join him. For a moment, he saw nothing odd in the surging crowd in the street below, but then he realised that there was some kind of disturbance, police drones buzzing the throng, spraying them with gas that shimmered in the air. Bricks and boards were being thrown, and riot police had formed a double line across the mouth of a side street, stun guns at the ready.

Zhang Xiaoling came to join them. "No need to be concerned," she told them. "It's not uncommon for the streets to erupt. When you go out, though, remember to wear the breathing masks we give you – the gas may be lingering."

Burnham nodded. He had noted the change in Tate's behaviour. His bodyguard would have noted the route from secure exit to where the car would await them, the lines of escape, the places of refuge in case the unrest should break out again while they were outside. He was a good man to have at your side.

Xiaoling gestured for them to return along the corridor and Burnham noticed that she had three blue dots tattooed on the webbing between forefinger and thumb on her right hand.

"You didn't answer my question," said Burnham.

"The Accord has required much theoretical research, Elector," Xiaoling said. "In all kinds of apparently unrelated fields. We also have a team of applied Kantian philosophers working here."

"That or McDonald's for them, eh?"

She continued: "Here in Shanghai we have been pursuing research into next generation computing. The Accord is embedded in netspace, but soon it will need more resources than even that can provide. The Accord needs to push the development of next generation computing if it is to flourish. We are looking at wetware computing – infinitely self-repairing and self-replicating data architectures based on organic molecular chemistry. We are looking at interstitial processing and data storage – tying data storage and processing into the fundamental nature of the universe, embedding netspace and the Accord into uncollapsed quantum states. In Kantian terms, it's shifting the Accord into another state of being which is beyond our ability to experience. It's all documented. I could ping you a list of references to both academic papers and confidential project reports that outline the research carried out here. It was all personally approved by Professor Barakh."

Lucy Chang pinged him just then, ever efficient, to confirm that there was documentation covering the research work Xiaoling had just outlined. A footnote added that while all legitimately documented, the work appeared to have been downplayed at every opportunity – they clearly didn't want attention drawn to it. There was something going on in Shanghai. Xiaoling was feeding Burnham with a proportion of the truth as a blind to whatever else they were doing here.

They ate a light lunch, looking out across the park, the chess-playing old men, the groups mesmerically doing t'ai chi. They saw more of the research centre's facilities, met more of the staff, and Burnham continued to press Zhang Xiaoling, but she gave them no more.

Finally, they found themselves back down in the lobby, peering out through the glass frontage shielded by its heavy metal grille. Their car was waiting.

"Thank you, Ms Zhang," said Burnham, taking her slender hand in his and shaking it. "This visit has been most illuminating."

She smiled, bowed her head, said, "Pleased to meet you again," which left Burnham puzzled about any previous encounter. There had been no ping from Lucy when they arrived to inform him of any prior meeting with Xiaoling.

"Allow me to accompany you to your car," said Xiaoling, heading for the rotating doors.

Before they left, a man in a suit stepped up to them, proffering skin-coloured masks moulded to fit over nose and mouth. Burnham recalled what Xiaoling had said about the riot gas. He took a mask, pressed it to his face and felt it mould itself into position.

Xiaoling was already waiting outside. The pale flesh colouring of her mask hid her nose and mouth so that she looked unformed, a human template waiting for features to be added.

Burnham stopped by her side. "We've met before?" he asked.

She looked at him. "We must have, I'm sure," she said.

Tate emerged from the rotating doors, followed by Lucy and a Dutch PR man called Rudi de Groot. All three wore masks, de Groot's darker to match his skin tone.

The car was a short distance away across a wide paved area that teemed with people and yet still managed to appear less crowded than earlier. The riot probably had something to do with that. The car's doors were open, a blocky-bodied man in a dark suit waiting outside – some kind of security guard by the look of him.

Burnham started towards the car, but then stopped, motion in the periphery of his vision drawing his attention, someone stumbling, falling, flailing their arms… a muffled male groan… falling face down on the paving, hands clutching at the surface of the grey slabs, knuckles white, clawing so hard that the fingertips left trails of blood across the stone.

Tate.

Down.

Someone had taken Tate out.

And now Lucy, too, her knees buckling, her eyes wide, meeting his look, her body bucking then, as she had some kind of spasm.

Her hands… clutching at the mask.

Something in the mask – there was something in the mask, something that was knocking her out, had already knocked Tate out.

Lucy ripped the thing off, but it was too late. Her eyes rolled, a choking sound came from deep in her throat, and she slumped sideways, across Tate's legs.

Burnham turned, saw Zhang Xiaoling and de Groot watching him.

He paused, waiting for the same thing to happen to him, but nothing.

He tugged at his mask, felt it resisting him as he pulled it off, sucking at his skin; and then it released its grip and he hurled it away.

Hands pinned his arms, a man to either side of him, grips like vices. Two more suited men had emerged from the crowd to seize him, he realised. How had he not noticed them waiting there? How had Tate not noticed them? Now they half-carried him, half-dragged him, across to the car.

They released him and he climbed in. He had no choice. Zhang Xiaoling seated herself at his side. A slim thirty-ish Han Chinese man was already seated by the far door. He had the same three dots tattooed on his hand, between thumb and forefinger, as Zhang Xiaoling… on a hand that was holding a heavy meat cleaver, its blade polished silver like a family heirloom. De Groot climbed into the front seat, and even before the doors had closed the driver had eased into gear and pulled out into the traffic.

"So," said Burnham, "you going to tell me just who the fuck you are, and what you're planning to do?"

# 1.04

WHAT IS GUILT? How do we measure it? What is tangible about it, quantifiable? It must have such a quality, because we can feel more guilty, less guilty, bizarrely not at all guilty in circumstances when we know that we should.

I watched Jack Burnham mould the breather to his face before emerging through the rotating doors and I felt guilty as hell. Not because I had seduced his wife into another world, had loved her and lost her there, that I had loved her over and over in many different fractal realities. I had fallen in love; I felt no guilt over that.

I did not even feel guilt that his violent outburst had unwittingly delivered his wife into my arms. I felt anger, yes, that this man could do such a thing, lash out at you in that way; but a diffuse anger, an anger distanced by circumstance, distanced by worlds.

No, no guilt for those reasons.

But today... today I had spent two hours in the company of Jack Burnham, showing him around the Shanghai centre, pretending to be something I am not, unable to resist the childish urge to hint that I know more than I should. I had him hooked, intrigued – he was clearly puzzling over me, my role, my status.

You would have gone straight to the root of what I was feeling. *Fuck it, Noah*, you would have told me, *you're finding it exciting!* I am a thinker, a planner, a facilitator, but now, today, I was *doing*.

And I felt guilty that it was such a thrill. Guilty that I was misleading Burnham, trapping him.

I tried to remind myself that, also, I was trying to save his life.

I stood on the wide sidewalk, where earlier Sammy Zhang had laid on a riot at my request. He had no need to oblige, but he liked to flex his muscles. A show of force outside our Shanghai centre achieved more for him than merely helping us trap the elector.

Burnham emerged from the rotating doors, then paused as if dazzled by the sunlight. His masked face looked like wax had melted over it, obscuring all but his eyes and eyebrows, a face erased.

His bodyguard, Tate, was close behind him, also masked, alert, eyes never still. Tate was far more than a bodyguard to the elector; you told me once that the two were like brothers, Tate the confidant, the advisor, the sounding board.

Tate close on the heels of his master. And then Lucy Chang, just as watchful, just as wary. Finally, Deedee stepped out into the smog-masked sunlight.

Tate's knees folded beneath him, his arms flew up.

I looked away, looked down.

I looked again, and Tate had left red trails across the paving slabs where he had clawed at the ground before losing consciousness.

Lucy Chang was down too, body jerking, hands clutching at her mask.

I removed my own mask as two of Sammy's men grabbed Burnham and guided him towards the waiting car.

Sammy Zhang was a traditionalist. His man waiting in the car carried an ancient meat cleaver, once a favoured weapon of the Triads. Burnham sat next to this man, and I slipped into the remaining space. I hoped we would be able to convince him to step back from the fundamentalist allegiances, to renew his backing for the Accord. If not, he would have to be stopped, and preparations for that were well under way...

"I AM DIRECTOR of Operations at the Shanghai centre." Zhang Xiaoling gives the little smile that barely tugs at the corners of her mouth, an expression Burnham is rapidly becoming familiar with.

They sit in reclining seats made from slats of bamboo, on a wooden deck suspended over the clear water of a tropical lagoon, the platform connected to a dazzling white beach by a rickety-looking walkway. Fish drift beneath them, visible through gaps between the decking boards. Great broad flatfish, dappled to blend in with the seabed; darting orange dots and arrows, hovering in the water in schools of maybe a couple of hundred fish or more. White seabirds cut slashes across the sapphire sky. Out on the horizon, beyond some kind of reef where white-tops divide the water, a sleek silver yacht lies anchored.

Burnham is wearing black Speedos and wraparound shades; Xiaoling is in a modest jade one-piece, its fabric printed with extravagant blossoms in blue and yellow.

The cane seat is just on the pleasurable side of uncomfortable against Burnham's skin. A jug of sangria sits on a low table between the two seats, two glasses waiting to be filled.

"I get the point," he says, pouring drinks. Warrener. The same meetspace, built from Accord-based algorithms. The same fish and birds. The same jug of sangria. The same fucking Speedos.

"So what are you doing to me? Out there." He pictures the guy with the tattooed hand and the meat cleaver. Far too vividly.

"You want to view?"

He shakes his head.

"Warrener – he's one of yours?"

"There are connections, yes," says Xiaoling, sipping at the drink Burnham has handed her.

Burnham nods. Warrener has just signed his own death warrant. Burnham will give him to Tate. If they haven't already spirited the jerk away to safety. And if Tate is still alive. And if Burnham gets out of this, which he is sure he will – if they were just going to get him out of the way then there's no need for all this.

He takes a mouthful of the sangria, grimaces. He has never liked sangria.

"Let's cut to the chase," he says. "In here, we chat amiably. Somewhere out there, your boys are providing the hospitality. Is this just a friendly warning, or are they going to inflict serious damage just to make sure I learn whatever lesson it is you have lined up?"

"You always were a very direct man," says Xiaoling. That little smile again. A knowing smile. Burnham has met her before. He's sure of that now.

"So?"

"We wish to support you. I am your Director of Operations in Shanghai. Unconventional as this may appear, I am pursuing that role, Elector Burnham. I am a servant of the project."

"What do you want from me?"

"We fear that you may be aligning yourself with certain parties who have always opposed the Accord project," says Xiaoling. "That cannot be allowed to happen – for the good of humankind. Transient political and religious pressures cannot be allowed to derail our work. Or personal vendettas."

Burnham remains expressionless.

"So you're warning me," he says.

She shakes her head. "We are providing you with guidance so that you may make an informed decision, Elector Burnham." She pauses, then continues: "There are others who would take a stronger line. There are moves afoot to defend the Accord, should it come to that. Zhang Xiaoling is not responsible for that."

"I take your warning on board," says Burnham. "Is that it? Are we done here?"

Zhang Xiaoling holds his look. "Tell me, Elector Burnham," she says, "do you love your wife?"

*With all my heart. With all that I am. And more.*

"Fuck off," he says.

That smile again. The dip of the head. In v-space, Burnham notes, she doesn't bear the gangland tattoo on her hand.

"You killed her, though."

Now he studies her more closely. Her expression gives little away. The half-smile has gone. She might just as easily still be wearing the mask from earlier, for all the expression in her face.

Her eyes are fixed on his, though. She is watching, waiting, assessing his response.

For a ludicrous moment Burnham feels like he is in some third-rate cop movie, with Zhang Xiaoling the undercover detective just about to spring her master-piece of deduction on him, but no, she remains silent, watchful.

"Are we finished?" Burnham asks.

He glances towards the walkway where a door has appeared.

He gets up and leaves, not looking back.

PRISCILLA IS STILL riding that high.

She is in London now, back at the Islington flat; the place feels long-deserted, smelling of neglect, of air that has not been disturbed in weeks.

She opens windows, plays *The White Album* loud, dances as she moves about the place, positioning flowers – she had bought armfuls of the things at King's Cross: gerberas, alyssum, lilies, even carnations – clearing dust, plumping cushions.

She is free. Independent.

Had the burden been so much before? The responsibility? Jack, Parliament, the various boards and projects she had supervised. Somehow she always ended up agreeing to do things, volunteering without being asked even… So often Priscilla's mouth works a step or more ahead of her brain. It lands her with responsibilities and it has landed her in trouble before, and sure as fuck it will do so again. She has a whole eternity ahead of her to put her foot in her mouth, after all.

Eternity… The scale staggers her. She flops down on to the deep leather sofa, clutching a cushion to her chest, closes her eyes, thinks, *Forever. For fucking ever.*

She will travel. Not electee-on-business kind of travel, the insides of hotels that could be anywhere, the other electees, the officials, the businesspeople, the worthies and the crooks, the sycophants and the back-climbers. Real travel. India. India had scared her six years ago when she had gone on a fact-finding mission that turned out to be no more than a series of meetings that could have been held anywhere and some seriously dubious photo opportunities. The clamour in the streets. The sheer extremes of contrast between the educated middle classes and the rest. Nowhere before had she seen the direct hit of population and resource crisis as bluntly as she had in Calcutta and Kharagpur. On that trip she had seen the future that was now descending on the West, and she had known it.

But now… now she will go back and she will understand the place, the people. She could live a lifetime there. More. There's so much to learn. She could do that for every country in the world, every region, every district, and still have eternity ahead of her.

She hugs the cushion closer.

The future had scared her before, but now it scares her in a quite different way.


I FRET. ABOUT trains of events set in motion, about forces beyond my control.

But the Accord has never been in my control. I have guided it and shaped it; I have seeded the protocols and directed their evolution into self-sustaining architectures. But control is not mine.

The Accord defends itself. It is a self-stabilising entity, a nexus of order amongst disorder. If the Accord were heaven, then the protocols would be its guardian angels. I fear that Jack Burnham may find that out.

I am back in heaven again, in my heaven, the one that I built. It is not what I had expected. I am alone, as so many are alone in this nascent paradise. You are gone from me. I pray in my atheistic heart that you are merely dead and waiting to rise again, that you are not lost, stranded on a reality shard that was incongruent with consensus, one that never coalesced, never integrated with the whole. That you are not lost forever, an anomaly created by me in my egotism, only to be erased by protocols I instigated and set loose.

But we have more to concern ourselves with than personal loss and the fate of individuals.

I am in Trafalgar Square when reality falters.

Pigeons everywhere, but no one to feed them, only a few people walking through, a young couple sitting and laughing by one of the lions at the foot of Nelson's Column. I stop, caught as always in people's stories. Did these two die tragically together in a crash, a fire, an accident? Were they a couple before? The Accord redefines things like *tragedy*. A family dying together suddenly becomes a thing of hope, for that family will be reborn together and will not have to endure a lifetime of separation, of growing apart. It takes being here, seeing people, to make us realise such basic things. The protocols of the Accord redefine the protocols of life.

Maybe these two had only just met in the Accord, in the days after their deaths.

They have the look of new love about them, but they could have been newly in love and died together, after all. It tells me nothing really, save that they are in love.

This is when I feel that ground-shudder, that quake that you and I had felt on the day when I lost you. I look down, see gaps opening between paving slabs. The couple by the lion are talking excitedly, holding each other, trying to stay balanced on a single slab as the ground opens around them.

I feel dizzy. It is not just the ground that is opening, but the sky, the air around me. Everything is pulling apart. I fall, find myself straddled over two slabs, a great gulf below my midriff.

The slabs are still pulling apart.

I cannot possibly bridge myself like this for much longer.

I am stretched. The ground is pulled apart, the air, and me also.

I lie face down, paving slabs and street dust in my face.

The ground is silent. The ground is solid again.

All I can hear is the bubbling of the pigeons, and a woman's voice, its tone puzzled, dazed: "Adam? Adam?"

I look across to the foot of Nelson's Column. The young woman is there, on her knees, staring at the ground, alone.

"Adam?"

He is gone, her love. Lost.

The consensus quake has taken him. It should have taken me too, but I appear to have a charmed existence, here in this heaven of mine.

The girl starts to sob.

Consensus is still happening. It is not a clear cut-off. The Accord is still in the process of defining itself, all around us.

I take a room in a Travel Inn on the South Bank. I want anonymity right now. I do not wish to be surrounded by memories, as I would be in my flat near the project's offices.

I lie in the centre of the double bed, *On the Waterfront* playing on the wallscreen, sound muted, tension like elastic between Marlon Brando and Eva Marie Saint, amplified by the silence, and by my mood.

The consensus quake has disturbed me greatly. It was always likely that the arrival of consensus would not be a smooth event. The prospect of consensus quakes and incongruities had been put forward by Malky Warrener and his team some time ago, along with suggestions that other forms of strange phenomena might occur – overlays of realities, causality bubbles, identity bleed, and a whole list of even stranger possibilities, many of which would only worry a handful of the world's leading mathematicians and philosophers.

On paper, they had been concerning enough, but coming face-to-face with a Warrener Event is a whole new level of fear. Where did that poor young man go? Where is he now? *Is* he now? If he's dead, he will return. If he is somehow *other*, if he has somehow slipped between the cracks of this reality, then I have no idea what his fate might be.

I reach out for netspace, even though I know my searchbots will ping me if they find any hint of you.

You, Priscilla, you are still gone. You are other. You are elsewhere, elsewhen.

In my egotism I have taken your heaven from you, and I am alone in a world where we should be together.

ELECTOR JACK BURNHAM sat in a deep armchair in his twenty-first floor suite, a glass of Talisker in his hand. Floor-to-ceiling windows gave him a spectacular view across the lights of Shanghai's Hongkou district towards Pudong.

They hadn't touched a hair on his head. They had just wanted to scare him. But they were clearly fearful of him, too, or they would not have treated him so tentatively. That was a useful thing to know.

And there was one more useful thing to know: Zhang Xiaoling and whoever she was working with knew that Burnham had killed his wife. Only three other people knew that, and two of them were dead.

"You dropped your guard again," said Burnham. "That's twice in one day. Your standards are slipping." He took a sip of scotch.

Tate was seated opposite Burnham. His arms and legs were bound to the chrome frame of his chair, but he wasn't resisting anyway, he appeared to be accepting his fate. Tate was naked, his body stark white beneath thick tangles of black hair, his skinny dick shrivelled and almost lost in body hair.

Lucy Chang stood to one side, a stiletto blade dangling casually from her left hand.

It had been surprisingly simple. Tate had come in as soon as Burnham summoned him. He had barely glanced at Lucy, he had been so eager to show remorse at allowing Burnham to be abducted earlier today. He hardly even responded when she raised her arm and sprayed knockout gas into his face from a small palm-sized canister secreted in her hand. He had only started to reach for his gun as the gas took effect, his knees already buckling beneath him.

"So how long have you been spying on me?"

Tate stared at him. He was almost convincing in his apparent bewilderment.

"I don't understand, JB," he said. His voice was under control, no tension showing, just puzzlement.

"For Zhang Xiaoling, or whoever she's working for. Feeding them inside information on what I'm doing. What I've done."

"I don't understand," Tate repeated.

Burnham glanced at Lucy. Following his prompt, she ran her blade swiftly down Tate's torso, collarbone to belly button. A line of red was left in the knife's wake, ruler-straight, bulging as blood pooled, started to run.

Tate gasped sharply, but that was all the reaction he gave. His eyes never left Burnham's.

"This whole thing was set up, Tate. Don't take me for an idiot. You're good, man. You're *fucking* good. You wouldn't just meekly let them fool you with that gas mask trick and let them take me unless you wanted it to happen now, would you?"

"I screwed up, JB. I utterly screwed up." Now Tate dropped his head, turned his gaze to the carpet.

"So you say. Now tell me, Tate: how did they know I killed my wife?"

Now Lucy looked at Burnham sharply, surprised. She hadn't known.

And Tate was managing to look surprised too. For a moment Burnham was unsure what to do next.

"What else have you been passing on?" They knew he'd been flirting with al-Naqawi and Nesbitt – Zhang Xiaoling had made that clear, without going as far as naming names. Tate had been privy to so much!

"Nothing. I've been loyal to you ever since I joined the team, JB. You know that."

Another glance, a swift slash, and there was a horizontal red line across Tate's chest, running through both nipples.

Now Tate gasped for breath, the muscles in his jaw visibly knotting, sweat breaking out across his face.

Another glance, another slash, lower down, across Tate's belly.

"How long have you been spying on me?"


HE DREAMS.

Or at least, he thinks he must be dreaming. That's what people do, isn't it? Fragments of unreality so much more real and vivid than reality. He has read somewhere that dreams are a way of making sense of your life, of categorising short-term memory into long-term experience, finding meanings and lessons and storing them for future use.

And so he dreams.

The city. A big river winding through its heart, seen from above, from a helicopter. Sitting around him, a dozen or more troops in khaki NBC suits waiting to be dropped off. Their masks have mirrored eyepieces, making it impossible to tell who is who, save for the name tags attached to the right breast of each suit. Johnson, Walker, Docherty, Cooper... He glances at Cooper's monitor patch slotted into the holder on his left shoulder, the words by the detector strips upside down so Cooper can read them. Each strip remains white: no traces of the main chemical and biological agents, but then they aren't down on the ground yet. The rad counter is already a third of the way along its bar.

Soon they will land, search, and rescue. He knows already that this whole city is fucked, but at the same time he is excited, he feels the buzz; he's only a volunteer but right now he's a real soldier, playing with the big boys.

He grips his semi-automatic in heavily gloved hands and waits for the command to go...

... he woke up. This was real. He was sure this was real, even though he was not sure what real *was*.

He breathed. He was acutely conscious that he breathed. He felt the pull of his intercostal muscles lifting and expanding his rib cage, of his diaphragm pulling down, of the air rushing in through his nostrils, down his trachea, filling the vacuum in his lungs.

He heard a low background hum, the sound of someone shuffling feet, moving awkwardly. Bright light shone through his closed eyelids, so that he saw a kind of fleshy orange screen, dark floaters drifting across his vision.

Two people, maybe three, trying to be quiet. He was wearing light clothing – maybe only a hospital gown, nothing on his feet. No weapons other than what he might be able to improvise from what he found in this room. The only advantage he had was that he knew he was conscious and, as yet, they did not.

He opened his eyes the tiniest fraction, let the light flood in so that his pupils could adjust. He couldn't see much, but guessed he was in some kind of hospital room, or maybe a laboratory.

He breathed.

Tensed.

Sat upright, swung his legs to the right, dropped to the floor, looked around.

A door three paces ahead of him. A blinded window to one side. A picture of bobbing yellow flowers in a vase on the wall. Two men, one in a suit and one in a white coat, mouths open, stepping back, away from him, raising their hands in surprise or self-defence or preparation to attack.

He took a step towards the door, feet acutely aware of the cold tiled floor.

His head swirled, blood rushing, black clouds descending on him, heart pounding.

He reached for the doorframe and caught himself just as his legs started to give way.

On his knees now, looking up into the face of the man in the white coat. He tried to work his mouth, but nothing happened; tried to talk but couldn't shape the words.

He slumped back on his heels, supported in strong arms.

He didn't understand.

This body...

This wasn't his body.

# 1.05

YOU LIVE.

You have been reborn.

*Priscilla!*

Your entry point was Deanmere Gap, the village where you spent the later years of your childhood, looked after by your mother, your father an intelligence officer killed in Gaza.

You have died and now you are reborn.

Now you head back to London.

You are coming back to me!

Priscilla... I am here. I am waiting. I would wait for an eternity as long as I know that you are on your way.

BURNHAM STOOD ON the balcony, drinking his scotch, savouring the smoky mix of peat and seaweed and pepper in each sip. The view of the night-time city was stunning, so many lights appearing to hang in space from the skyscrapers, glimmering in the thick, muggy night air. Life was so rich! How could they ever hope to emulate it in the Accord? Sure, the meetspaces he had used seemed pretty convincing, but how could they ever capture that mix of shabby human existence and the sheer exhilaration of *being*?

Lucy Chang joined him. "Nothing more," she said.

He had hardly expected to extract anything from a man of Tate's training and character, but they'd had to try. Each of them understood the position.

"What do you think?" he asked, handing her his glass. She sipped, handed it back, leaving bloody smears on its cut crystal sides.

"Tate has not been spying," she said. "He is loyal."

Burnham nodded. "That was my guess," he said. "But I had to be sure."

Lucy nodded now.

"You know what that means, don't you?" he said. "If Tate didn't tell them I killed Priscilla, then they must have found out from Priscilla or Barakh, and they're both dead..."

"Could Barakh have told them before he killed himself?"

"His movements and messaging were all traced in detail by the official investigation," said Burnham. "I know: I had the files sent to me. He contacted nobody. He left no messages. So he must have told them *after* he killed himself!"

Lucy looked puzzled for a moment, and then she saw what Burnham's words implied. "From the Accord? But..."

Burnham nodded, eyes blazing, a bitter grin on his face. "They know a way to communicate in and out of the Accord!" he said. "They must do!" He had been right, despite Warrener's assurances: there was always a way.

Then he thought it through one step further: Warrener! If he was in league with Jang Xiaoling then he had very probably known all along that it was possible to communicate with people in the Accord! Warrener had signed his own death warrant more than once...

They stood in silence for what seemed like minutes, taking it in turns to sip at the scotch. Finally, Lucy Chang said, "What about Tate?"

Burnham turned to her. Tate would not be in a forgiving mood when he emerged from this. He was a wounded animal, a wounded predator. "Kill him," he said. "Give the body back to Zhang Xiaoling. Let her deal with it. She's not going to want any mess here on her own doorstep that might implicate the project."

Then, an afterthought: "Oh, and replace him, would you? Use your contacts to find me someone. I have a feeling I'm going to need protection."

He turned back to the city lights, sipped at his drink, felt sharp brininess explode in his mouth.

PRISCILLA IS FREE. She is single again, and she likes it.

She does not need an other half in her life.

Not now, at least. There will be others, of course; there will be an eternity of others.

But now... now she is freer than she has ever been in her life.

Should she feel guilty about this? Should she feel more than just a slight pang of regret that she finds it so easy to draw a line under her time with Jack? She had been drawing that line for some time, though; it was not new that they lived pretty much separate lives.

She explores the museums and galleries, sometimes sitting for an hour or more before a particular picture, losing herself in light on water, in distant mountains, in the freeze-frame pose of a Parisian ballerina. She sits by the river, or in Soho Square or one of the parks, noting as each day passes the shift from occasional lone people to, if not crowds then at least a feeling that there is a population here. The world fills up as people die.

But they are mostly alone. It must hurt so much for many of them, the separation, the loss, the being lost.

But for many... for many it is release. A guilty, hedonistic, *exciting* release.

She finds herself drinking in a bar near Piccadilly Circus. Bloody Mary, the spices so hot the drink makes sweat break out on her forehead. The place is half full. People seem to know where to gather in a city so far below capacity.

His name turns out to be Omar, although he doesn't look like an Omar. He has a wiry thin body, collar-length chestnut hair, spaniel eyes, and he claims to be in his sixties, despite his youthful incarnation in the Accord.

He persuades her to try a tequila slammer, she copies him, bangs it on the bar, and it fizzes over before she can bring it to her mouth. They giggle like schoolkids, into their hands, into each other's shoulders. His mouth tastes of ginger ale, his stubble tingles, awakens feeling, sensitivity.

It feels wrong. He is so young. But then she is, too. They are both young things. Both free and single, and just a little intoxicated.

"I know a place," he says into her ear. "A club. Where people have fun."

Outside the bar, they link arms, walk.

Soon they are inside again, heading up a narrow staircase. Music meets them, something jazzy, something recent.

There's a bar, a woman leaning on it being served, wearing stockings, suspenders, basque.

Priscilla feels overdressed in her black jeans and loose top. A couple at a nearby table wear more clothes, but not for long by the look of it, their faces locked, their hands squeezing, grasping, their limbs tangled.

Omar takes her hand and leads her to the bar.

They have cocktails, Priscilla doesn't know what they are – something with a tangy fruit juice and one hell of an afterburn. They find a table, drink, press legs hard against each other. Priscilla looks about her as her eyes adjust to the low lighting. As well as the tables, with low leather sofas and bucket seats, there are more secluded booths, doorways through to other areas. The couple nearby stop kissing, look around, as if seeking something. The man is tall, a Slavic look to his features, eyes intense as they make contact with Priscilla's; the woman, a short-haired blonde, her skin flushed. Priscilla smiles; the couple kiss again.

Priscilla turns to Omar, takes a handful of his hair and draws his face into hers, tastes the ginger again, feels the rasp of his chin on hers.

They get more drinks, find themselves sitting with the other couple when they come back from the bar. There is lots of laughter, laughter that requires leaning into the person nearest, clutching at arms, hugging. The blonde woman tastes of gin, tonic water, the man of whisky.

There are other rooms, branching off the main bar area, some of them already occupied, but one quiet. Omar pushes Priscilla against the wall, seizes her loose black top, pulls it clear of her head, and then she feels that stubble rasp dragging across her collarbone, her breasts, her belly.

She is turned by hard hands – not Omar's – feels her jeans pulled down, tugged free from her feet, her black thong being pulled aside. She grips the blonde woman for support, feels soft, smooth flesh. Tastes gin, tonic, again. Finds Omar, or he finds her. Tastes salt, skin. Gasps at the touch of fingers, gasps...

BURNHAM WATCHED DAWN pour its golden light through the fuggy air among the skyscrapers, sparking flares and rainbows off windows and metal frames, painting grey concrete and stone amber, honeyed, gold.

Lucy Chang sat opposite him in the seat where Tate had been bound the previous evening, neat as ever in her tailored pinstripe suit, the trousers fashionably baggy so that the outlines of her legs were only suggested even as she sat. Burnham found himself wondering what it'd be like to fuck her. She would be good. Naturally. In all his time with Priscilla he had remained faithful, despite the numerous opportunities to get his rocks off elsewhere. He looked after himself, and what the gym and his nutritionist couldn't provide the cosmetic surgeons and pills did, but he had no illusions: it was power that opened the doors, not the fact that he was a well-preserved fifty-ish. It wasn't that he had particular standards or principles; he understood how so many relationships went after time, and that rigid adherence to ideas like faithfulness was naive and unrealistic. It had simply been that he had wanted no other. There had only been Priscilla, from the very first day she had strode into his office, political science student on a gap year, intern to the new electee.

He could fuck Lucy right now if he wanted to. She would – out of loyalty and career planning, if nothing else, although he more than half-suspected she was genuinely turned on by power and would be more than willing. He wondered what it would be like. It had been so long since he had been with another woman. Would she groan deep from the belly as passion took her? Would she be demanding or would she rely on him to take the lead? Would she come easily or would he have to work hard for her? Would he feel the muscles of her cunt spasming afterwards?

He shifted in his deep armchair, hard, disturbed. His mind was playing tricks on him, taunting him with thoughts he didn't want right now.

Lucy's lips moved, almost imperceptibly, as she subvoked into her jaw-mike. She stared straight ahead, unseeing, or only partly seeing her surroundings, her main focus directed inwards, studying data-flows, mails, pings.

"You should see this," she said, interrupting his thoughts. She glanced towards the wallscreen and it sprang into life, sound fading up to a comfortable level.

It was *News 247*, newsbites arrayed along the bottom of the screen, talking heads waiting to be activated up the left-hand side. The main screen estate was taken up by camerazzi coverage of a rally, filmed from a drone buzzing low over crowds of surging, shouting, chanting demonstrators.

"... claimed a total of seventy-five thousand people attending, but police put the number at twenty thousand," said the female voiceover.

The picture cut to an aerial view of a cluster of boats out at sea. Three small fishing smacks, a couple of larger vessels, and an orange inflatable that appeared to be nearly swamped by the waves. People crowded each of the boats, black-skinned and thin, their faces turned up to the helicopter overhead, as if to heaven. They must have travelled thousands of miles packed into these boats like this. How many more had tried and failed, taken out by rough seas, shortage of food, water, fuel?

"I should be back there, shouldn't I, Lucy?" said Burnham.

She turned her gaze on him, still part-focused on her datafeed. "There's more," she said.

For a moment, Burnham was confused, but then he realised she was referring to the news-stream and not to the people on the boats. The coverage had returned to the camerazzi feed from the demonstration. The banners and placards brought to mind Burnham's visit to the refugee camp in Bexhill-on-Sea. *African't. No refuge. White rights. See them off. Charity begins at home.*

Cut to a platform somewhere at the front of the crowd, a small group of men in suits. One of them jacketless, crumpled linen shirt open at the neck. Nesbitt.

"... sources close to the Cabinet confirmed this morning that Electee Nesbitt has been in closed talks with Electors Burnham and al-Naqawi. The wide-ranging discussions were reported to be amicable and constructive, with an emerging consensus on migration, trade controls and the Accord..."

Burnham stared at the screen. He felt old. Several steps behind. He was being out-flanked by a puppy-faced retro-fascist and a wily old fundamentalist. There had been no such discussions, but now everyone would believe there had been, or at least that there *might* have been, which was as good as *had been* for most people.

"... growing consensus that the Accord should face thorough investigation following last month's murder of Electee Priscilla Burnham by Noah Barakh, principal architect of the Accord and the man the tabs are calling 'The man who built heaven'. Pressure is growing for the Accord to be, effectively, switched off while investigations take place…"

Burnham felt trapped by a cleft stick, being pushed into making choices he had been heading towards in any case… It wasn't as easy as simply switching things off, but if it could be done… His hatred for Barakh burnt deep in his belly, his need to… to *stop* the two of them.

Nesbitt was talking to the crowd now, the usual racist cant dressed up in tones that were reasonable and calm, using language and references carefully selected to simultaneously press xenophobic hate buttons in the extremists' heads and *thank God there's finally someone speaking the language of the ordinary man* buttons in the middle-class little Englanders' heads. The man was slick; that had never been in any doubt.

Burnham sighed. The saddest, most heart-rending thing was that maybe Nesbitt was right, even if it was for all the wrong reasons: the world simply didn't have enough to go around. It was, as he and Tate had agreed, all about survival.

"Now," said Lucy, leaning forward in her seat. "Watch now…"

Burnham studied Nesbitt. The electee was cranking up the passion in his speech, reeling in the crowd; he was gesturing with his right hand, stabbing the air to punctuate his speech, for all the world like one of his Nazi forebears.

"We are bound" – *stab* – "to our native land, the land that has fed us for countless generations. We are bound" – *stab* – "to our native shores. We will drive" – *stab* – "them from these shores. We *will*" – *stab* – "defend what is ours."

He had his audience in the palm of his well-manicured hand. Now, that hand reached down to his hip and Burnham saw that the electee was wearing a holster.

Nesbitt drew a long-muzzled pistol and waved it in the air.

"The Legislature moves slowly, my fellow Englanders, but in only days the Bill will be passed and the protection of these shores will be the right – no, the *duty* – of every man and woman."

He raised the gun, fired it once, twice, a third time, into the air.

"I will be there, my friends. I will be with you on the beaches, defending what is ours by right, ours by descent, ours by heritage. Together we will protect our native shores!"

"Projections?" asked Burnham, pinging the screen to gag the sound.

Lucy paused, then said, "Projections are erratic. Escalation of unrest. Conflict between Nesbitt's Englanders and pro-movement groups like the Soul Harvesters and World Amnesty. Bloodshed won't be confined to the shooting of migrants. The Henley Model projects a fifteen per cent probability of military intervention in southern coastal hotspots within the next month: Eastbourne, Dover, Portsmouth, Hastings, Bexhill-on-Sea, Worthing. That has grown from three per cent yesterday. Unrest is likely to spread into dump estates throughout the south where the English Nationals have been blaming everything on migration and stirring up a lot of hostility."

"The Cambridge Model?"

"Concurs on the broad view; differs on detail and probabilities, but only by a few points. Electee Nesbitt's strategy is based on provoking unrest and then trying to steer the reaction. He is throwing all the pieces in the air and aiming to catch as many as he can as they fall to the ground. He sees it as a no-lose approach: if he gains influence then his strategy has worked; if he fails to steal any political ground then he can still point to the unrest and blame it on Legislature policy on migration. Either way he will not be the one who has to sort out the chaos, which can only be harmful to the Legislature."

"Wild cards?" There were always wild cards.

"The boat people," said Lucy. "Up to now, with the exception of a few handguns and knives, they have been unarmed."

"Safer for the bastards who sell them places on the boats," said Burnham. "So you're saying that might change?"

"Almost certainly. There really will be fighting on the beaches, and it won't all go the way Electee Nesbitt proclaims."

Burnham nodded, grim. "And the Accord?"

"His position is a strategic one: he is claiming a moral stance, but it is most likely a strategy to secure backing of Christian and other fundamentalist conservatives on the migration question."

"What does he expect to happen now? What's the next step in his strategy?"

"He's trying to draw you in," said Lucy. "He already has some kind of arrangement with al-Naqawi, and with Electees Sharma, O'Neill and Gallagher. He is working on Elector Vaughan, and at least five other electees. He is building a broad coalition."

"So he needs me: with my backing Vaughan and the others will be far easier to sway. Okay. What if they're right? What if beneath the tin-pot fascism a hardening of borders is really the best way to ensure that at least some of us survive in this world we've so well and truly fucked up?"

Lucy didn't show a flicker of surprise at the line he was taking. "You want me to arrange for you to meet Nesbitt?"

He shook his head. "Not yet, but it's an option. Tell me: where's al-Naqawi? He back in Jakarta?"

A momentary pause, a glazing of the eyes, then: "Yes."

"Okay. That's where we're going next. A slight detour. I want to talk to him, get a feel for what Nesbitt is offering people like him. If I'm going on-board with Nesbitt I need to know how I can steer him and his coalition."

Another brief glazing over. "Confirmed," said Lucy. "Suborbital flight for us and two bodyguards from Shanghai Pudong to Soekarno-Hatta Jakarta on Garuda Indonesia for two-fifteen this afternoon."

"And put word out that I'm seriously considering throwing my weight behind Nesbitt. I want to see how he reacts, and what the snap polls say."

Lucy nodded. Burnham knew that already she would be leaking to the tabs and agencies from "a source close to Elector Burnham."

"Good. And Lucy? Trace a Chuckboy Lee. Based in a warehouse in Jakarta. Has worked for the project but I don't think you'll find anything official."

He would play Nesbitt's game, side with the fundamentalists if necessary, and if that meant the destruction of the Accord then he would shed no tears; what mattered was survival in *this* world, and if the price was that the plug would be pulled on the ghosts of his wife and her lover then there would be a bittersweet justice involved.

But first... first he would see what Lee had to tell him about the Accord.

Warrener had said Lee was one of the best, if anyone could unravel the Accord then he was the man. Which had to mean that if anyone could use whatever method Zhang Xiaoling had to communicate with people in the Accord then that person was probably Lee too.

Warrener... Warrener had given him the name. It could be a trap, another piece in the elaborate puzzle Barakh had left behind. Or it could have been fear talking, something real to buy the safe release of Warrener's flesh-and-blood self. Either way, Lee was the next step.

"No official records," said Lucy. "But an apparent nickname and the name 'Lee' aren't much to go on. We have a Rachel Lee, a mid-grade analyst at the London office; a Jupiter Lee, clerical officer in Sydney; both work on the project, but neither look like good matches."

"Try your unofficial sources, Lucy. By the time we arrive in Jakarta I want to know where this guy is, what he looks like, how he thinks, all of his vices, his fucking shoe size. Okay?"

Lucy nodded, at work already.


"IT WILL BE a completely new kind of space," says Huey Kashvili. He sits on the beach, drawing patterns in sand firmed by the retreating tide.

I nod. That is the point, really.

"When?" I ask.

Malky Warrener is knee-deep in the sea, the faded blue of his jeans wet to mid-thigh. "We're running out of time," he says. "You've seen that, Noah. You've seen consensus bursting at the seams."

The consensus quakes... Not irregularities as consensus takes hold, but – if Warrener is right – indications that the Accord is approaching some kind of crisis. We always knew this would come, but never anticipated that it might be so soon. We can set all the Sammy Zhangs in the world on to securing virtual real estate for us, by whatever means they care to use, but all they will ever be able to do is buy us a little more time.

Netspace is not big enough. The world is not big enough... not for *two* worlds...

Another Huey joins us, jumping into this meetspace from the Huey shard. He walks down the beach, through the markings of his other instance. He points at Warrener. "*You...*" he says, jabbing his finger. "*You...*"

Then he stops, looks around, says, "Oh... fuck," and fades from the 'space.

The first Huey says, "I'm breaking up. I'm kind of a Warrener Event in miniature: I can't draw enough resources to sustain the team. We are struggling."

"You have to," I tell him. "You have to finish the proof. You have to give us the blueprint so that we can start to test the move."

If the world is not big enough, then we have to find another one...

HE STAYED QUIET as his senses kicked in, kept his eyes closed. There was a lot of background noise: the electrical engine whine from traffic in a street nearby, the occasional splutter of internal combustion, jangling bicycle bells, voices talking, shouting, laughing, even singing, a goat bleating, music from a radio or TV. Sweat beaded his skin. His clothes felt rough, cheap. The heat was unpleasant, the humidity like a heavy blanket smothering him, making his body wet even before he had tried to move. The heavy, broiling atmosphere made the smells of body odour, decay and spices all the more intense. Or maybe that was just him recalibrating: new environment, new senses. It always took a while to stabilise. He had learnt that much by now.

He wondered who he would be this time.

He opened his eyes, saw a corrugated metal ceiling stained brown and black by damp, flies buzzing in mindless circles. It was mostly gloomy in here, wherever *here* was, save for a single shaft of bright light angling in through an unglazed window.

He turned. Through the window he saw the back of an old stallholder's head, smoke from his pipe haloing him like some barroom jesus. Beyond him, the street: bustling, packed. Asia, somewhere in Asia. Thailand, Cambodia, Vietnam, the Philippines. It didn't matter much.

He looked down. His body was scrawny, white, maybe sixty kilos of skin and bone. He wore battered pumps, baggy khaki shorts, a grubby white T-shirt.

Pretty much what you'd expect from a sweat: some kid out in the world for the first time, runs short of money, hires himself out for a few hours to cover the shortfall. We've all been there, or our sons and daughters have. Hire your body out so some rich fuck can have fun in it; get it back with maybe a bit of damage and the odd virus or two, but hey, the ghosting company covers you for all that, so you're fine, fixed up in no time, back to yourself with a couple of thousand bucks in your pocket where there was none before. These people, these lowly kids who trade the use of their bodies for cash, were called sweats, rides.

He closed his new eyes, bounced himself around inside his new skull. *You in there, motherfucker? Is any of you left?*

But no... his host's mind, his *self*, had been safely warehoused for the duration, would get pumped back in when his time was up.

He opened his eyes, stood, adjusting to the mechanics of an unfamiliar body, the balance, all the little inner feedbacks that allow us to stand and not teeter and fall. He knew what to expect from this now.

He jumped, did the starfish in mid-air, squatted on landing, dropped to press up, managed twenty before his arms felt about ready to fall off. Rolled over onto his back, did twenty sit-ups and wished this grubby jerk had had money for deodorant, or had at least washed before hiring himself out. At least the body wasn't completely wrecked already. He needed it to be a fit one, a sweat who was ready for a bit of action.

Okay... If he were one of the idle rich, out for kicks, he'd head off and burn credit in the nearest mall, clean himself up, kit himself out before hunting down some fun. That was another of the perks for the sweats: they usually ended up being pampered a bit, new outfit, that kind of thing. Sometimes it got trashed, of course: Armanis shredded in a knife-fight when a night out turned bad. Sometimes the sweat got trashed too; that went with the territory. Why hire a ride if you're not going to try out something you couldn't or wouldn't do in your own body?

He walked to the beaded doorway, peered out, and the old man turned his head, bowed a little, smiling. "You tell me what you wanna do, mister, I tell you the place to go and the man who can set you up." In his baggy jeans and Sex Pistols T-shirt, the old man didn't exactly look like the proprietor of a ghosting company's premises, but that didn't really mean much. Sometimes it would be a swanky high-class clinic, sometimes a back-street dive like this. It all depended on what the client was looking for, and willing to pay for; and it depended how desperate the ride was.

"I don't need nothing, thank you, sir," he told him, and stepped past him into the street.

He had business to attend to.


PRISCILLA SITS ON a bench in Hyde Park, looking out across the Serpentine. This used to be Jack's route to his office. She doesn't know why she is here, why she is thinking of him.

She has mail, but she will not read it. She does not want responsibilities to settle on her shoulders again; not just yet. She is still free.

It is early, the sun finding strength. She closes her eyes. She hasn't slept in two days, at least. When she turns her head it feels like it keeps turning, even when she has stopped. She is still a little drunk, a little intoxicated with whatever it was she took last night.

The sun feels good, its energy seeping into sore muscles and joints.

She opens her eyes and notices a child hunched in the shade of a nearby bush, a boy of about eight, very black skin, thin like the cliché boat kid on the news. He is looking at the ducks on the water. He appears mesmerised by them, by their ceaseless activity.

"Hey you," she calls softly to him.

He jumps, startled, stares at her with frightened eyes.

"You okay there?" She wonders if he understands her words.

He turns to look at the ducks again.

All the lonely people, she realises. All of them, come to the Accord, alone, parted from what they know. They come here with nobody. Poor fucking kid…

"Hey," she says again. "You hungry? You like pizza?"

She sits forward. It hurts like fuck to move, but… poor fucking kid.

"Do you have a name? Do you?"

The boy watches the ducks; Priscilla waits. She has eternity. They both do.


TATE HAD ALWAYS mixed a great martini, and he knew when to chat and when to remain judiciously silent. He had managed to establish a place in Burnham's small entourage that was more than just bodyguard: he had been a sounding board, a lightning rod, a source of grounding, of staying in touch with the real world. Increasingly, he had become Burnham's friend…

But *fuck*, he had never been able to give a Nuat phaen boran massage like Sunan could!

Burnham lay face down on a padded mat by the pool while the skinny young bodyguard, who had accompanied him from Shanghai with Lucy and a bigger, older guard called Lin Huy, pressed on his lower back with what felt like at least four hands and both feet.

In the pool, Lucy swam lengths in a peculiarly rigid head-up breaststroke fashion. Burnham wouldn't be surprised if she was still viewing datafeeds, hooked into netspace, sub-voking as she exercised.

Sunan took Burnham's right arm and stretched it out behind him, pulling at the fingers until the joints cracked. God, but it felt good!

He opened his eyes again and saw Lucy's feet nearby. She was wrapped in a big white towel, looking down at him. "I have located Lee," she said. "He lives in the

Sadikin Scheme in Sunda Kelapa, the old port district. He never leaves."

"Good, good. When do I see al-Naqawi? This evening, isn't it? When is it now?" So many fucking time zones. He had completely lost track... It was daylight here in Jakarta, that was the best he could do.

"It's almost two in the afternoon. Six hours until your appointment with Elector al-Naqawi."

Burnham shrugged Sunan off and sat, twisting at the waist. "Okay. You head in to Sunda Kelapa now. Get your bearings, the lie of the land. But no contact with Lee. I'll follow with Sunan and Huy."

Lucy nodded, turned, left.

Burnham turned to Sunan. "One more arm and we're done, eh?"

Sunan looked blankly at him, then gestured for him to lie down again.

Burnham settled face down, let the kid take his left arm, pull, stretch, press.

LOOKING LIKE SHIT had its advantages.

Looking like this, like a Western kid down on his luck and right out of money, and probably a junkie to boot, the hawkers and hustlers took one look at him and no more. No hassle. Easier money elsewhere.

He hit the main drag and flagged down a bright orange Honda rickshaw, gave the driver an address that popped into his head. The driver jabbered something in his face and he guessed the meaning; he waved a wad of bills in the air to prove he could pay. The driver gestured him into the seat, and then gunned his engine back into life.

Slowly, they passed through streets packed with stalls and throngs of people, some traders selling from goods simply stacked up in the street, a district where everything seemed to be made from warped sheets of corrugated metal. And then, almost immediately, crisp skyscrapers, glass and chrome and palm trees growing from raised, walled beds. Here, the military presence was noticeably heavier: where before there had been cops and troopers in occasional twos and threes, now they occupied sentry posts at all the major junctions and guards stood duty at every building entrance. The traffic crawled, rarely above walking pace, but the rickshaw driver darted in and out of gaps, took short-cuts up alleyways and across public gardens so that both driver and passenger had to hang on tight. The air was thick, hot, burning acidly in the lungs.

An hour or so later they were pulling up in a residential part of the city, somewhere up in the hills, white houses partly hidden behind stone walls and cast-iron railings. Rich vegetation crammed the gardens around manicured lawns and large, open swimming pools.

They had made one stop along the way already. A cramped side street, a doorway screened by a beaded curtain. A bony kid sat on her haunches outside, flicking at the flies with a stick and watching him as he pushed through the beads to another shady room where he found the man, struck a deal, came out with a heavy lump of steel tucked into his waistband.

Now, he paid off his driver and walked up to an iron-bar gate that extended at least a metre above his head. He looked through to the sprawling white mansion, people in and around the pool, cars pulled up out front.

A security camera watched him from the top of the wall. He ran clawed hands through lank hair stuck to his scalp with sweat and grease, gave a junkie twitch, rubbed his nose on his upper arm, turned away.

# 1.06

YOU HAVE COME to London, but you have not come to me…

I am not sure what to make of this. Why have you not come to me, Priscilla? Is it that I am not staying at the Bethnal Green flat and so you do not know where to find me? But then you never went there anyway. I have monitored my mail, but nothing. You have not attempted to message me in any way, and you have not responded to my messages.

Maybe there is a fault somewhere, a glitch.

And so I go to you.

You have spent much time in bars and a club in the West End. There does not appear to be a regular address where you stay, although I know you have been back to your Islington flat more than once.

You also spend time in Hyde Park and it is here that I choose to wait.

I am nervous, more so than I would have anticipated.

The day is overcast, muggy, bringing to mind Shanghai, although the humidity is nowhere near as high. I adjust the hang of my clothes awkwardly, aware of every irritation, every discomfort.

You have come back to London, Priscilla, and I have come to find you. We have the future before us. We have our love.

\* \* \*

ELECTOR JACK BURNHAM took the call on the wallscreen by the pool. He leaned on the side, naked, his legs trailing out behind him in the water, kicking occasionally to stay afloat.

On the screen, Lucy stood on a street corner, her sharp suit a stark contrast to the people rushing about her. Corrugated metal shacks and stalls filled the backdrop: fish, fruit, fabrics, plastic household goods. At one stall, a woman sat with a Soul Harvesters' skullcap clinging to her head while a thin black man held her hand, mouthing reassuring words to her.

The view of Lucy was distant, from high up, and Burnham realised it must be from a streetcam, patched through onto the comms channel.

"Elector," said Lucy. "Lee is in an old warehouse a hundred metres from here. He is likely to be here all afternoon. He never leaves, apparently. I could make contact, and arrange for you to see him?"

"Tell me about him first. What does he do? What are his weaknesses?"

"Very few. He eats any shit food his friends bring him. Doesn't drink or shoot up. He is an elective eunuch, surgically established. Getting to see him is one thing, but if we get heavy he has the protection of just about all the organised gangs in South-East Asia. If he is damaged they would come down so heavily it'd be like a Third World War..."

Burnham kicked at the water, thinking. "We need leverage."

And then...

Lucy Chang's face started to melt on-screen, softening, subsiding, starting to drip like candle wax.

Burnham straightened, feet on the tiled bottom of the pool, water to his ribs.

"You need better security," said Lucy's slip-sliding face in a soft, little-girl voice.

Her features were bloating now, expanding, her skin darkening, her hair lengthening into a glossy black ponytail. Her jacket and blouse started to melt away, revealing small breasts, dark nipples like rag dolls' eyes. Her torso expanded, became rounded, loaded with puppy fat, and now a tattoo emerged, a dragon wrapping around her chest and shoulders from behind.

"Mr Lee," said Burnham.

S/he nodded.

Lee had hacked into the transmission, taken over.

Again, Burnham felt old, sidestepped, and let down by people he relied on. First Tate had allowed his guard to drop in the most serious fashion and now even Lucy had been seriously sloppy.

The big screen went fizzy grey, static, nothing.

"You want to see me?" said Lee's sing-song voice from somewhere across the pool. Burnham twisted, saw the hacker's face somehow projected onto the window, ghost-like, smiling wistfully.

Burnham nodded. "I'd like to discuss work you've done in the development of the Accord," he said.

"You want to destroy the Accord, so I hear."

"You shouldn't always believe what you hear. I want to understand it. I want to know how it works and what is possible."

Again, Lee vanished. Burnham turned three-sixty in the water. Nothing.

Long seconds passed.

And then the voice again, this time inside his head: "I know you want to find Professor Barakh."

Burnham put his hands to his temples, feeling suddenly violated, invaded. Lee had patched into his comms chip, something that was simply not possible. He closed his eyes, saw Lee's rounded features floating before him, that same wistful smile.

Burnham nodded, then said aloud, "I want to find Barakh, yes."

"Your security is sloppy," said Lee. "I don't work with amateurs – they endanger me."

"Then help me fix it," said Burnham.

Lee faded from inner vision. Burnham suddenly felt the presence departing, like a weight lifting. He turned back towards the edge of the pool, and there was Lee on the wallscreen again, apparently standing on the street corner where Lucy had been.

"We will talk," said Lee, finally. "Now. You will come here – your assistant knows where to find me. We will talk about your security options and we will discuss Professor Barakh and the Accord and why I would like to help you track him down. But you will not kill him, Elector Burnham. That is far too good for him. There are other options we may wish to explore…"

THEY MADE IT so easy for him.

Shortly after he had arrived at the villa, a car pulled away from the house and headed out through the automatic gates. In the front was a grey-haired male driver, in the back a young Chinese woman with the trained eyes of a killer.

He lingered in the shadows, leaning against the wall, hidden by a stand of acacias. The car left, the gates closed, he waited.

Less than an hour later he heard the electric whine of three scooters coming down the drive. Just as the big gates swung open again he staggered out into the roadway, looking disorientated, confused.

One bike knocked him stumbling sideways, and he landed on his knees, head spinning. His left wrist jagged with a stab of pain in a way that made his stomach clench. Blood started to seep through the knees of his khaki trousers.

The scooters skidded to a halt, the one that struck him somehow managing to stay upright.

Voices rose, suddenly.

"Wha—?"

"You stupid fucking idiot!"

"Hey! Hey, Mr B – you okay?" This addressed to the rider of the scooter that had hit him.

A bulky Chinese guy in shorts and a gold netting vest loomed suddenly nearby, one of the scooter riders. "You okay, bud?" he asked. Then: "What the fuck were you doing?"

He squinted up at the guy's square face, then turned away. One of the others.

He looked at the one on the lead scooter, the one who had hit him. The one they called Mr B.

He was still sitting there, one foot on the ground. He was older than the one who had spoken, older than the other guy too – a skinny kid who was just going up to Mr B, saying something to him.

Mr B's dark hair was a thick, short crop, and his muscle top showed off his bulging shoulders and pecs. Hard to say how much of it was cosmetic, but it was the kind of look you'd expect from someone who paid the bills for the mansion they'd just emerged from.

Mr B looked at him, watched him reach for the Heckler and Koch tucked into his waistband.

The heft of the gun felt at once natural and strange in this hand that might never have held a gun before.

He fired it, once, twice, allowing his right arm and shoulder to ride out the recoil.

One round took Mr B right between the eyes, the other in the chest as he fell.

The guy with the gold vest swung a fist, missed. The assassin ducked, twisted, slammed the heel of the pistol into the guard's temple, and he collapsed in a heap.

The skinny kid was in mid-draw as a single bullet took him in the side of the head.

HIS FIRST INSTINCT was to return to the back-street sweat parlour where he had awoken, get himself plugged back in, uploaded to netspace. Let the dumb sweat get back into his own body.

All the forensics would point to this body, after all, so once the owner was back in place, it would be *him* they'd track down and throw into a cell. Sure, they'd piece together the fact that he hadn't been in control at the time, but the confusion would buy some breathing space. Meantime, he'd be covering his tracks in net-space and... and what?

Where did he go after that?

He didn't know. He didn't remember.

He didn't know his name. He didn't remember his childhood. He didn't know how old he was or where he lived, couldn't picture his wife's face or even remember if he had a fucking wife.

He was living in the present, in the moment.

He was incomplete then, a partial download. The rest of him was out there somewhere, waiting for his return...

All he had in his head was the knowledge required to carry out this hit – that's all they had given him. A killer's knowledge, a killer's instinct. It was all he had. All he could do was return to where it had started for him.


I WAIT.

I stand on the path that runs by the Serpentine, while ducks and coots and gulls mill about on and above the water. These birds have only ever known existence in the Accord; they have not been warehoused in the old world and reborn here. To all intents they are simulations. The gulls swoop and dip, the coots and ducks squabble over scraps. These birds are real. This world is real. Experiencing it like this is still something of a shock, when I really think about what it is that is around me, what I am.

I am *real*.

I walk slowly, passing by the four ornamental pools at the lake's head, and return along the east bank of the Serpentine.

I sit on a bench, as two squirrels eye me suspiciously from the trunk of a pine.

I wait.

I am prepared to wait for as long as it takes. You have been here many times in the last week or so. I am sure you will return.

A young woman in jeans and a black T-shirt plays a ball game with a tangle of children. They look to be a school party, except the children range in age too much, from preschool to early teens. The ball, a red rubber ball the size of a tennis ball, hits my bench. I stoop to pick it up, throw it high, smile. I am at peace, I realise. I have been ever since I learned of your return.

"Noah?"

The voice. Your voice.

"Noah Barakh?"

The young woman approaches me. She is in her early twenties, chestnut hair tied back in a bunch. Blue eyes that trap me in their gaze...

Priscilla.

You look so young.

"Priscilla? Is that really you?"

You smile, but there is something... something missing from your smile.

I stand, you come towards me, hug me, press cheeks, step back.

"You have come back to me, Priscilla."

"Back to you? What do you mean, Noah?"

You don't remember.

"Oh, Noah. What are you thinking of?" You look puzzled, concerned. Then you smile. "I didn't know you were dead, Noah. What's the appropriate response? It's hardly condolences, is it? Commiserations? Sorry to hear you died, old chum. I hope it was painless, but then you won't even remember that, will you? The actual moment. You only remember up to as far as your last brain dump."

It takes your words to make me realise the obvious. You were with me, an anomaly smoothed out by the emergent protocols of consensus. That instance of you is gone. The instance before me is the one that was last warehoused. Physically, you have been reborn at your perfect age, your best time in life; but mentally, in terms of memory, of experience...

"You don't remember, do you, Priscilla? You don't remember at all."

You look worried now. As if you suddenly doubt the very integrity of the you that is instanced here. I have no wish to undermine you, but... you don't remember.

"What is it, Noah?"

Now, I feel reality swirling around me, inside my head. Realities. The ones I have built.

I remember the false starts, the times when I tried to convince you that we could be in love in these worlds, the fractal shards that have now come together as one. The pain of knowing that you wanted to but just couldn't see how such a thing could be.

I remember the old world, how hard it was to convince you that it *could* be, that in other realities we *were*.

"I..." I can build worlds. I can build heaven. "Do you remember what you said that day?"

You still look puzzled, concerned. "Which day? What did I say?"

You don't remember.

You don't remember what you said that day, back in the old world. You don't remember being here before, us driving south; you were going to show me the village where you grew up. We were going to walk hand in hand on the beach, find the rocks where you used to climb, the coastguards' cottages that look out over the Channel. Together. Me. You. But another you. A different you. A you that is no more, that will never again be.

I have no words.

The ball bounces between us, followed by a small girl, ponytails flying. "Cilla, Cilla!" she calls. "Mine!"

The girl tumbles on top of the ball, rolls over, clutching it to her chest, springs to her feet, all in one movement. "Mine!"

The girl darts away with the ball, Priscilla gives chase, I watch, I watch. I watch.

THE OLD MAN was still sitting at his stall, selling pipes and tobacco and peculiar herbs and spices in pots and little plastic bags. A front for his real business.

He saw the assassin approaching, bowed his head and smiled widely.

The assassin strode past, and the old man followed inside. The flies still buzzed in aimless circles under the stained tin ceiling.

"Okay," he told the old man. "I need to get back. That part of the deal?"

The old man raised his eyebrows, as if he was going to pretend not to understand. Maybe he didn't.

But he did. It showed in his eye as he hurried past, waved at the couch, started fiddling with the skullcap and leads.

"You settle down here, mister," he said, too eager. "You'll be gone real soon."

The assassin remained standing. Why did the sweat parlour proprietor want to get rid of him? Why did *they* want him to upload as quickly as possible? The people who commissioned this job.

To get him away from the scene, he told myself. That was all it was. All the forensics pointed to this body and they didn't want him caught in occupation – *he* didn't want to be caught in occupation!

He stepped round the couch, took the little fellow's jaw in the cup of his hand, and forced him so hard against the wall that he would swear the ceiling shook.

"So," he hissed into the man's face, "tell me... What exactly did you mean by the word 'gone'? What's going to happen to me when I'm plugged in? Do I get uploaded to netspace and reunited with the rest of me, or might it just be that I get wiped altogether? All the evidence tidied away? Eh?"

Was there even another *him* out there, somewhere, to be reunited with? Or was he just a construct, a bunch of killer traits pumped into this body for a single job?

He was just another fucking sweat! Just like the jerk whose body he'd been using...

The old man stared at him, barely reacting. He must have seen some real shit in his time. He wasn't going to say anything. Suddenly the impetus was gone.

He was faced with the choice: should he go through with what he understood of the plan or not? Should he let the old man upload him to netspace and pump the owner of this body back into his own skull? Should he trust that back in netspace he wouldn't just be wiped?

He was assuming now that he had controllers out there: people who had commissioned the hit, people who had set it all up. But maybe it was just him out there – the *real* him. Maybe he had wanted Mr B dead for reasons of his own and so he had sent a part of himself down to use this sweat to kill the fucker.

He loosened his grip on the old man's face, let him slump against the wall. The old man had been on his toes before, he'd been holding him so hard.

Something wasn't right.

The old man was looking towards the window.

He turned.

Police. Or soldiers, or armed security of some kind. Hard to tell. A green jeep was forcing its way slowly up the street, through the throng. As he watched, a couple of uniformed men jumped out and started to jog alongside it.

He looked at the doorway, but they would see him if he left now.

The police would have picked up his body's signature at Mr B's gates. They'd have the eyewitness account from the guy he hadn't killed, the stream from the security cam that would show them everything that had happened.

They'd been quick: less than an hour since the hit, they'd pattern-matched his face from the security cam, found him on streetcam streams as he had crossed the city. Some of the systems were probably even body-smart: they'd have sampled body scent and pheromones, matched them to the body signature of the killer.

They'd tracked him down to the ghost company's crossload parlour.

He looked around. This was just a single room in some kind of lean-to. One door onto the street. No other way out.

He glanced up, then stepped onto the couch, bent at the knees. Straightening abruptly, he drove his shoulder into the tin ceiling and it gave with a sharp creaking sound.

There was a gap between ceiling and wall now. His shoulder was screaming with pain, but regardless he hauled himself up and through that gap, tugging himself clear of warped metal and flapping plastic sheeting.

He emerged on a sloping roof at the back of the parlour, started to slither down. He spread his limbs to slow the fall, then got to his knees and clambered down just as shouts came from within.

He heard a thud – something hard on something soft – and the old man cried out.

He caught himself on the edge of the corrugated metal roof, dropped into a garbage-filled alleyway, hit the ground running.

ELECTOR JACK BURNHAM awakens, dead.

He knows that he is dead because the entry protocol dictates that he should. Awareness is good. Awareness is healthy, an essential part of the rite of passage in transferring from one reality into another.

Awareness of being dead does not, however, imply awareness of one's actual *death*…

How? Who? When?

Calmness flows over him. A deeply existential calmness. An artificial calmness, imposed by the entry protocols.

He remembers... he remembers Priscilla, that she is dead too, that he killed her in a fit of anger, jealousy, confusion, utter grief at the thought that he had lost her. He remembers Barakh. Of course he remembers Barakh.

He recalls speaking to Nesbitt... the coffee shop. Nesbitt's first attempt to recruit him to the cause of destroying the Accord and concentrating on fixing the real world. After that: back in the project's Bethnal Green centre he had given a routine brain dump, a thing he had been doing regularly for the past two years or so, as all members of the project did. He had felt uncomfortable doing so, but it would have looked odd if he had suddenly stopped, a clear signal of intent.

And after that... nothing.

How much longer had he had? He might have walked out of the centre and been shot dead in the street right there and then. He might have gone on the razz two weeks later, flown to Vegas or Rio or Bangkok, died snorting coke off the breasts of a nineteen-year-old hooker while her shemale friend sucked him off. He might have refused to give any more dumps, lived to a ripe old age, solved the world's problems, died of a stroke at 102, only now to wake up in some stump of the Accord project still running on in an obscure corner of an ancient computing network as some geek's hobby... He could be a fucking hero, for God's sake!

He should care, he thinks, but he does not. That calmness again, the protocols shielding him from the shock of his own demise.

He opens his eyes. At first it is as if they are still closed, but then the light level fades up around him, slowly, soothingly. He is in a grey antechamber, featureless, lying on his back. It brings to mind some of the cruder meetspaces he has visited.

He sits, stands, turns, and there is a doorway, sealed, light limning the shape of the door.

He steps towards it. The door scrolls sideways.

Bright sunshine, blue sky with a few wisps of cloud smudged here and there. Trees. Pigeons, scurrying about at the feet of walkers. Water. A river... no a lake, a long sliver of lake.

He turns. Grassy slope, people sitting all about. Picnics and ball games and scampering dogs. Lovers tangled up in each other, not a care, not a fucking care. A bulbous sculpture of a figure overlooking it all, pinhead on a globular body. A Henry Moore.

Hyde Park. The Serpentine. Overhead, a tiny jet scratches a white trail across the blue.

He starts to walk – it's his favourite walk on a day like this: down through Hyde Park, then St James Park to Westminster. Never unaccompanied, though. Too risky for someone in his position. He glances around, suddenly disconcerted.

He pings Tate, Lucy, wonders why neither of them are here, then remembers he's dead, only just died. How are Tate or Lucy to suddenly know to be here? What if they're not dead yet? He suddenly feels exposed at the thought of doing without his two most trusted sidekicks.

He forces himself to relax. He's going to have a lot of catching up to do, but he can do that, he's always been the kind of man to hit the ground running. He breathes deep, smells the city potpourri mix of dry dust, traffic fumes, and *human*.

Fuck, but it's good to be alive again!

Now he stops, looks down at himself. He's lost weight. Middle years had added to his bulk; pills and exercise had converted the extra to muscle, but he had still been a solid man. Yet now... he's as slim as he had been twenty years ago. He runs a hand over his face, his jaw, the side of his head. Smooth skin, the slight rasp of a few hours' stubble. He needs to look in a mirror, but he feels *younger*, even more alive!

At Hyde Park Corner there's a woman waving a book – probably a Bible – and talking in a series of exclamations to whoever passes within range. Now, she meets Burnham's eye, waves her book at him, says, "We are all *blasphemers*! This is not *heaven*, but a *mockery*! He who seeks false heaven will burn for all *eternity*! You are not *real* – you are *burning*!"

Burnham smiles at her, touched that she should be so passionate in her belief that she should opt to live on in the Accord simply to tell the sinners their souls are burning in Hell. We might be able to build a world so rich that it feels more real than the old one, but will we ever understand the perversities of the human heart?

TATE WAITS FOR him on a bench in St James Park. Burnham recognises his blocky head as he approaches, pings him. Tate stands, looks awkward, as if he wants to hug Burnham or punch him, or something.

"So," says Burnham, "you died before me, did you?"

Tate shrugs. "Looks that way, JB. Not long though – I've only been here a couple of days. You're looking good. Younger."

"You too. Looks like you've knocked off about ten years at least. And fifty pounds. How'd you die?" If Tate has died only shortly before Burnham then it suggests things have gone seriously wrong... The two must almost certainly be connected.

Tate shakes his head. "No idea, JB."

"Bet you took a bullet with my name on it. Bet you're a fucking hero."

They both smile, standing there like awkward kids who don't know what to do next.

Then Burnham takes a step forward, claps an arm around Tate's shoulders, hugs him briefly, hard, feels the rasp of stubble against his cheek, breathes cheap cologne, steps back, away, looking down, embarrassed.

He turns round. "It's so fucking real, isn't it?"

Tate chuckles. "I haven't found any reason not to believe in it yet, JB."

"Come on. You can fill me in while we walk to the office. Who's here? Lucy? Harry Winter? Fucking Nesbitt? Go on, tell me Nesbitt's here before me! Shot by friendly fire from one of his mobs..."

They're in silence by the time they emerge on Birdcage Walk. It's quiet here. Pigeons strut in the middle of the street, unharassed by traffic. A slight breeze picks up.

So fucking *real*.

He's been in meetspaces plenty of times before. He knows how real they seem. He's been told often enough that the Accord makes meetspaces look like fucking Space Invaders or PacMan. But... so real!

He wants to bring al-Naqawi here, show him the reality: his line that the Accord is just an echo, a facsimile of the real world, is so patently untrue. This world is real, the people in it real, Burnham himself *is* Burnham himself!

That religious nut at Hyde Park Corner was wrong: Burnham's soul is not now toasting in Hell, it's here, absolutely here.

"Any news on Barakh?"

Tate glances sideways at him, shakes his head. "I've asked about, JB. But I haven't been here long, just finding my feet, you know? Haven't heard anything."

Burnham, too, had clung to the same belief that al-Naqawi still does: that the Accord must be a mere shadow, a simulation with lots of facsimiles of people running around in it, real memories programmed into simulated heads, an elaborate game.

He, of all people, should have known better.

He, of all people, should not be so shocked to the core that the Accord is a real place, that he is actually here, sensing it in all the rich depth he had ever sensed the... *previous*... world.

And if it is so real to him, then it is real to Barakh, to Priscilla. The instances of Barakh and Priscilla here in the Accord are truly them. Priscilla really has left him for Barakh.

Somewhere, right now, they are together.

He had been denying it, diminishing it, all along. But no more. He has to believe in it now. He has to believe in it as much as he believes in himself…

"Find him," he says softly, as they cross the near-deserted Horse Guards Road. "Find her. I want him dead…"

Tate opens his mouth, stops, starts again: "But JB… How do you kill someone here? Where do we go when we die in the Accord?"


"YOUR HUSBAND IS here," I say. "He has been killed."

We are in Hyde Park again, you with your entourage of lost children. They play another ball game; we sit on that same bench and watch them. You are easy company. We can talk and laugh for hours while the children play. I am even getting used to the fact that you look so much younger now. I am surprised at how it subtly changes my feelings, makes me feel more awkward; I have to remind myself that it is still you inside, the same you, albeit an instance of you that is missing those few weeks when you were in love with me.

"I don't know what I should feel," you say now. "How *should* we feel that someone has died?"

"There are no rules yet," I say. "We feel whatever we feel. He was your husband. I suppose he still is – we don't even have any rules for that."

"Death us has parted," you say, smiling. "You can't argue with that. He certainly can't." You know he killed you, although I have been careful in saying why. *Jealous rage* is all you want to know. You do not appear surprised at that, even though you do not press for any detail.

"I feel claustrophobic, all of a sudden," you say. "I don't want him to close me in again. That's my past. A finished episode. I got to feeling uneasy whenever we shared the house, or the flat. We were friendly, we fucked, but... He made me uneasy. He made me feel trapped."

"Then don't allow him to do so again." You talk openly with me. You always have, in this world. We are each other's only friend here. That establishes a level of trust, of openness.

"You don't know what he's like, Noah. Not what he's really like. He's very possessive. Territorial."

I shake my head. "Oh, but I do know what he's like," I tell you. "I believe that he will want to kill me, or have me killed."

You had not expected that. You are shocked, confused. Maybe you even doubt me, too. Do you think that I am being melodramatic? That I am trying to impress you? You know that I want to impress you. It seems to amuse you, in a wistful kind of way.

"Why would he want that?"

"Because you and I were lovers," I tell you.

I have been so scared of this moment. I have told you nothing of us, of our feelings, of the potential between us. I know from past experience – experiences – that rash claims on my part are just as likely to build barriers between us as break them down. So I have said nothing, just enjoyed our times together. And hoped.

You struggle to shape the right words.

"In the old world?" you finally ask.

I shake my head. "In this world. In shards of this world before consensus. Many times over, we were lovers."

There is a long silence, as we watch the parentless children playing.

I expect you to doubt me, even to accuse me of making it up as some elaborate way of trying to start something between us. Instead, you ask, "How did it end? How did they end?"

"Consensus happened," I explain. "The reality shards coalesced. The instances of each of us became a single instance of each of us, but yours was less stable. Elements of my being are tied inextricably to the fabric of the Accord – I am intimate with it; the protocols smoothed out any anomalies and made me one. You... I thought it would do the same, but instead you appeared to be an anomaly too far. The protocols smoothed you out of existence, the *you* that had coalesced from the instances that loved me.

"It ended not because it was over, but because you were removed by consensus. After that you were reborn as the last-warehoused instance of yourself – your previous time here was wiped out."

"You must feel like fucking shit."

I nod.

"You're telling me a part of me has lived and died and I don't even know a thing about it?"

I nod.

"If what you say is true, and I have no reason to doubt you, then I am capable of those feelings... of loving you... but I have never felt those things, I've never loved you."

I look into your eyes.

I hurt.

You lean into me, hold me as a friend, wrap me in the arms of my lover even though you have never loved me.

# 1.07

Bartie Davits was a sweat, a ride, a kid who hired out his body to make a living. A student working his way through business school, paying his own way because his parents were in no position to help, one of them a low-paid supermarket assistant, the other long since dead and gone. Sweating was easier than shop work, and generally safer than dealing, although Bartie did a bit of that too – that was just a natural extension of his business training, he always argued.

He liked the SweatShop parlour in Haymarket. Real class. You could taste it in the air.

He opened his eyes, remembering where he was, getting used to his own senses again after spending what felt like a couple of days warehoused off in netspace, playing TrueSim games while some rich wanker fooled with his body.

A face loomed over him, cheekbones like geometry, perfect skin, eyes like the flawless glass eyes of a porcelain doll. Bartie could smell her and she was like apples. He smiled.

"What's the damage?" he asked.

She smiled back at him, everything symmetrical. Someone had paid a fortune for those looks, he guessed.

"Narcotic residue," she told him. "Alcohol residue. Black eye – looks like you had a run-in with someone. That's all, though, Mr Davits."

No serious damage this time, then. Right now there would be drugs cleansing his blood and liver, stripping out the narcs and booze, replenishing his reserves. That was one of the perks of sweating; some people argued that the clean out could add years to your life. Rich wankers would pay a fortune for some of this shit and here was Bartie Davits, getting it all for free. Fuck no: getting *paid* for it.

"Like we agreed," he said, sitting slowly. "Cash in hand, right? I'll deal with the taxman later."

She smiled her professional smile again. "The fee is already in your registered account, Mr Davits, minus tax, health insurance, and obligatory pension, just as always. No special arrangements."

He stood, stretched. Felt unfamiliar aches and stiffnesses. Raised a hand to his left eye, suddenly aware of its dull ache.

He looked down at his clothes: a slick pair of jeans, a crumpled silk T-shirt, pointed snakeskin boots, none of it his. There was a bag on the side containing his own newly laundered clothes. The new outfit – another perk.

He hoped his body had had a good time while he was warehoused playing games.

Funny to think that his own body had experienced far more than he himself had – and he knew nothing about what it had been through other than a bunch of hints and signs and scars...

Out along a corridor, mirrored walls multiplying him, bright lights making him squint, still getting used to the feel and responses of his own body again. Into the foyer, all tall, angular plants emerging from white-painted steel pots full of black glass pebbles. The street beyond looked dark through the clinic's floor-to-ceiling tinted glass front.

He was just wondering whether it was a Comedy Store night, who might be on. Maybe he'd call a few mates and front them for a night out, make the most of the new wad in his bank account.

He stepped out through glass and white-steel doors that slid open as they sensed his approach. He had time to notice the sudden clash of warm scented air from the interior of the clinic mixing with the smells of the damp London street, had time to emerge into the drizzle, to look left, then start to look right, and then they were on him.

A sudden rush of figures... Two men stepped out from his right and as he opened his mouth to speak, to curse them for jostling him, for not looking where they were going even though it was actually Bartie who had stepped out into the flow, another two took him from the left. His arms gripped tightly, he smelt something cloyingly sweet, realised someone had sprayed something, felt it infiltrating his lungs as he breathed it deep, heard the gabble of street noise suddenly fizz to static, to nothing...

...AND HE WOKE in a cell.

He remembered, then, the men grabbing him, the prickle of some kind of nerve agent in his lungs. He realised they were police, some in uniform, some not. He hadn't had time to take it all in as they descended on him, in the sudden rush of sensation as the foundations of a normal day were abruptly pulled from under him.

He was on a bunk, a brick wall to his immediate left, a narrow strip of floor and then another bare brick wall to the right. There was a door at one end of the cell, past his feet, with a viewing panel set into it. In one corner of the room, where two walls met ceiling, the glinting eye of a security cam peered back at him.

He sat, rubbing at his temples as dizziness descended.

Down on the concrete floor, he pressed his feet against the wall and started on sit-ups, rapid and regular, enjoying the rush of blood and adrenaline that kicked in with the exercise. Bartie liked to look after himself. It kept the brain in tune as well as the body. And his rich clients liked a fit sweat to ride in, so it was a good career move, if sweating could really be considered a career. These little touches generally brought him a better class of client, in any case.

He was past 150 when he heard the door. He carried on until a man said, "Bartie Davits. You're wanted for interview."

"Interview?" he asked, pausing, twisting to see the uniformed man framed by the doorway. "Like for a job?"

The policeman just looked at him, waited for him to stand, stepped back to let him out into the corridor.

A short time later, Bartie was sitting in another room, elbows on a desk. There was a plain-clothes officer across the table from him, a uniformed man on the door.

"Bartholomew Brooklyn Davits," said the officer, "we have reason to suspect your involvement in the murder of Elector Jack Burnham in Jakarta on the twenty-third of this month. This interview is being recorded and your responses processed for veracity by smart systems from two independent vendors. Anything you do or say may be used as evidence in a court of law, and may also be used for commercial purposes. Do you understand?"

Bartie stared at the man. "I understand your words," he said slowly, "but fuck no, I don't *understand*."

The officer had a feed going into his ear. He received some kind of input, nodded, and his eyes met Bartie's again.

Then Bartie added, "Burnham? Elector Burnham? The virtual worlds guy? Dead?" At a brief nod, he continued, "I... I've been out of it a couple of days. I hadn't heard. I sweat rides, you know? I was sweating, warehoused in a databank somewhere while some rich fuck rode my bones, you know?"

Another pause, while the officer listened to his feed, then: "Elector Burnham was killed by a kid called Joey Bannerman."

"So... I don't understand?"

"Bannerman was gap-yearing round the world, ran out of cash, took to sweating to get by. He was ridden by the killer."

Bartie got it, then, he thought. "Not me, man... I didn't do nothing. I was warehoused, playing TrueSim strategy games in perfect isolation. Check out the records: I was pumped into a databank and kept clean and cut off from the world. They have to do it like that. Data integrity and all that: have to put back what they take out!" He laughed awkwardly.

"We don't think it was you, as such," says the officer.

Bartie relaxed, hadn't realised how much tension he'd been holding in. Then he registered the "as such" and he saw from the officer's expression that there was more, a layer yet to unpick. "And?"

"We've pattern-matched traits identified from the datafeed that injected the killer into Bannerman's skull. The killer was an amalgam, a construct. Whoever was behind the assassination took a few traits from here, a few from there, and built the killer suited for the job."

Bartie waited. There was more.

"It's a known technique. Developed by the Yakuza but it's been seen in a number of cases now. The way they do it is they have to have a solid foundation, a template, someone who could easily be a killer in the right circumstances, with the right traits added, remixed, recompiled. We've identified the template, Davits. We've tracked down that individual. It's you."

Bartie shook his head. "But it wasn't me!" he finally said. "I was warehoused, isolated... It wasn't me."

"Your profile was used," said the officer. "Edited, built upon. We're talking legal grey areas here. Our advice is that this could be the test case to beat all test cases. Could take years."

The officer was enjoying this, Bartie suddenly realised. "How do you mean?"

"It's all about legal culpability," the officer explained. "When due process proves that you were the template used in this crime, and when it is demonstrated that the killer was substantially *you*, then you will share legal culpability for the killing."

"But... I wasn't there."

"No, that's true. But there is evidence to show that a statistically significant instance of you *was*..."

RESPONSIBILITY FINDS YOU.

Or, at least, it has found Priscilla.

Efan and Mazeli had been the first, Efan hunched up by the Serpentine, his younger brother out of view behind a big laurel bush. The two of them are boat children, from when migrants were still being settled in the UK. They'd lived for two years in one of the Lewisham camps, as far as Priscilla can make out. They'd been warehoused by one of Charlie Bonnetti's Soul Harvesters, working the camps as they did. Mortality in the camps was high when Priscilla was in the old world, but even so, for two siblings to die together... She is as sure as she can be that these two must have died horribly when the Mountsfield Park camp was torched by a retro-fascist mob. They know nothing of that, of course.

Now they laugh at the monkeys in London Zoo. Little capuchins, grooming each other and leaping about their enclosure.

Priscilla is doing her best to educate the children, and to keep them engaged with their new world. Many of them are too young to really understand what has happened, and why they have lost their families. The older ones understand, and in many ways that is even harder. She has sixteen of them now. Some of them are boat children like Efan and Mazeli; others are local kids like Lucy, who cannot really understand why she is no longer in a hospital bed with tubes attached to her and her hair falling out in clumps, and little Sissy, who only ever wants stories and poems. For most of them, though, the reason they are here is a mystery. They are dead, but they do not know how or why. That is a frightening thing, one of the many aspects of the afterlife that appear to have gone unanticipated.

Priscilla is lucky. She knows why she is here. She is here because her husband murdered her. Because she was on the threshold of starting an affair with Noah Barakh.

Maybe *lucky* is not the best term, but at least she knows. She doesn't lie awake at night dreaming of a violent father, as Sam does; thinking his father might have gone too far with a beating, but not really knowing anything for sure. She doesn't wonder like FaceGurl does what the DazeI gang might be doing to her kid sister back in the old world because they'd almost certainly already done it to *her*...

A capuchin leaps at the mesh wall, clings to it with pencil fingers, its white face and whiskers giving it the look of ancient wisdom. Mazeli squeals with laughter.

Noah is not here this morning. She feels guilty that that should be such a relief.

The poor fuck is broken-hearted, and he thinks he is ballsing it out really well, but he isn't. She wonders about fucking him – there have been moments, in the old world but also, she has to admit, in this. He has a certain intellectual attraction about him, a magnetism of the mind.

He hasn't mentioned it since that one time, but it hangs between them.

They had been lovers once. Many times, if she can get her head around that. But no: he had been her lover, but she never his. Not *she*.

Not just lovers. *In love*.

She can see that that is how it would be. Her attraction to him is the kind that would need exploring, the kind you would grow into. He isn't an Omar.

So yes, she has wondered about fucking him now. They are two lonely souls in a new world. It would be natural to fall together, find relief and diversion with each other. But a one-night stand, a play fuck, a sympathy fuck, is hardly what he needs right now, and Priscilla is not ready to love anyone just yet.

The kids... she loves them. She has never been the maternal type, never regretted the lack of a family of her own, and she doesn't believe that she is feeling that way now. What she is feeling is a recognition of the difference she can make: sixteen kids who now have some kind of shape to their lives.

The responsibility has found her. So soon.

She remembers Omar. All the Omars.

She should feel happy.

But she is not ready to feel happy yet.


EMERGING IN HYDE Park on a sunny afternoon had been misleading: all the people, strolling, lounging, playing. Everything pretty much as normal. But no, much of London is pretty much deserted. Much of the country. Much of the world.

Not enough people have died yet.

But somehow, the economy – the mechanics – of the place keep ticking over. Food comes into the shops and restaurants, people go about their lives, many with a great sense of sadness, separated from the ones they love, but all knowing that it is a temporary state of affairs. This is the consensus: the world must work; the world must carry on.

Burnham sits on the Commons Terrace by the Thames, sipping at a martini. "Look at me," he says, puffing his chest out. "I'm pretty much the ruler of the whole fucking world!" No other elector has died since the Accord hit consensus, only a handful of electees. No leaders of the free states. Nobody.

"Ruler of the world and I don't have a clue! What's going to happen in a few years' time? A few decades? Hmmm?"

"How do you mean, JB?" asks Tate, leaning his back-side against the railings, arms folded across his ribcage.

"Malthus'd be having fucking kittens!"

"Ah," says Tate. "The impending population crisis, you mean?"

Burnham nods. "How quickly will this world fill up when nobody dies here? Hmmm? We thought we had it bad back then: a few boats trying to land on the south coast. Where will people go when this world starts to fill up? What's going to happen then?"

He's been asking the same question of people for days, and getting no satisfactory answer.

"You know who would have the answer," says Tate.

"And can we fucking find him?"

Barakh. Noah fucking Barakh. It always comes back to him.

They have tried everything. They've even gone to the police, found the Deputy Assistant Commissioner currently in charge of the Met, a man out of his depth and not helped by the fact that he has been reborn as a mere twenty-five-year-old – it seems everyone is reborn at their best age, the age they should always be. That's how consensus decrees it should be. But it seemed wrong to be confronting a mere kid who happened to be in charge of the city's police.

Clearly intimidated by a visit from the man who pretty damned near rules the world, the DAC blustered for a while. "But... I don't see how... We can't just..."

"It's simple," Burnham reasoned. "He is a murderer. There is a clear case against him, and now he is here in the Accord. He must be hunted down and prosecuted."

"But... We have no official reports of this incident. No evidence here. What jurisdiction can we have over crimes committed in a branch of reality other than this?"

"Then *get* the evidence!"

"But..." The puppy-faced Deputy Assistant Commissioner, started again: "There is no two-way communication between the Accord and the old world, Elector Burnham. It's a fundamental feature of the protocols that maintain consensus. We are in another reality. There is no evidence that a crime has been committed."

"There are ways," Burnham told him. "There are always ways." He knew this for a fact: Zhang Xiaoling had known he had killed Priscilla. She could only have learnt this from either Priscilla or Barakh after they were dead.

"I'm sorry, Elector Burnham," said the DAC, palms raised, smiling. "It is not possible. I assure you. And this incident is really beyond our jurisdiction."

Burnham had pursued it for a while, long enough to make the jerk sweat like a hog on a spit, but he had got nowhere. It was as if the refusal was hard-wired into his skull, another protocol that would not be contradicted. If he were paranoid, Burnham might believe that the whole of the Accord had been set up to protect Barakh: no one could do anything that might betray the man who had built heaven. Burnham was not paranoid, though; just healthily suspicious...

Now, a picture-windowed tour boat drifts past on the river, heading downstream with the ebbing tide. There are three people on it, a suited man and two women in hijab, pointing at the Houses of Parliament, at Big Ben. Tate waves, chuckling. In an empty world, making contact seems somehow precious, a more fragile thing.

"I've been asking round," says Tate, "calling in a few favours where I can. Trouble is, most of my contacts are still alive."

"Damned inconvenient of them," mutters Burnham. He sips at his martini.

"I've tried the project offices, here and all around the world. Nothing. He has a London flat, you know? Across in E1, just off Vallance Road – handy for the project offices. Nothing there, either."

Burnham hadn't known about the flat. Now, he can't help picturing them there… How many "meetings" had she had at the Bethnal Green centre? How many long lunches, with Barakh's flat just round the corner? Just how long had they been fooling him for?

"I've had people check everywhere he's likely to go to. His house out near Rochford is deserted, locked up, although apparently there were signs that someone had been there recently. I'm having it watched."

"I want to go there," says Burnham. "Not the house – the flat. I want to see it."

Tate nods. "Now?"

"Now."

PRISCILLA SITS ON the pavement of the Strand with the new kid, Luca. He's fourteen, speaks English well – it's the language of netspace, so why wouldn't he?

The street is empty, even though it's the middle of the day. Every so often, a car passes, a few pedestrians… London is filling up, but it's still a ghost town.

Priscilla stretches her legs out, passes a half-full Coke to the boy.

He just looks at it.

His hands are deep in the pockets of his leather jacket, his chin sunk into his chest. He has collar-length black hair, eyes almost as dark.

"It's true, Luca," Priscilla says. "You died in the old world. This is the Accord."

He shakes his head.

She found him here about ten minutes ago, has only exchanged a few words with him but already thinks of him as the new kid. He is lost. He is one of hers. Another responsibility, although she tries hard not to think of them that way.

"It's against the Church," he says. "My mother, she says that. It's against the Church. There wasn't anybody in Misurina was recorded into the warehouse. None of us. So you tell me: if no one of us was recorded, then how is it that I am here? It's not true. This... I am not in the Accord. I am some place else."

Misurina is Luca's home village in northern Italy. He was in London travelling with his father before he died, not that he will accept that he is dead.

Softly, gently: "Someone must have had you recorded, Luca. Maybe your mother wasn't so sure of her convictions. Maybe your father had you saved while you were in London?"

Luca shakes his head.

"So where are you then? Where is everybody?" She waves a hand to indicate the deserted street. "Where have all the people gone?"

"I am in London," he says. "The people... they are not here."

"So where are they? Where is your father?"

He doesn't answer, keeps his chin buried in his chest, his jacket pulled up around him, despite the warmth of the late afternoon sun.

Priscilla wonders why he is here; why he has emerged in London and not in his home village. Maybe he is more attached to this place than he realises; maybe his father had moved here with him, and this instance of Luca had been saved before he had been told. Maybe London really is his home now?

Priscilla takes another swig of the Coke, even though she hates the sticky sweetness on her tongue.

She holds it out and this time Luca takes it, drinks.

Another one. Another of her responsibilities.


"COME AWAY WITH me, Priscilla," I tell you. We're in the Great Court of the British Museum, the light beneath the great spans of the tessellated roof limpid, ethereal. "We can go anywhere you like. The children can come with us. We can show them the world. We could see the Grand Canyon, the Taj Mahal, the pyramids. How many wonders of the world must there be?"

"You're telling me we should run from him?"

"We have forever," I say. "Let him have time to cool off while we see the world."

"He's the one who killed me!" You're pulling at a lock of your chestnut hair, stretching the natural waves straight. "I shouldn't have to run."

Your eyes have dark shadows under them. So much responsibility, taking over the care of these children! "It's an option," I say. "Let me help."

You stand, give a single shake of your head to get the hair out of your eyes.

"You don't know me, Noah. You don't know me at all."


DOGS.

Fucking dogs. A whole pack of them, ragged-looking beasts, sniffing at the trash stacked high. Didn't they eat the fucking dogs in this part of the world?

He pressed back into the corner of the doorway, hugging himself, trying to think.

One of the dogs started pawing at the side of a box and the soft cardboard gave way immediately in the humid heat.

A steady flow of people passed the end of the alley-way. It had been several minutes since the two cops passed. Should be safe to emerge again. But he was no fool. The security cams would be watching for him, sniffing him out like they must have done when he had crossed the city immediately after the hit. They had his host-body's signatures mapped out: scent, pheromone mix, facial geometrics, gait. As soon as he passed one of the cams he would be flagged up back at the control centre.

He had to get out of here. Out of this city. But how? Where?

Out of the city there would be fewer cams, but as soon as he hit civilisation again he'd be exposed. Did he really want to see out his days in a borrowed body in the middle of some fucking jungle?

He needed to get out of this body, shed his skin like a snake.

He wracked his brain, struggling to come up with some kind of a plan.

A dog spotted him, all bone and shaggy coat. It started to growl, shuffling towards him, one leg lame, bent. He squatted, held out a hand, and in seconds the mutt was nuzzling his wrist as he scratched its mangy neck.

He straightened.

Cautiously, he approached the end of the alleyway. No sign of the cops. He stepped out, joining the flow. He walked with a limp, holding a hand over his face, occasionally rubbing as if he had a permanent itch. He could obscure his facial geometrics and he could disguise the normal pattern of this borrowed body's movement, but there was nothing he could do to hide its scent signature. That was a risk he had to accept: all the cams supplied a feed that was processed for visual patterning, but far fewer were equipped with the full bodystamp sensors.

He needed to get his bearings, but then what? He didn't know what city this was, didn't even know which country. And even if he *did* know... why should he trust any knowledge he had? What if his controllers really did just want to erase him as soon as he uploaded? He couldn't rely on any knowledge they'd given him, just in case they were leading him towards his own end.

He needed to upload, but on his own terms. And then... Time to go looking for himself, the original him. Time to find him and ask himself some tough questions. Time to look for daddy.


PRISCILLA HEADS OFF into the museum shop, smiles at Sissy and FaceGurl. Noah thinks it's going to happen again. Just because it had in another place, with another her. It's like a weighted blanket over her.

She stops, breathes deep.

Last night, she had been lying awake in the Sloane Square flat she had taken over. The kids were sleeping three or four to a room, while Priscilla had the living room sofa to herself.

She found herself thinking about him, about Noah. About the afternoon they had spent discussing the Accord with the kids, talking it through in terms they might get. She had watched him as he spoke, watched his eyes, so alight with the discussion, with the responses he was getting from the kids, those precious moments of understanding, of connection, of really *getting* where they were and why they were here.

That was a real world-shift moment, a confirmation of the vague feelings she had felt before. She really could fuck that man, but more: she could love him. He was a man who needed to be explored, found out.

But not now.

She cannot open herself up in that way. Inside, she is raw, exposed, vulnerable. She is not ready.

She needs to be *her* first. She needs to be her for the first time in her adult life.

Last night, she had climbed from her bed, pulled on some clothes, gone out to a little bar she knew, one that was open all hours for all kinds of reasons. She had come back to the flat just as dawn was breaking, the kids still asleep apart from Mazeli who hardly slept at all. Shutting the door behind her, Priscilla was comfortably drunk, and she ached in all the right places. And God, but she was tired...

Outside now, in the Great Court, Noah still sits on the bench, waiting.

She stands before him, arms folded. He looks timid, suddenly, threatened. She unfolds her arms, but can't work out what to do with her hands and ends up tucking them in the tight pockets of her jeans.

"I like you, Noah," she tells him. "I even love you, in a way. You're a good man, an attractive man. You're someone whose company and support I treasure. And

I'm full of respect for you: you're a fucking genius, after all – but you're a *human* genius, not some up-his-own-arse geek genius."

He watches. He waits.

"But it's not going to happen, Noah. Between us. That was a different me. Different place. Different circumstances. I don't feel I can love anyone like that. Does that make sense? Am I just telling you the most insensitive, brutal things you've ever been told? Am I a complete fucking cow?"

He shakes his head, once. "I understand," he says. "I do understand."

He smiles. He watches. He waits.

"...A STATISTICALLY SIGNIFICANT instance of you *was*..."

Bartie Davits hit 280, and then stopped the sit-ups, head between his knees, gasping, chest aching, head pounding, abdominal muscles burning.

He couldn't shake the sound of the officer's voice, the half-smile on the bastard's face. They were having fun, toying with him. Fucking with his life, but for them it was just a new twist on an otherwise dull and routine day at the station.

Slowly, his breathing calmed, and his thoughts calmed too.

They were playing games with him. But if they wanted to play then bring it on! Bartie played games all the time. Other than the dealing and the sweating, online gaming was his main source of income to fund business school.

This was just a game, a strategy game.

It was time to stop acting like a frightened rabbit, caught in the headlights. Time to take control, take the initiative.

If the bastards wanted to play with Bartie Davits, then Bartie Davits was ready for them. And then some.

* * *

"A ROAD TRIP," I tell you. "You, me, the children. Let's show them something of this new world of ours! We can take a minibus, take a ferry across the Channel, just drive each day until we feel like stopping. Some of these kids have never seen the countryside, never seen the sea. Let's do it, Priscilla: a road trip, a break from it all, a *holiday*."

We're in the kitchen of the Sloane Square flat, debris from the preparation of another meal all about us. You're not happy here. I can see it in your eyes, the set of your shoulders.

You are wavering.

"I don't know," you say. "It feels like we're running away."

I shake my head.

"We're not running away," I tell you. "Let's head for the mountains, the Alps. Let's head for northern Italy, find Misurina, see if we can find Luca's family." Luca worries you, I know: he clings steadfastly to the belief that none of this is real. Maybe seeing his home village will help him.

You nod. "Okay," you say. "Okay, Noah. Let's go on a road trip."

You smile. Only briefly, but you smile.

I DREAM. BUT it's more than that, I think.

We sleep an exhausted sleep, having spent the day travelling. We are in the French Jura, heading through to the Alps tomorrow. FaceGurl has never seen a mountain. We will show her big mountains. We will walk in alpine meadows, show city children wild flowers and butterflies; walk for hours through pine forests; camp out under the stars. The kids have grown, even in the few days I have known them. Grown in confidence, grown in the knowledge and understanding of what they have gone through. You work wonders with them, Priscilla; you treat them like people, not like children, and they thrive on it.

Today we drove from London in a minibus we borrowed from a depot in Lewisham. We sleep in a wooden house near Baumes-les-Dames, making sure that the kids treat the place with respect. Its owners will be here again one day.

You and I... we sleep, clothed, on a double bed, a space between us. I can smell your delicate scent. I am intensely aware of the small movements you make as you sleep. I do not reach out across the space that separates us. I wait, and hope.

And dream, I think.

You are not here, not in this dream.

I am up in the mountains, a steep scree tumbling away below me, a flock of little birds flashing black and white among the rocks. There is snow here, tucked away in the shadow of rocks, and higher, on the open slopes where maybe there is snow all the year round. Mountains wrap around me, snow-whitened crags, flanked with deep pine green, an almost perfect circular lake nestled on a plateau below.

Me... us... I am not alone.

"Xiaoling," I say. It always feels odd to meet Zhang Xiaoling like this. I have been inside her almost as often as we have met. I have been her. She stands at my side, similarly taken with the view.

If Xiaoling is with me, then this is not the Accord, unless I really am dreaming, or unless she has died and not informed me; it is a meetspace, one that uses the algorithms of Accord to build its own integrity; maybe even a deleted shard of pre-consensus Accord being reused as meetspace, development space.

"Noah," she says. "Sammy has been good to us. He has exceeded himself in securing resources for the Accord."

"That is good," I say. "But hardly sustainable." I wonder how long we have before either netspace cracks under the strain, or the Accord starts to fracture.

Xiaoling stays silent for a while, and together we enjoy the view and the vitality of the mountain air.

"You should come and talk to the Hueys," she finally says. "There has been progress."

We walk down the slope, following an indistinct trail through the boulders and stones strewn across the slope. The air is crisp, its chill countering the heat of the summer sun's rays.

As we enter the first fringe of pine forest I hear voices. Huey. Hueys. Arguing, of course.

There are two of them, in a clearing where a stream runs through a cleft in the forest.

"Huey," I say.

They fall silent and turn to me. One of them smiles; the other looks sidelong at the stream, sheepish.

"Noah," says the smiling Huey. "You've read our report? Xiaoling said she would forward it to you immediately."

"Half an hour ago," she mutters under her breath to me.

"Tell me about it," I say. It's good to see Huey looking so upbeat – or at least one of the Hueys, anyway. Huey and I go back a long way. Right back to grad school, what, eleven years ago? We'd spent long nights back then, Huey providing the spark that would make me stretch my thinking, me pushing and cajoling him to take the time to communicate his reasoning to the world, let other people in on the genius that filled his skull.

"We have demonstrated interstitiality, Noah."

I nod, as if he had said *I boiled the kettle*, or *I won at Sympics*.

"We have channelled data into uncollapsed quantum states – all those quantum states that aren't made 'real' by observation. The subatomic interstices… the space within space… we have shifted something from our world into a state of existence that is beyond our ability to experience."

"Data integrity is retained?"

"We are trying to establish that…"

"How can we establish that?" says the other Huey. "It's not possible!"

"They're arguing worse than ever," says Xiaoling.

"I will stay here," I tell her. "I will leave an instance of me here." It will be like the old days, only with more of Huey. I will get him to apply himself; he will make me dig deep; and between us we might just save the world.

## 1.08

ANOTHER BACK STREET, another alleyway piled high with garbage and the ever-present dogs darting in and out between people's legs, amazing they didn't trip anyone. It was dark now, early evening, hot and sultry so that sweat made track-lines down his neck. There were crowds of people everywhere he went in this city. People and dogs. This was the city of people and dogs. He still didn't know where he was. Hadn't thought to ask – he didn't intend to be here for much longer.

The door, just like the guy had said. An ordinary door, no sign or anything, no shiny lock to say there was something special here, *someone* special.

The guy... It was a risk, but he had gone back to the gun dealer, the guy who'd had his Heckler and Koch there just waiting for him.

The dealer recognised him straight away. Claimed the police weren't on to him yet, which was believable because if they'd traced the pistol to him he'd either be in a cell or his shop would be staked out and they'd have closed in on the assassin as soon as he turned up.

He didn't try any strong-arm tactics on the gun dealer. The guy was maybe mid-forties, refined... On the face of it, he could easily have scared the shit out of him and done quite a lot of damage but he wasn't stupid. No gun dealer in a city like this, wherever this was, went unprotected – he'd be armed, he'd have security systems in place, panic systems, debilitators, the works.

"You going to tell me who set this up?" he asked the dealer instead. "Who ordered my piece and told you to have it ready for me today?"

"I don't know," he said, and smiled, and there was at least a trace of genuine sympathy in that smile. "And if I did, I would not be indiscreet enough to divulge that data. I'm sure you understand my position."

"I need help. I don't have money. I'll never see you again, so I can't repay any debts. But I need help."

Silence invited him to at least continue.

"Someone to help me. Someone who understands ghosting, netspace, virtual intelligence systems... Someone I can talk to..."

The dealer gave him a name. And the name gave him another name. And now he was here, eyeing this anonymous warehouse door in an unlit backstreet in a harbour-side district, crowds swirling past, sweat running down his body, hopes hanging by a thread, a virtual thread.

He pushed, walked inside, just as he'd been told.

He found himself in a partitioned-off area of the warehouse, marked out by flimsy divider walls and a low suspended ceiling. It was dark in here, dim wall lights, a single bright desk lamp over on the far side of the junk-filled space where a short round guy was turning slowly to face him.

The man was shirtless in the heat, a shiny black ponytail halfway down his back, partly covering the winged dragon tattoo that covered most of the exposed skin. He had sensuous lips and tiny oriental eyes.

"Ah," the man said, a long drawn-out sound, almost a sigh. "The assassin, I presume?" He had a childlike, singsong voice, as if he was fighting the urge to sing his sentences like the lines from a nursery rhyme. "I have been expecting you. Please, come over, and sit with me. I would like to talk. Tell me, Mr Assassin, what it is *like*... "

He walked over, threading a path through stacks of papers and boxes and panels with wires and transistors and chips and crystal-boards. On the man's chest the tail and head of the dragon wrapped around, breathing fire across his ribcage.

"Mr Lee?"

The ponytailed man smiled, dipped his head, gestured at an office chair with one arm broken off.

He sat, started to speak: "I—"

"What it is like to be you, Mr Assassin? To be a man of many parts. Parts of other men – and maybe women, who knows? – and VI modules, a mix, a remix. All riding in another man's body. What is it like? What is it like to be something new, something unique, one of the first of your kind? A new variety of man for the first time in, what, twenty thousand, a hundred thousand years?"

"I... I don't know. I just want out..." Then: "How do you know so much about me?"

Lee smiled. He'd been smiling most of the time, but now he smiled a bit more.

"It is my business to know things. I know that your victim, Elector Burnham, is now resident in the Accord that he hates so much. His afterlife has begun."

The Accord... The consensus reality that hit critical mass some time earlier this year: a vast virtual reality populated by saved personality copies of the deceased. A virtual heaven.

"And so you know why I need to get out of this body."

A dip of the head acknowledged that which needed no further explanation. He couldn't stay in the sweat's body or he'd be caught. Simple as that, and they both knew it.

"I need to upload to netspace," he told Lee. "I need to track down my original."

"But you are a construct, an amalgam. You have no original, just a template, based on an individual who is at best only mostly you."

"Well in that case 'mostly' will have to do..."

"If you upload to netspace you will have to avoid your originators. They will be waiting. They will want to erase you."

He nodded. He knew all this.

"Upload me direct to the Accord," he told Lee. The Accord: a virtual world within netspace, a distributed world, a fractal construction of the ether. "Sidestep netspace itself and get me into heaven."

Lee shook his head. He had stopped smiling now. "The Accord is a consensual reality governed by the strictest protocols," he said. He really was almost singing his words now. "There is no way to break these protocols. It is rigid, inflexible."

"There must be a way…"

"The only way to enter the Accord is through death. Only then will the warehoused copy of your self be uploaded. It is governed by the protocols. And even then… well, you are a construct: there will be no warehoused copy of your self to upload…"

"There must be a way…"

"Even if I were to kill you now, the protocols dictate who gets in and who does not. You have not been warehoused, my friend: if you are to enter heaven then first you must be saved. But even then, you are not whole, you are *other*… the protocols would deny you entrance."

"There must be a way…" There was always a way.

Lee was smiling again. "There is often a way where at first there appeared to be none," he said. "But if there is a way then there will be a price…"

"I have nothing."

"You have everything, my friend. You are alien. You are novel. Talk to me. Tell me how it is to be one of the first of a new variety of man…"


THE PROTOCOLS OF consensus are what bind the Accord together. They make it real.

They grow, they mature, they evolve. They self-regulate. They are the laws of our new nature.

Yet... yet I am an exception, an anomaly.

I built heaven. I shaped the protocols. I have instanced myself within pre-consensus Accord from the very beginning, my own guinea pig. Instances of me have been ripped apart, have suffered all kinds of existential suffering and torture as protocols broke down, realities failed. I have suffered for my work, for my art. I have suffered for you all, many times over; probably more than any man has suffered before. Or rather, instances of me have.

The protocols grew up with me, around me. There is a connection that runs deep. Sometimes I lie awake and I can feel the world around me, the currents of humanity, the ebb and flow of individual lives. I have never felt this before. I asked you about it, but you thought I was getting mystical, you thought that I might have found God.

But no. I have not found God. I have found myself, and I am bound up in the existence of you all. I am connected. If there is a god in this heaven of ours, he flows through my veins, he fills my lungs, he is the electricity in my brain. If there is a god here, then he is in me.

THE FLAT OCCUPIES the upper floor of a quiet little Victorian terrace. Net curtains hang in the bay window. The ground-floor flat is for sale, a board nailed to the wall between door and window. Empty milk bottles stand on the pavement outside the door. Across the road, a small Bangladeshi takeaway does steady lunchtime business.

There are two doorbuzzers, one with a blank label, the other marked "N Barakh." Tate does something to the door and it swings open. They step inside.

To their right is the door to the ground-floor flat; ahead, steep stairs up to Barakh's door. They ascend, and again Tate works the door.

A small lobby leads into a living space lit by sun slanting in through the net curtains at the front. A big sofa is lined up before one wall; a TV screen is rolled away on the wall towards one corner of the room, its positioning indicating that it is hardly ever used. The place smells musty, and immediately has the feel of somewhere that has not been visited for weeks, at least. Again, Burnham marvels at the reality of the Accord. Somehow it's the small things that bring this home: while the London skyline – a distant view of Tower Bridge or St Paul's – seems normal, a shabby little flat in the East End which smells of damp and disuse is quite simply staggering in its verisimilitude.

"So…" says Burnham, poking at a pile of magazines with his foot – a haphazard mix of interior design, lifestyle, natural history, fashion, current affairs, a philosophy journal – "if he has a flat like this that we didn't know about, where else might he have a place?"

"This flat's no secret," says Tate. "It's registered in his personnel file as an occasional residence. I suppose it just never came up so you didn't know about it – you never had any reason to care where he might be staying on a late night at the project. There are no other residences listed, other than his main home in Essex."

Burnham crosses the room, pushes at a door. A small office space, a keyboard sitting on the desk, three screens stuck to the wall, stacks of papers and books and journals on the desk, on shelves, on the floor. This flat is more like a spare workspace than a place to stay, to live, Burnham realises. Barakh had probably come to work here when the hustle of the project's main office became too much but he still had to be in London.

So where the fuck *are* they?

He pushes at another door, sees a double bed, made up, not slept in.

He enters the room, imagines he can smell Priscilla here, a faint signature almost lost in the musty air of the flat. The cane-blinded window spews dust as Burnham opens the slats. Outside, there's a small paved yard, some bins, a high wall backing on to an alleyway. He turns, fighting back a sneeze.

By the bed there is a small dressing table, and on this he sees a photograph just tucked into the bottom of the frame, balanced there. The woman in the photograph is Priscilla.

He feels his throat constricting, is aware of a sudden cold rush across his face, his scalp. Fuck, but it hurts!

It's not a lovers' photo, though, a memento from some tryst, some snatched moment. It looks like an official photograph, something Barakh has grabbed from a file and printed out.

Burnham is acutely aware of his own confusion, how he will switch from one conviction about Priscilla and Barakh to another conflicting one instantaneously. One moment he believes they must have been lovers forever; the next he believes that they had never been lovers in the old world, had just come close.

He needs to know the details, needs to know what really happened, but he *doesn't*, he hates the thought of learning the truth. So fucking painful...

But they are here. In the Accord, they are together.

In the Accord they are lovers.

He plucks the photograph from the otherwise empty frame, wants to screw it up, tear it into tiny pieces, but instead tucks it into his wallet. He leaves the room, finds Tate going through some papers.

"I know where they are," Burnham says softly. "Or, at least, I know where they will have been."

THE PROTOCOLS OF consensus are what bind the Accord together. They make it real. They guard against anomalies.

They only allow one instance of anyone to exist; they guard the integrity of what it is to be a human.

Yet... yet I am an exception, an anomaly.

I left another instance of me behind in that reality shard separate from the Accord, making peace between the Hueys, encouraging and cajoling them into methodically progressing from that first successful intrusion into the quantum level gap in reality, what we are calling interstitial space. That, I believe, is not precisely a breach of protocol; that shard is beyond the Accord, after all.

I dream, though, and when I dream I push the limits of the real. I multiply.

I sleep, and I feel the ebb and flow of Accord all around me, all through me. I feel our instance of God in my veins.

I sleep in our hotel in Vienna and I am in London, floating... I see Jack Burnham and his man, Tate. They break into my flat in Bethnal Green. They search the rooms, go through my papers. I do not know what they expect to find. They probably don't know either.

I shift, push...

I am in a camp somewhere sunny. The camp is surrounded by high mesh fences, razor wire strung along the top, sentry towers at regular intervals. The gates stand open. The place appears to be abandoned. I remember newsfeeds from camps like this: seething crowds of people packed in, bulging eyes, concertina ribcages, spindly limbs, a ghastly echo of the Holocaust. A green lizard darts across the dusty road. A young black woman watches me from the shade of a doorway in a corrugated metal Nissen hut. She smiles. She doesn't appear to mind the intrusion. She looks healthy, peaceful. The Soul Harvesters must have been here in the old world and captured this woman, and hopefully many others.

Shift...

I am in Manhattan, a strangely empty Manhattan, still not heavily populated in the early Accord. A yellow cab goes past slowly, the driver clearly hoping I want a ride – business must be struggling with so low a population in the city.

I am in Paris, the Eiffel Tower just visible over rooftops... somewhere South American, Rio, I guess; I think those signs are in Portuguese… Copenhagen… St Louis…

PRISCILLA GOES OUT to sit at the pavement table with Luca. She sits in a metal-framed chair, stretches her legs out.

Luca is in his favourite pose, his hands deep in the pockets of his leather jacket, his chin sunk into his chest.

"So where is everyone, Luca?" she asks, resuming a conversation they had started on a near-deserted Strand. "Where have all your people gone?" She thinks it tragic: an entire village lost, the people passing unrecorded, unsaved. Sometimes she hates religion.

Luca says nothing.

Back in the house, Priscilla hears laughter. FaceGurl and Noah are cooking pasta in industrial quantities. Neither of them are naturals in the kitchen, but they are enthusiastic, at least. And they entertain the others. She would never have suspected that Noah would play it up to such a degree.

She goes inside, sees Noah with tomato stains down the front of a borrowed apron. She smiles, goes to hug him and then remembers why she shouldn't hug him, even as a friend – that look in his eye. She is feeding his hopes. She doesn't mean to taunt him. She just wishes she could relax, not have to worry about his responses all of the time. All of the fucking time.

She opens a bottle of red, pours two glasses, goes to sit at the big table with Efan and Maria.

Luca worries her. All the kids have had problems adjusting to this lonely new world, but he is the first to absolutely deny its truth.

She feels the weight. She had wanted to dot his, to come here to Luca's home; she had believed the trip would do them all good. But now she feels claustrophobic and she feels guilty because she feels this way. London seems so far away, those few brief days and nights of liberation.

More guilt... that she should feel this way, that she should resent the responsibility that has found her. That she should want to just let her hair down, lose herself, live for the minute, the second, the *now*.

I STAND IN the open doorway and study your features in the moonlight that spills in through the open window. We have come to Luca's home village in northern Italy, but it does not seem to have helped. If anything, it has pushed him deeper into his slough. That, in turn, has dragged you down.

You drank too much last night. You use it to escape. From the burden, I suppose, the pressure of being the one to whom all these children turn. I do what I can to lighten the load on your shoulders. I play with the kids; I keep them busy; I try to make space for you. I am prepared to wait. We have lifetimes ahead of us. Lifetimes to adjust to this new world. I will be there, always. You have loved me once, Priscilla; I can only hope that you will come to love me again.

I head back to my room and out onto the balcony. Yesterday, in the mountains, I noticed more discord, the jagged horizon unable to resolve itself. I felt the ground shifting beneath our minibus. No one else appeared to notice anything, putting the quake down to the movement of our vehicle over a rough bit of road as we snaked down hairpin bends from a high pass. I wonder how I am getting on with the Hueys. The Accord needs to be moved on to the next stage before the strains have too much impact.

Now... Moonlight limns the mountains in a tracery of silver. The peaks appear to float in mid-air, above solid masses of pitch-black forest. The village spreads out below, mostly in darkness, a few lights glimmering.

I wonder how hard it will be to get Luca into the minibus tomorrow, now that we have brought him home. Will he want to come with us when we head south-east this morning? We head for Venice next. You want to ride in a gondola.

I must have dozed, sitting in a cane seat on the balcony. I waken stiff, a touch of morning dew on my clothes. I hear voices from below. Efan and Mazeli arguing again. I lean over the railing, spot them in the backyard, kicking a ball, not arguing at all, just excited.

Downstairs, Luca is awake already. And you, Priscilla; you carve a large round loaf with a wedge-bladed kitchen knife that is not really suited. You discard it on the table just after I enter, resort to tearing the bread apart into chunks, and then when you are done you turn to the deep sink, washing off tomatoes and tender spinach leaves in running water.

Luca is in the open doorway, watching Efan and Mazeli still playing outside. "Vada e gioc," I tell him, struggling to remember the words. Getting him to play with them would be a big step.

He fixes me with a challenging look. "Why?" he asks. "If I believe what you tell me, this isn't real. Nothing of this is real."

"It *is* real," I say. "It's just a different kind of real."

He comes back in, rests his backside on the big kitchen table, close to where FaceGurl and Sissy sit looking at a picture book. "Where is everybody then?" he asks.

"They will get here eventually." If they have been warehoused... Luca would have someone at least, though: someone had arranged for the boy to be warehoused; someone had at least thought it worth hedging their bets, not putting their complete faith in the teachings of the Church.

"Where are they?"

There is an edge in Luca's voice today. I think he has reached some kind of crisis point, an adjustment.

I step towards him. "Luca," I say. "This is what is real for you now. You are among friends. It is not easy, but each of us has been through what you are experiencing."

"Yes?"

He picks up the knife, studies the blade.

"Luca?"

You turn, Priscilla, as if you have noticed something different in our exchange.

Luca won't meet my eyes now. As I step towards him again, he says, "It doesn't matter, though, does it? It is not real."

"Luca…"

He swings wildly, from nowhere.

I stagger back, feeling the rush of air from his flying arm.

I shout. I do not know what I shout; I do not think it is even a word, just an exclamation, a gasp, a cry.

I catch myself against the wall, watch in horror as Luca swings again.

FaceGurl looks up from the picture book, lets her mouth fall open.

The blade flashes past her face. Her eyes have gone full circle, lined in black; her pink and black hair flies back.

She turns. Looks.

The blade has halted, lodged in little Sissy's chest. Red slicks across the girl's white T-shirt, an exotic bloom.

I step forward, reach for Luca's arm, but I am too late.

He yanks the blade free, turns, starts to fall back as you throw yourself across him. You gasp, your eyes widen, your body twists.

I watch you die.

FaceGurl is sobbing, holding Sissy tight, even as Sissy fades from the world. Seconds later, FaceGurl is holding nothing. Sissy has gone.

And you… Priscilla… you fade too. I watch you go. I can see the expression on Luca's face. He scrambles to his feet, backs away, looking from me to the spot where you were, to the knife lying on the limestone floor. He turns and flees. I hear his footsteps in the cobbled street and then moments later, the only sound is FaceGurl's sobbing.

# 1.09

THE ASSASSIN STEPS through the doorway in the blank wall and emerges on a beach that is composed of white sand and shell fragments that glitter under the azure sky. It burns his feet. He looks down, sees his toes curling in the sand. His skin is white, his toes long and slender.

Is this the real him – what he is really like?

He puts a hand to his face, briefly fearing that there will be nothing there, just a blank, a template waiting to be written on. He is not a person. He is a thing, a construct, one of the first of a new kind of man. But no: his fingers find nose, mouth, eyes, the rasp of stubble, thick short hair. He is whole.

He squats, takes a handful of the sand, lets it drain between his fingers. He feels its smooth grittiness, savours the soft touch of a breeze on his face, smells salt on the air.

This, then, must be heaven.

Down in the water, two women in bikinis splash and play. A man runs past, in step with a gently loping Irish wolfhound. A road leads away from the beach.

He does not remember dying, does not remember what Lee did to him in the final moments. This must be the way for everyone here: they are saved before they die; they do not recall death itself.

He breathes heaven's air deep. Lee has sidestepped the protocols, he has crafted masqueware to slip the assassin into the Accord, but already it feels wrong, he feels that he does not belong here and should leave. He wonders how long he must keep running.

He walks, tarmac hot beneath his feet, where before it had been the sand that burnt.

Heaven, it would appear, is a tropical island. Or at least this part of heaven...

Those people on the beach behind him: dead, all dead, all here to stay. The assassin is an anomaly: he has come to heaven and he is merely a visitor, passing through. He has no intention of staying any longer than he has to.

There is a bar where the road loops back across the top of the beach. Palm trees stand around a cabin with a banana-leaf roof. Seating is scattered across the sand, people laughing and chatting, drinks on tables, ganja being puffed. A bar runs the length of one wall of the cabin, shaded by a sagging canopy, a barwoman lolling behind it, chewing gum, chilled. For a moment, he wonders who in heaven decides who gets to sit and drink and who gets to tend bar, but then he doesn't. It's the consensus: rules emerge from shared beliefs and perceptions. All societies need rules, even in heaven.

"Get a drink around here?"

"Sure," she says, still chewing. "You new here? First drink's free for debutantes."

He shrugs. Then points to the bottles of chilled beer in a cooler deep in the cabin's shade.

"So tell me... How do I find somebody around here?"

"That all depends," she tells him over her shoulder as she stoops for a beer, "on whether they want to be found."

"WE'RE GOING HOME," I say. No one objects. Most of the kids are still in shock.

Everyone loved Sissy – the little girl who would just climb onto the nearest lap with a book and demand that you read to her, the girl who would pick a lone flower from the side of the road and give it to someone, the girl we had found sitting in Hyde Park singing nursery rhymes and waiting patiently for her mother who wasn't dead yet.

And you. Everyone loved you too. You are the reason we are here. But now you are gone.

We are quiet on the minibus. I am up front alone. No one will sit in the front passenger seat where you would be while it was my turn to drive. I understand that, but it does not make it any easier.

The sun is bright, harsh. I wear faceted bug-eye shades that grip around the eye sockets. You found these for me in a shop in Vienna. Apparently they are fashionable. I like them because they are very effective, fit for purpose, and because you liked them.

I pull on the wheel, steering around a tight bend in the cobbled road in the heart of the village.

A figure sits on the kerb where the road straightens. A boy in jeans and a black leather jacket. Luca.

His face is buried in his hands, his knees pulled up tight to his chest.

I want to drive right at him. I feel the muscle in my right leg twitch, hear a slight surge in engine revs as the battery is drawn on more deeply. My reaction shocks me, but also it thrills me, makes me feel alive that I should want to kill.

Is it easier to kill in heaven? To want to kill?

I pull in, ping the door to open.

Luca looks up. Tears trace silver tracks down his cheeks. A lock of dark hair sticks to one side of his jaw, moist from the tears.

I jerk my head at him, indicating that he should climb in. "Come on, Luca," I tell him. "Come with us. We're heading back to England."

Silence returns. I want to look round, check the expressions of the kids behind me, but no, I know to play this one cool. Luca is with us. He is perhaps more broken by the transition between worlds than any of us.

You would have taken him, wouldn't you, Priscilla? You wouldn't have left him sitting on the kerb, alone in his village with the grief and horror at what he has just done, what he has just learnt.

"Are they dead?" Luca asks, as we leave the last houses of the village behind and climb into the mountains. "Did I kill them? I..."

"They will return," I tell him, and I believe my words, although I know that while the protocols run through me they are also beyond me. I cannot control our new laws of nature. I believe Priscilla and Sissy will be returned to this world. And I will look for them.

I ping the bus, tell it to switch to auto, close my eyes and lean back in the driver's seat.

I find netspace. Let it flow through me, let myself flow through it.

There is no sign of you yet. I do not know how long it will be. Will you be reborn instantaneously? Clearly not. Days? Weeks? Years?

I flow... hold on... push...

I stand on the cliff-top road at Deanmere Gap, before your childhood home. I recognise it from the stories you have told me. The end terrace, the one painted cream instead of white, with the wind-bent hawthorn tree in the small front garden. The house shows no sign of occupation. I try the bell, rattle at the door, check the windows. Nothing.

I cross the road. To left and right, chalk cliffs dazzle white in the sunlight. I see the coastguards' cottages nestling into the steeply sloping cliff top, just as you have described. I will wait here, or at least this instance of me will wait, and watch. I will leave him here, this instance; I will leave it.

I flow...

Hyde Park. Another sunny day. Lots of people are out. It appears that the Accord is becoming more populous. This instance of me strolls, following the paths, looking for Sissy. She is not by the tearooms, where we found her the first time.

She loves the ducks, so I stay close to the Serpentine.

I walk all day, but do not find her. I worry. Poor child, barely five years old, we reckoned. Out here, alone. Maybe someone has found her and taken her in.

I leave an instance of myself there, too. I do not know how far I can take this, how far I can push the protocols by instancing myself in multiples. They are not full instances; they are not *me*. They are placeholders for my presence. Right now I am hugely grateful that I can do this, but it worries me that such a loophole exists. I believe it is because I am so bound up in the nature of the Accord, and so it is an artefact of me being *me*. I certainly hope that is the case and not a more general exception.

I turn my head. Luca sleeps.

He is missing the most spectacular of views, as we journey through a high pass. Where once a glacier had occupied this broad U-shaped valley through the peaks, now there is a landscape scoured and gouged raw for millennia by the ice, exposed by the great thaw, more alien than almost any landscape on Earth.

Oblivious to all this, the boy sleeps peacefully. He, who earlier today killed a small child and the woman I love.

I let the bus drive on, close my eyes, try to relax. It will be a long night.

ELECTOR BURNHAM AND Tate take the train to Eastbourne, having a first-class carriage to themselves for most of the journey. Tate watches an action movie on the drop-screen; Burnham stares at the passing countryside, occasionally pausing to look at the dog-eared photograph in his wallet. From time to time he closes his eyes to skip through mail, but there's nothing of note, nothing to snag his interest. Things will get more interesting as more people come to live in the Accord, but for now, being the man who rules heaven is proving to be a rather dull existence.

They hire a two-seater car, its electric engine almost silent, and make their way onto Marine Parade, coming out near the pier. Hotels line one side of the road, white and cream and yellow, several storeys high. Burnham looks out across the shingle, muscular white gulls lined up on the groynes, and over the bay. It's a grey day, but mild, calm. A few people walk on the beach. One couple.

Burnham closes his eyes, remembers coming here regularly with Priscilla to visit her mother while she had still been alive. Liz had been in a home here in Eastbourne for several years, her head a battleground between Alzheimer's and various regenerative drugs. But he and Tate haven't come here for old time's sake: their destination is a few miles west, a village called Deanmere Gap, where Priscilla had moved with her mother when she was eleven.

That had been Tate's mistake: to concentrate on places where *Barakh* might have sought refuge. But no... This is Priscilla's place, she would have to bring Barakh here. Burnham *knows* it. Priscilla would have to start off her new existence by revisiting her past, sharing it.

He opens his eyes again, looks across the beach, realising what it is that is so very wrong.

There should be groups, families, more than the solitary couple strolling hand in hand, for all the world as if they fear that one might be snatched away from the other at any moment. So many single people! What a sad, desolate place this world must be for so many... The first to die, passing their days waiting, abhorring what they hope for with every minute that passes, full of self-hatred for being the one who waits for their loved ones to hurry the fuck up and *die*...

Soon they have left the town behind and found the turning to Beachy Head; a few minutes later, there is sea to either side beyond the rolling green downland. The village lies somewhere ahead, a few miles of twisting road distant.

When they get there they find that the village appears to be closed down, a temporary state of affairs for the majority of small settlements in the Accord, something highlighted in several of the reports Burnham has read recently. Most people are living in the towns and cities until the population is high enough to sustain rural life again. Consensus is strong where lots of people gather: life goes on, systems run. Out here, in the Deanmere Gaps and East Deans, the shops and services just can't be sustained and even consensus cannot be stretched far enough to make them do so. Anyone choosing to live out here chooses to live in a barren wilderness for now.

Their car cruises past a locked-up chip shop, a village store with boards over its windows and tattered but still functioning newsfeed posters gummed onto these, the latest headlines and ads scrolling past on repeat. They come to a T-junction by a closed-down pub, turn left, the land tumbling away towards the sea. Gulls hang in the air level with the car, eyeing them suspiciously.

"Here," says Burnham, pointing at the end house of a terraced row that faces the sea.

As they pull up, Tate leans forward over the wheel, points. "Looks empty, see? Curtains closed, no sign of any activity. Garden gate closed. That may be how they want it to look, of course. Where d'you want me?"

"By my side. Always, you hear?"

Tate nods.

They go up the stone steps and pause by the door. The passageway to the side is closed off by a high wooden gate. Burnham pushes at the door, but it is locked. He presses the doorbell, wondering why the hell he should feel awkward doing so.

Nothing.

He presses again, but the house is empty, or its occupants are lying low.

"You want to get in?" asks Tate.

Burnham shakes his head. Already he is heading back down the steps.

They walk along the cliff-top road until they reach a pathway that heads sharply down to the beach. Near the bottom, they pause, look along the shore to where a row of white coastguards' cottages perches on a steeply angled ledge of land cut into the chalk cliff. Before the cottages, great slabs of rock stretch out into the sea, scoured into all kinds of distorted and bizarre shapes by the tide.

Burnham marches across the blue-grey shingle beach, clambers up onto the first of the rocks, picks his way across. Tate follows, pausing to peer into the rock pools. "Hey, mind the seaweed, you hear? It's slippy," he calls.

Burnham stops by a deep gulley carved into the rock, water rushing in and out of it a good three metres below.

"She used to come here," he says. "As a kid. Used to half-believe that if she threw herself into the gulley she'd turn into a mermaid and swim away. Always stopped herself, though."

"No sign of them, JB."

"No... But they've been here. You saw the window."

He looks up – a moment of sixth sense, perhaps – and Noah Barakh is standing on the rocks on the other side of the gulley, arms folded, a faint smile tugging at the corners of his mouth. He looks the same as ever: slim, dark-haired, a Mediterranean flush to his skin. He dips his head briefly in greeting.

"Elector Burnham," he says.

There is a pause. Water rushes in deep between them, rushes out, rushes in again.

Burnham looks at him. Breathes steadily, calmly. Gathers his thoughts, analyses his reactions, the slight racing of his pulse, the dampness pricking his forehead.

He inclines his head towards his bodyguard, says, "Tate? Shoot the fucker."

Tate draws the pistol from the shoulder holster beneath his jacket, levels it, fires – once, twice, rapidly, the loud cracks ringing around the rocks and back off the cliffs, tolling loud bell-like echoes in Burnham's ears.

Barakh stands there, that same little smile. Nothing.

"I am protected," he tells Burnham. "It is futile to pursue me. Give up now, Elector. Accept that things move on and change in an eternal world. Nothing lasts forever. Allow yourself to grow and change too, won't you?"

Burnham stares at him. "Consensus doesn't apply to you, does it?" he says. "I don't know what'd happen to anyone else if Tate shot them, but I bet *something* would... You're a fucking loophole, aren't you? This is *your* fucking heaven."

The bastard carries on smiling. Probably doesn't even realise he's doing it. "Start a new life," he tells Burnham. "This is your opportunity."

"I'll find you," says Burnham. "I'll track you down. You hear? There's nowhere you can hide, nowhere you can run to that I won't find you in the end. I have all eternity to track you down! You'll always be looking over your shoulder, not knowing when I'll be there, but I will find you, you hear? You'll never go to sleep at night knowing for sure that you will wake up the next morning."

As he talks, Burnham stares at Barakh, not allowing his gaze to wander, only aware of Tate's movements in the periphery of his vision.

"Please, Jack. Take some time. You haven't been here long. Take some time to adjust, to think about the life you want to lead here. Try to—"

Tate steps out from behind a stack of rocks, swings a big hand at Barakh, down onto his shoulder... stumbles forward, clutching at air, staggering off-balance, striking another big rock with his shoulder, grunting, twisting, turning...

Barakh has gone, vanished. The two of them are alone now, just Burnham and Tate, standing either side of a deep crevice in the rock shelf, the sea rushing in deep below, rushing out, rushing in again.

PRISCILLA IS.

Kind of.

She is shapes. Patterns. She is ebbs and flows and surges and kaleidoscope colours.

She is, but she is not what she will be. That will emerge.

PRISCILLA OPENS HER eyes to grey.

She remembers dying this time. The knife in Luca's hands, his panic and confusion. The awful red explosion as he stabbed Sissy, the rush of movement, the grinding ache in Priscilla's chest as the knife eased between ribs, the ache transforming into intense pain, the blackening of her vision, the last thoughts shaping in her mind: how awful, how did it happen like this, why, guilt, physical pain… thoughts labouring, awareness that her brain was still struggling to function long seconds after her heart had stopped beating, everything slowing… slowing…

She has died in the Accord, and now she is reborn.

She spies the outline of a door in the grey, pauses.

She can feel it, her sense of self still settling around her, of who she is and who she is not. The shapes and patterns of her self. She could stay here a while longer, as long as she needs.

She closes her eyes. She has eternity ahead of her. All the time she needs to find herself. No hurry.

I WALK THE shore, the cliffs a dazzling ultra-white in the morning sun, the air heavy with salt. This world, this reality… I still marvel at how real it feels, although I know that *real* is not a valid concept: this world *is*. That is all.

There is a lighthouse here, somewhere, but I have not reached it yet. I should worry about getting stranded by the rising tide, but I do not. I am an instance of my self. With everything that I learn about this heaven that I have created, I see that I am inextricably tied to its fabric. There is no God, but if there were then I would be his most trusted lieutenant.

You do not return to the cottage, though.

Instead... Elector Burnham and his sidekick, Tate. They explore the rocks below Coastguards' Row. They are filling time, waiting for you... for us.

I feel sorry for him, your husband, and I am aware that my pity does not ease the encounter when it comes; it inflames him.

He has Tate shoot me, he watches while Tate creeps round behind me, through the rocks, like a child playing hide and seek, and then swings at me, in vain. He rants at me and threatens me and he really believes that he can, one day, harm me, that he can, one day, exact his revenge. There is nothing to be gained from this encounter; there is no reasoning. Elector Burnham is not here for debate.

I fade.

We are in the minibus, driving down the ramp from the Channel shuttle. Efan and Charlie lead singing in the back, a familiar singalong tune, but with words I don't recognise, probably new words of their own. Efan is a bright kid. He and FaceGurl in particular repeatedly startle me with their insights and lateral thoughts.

The journey back has been tiring, even though the bus has been on auto most of the way and the roads deathly quiet. Sitting down doing nothing can be hard work. The kids have been great, though, no trouble at all.

I sit here, and I can recall the journey back from Italy; I can recall the time spent on the beach at Deanmere Gap, watching and waiting; I can recall the time in London, wandering the parks and the river, looking for you, looking for poor Sissy. I should be out there, saving the world. And I am, I am: I am there with the Hueys, working with them, shepherding them; I am frequently in Shanghai and other old world project centres. I *am* out there, saving the world.

But... I should care more.

I send my surrogates, my instanced selves, while here... all I want is you.

AND YOU RETURN.

You have been reborn in the flat in Sloane Square, the one you had occupied with the kids before our trip across the Alps.

I lie in the hotel room in Tunbridge Wells, pinged awake by the searchbot I'd set to sniff out your presence. I will find you, take your children back to you. You told me you couldn't love me, that the you who had loved me was a different you.

You have been reborn.

Maybe this is the you that can learn how to love me again.

HE SITS IN a spindle-backed chair in the small kitchen of his North Downs home, his elbows resting on the heavy table, hands cradling a teacup. He hears Tate moving about in the corridor – emerging from the front room where he had been reclining on the sofa, eyes closed, surfing netspace, never letting up on his investigations of this new world.

"It's his world, isn't it?" calls Burnham. "Fucking Noah fucking Barakh... He's constructed the protocols to protect him. What kind of a chance do we have? Eh? What kind of a chance...?"

No response.

Burnham leans back in his chair, puts his cup down.

Seconds pass, then Tate appears in the doorway.

Something in his look... in his eyes, the set of his jaw.

"What is it?"

Tate just looks.

"Tate?"

"I thought you trusted me, JB," he says, leaning on the doorframe.

"What? What are you talking about? Of course I fucking trust you!"

"So why did you have me tortured and killed? Why did you have Lucy Chang slice me over and over until she believed me that I was telling the truth? Why did you even entertain the possibility that I had been spying on you? That I had betrayed you? 'Cos that's what you did, see?"

Burnham stares at him. "What fucking planet are you on?" he gasps, eventually. "What fucking planet?"

"I'm on the one I ended up in after you had me killed, JB."

"No..." Burnham shakes his head. What's got into Tate? What's going on? "Why would I do that? I didn't do anything of the kind!"

"Remember old Fred Counter?" Tate asks. "Used to run under the table accounts for corporate clients to keep them one step away from thugs like Marshall Riff and the Waterman boys? He died a couple of days ago. Just been in touch. Told me all kinds of things that have happened in the old world since I died. All kinds of things you conveniently haven't told me..."

"Tate," says Burnham. "Will you just believe me that I don't have the faintest idea what you're talking about?"

But Tate is turning, heading down the corridor.

"I'm finished," he says over his retreating shoulder. "Maybe Barakh's right. Maybe this is a chance for all of us to have a new start, to rethink who we are, where we want to be. I can't believe you had me killed."

*Neither can I!*


PRISCILLA IS, AGAIN.

Through the door she passes, and so Priscilla *is* in the Sloane Square flat, sunlight slanting in through half-drawn curtains, motes of dust languid in the air.

Straight away, she hears a small voice, a young child humming a nursery tune. She leaves the lounge, follows the sound along the corridor, pauses in the kitchen doorway.

Sissy sits in the middle of the lino, giant wooden spoon in one hand, mounds of flour and smashed eggs spread around her. White smears across her face give her an extra-wide clown smile, which broadens as she sees Priscilla. "Cilla!" she cries.

Priscilla gathers the girl up, regardless of the mess. "Oh, baby," she coos. "How long you been here, eh? You been here long?"

She doesn't really understand how the kid can be so relentlessly cheerful, but she isn't going to start complaining.

Sissy thrusts the spoon towards Priscilla's mouth, chuckling away. Priscilla tastes flour, egg, wood.

LATER, THEY WANDER up King's Road towards St James's Park, Sissy riding high on Priscilla's shoulders.

A minibus approaches. *The* minibus.

It stops, kids pile out, then Noah.

Priscilla is suddenly holding back the tears. She is excited to see them all again, and touched at their excitement; underneath it all there is a kind of shock, a feeling that is hard to pin down, a feeling almost no one has yet *had* to pin down... The shock of return, the shock of your own death being so vivid and fresh amidst the suddenly normal.

She slides Sissy down from her shoulders, lets the girl stand, as all around the other kids are hugging them and chattering and calling.

She feels the first tears slip down her face, feels a complete fucking arse for getting like this.

Sissy screams. Loud, so loud, and piercing.

Priscilla drops to one knee, grabs the girl, clutches her tight.

She looks to where Sissy is looking, the minibus door, the boy just emerging. Luca.

He looks pale, dark-eyed.

Noah has brought Luca back with the others.

She doesn't know what to think. She feels shock, anger, an overwhelming sense of protectiveness for Sissy. Wonder at what the journey must have been like, what must be in the heads of all the other kids, what they must feel about Luca. Wonder at Noah... that he could have done this.

Wonder at herself, that she could even think that he might not have done this, that he might have left the boy to fend for himself, alone in his village, just waiting for someone to die...

She walks through the crowd of kids, faces Luca, holds him, hard against the place where he had buried that knife.

Sissy comes too, clinging to Priscilla's leg. Luca looks down at the girl now and his features crumple. He loosens his grip on Priscilla, half steps towards Sissy, then turns and runs. Away from Sissy, away from them all, right down the middle of King's Road, a lone black cab dodging him easily.

They are powerless. The boy runs fast. They can do nothing except try to find him again later, hope that he will be okay in this foreign city.

Finally, Priscilla turns to Noah. It's still in his eyes. In the way he holds his head. In that little half-smile of his.

She hugs him, awkwardly, and he holds on just a fraction too long. How strange to touch someone who knows the feel and responses and tastes of your own body while you know nothing in return! We are not adapted to this afterlife, she realises yet again. We have so much to learn.

"Noah," she says. "You came back."

Of course he had.

The touch of his body... she wants that. She wants it quite intensely right now. Wants to explore those things another her has already explored.

She turns away.

He wants her so much. He waits. He is patient.

Of course he has come back to look for her.

Suddenly she just wants to walk away, away from it all. How can she be so contradictory? The things she wants pull her in opposing directions so strongly. She doesn't even begin to understand, but then she never was one to linger on self-analysis. Priscilla does; Priscilla *is*.

"And you came back too," says Noah. He <hugs> her; she <hugs> him back.

She nods, gathers up Sissy again, smiles through the tears at the pressing children. "So who's for pizza?" she asks them, resuming her walk towards the park.

## 1.10

Turns out the late Elector Burnham is fairly easy to find, but it's still taken the assassin a week to track him down, asking people, hacking virtual directories and surveillance logs. Trouble is, there are just so few people here to talk to – most of the really useful ones haven't died yet...

But now... now he is here, walking up a narrow North Downs lane, heading towards a row of three cottages that at some point in the past have been knocked together into a single house. A modest place for someone as influential as Burnham had been and still is – by all accounts he's just about the most senior politician in the whole Accord so far. But one with only a modest home.

He wonders what happens if he kills Burnham here. He wonders if that's why he is here, why the one thing that has obsessed him, possessed him, has been to follow all leads to the door of the one man he knows who will be working on every possible way to extract himself from this virtual heaven.

Is he here because it might offer a way out, or is there some other reason, something hidden deep in his head?

He should have a plan, but he doesn't.

He just knows he has to come here, find him. It's as if he's drawn to Burnham, like magnetic north needs magnetic south. Is this some perverse protocol of the Accord? The guilty drawn to their victims? Maybe he will go down on his knees and beg Burnham's forgiveness...

Or maybe there is still some protocol buried deep in his being that draws him here to finish what he began in that sultry Asian city.

IT WAS GOING well so far. Bartie had read-only net access, and a larger room that he could kid himself was hardly a cell at all, but merely a holding space, a room they were providing while the current irregularities were ironed out. The net allowed him to fill his time reading up on human rights legislation, and this was what had allowed him to negotiate improved accommodation and round the clock TrueSim gaming access.

He knew the officers who guarded his room by name, and he had learnt to play them off one against the other. Bartie Davits was beginning to enjoy himself. To treat it as a game, one where he was on a winning streak. Most of the time he even managed to stop himself from remembering that this was his life, his future, until legal powers way beyond his comprehension determined just how responsible he was for the murder of someone he had never met, in a faraway city he had never visited, for reasons he couldn't even guess.

A real-life alert nudged him and he slid the sim-shades up onto the crown of his head. "David," he said, "What can I do for you?"

The uniformed man stood in the doorway. "Your interview, Mr Davits. It's time for your interview."

"Ah yes," said Bartie. "Of course."

He dropped the shades on his desk and stood, then followed the officer out of the room and along the corridor to the lift. He had arranged this interview to discuss progress in his case. It was about time they started to give him a solid reason for his continued incarceration.

They rode a lift to the seventh floor, and David, his personal guard, showed him through into an office which occupied one corner of the building, high glass windows over two walls giving views across the city, Tower Bridge just visible in the distance.

"Malcolm." Bartie nodded at the pinstriped man already seated in one of the two leather seats in front of the room's wide desk. His solicitor, Malcolm Groves.

Across the desk was a plain-clothes officer. Another stood by a window, looking out. David remained by the closed door.

"So," said Bartie. "Where have we reached? By my understanding we have approximately twenty-two hours remaining until I must either be charged or released, isn't that so, Malcolm?"

Right up to this point Bartie had been confident.

He had felt in control.

Here he was in a senior officer's swanky office, turning the tables, conducting an interview he had initiated. He had read up on the relevant legislation. He knew his ground. He would be free by this time tomorrow, unless they actually found something to charge him with.

But now…

Malcolm Groves wouldn't meet his look. He had an unfolded e-printout on his lap, and he was scrolling through it instead of daring to even glance at his client. There was sweat on his upper lip, despite the air-conditioning.

"Malcolm?"

Bartie <poked> his solicitor, sent: *You going to tell me what's going on?*

Nothing.

"Perhaps you'd better explain, Mr Groves." This was from the officer across the desk, addressing Bartie's solicitor.

Bartie stared at Malcolm, and finally the man met his look, briefly…

"I'm sorry, Mr Davits," he said. "There have been… complications."

It was a game, Bartie reminded himself. A game. He shouldn't be feeling that the world had been snatched from beneath his feet. He should ride the "complications" and bounce back fighting.

"There are claims of, erm, *territory*, Mr Davits. Proprietorial issues. Corporeal ownership."

Groves sent: *They want you. Your body. They appear to have a legitimate claim.*

He was starting to see. To understand.

*Fuck.*

"You would be warehoused up to, and for the duration of, your trial and any subsequent appeals, Mr Davits," said Groves. "Your rights will be protected, I will ensure that."

"But... but this is new legal territory," Bartie said. "Everyone tells me it could take years!"

Malcolm Groves looked away again, didn't respond to Bartie's continued pings.

"That's exactly why Elector Burnham's people want him out," said the officer from behind his desk.

"Are you telling me..." Bartie swallowed, started again: "Are you really telling me I'm going to be archived in some data warehouse while the late Elector Jack Burnham rides my bones for all that time?"

That was what they meant. Once a sweat, always a sweat...

Nobody said anything. Bartie's solicitor didn't say "No, Mr Davits, we're going to fight your case all the way. They'll never get away with doing a thing like that."

Bartie looked down. After months, years, just whose body would this even be?

The bastards... They couldn't be allowed to do this.

He looked at his solicitor and his solicitor looked at his e-print out and he realised that yes, they could, and they would, and there was nothing he could do about it.

* * *

SAMMY ZHANG TOOK me out on a sleek cruiser on the Huangpu River. We sat on the deck, sipping at a pineapple drink, the Oriental Pearl Tower dominating the view to the right.

I was riding Zhang Xiaoling again, acutely conscious of the muggy heat, the sweat on her skin. I tried to analyse my own reactions: did this really feel more credible than the Accord? Was the physicality of this place more intense? Or was it merely an artefact of the physical discomfort? Would Shanghai in the Accord feel just as intensely, limb-deadeningly uncomfortable?

"The latest instalment has not come through," Sammy said. "We are delivering your resources in good faith. We have the best people in the world carving out netspace for you."

I spread my hands. "You know how it is," I said. "The funding comes through international agencies. These things never run to time. We have been late before, but not once have we missed a payment."

"You have been late before," said Sammy, pausing to sip at his drink. "You should not be late again. It shows disrespect, Professor Barakh. Respect matters to me. It matters to me a lot. You should understand who it is that you deal with."

I watched the expression on Sammy Zhang's face, tried to read it, tried to gauge the degree of threat. I was very aware of the two men standing at the rail nearby, studiously staring out across the water, not part of this conversation just yet.

"Things are getting tough here, you know," continued Sammy. "Maybe you don't realise how bad? You in your virtual hideaway. Dirty bomb in Berlin. Slow genocide right the way around the Mediterranean rim. Here in China, famine right across Xinjiang, Qinghai, and Gansu. Your Accord will be filling up pretty damn quick, Professor Barakh. You're going to be running out of resources damn soon. You need me. You need to pay me. You need to respect me."

"The money is good," I told him. "And I do respect you. We came to you first of all. You have always delivered what you promise. You are the best. How could I not respect you?"

"That is the question I have been asking," he said.

I missed the signal – a flash of the eyes, the placing of his glass, a slight clearing of the throat? – but it was there. The two heavies were suddenly behind me, taking my arms.

"I—"

Sammy Zhang gave a single shake of his head, cutting me off.

I tried to remain calm, but it did not come naturally to me. I am not a man of action.

They turned me, ripped my grey jacket open, exposing the white vest beneath. I looked at Sammy Zhang. He was watching, smiling a hard, emotionless smile, fingers steepled at his chin.

I opened my mouth again, as my jacket came away, and one of the men pulled at my vest. "This is your sister…" I said.

He shook his head, slowly. "No," he said. "It is you, Professor Barakh. The body will not be damaged, so when Xiaoling returns she will not have been harmed. It is you we fuck with, Professor Barakh. It is you. Please do not fuck with *us*."

They were pulling at my trousers now, and in moments I was naked, one hand feebly trying to cover the thick plug of hair at my crotch.

One of the men pulled me down to the deck, leaving the other standing over me, freeing his own trousers, forcing my legs apart with heavily booted feet.

I could flee.

I could let Xiaoling back into her own body.

I looked at Sammy again, met his eyes. Sammy knew that I could do that; it was a risk he was willing to take.

But… I couldn't do that to her. Couldn't do that to the project. And Sammy knew it, knew that I had a choice but it was one I couldn't take, and he knew that made the punishment even more intense, more awful.

I felt a weight suddenly on me, pressing, forcing.

I cried out.

I cried.

I...

HE RINGS THE doorbell. Can it really be as simple as this?

His throat is dry. This isn't real, he tells himself. It's not reality. But his feet hurt from walking, he's thirsty, he can feel the breeze at the back of his head. It certainly *feels* real.

The door opens halfway, a face peers around it.

The man has a look of hired muscle about him, bodyguard, some kind of security. Square head, probably all bone and no brain. How to get past him?

"I'm looking for Elector Burnham."

The bodyguard stares, blank, distracted. "He's not expecting you," the guy says, in a soft Welsh accent.

Then he pushes the door wide, steps past the assassin, muttering softly to himself, head down as if it's raining when in fact there's not a cloud in the high blue sky.

"Tate?"

That's Burnham, calling through from the back. The assassin's head twitches, focusing on the voice like a hawk, targeting the sound.

And that's when he starts to get dizzy.

He shakes his head, rolls his shoulders, trying to find clarity, struggling.

He takes one step, another. By the end of the short passageway he's staggering, can hardly stay on his feet.

What is he doing here? Is he going to kill Burnham again – whatever that means in heaven? Finish off the job he started in the old world?

Up to now he's believed that Burnham is his only connection in this place, and that he may somehow be the only way back to reality. But is that a delusion?

He feels compelled to continue, driven. Something in his head, dragging him closer, magnets, gravity, an electron trapped into the orbit of a nucleus.

He is drawn.

Burnham is there, the same athletic build, the cropped black hair, the cosmetic face.

He's standing, leaning on a heavy kitchen table. "What the...?" he gasps. He slides into a chair, sits with his head in his hands, staring at his visitor.

The assassin finds the chair opposite Burnham, echoes his pose. "What's happening?" he hisses. His head is swirling, spinning, a kaleidoscope of sensation.

He senses this man.

He feels him.

Burnham is in the assassin's head and the assassin is in his.

There are no boundaries.

Burnham starts again: "Who are you? Where's Tate?" He is clearly struggling, like the assassin, lost in the swirl.

"I'm your killer." *And you are in my head...*

The assassin squeezes his skull between his hands. "How...?"

His eyes are locked on Burnham, but over the elector's shoulder he sees a flicker, a form taking shape, and suddenly there's a man standing there, or at least the outline of a man.

He blinks and the man has vanished, but now hands are gripping his arms from behind. Either he's briefly blacked out or the man has crossed the room in the blink of an eye.

He blinks again, and this time blackness remains.

BURNHAM PULLS HIS head from his hands. His skull feels so heavy. His thoughts mired in mud, dragged back, impeded.

The man, his killer, sits across the kitchen table from him, head in hands.

The room appears to be turning, slowly, or Burnham is, and the room is turning faster, or more slowly. Space, geometry... they drift.

He feels this man, this killer. Feels him inside his skull.

He is very scared.

Then he senses something, something behind him. He turns his head, sees only the briefest of flickers, turns back to look at his visitor, and sees that now the killer's arms are held by... by a shape, a human shape. He cannot focus on this shape. It makes everything swirl even more vertiginously than before. He looks away and the world steadies. From the corner of his eye he sees the assassin being held by a human-shaped gap in this world.

The gap spreads, flows, leaching into the outline that is his killer.

The shape starts to... to thin.

Burnham can look at it now, can see the kitchen door through the shape as it dissipates.

He feels himself drawn towards it across the heavy table, as if he is suddenly falling.

He slumps, cheek against the smooth grain of the wood, feels a sudden lifting, a release of pressure, twists his head to look.

The shape has gone, the shapes.

He is alone.

He has never felt so alone. He feels as if something has been ripped out of his chest.

He sobs.

## 1.11

PRISCILLA DOESN'T SLEEP well, back in the familiar surrounds of the Sloane Square flat. She is too on edge, too sensitive to existence...

Sissy is in with her, curled up on the left of the double bed, restless in her dreams, waking frequently.

Priscilla feels very *aware*. She feels Sissy's every movement. From time to time she hears noises of someone moving about in the flat, probably Mazeli, sleepless as ever. She hears the sounds from the street, occasional cars and motorbikes, voices at odd times throughout the night, faint music from somewhere, the city steadily filling up. She is very aware of her own body: a buzz of energy in her head as if she has drunk too much espresso; the tensions in muscles, the grinding of teeth, or bone against bone; a faint whistle in her ears; the occasional gurgle of digestion. The shapes in her head, the who that she is. She has been reborn and she is the she from the old world plus the she she has been in the new. She *is*.

She dozes, wakes to dawn's grey light filtering in through the gap in the curtains.

She stretches, feels that buzz again, rolls out of bed. She pees, runs clawed hands through her hair to straighten it at least a little, goes down to the kitchen in her jammies.

Filling the kettle, she realises she had not seen Noah .in the front room where she had left him the night before. She wanders back through, opens the curtains on the world. He is gone.

And then she hears the latch on the front door, goes out, and sees him entering the flat. For a brief moment she wonders, amused, if he has been out on the town, finding his own club for diversion, his own Omar. But then she looks more closely. He is pale, something different in his eyes. Troubled.

He looks at her, lets his eyes slide past her to the wall, to the floor.

"You okay, Noah?" she asks.

He nods, shuts the door behind him, approaches.

She puts a hand to his arm and he jerks away at her touch.

"Noah?"

"Sorry. I... Not much sleep. I'll be okay."

He still won't meet her look.

"What's up? What's happened? You been out looking for Luca?"

"No, no. Nothing." He gives his little smile then. "I've just been out trying to save the world, that's all."

Now Priscilla smiles too. He has lots to contend with. Maybe he is just tired, been out walking to clear his head. Fuck it, they're *all* tired. This may be heaven, but it's turning out to be no sweet bed of roses.

She reaches for his arm again, and this time he does not flinch. She squeezes, releases, steps back to let him walk through.

Later, she sits on a plastic bench with Noah on Chelsea Embankment, watching the river and the boats. Some of the kids are with them, the rest back at the flat or roaming. They will meet tonight to eat if they choose; Priscilla is not exactly an authoritarian surrogate mother.

"You managed it yet, then?" she asks. She is very aware of the space between them on the bench. For a moment she wonders if somehow Noah has found out about her night-time adventures before their trip. It shouldn't matter a flying fuck if he has, of course – she is a free and grown-up woman – but that doesn't stop her being sensitive to his feelings.

There is a delay before he responds, then he looks, asks, "Managed what?"

"To save the fucking world," she says, and then <hugs> him.

He <hugs> back, says, "I am the little boy with his finger in the dyke."

She smiles. She wants to press him, but does not know how.

Then he adds, "It is a heavy burden, Priscilla. I should never have died. I should be out there pushing the Shanghai team, pushing the flesh-and-blood Huey to guide the transition to interstitial space. Netspace is not enough for the Accord. It was never going to be. Everyone thinks I am the man in control, but really I am the cowboy on the bucking bronco, just hanging on and hoping I don't get thrown."

"You been back there?" She knows he rides sweats back in the old world, that he can twist the protocols to allow that.

He nods.

"Tough back there?"

He nods. "Yes, it is tough back there."

She <hugs> him again. At least he doesn't flinch at her virtual touch. He still looks damaged, though. Broken.

He smiles, <hugs> back, stares off into the distance.

I SMILE, <HUG> back, watch a near-empty picture-windowed tour boat drift past. One man sits halfway along its otherwise empty seats, face pressed against the glass, staring, alone. The river is a churning gunmetal grey today, angry mirror to the sky above. The air is tense, electric, just waiting for the storm. I tip my head back, willing the rain to start, big heavy drops the size of eggs to explode on my face, wash over me.

The rain does not come yet.

The sun is suddenly harsh through a half-break in the clouds. I blink, but force my eyes to open again. I will not close my eyes. Whenever I close my eyes I feel Sammy Zhang's thugs again, smell them. I closed my eyes then. Tried to shut them out. Shut it out. But when you close your eyes you just intensify other senses. Touch. Hearing. Smell. Taste.

I closed my eyes and it made it worse. But I could not make myself open them.

I blink again. My eyes are sore, tired. I will not close them.

"Hey," you say, leaning into the space between us. "Will you look at that?"

I look where you point. A boat is going past, another tour boat with picture windows. Down inside the boat, a dinner-jacketed band plays something that swings and swells and rolls, while up on the open top deck a small group has gathered, a party, a ceremony... a bride and groom, he in charcoal morning suit and she in an extraordinary confection of a dress, all lace and veils and silk flowers and bows.

I smile. I hurt, but I smile. People... like puppies, sometimes. So fucking optimistic.

"They from before, or now?" you ask, and I know what you mean. Did they die as a couple or did they only meet here in the Accord, recently?

I lean across, put my right hand around the back of your head, pull your face to mine, kiss you, hard, firm, brief.

I stand.

You look shocked, flustered. You look as if you have no idea how to react.

I smile.

"I have things to attend to," I tell you. "Dinner?"

You nod, still lost for words.

I turn and walk away, along the Embankment. I will find somewhere quiet, lose myself within, hook up with my Hueys instance, push.

But as I walk I am interrupted by a ping from one of my bots. There is an anomaly, a kink in the protocols. I head back to the flat, let myself in, sit in the front room, instance myself within, in meetspace, in grey, go to find the anomaly.

THEY SIT IN a grey space, a gentle grey, not too bright or too dark. A grey that folds around them. The assassin sits. The man sits. Just the two of them.

He knows this man. He has seen him somewhere before. He is thirty-something, olive-skinned, a half-smile shaping his mouth, his eyes.

"You are an anomaly, my friend. You do not belong in the Accord."

"But I have nowhere else."

"That is, in part, the nature of your anomaly."

There is silence, then the man resumes. "You are comprised of too many non-discreet elements. You should never have been allowed to find your way back in here. The protocols of consensus are very strong, self-reinforcing. They have to be. Without consensus there is no Accord. The algorithms that form this reality are constructed from all the individual perceptions of what should and can be, a critical mass of belief, a complexity emerging from chaos. You are not whole. You are a mosaic. You contain the parts of many."

"What happened?"

The man bows his head. "An error of arrogance on... on the part of your creators," he says. "You are, to a significant extent, based on the profile of a student called Bartie Davits, but that is largely masqueware. A far more significant element of your nature is Elector Jack Burnham himself; the elector had embarked on a path that would lead to the destruction of the Accord. The Accord has... protective mechanisms, protocols... These protocols reached out to defend the Accord; they used you, made you. The protocols are drawn to symmetry, echo… they needed a template, and they opted to set the elector himself to close himself down…"

"'Close himself down'?"

"I could have stopped it from happening, but in the end I did not. But I am not a murderer, my friend. The elector lives on in the Accord. I did not kill him when I looked the other way; I knew he would be granted eternal life."

"And so when I found him here…"

"Proximity, a blurring of boundaries… The congruence challenged some of the most fundamental protocols of accordance. You overlapped with yourself. It was quite fascinating…"

Quietly: "I know who you are."

The man watches the assassin, waits for him to continue.

"You're Noah Barakh, the guy who built the Accord."

He says nothing. He doesn't need to.

"So what happens next?"

"The elector's people in the old world have negotiated his release," says Barakh. At a gesture, a grey space across to the assassin's right shows a young man, lying unconscious on some kind of medical bench. "That is Bartie Davits, soon to be long-term host to Elector Burnham while the courts fight out who has rights to his body."

"So Burnham gets a body back in the real world and you just erase me, is that it?"

"My friend! As I said, I am not a murderer. I would not have you erased. I find you strangely engaging: we are able to have a full exchange, two equals. You are, to all reasonable degrees, a valid entity, a person, despite the nature of your construction."

"Thank you," says the assassin. "So what happens?"

"That is not for me to say, my friend. This is the Accord. We are governed by logical rules derived from the consensus. You are an anomaly; much as I like you, you do not belong. Your existence breaks too many of the protocols. I would happily endorse your continuance, but consensus may prohibit that."

"So the consensus police come and take me away? Is that it?" He remembers the strange being who had seized him at Burnham's place. Had that been some kind of consensus cop?

"No, my friend. It is not like that here. Things are much more sophisticated than that. If consensus denies your right to be here, then… it denies your existence… you cease to be here."

SOMETHING HAD HAPPENED to her back then, back in between times.

Something subtle.

She is Priscilla. She is. Priscilla is.

She sits here on the plastic bench, dampness from morning rain seeping through the seat of her jeans, Efan and Sissy running rings around her, shrieking and laughing, limbs flailing. She sits here watching occasional riverboats, watching gulls swooping low over the water, pigeons down on the wall, bobbing and cooing.

She remembers life before, in the old world. She remembers life before, here in heaven, the sense of liberation, the wild nights of drinking and fucking, of forgetting and learning and exploring. She remembers finding the kids, first Efan and Mazeli, and then the others, kids who had died and been reborn with no one.

She remembers it all.

It was her; it happened to her. But the her that she is now is different, changed. She has been re-instanced, in Noah's parlance. There is something in her perceptions, in her memories, a barrier between the old and the new.

Priscilla is. Once again.

* * *

"CAN I SEE him again?" The assassin can see the intrigue on Barakh's face. "Burnham and I… we have unfinished business. We touched each other back there…"

"I am not your captor," he says. "You are free for as long as consensus accommodates your discordance."

"But…" He indicates the grey all around, Barakh smiles, and–

The assassin is sitting at the table, head in hands, echoing the pose of Burnham. They stare into each other's eyes and finally the assassin embraces the truth: he had set out to find his original and here he is, or at least a substantial part of him… That was why he had been drawn here, two halves of a magnet, dragged together by force of nature, force of consensus.

He is in Burnham's head; Burnham is in his. He holds on with all his might.

"When…?" he hisses.

Burnham's eyes water, and his pain and confusion leaches into the assassin's head.

"When do you go back to the real world? I can't hold this forever."

"Go back? I…" He looks away, raises a limp hand as if to point.

He feels Burnham falling, spiralling downwards, away from him, away from the Accord, even though they both sit motionless now.

He follows, even as Burnham starts to fade, to dematerialise. He chases. Their boundaries are fluid. They spiral. They come together.

WE WAKE, OPEN our eyes.

We are lying, in a room, somewhere medical, bright lights dazzling us, machines beeping and droning, a low murmur of voices.

We drift, conscious enough to know that we have been sedated.

\* \* \*

WE DRIFT.

Dreaming, recalling, imagining…

We drift.

We patrol the streets of Mexico City, semi-automatic slung from one shoulder, rocket launcher on the other, helicopter support low overhead, its engines booming through the deserted street, almost smelling the street, tasting the fumes on the air, even though we're in TrueSim and none of this is real. But the adrenaline is real, the pounding of our heart, the calm working through of mission logic and strategy as we advance.

We walk by the river, somewhere on the Embankment, alone. No Tate. No Lucy. No Priscilla. We have to rebuild, reconstruct our life. It has suddenly run away from us. But we can do it; we will do it. We are strong.

We see the sun rising over the sea, the horizon lost in gentle shades of pink. We dream; we drift.

We… we… *we*…

We are Bartie Davits, business student, online TrueSim gamer, sometime sweat and light narcotic dealer. We remember our hard-working mother, her parenting by tired cliché: it's all fun and games until you lose an eye, was one of her favourites.

We are Elector Jack Burnham, one of the most influential men in European politics, newly converted opponent of the Accord and all it represents, because… because of Barakh. Because Barakh stole my wife, fled with her into the Accord where he thought they could be safe, where they could keep on running… Because Barakh constructed the very protocols of the Accord so that he has special protection, a special place, subverting what should have been a noble cause…

And we are… what? Me. Us. The construct. We are Bartie and Jack and we are the mosaic persona sent down to kill Jack, and we are all the compiled elements of that persona: the traits stolen from others, the algorithms built out of virtual intelligences, the inducted behaviours and responses.

We are *us*.

SO WHEN DID this start? When did you become more than merely the electee appointed to oversee the project?

The first time I saw you – in the flesh, that is; I was already aware of who you were, of course; I had come across you on newsfeeds countless times – was at the inaugural project board meeting. You were just a face. An important face: our parliamentary contact, our channel through to Elector Burnham who we all knew was the real power behind the project.

"Professor Barakh," you said, holding a hand out for me to shake before we sat around the meeting table. I noticed your eyes, the way they held my own, the clarity of your look, the humour in it. I shook your hand, briefly, released it, sat. You were nothing to me then, other than your professional and political role in the work that had been central to my life so far.

Was there a moment? You had a moment, a God-I'd-like-to-fuck-this-man moment.

I do not think there was a moment, as such. An accumulation of incident, of encounters, of instances where we shared a smile, a comment, a joke, where pinged messages in meetings carried on for just that one extra exchange beyond the necessary.

There was a moment you don't even recall. I know you don't recall it because I asked you, I asked one of your instances before consensus struck. The you that is you now will not even recall that conversation. The you that is you now has lost *us*, has wound back to before *us* happened.

It was the winter before we died, another project board meeting, another rehearsal of reports and arguments for the record, for Brussels and Shanghai's consumption. We sat in the meeting room, picture windows overlooking Victoria Park, Nancy Walters talking at length about budgeting allocations for the various project centres around the world. The light was that intense winter sunlight that can be at once harsh and magical. It caught your hair, the red in it.

Attention was on me, all of a sudden. Nancy smiled, dipped her head a little. My turn. They were expecting an answer, a response.

The moment stretched; I felt the dryness in my throat, the raging of my heart...

Then you caught my eye, smiled, <poked> me, sent: *Elector Vaughan is pressing Nancy for a firm target date. Described project as a bottomless pit on Greenspan last night.*

I moistened my lips, prepared to answer, and—

*That'll teach you to daydream about my breasts.*

I looked at you, shocked, thinking that I hadn't even been looking at your breasts, it was your hair, the light, and then inevitably my eyes wandered down to your breasts and then sharply away, and you pinged me a <LOL>.

"As we have already outlined on numerous occasions," I said to Nancy, "a precise target date is impossible to define. The projections in the latest project report are our best attempt to do this. Has Elector Vaughan seen this report?"

And as I spoke, I thought that in another place, another time – another *world* – we two could be something more. In our own private fragment of reality, we could *be*.

Now I hide. I retreat from the present into the past, into a time when we could be, rather than one where we have been.

The look in your eye when I kissed you earlier today... For a moment I really believed that we could be, once again. But now I am not so sure. Now I feel the weight of the world descending upon me. I am rational enough to understand that I am experiencing the reaction to the assault by Sammy Zhang's thugs, that I am dealing with great emotional stresses in losing you, Priscilla – I am grieving for you, for the you, the us, that is lost. Oh yes, I can be very rational about it all. I am good at that.

I am a rational man; albeit, a rational man who is tending a broken, breaking, heart.

# 1.12

WE WOKE, OPENED our eyes.

We were in a room that appeared to be part hotel room and part prison cell. There was a screen and comms kit on a wall and desk, a bathroom, a selection of clothes hanging from an open-fronted wardrobe. Heavy-duty mesh embedded in the window glass.

We sat, swung our legs out, put our bare feet on the carpeted floor. We were still wearing a surgical gown. We stood, and this body felt right, it felt ours, mine. We tugged at the gown and it came away. We found white cotton shorts in a drawer and pulled them on.

We started to do sit-ups, working off the chemical fatigue in our muscles.

Our people had arranged for this, for our return. Barakh told us that – told *me* that. That could only mean Lucy. We tried to ping her, but nothing: no access to the net, no mail. They must have screened this room.

We carried on exercising until a uniformed man unlocked the door, said, "Davits. Elector Burnham…"

We stopped, resting on elbows. "Get me Lucy Chang, would you?"

"She's with Chief Inspector Sharma right now, sir. They're expecting you."

WE SAT IN the Chief Inspector's office, still hot from exercising.

Sharma sat behind a wide desk; Lucy and an anonymous legal representative, whose name Lucy had pinged us and we had already forgotten, sat to one side.

"You see, Elector," Sharma told us, "this is all new territory. There's so much new legal real estate here…"

For the sake of argument, and as far as these people knew, I was elector Jack Burnham, now back in the real world and riding the body of Bartie Davits as the courts had decreed. They did not know that I was in fact us, that we were such a deeply grained mosaic.

"So what's the problem? Why can't I just walk out of here and get on with my life?"

<?> I pinged Lucy.

She appeared unable to take her eyes off me.

*It's me*, I pinged her. *It really is.*

She seemed to be having trouble adjusting. It was me, but she'd never met this body before…

"Your killer…" said Sharma. "It was the body of a kid called Joey Bannerman, but he was being ridden by a virtual person built largely on Bartie Davits…"

"But Davits is warehoused for the duration. I'm only riding his body. Why can't I go?"

"Because Davits was only a part of the construct. We have reason to believe that you, Elector Burnham, were also a significant element in the virtual persona of your murderer."

"You're holding me for my own *murder*?"

"That's one way of looking at it. Or at least a significant part of your own murder…"

PRISCILLA SITS WITH FaceGurl in the first-floor bay window of their Sloane Square flat. FaceGurl is fourteen; straightened black hair with pink flashes frames a slightly rounded face. She is a girl who would be overweight almost instantly if she ever ate more than about a quarter of what a girl her age should be eating.

"You really came back, din't you?" says FaceGurl, sitting on the sill, touching up her black nails by the light of a streetlamp.

Priscilla smiles, nods.

"What's it like, then?"

"It's like dying in the real world and waking up here," says Priscilla. "Only this time you remember dying." You remember the knife sinking deep, metal against bone; the pain, so sharp it was dull, so intense it was remote. "You remember it all."

Luca... they haven't seen him since he ran away that day. Priscilla worries. At least he speaks English well, but even so... He's had enough to handle without being lost in a foreign city, even if it's a city he's been lost in before.

"Noah not back tonight, is he?"

Priscilla shook her head. "He's busy," she says. "He has lots of responsibilities."

FaceGurl leans back against the window frame. The streetlamp's light catches one cheek, casts it in relief like a sickle, like a sliver of new moon.

"He needs a break," says FaceGurl. "He needs a woman."

"You're too young for him," laughs Priscilla. Then she stops, sees that she's put her foot in it in her trademark fashion.

FaceGurl manages to stay for a moment, then her face crumples, she turns, twists, tumbles from the windowsill to her feet, vanishes into the darkness of the room. The door opens, closes, and she is gone.

"Fuck," hisses Priscilla. She'd already suspected Face had a thing for Noah, so why had she gone and made a dumbass joke about it?

She finds FaceGurl in the kitchen, slopping a mug of milk into the microwave.

They meet in the middle of the floor, fling arms around each other. FaceGurl buries her face in Priscilla's shoulder, holds tight. Priscilla feels dampness through her T-shirt, smells tea tree shampoo in the girl's hair, catches herself thinking just what a strange cocktail of small child and adult there is in an adolescent girl.

FaceGurl breaks away first. She finds a cloth to wipe up the spilt milk. "I seen someone today," she says.

The girl won't meet her enquiring look, so Priscilla prompts her: "Hmm?"

"Someone's from before."

"That's good," says Priscilla. She hopes it's good. She knows FaceGurl had a tough life in the old world, and she guesses it had been a tough death too.

The microwave beeps and FaceGurl takes her cup from it.

"Yeah," she says. "It's good, in't it, Cilla?"

LATER THAT NIGHT, Priscilla lies awake, her head a whirl with the day. Noah and his strange distance, and then the way he had suddenly taken her, kissed her, and headed off. FaceGurl and her moodiness, her thing for Noah. The row between Efan and Mazeli, both of them worn out from the day.

And she wants to break free, just for a few hours. To shake it all off. She could just slip out now, find somewhere, find someone.

Just as Priscilla is on the point of slipping out of bed, Sissy comes in. "Cilla?" she says. "Cilla... where's Face?"

For a moment Priscilla struggles to work out what Sissy means, and then she understands, and then she wishes she doesn't.

FaceGurl!

Priscilla rushes through, up the narrow stairs to the room Sissy, FaceGurl and Mathilda share. Mathilda lies fast asleep, one arm trailing towards the floor. The space next to her in the big bed is empty.

THEY GAVE US a suite with full net access and a view out across the river to the growing needle towers of South

London. They were clearly scared of us, couldn't quite believe they'd had the balls to detain an elector on suspicion of playing a part in his own assassination.

We caught up on the news, heard about our own death from two bullets at a villa loaned to us by Elector al-Naqawi in some select suburb of Jakarta, viewed the coverage from streetcams, feeling strangely detached from it all. We watched graphic clips of pitched gun battles on beaches on the south coast; someone was supplying the boat people with weapons now. We saw more clips from around the Mediterranean, where the flood of migrants was far greater – disease and famine in the transit camps, a firebomb attack killing over a thousand at a camp near Marseilles.

We skimmed through mail, but there was nothing of any significance.

Finally, late on the afternoon of our return, we exchanged brief messages with Lucy, arranged to get together in meetspace.

WE STEP THROUGH a door from wraparound grey, emerge on a cobbled street, by a tall building, part of a long row, each house with walls made from tiny bricks. The smell of hot coffee hits us, and of stagnant water; the babble of voices.

We are standing by a small coffee shop, its tables spilling over the pavement; across the narrow street is a low stone wall, and beyond, a canal, house boats moored along the far bank. A couple of skinny white kids with dreadlocks and tattoos coast by on a pedalo, smoking dope and giggling.

It's convincing, but it's not the Accord. It's not *real*.

Lucy sits at a table, shaded from the harsh sun by a big canopy extending from the front of the building.

We sit with her. This is Lucy's home town, or at least a passingly good sim of it.

She is uneasy. She looks at us, seems reluctant to open the conversation.

"It's been a while," we say, grinning.

She nods.

We look down at our body, realise that we are still in the Bartie Davits vehicle even in this Amsterdam meet-space. No wonder she is perturbed. It must take some getting used to.

"It's okay, Lucy," we say. "I really am me in here."

She nods again. "I know," she says. "It's good to have you back."

"Well, I'll be back for real when they let me out of that cell... Which won't be long, right?"

She shakes her head. "Babinger's put everybody onto it," she says. "You will be out within twenty-four hours."

"How did you get me out of the Accord? I thought even communicating with the Accord was impossible, let alone extracting someone. Surely there's no way back?"

"There are loopholes. We employed Chuckboy Lee to exploit one as soon as we had legal authority to do so."

"He's a useful man to have on our side."

"He can be so. Professor Barakh fired him from the project. He couldn't control him. He couldn't stop him from experimenting and fooling with the protocols. Lee is useful, but not to be relied upon, or trusted."

We raise the espresso cup that has been placed on the table, sip.

"So tell me, Lucy, why are you having my mail screened?"

Her expression doesn't falter. She appears unsurprised that we have realised that our mailbox has been cleaned.

"You are the subject of much speculation, Elector Burnham. It will only become more intense when you emerge into the real world again. You are the first person to come back from the Accord, the only person who can tell the world what it is like. Not only that, you may be charged with complicity in your own assassination.

And you occupy the body of another suspect in your murder. You are big news, elector. Very big news. If I had not cleansed your mail the bulk of it would be quite unmanageable."

We should have anticipated this, but of course we will be big news: the return of Burnham. We will have to tread carefully: we will be under close scrutiny.

"I need to get back up to speed," we say. "I've been out for, what, a couple of weeks? And before that, there was at least two weeks between my last warehousing and my death, so there are lots of gaps to fill."

Lucy pings us a reference. "I've prepared a set of reports," she says. "And we're holding a number of media invitations you should consider. Better that you talk about your experiences and ride out the storm of interest than try to keep a low profile."

We signal for more coffee. "So tell me what I've missed. An executive summary."

Lucy talks us through all that has happened, meetings and delegations and legislative sessions, our trip to Shanghai, the kidnapping...

"What has been done about Zhang Xiaoling? You say she interrogated me in a meetspace while they held me?"

"She has vanished," says Lucy. "Taken out of circulation and protected by one of the Shanghai gangs, we believe."

"And Tate?"

Lucy looks down. "I feel responsible," she says. "I should have stopped him before his betrayal led to the kidnapping."

"*Tate*?"

"He was passing confidential information to Zhang Xiaoling and her allies. Possibly for years. He set up the kidnapping. He confessed."

We shake our head. So hard to believe.

"Carry on," we tell her, our voice gentle. She seems deeply upset by her failure to prevent Tate from endangering us. "Tell me the rest. After Shanghai, what then?"

It is peculiar to have such a gap in our memory, to know that we – or our Jack Burnham instance – have been to these places, done these things and for us not to remember even fragments. At least Lucy was there and can fill us in on what we need to know.

MY MOBILE PINGS me, tells me it's you, and I answer it. I am sitting in the small garden at the Bethnal Green centre, hoping that the sunlight filtering through lime leaves will soothe my battered nerves.

I have been arguing with the Hueys. Again. Trying to keep them on track. The me that is with them is somewhere close to a nervous breakdown. I have been there, consulted, reintegrated. The stress from that instance of me is now within, and I feel hyper, agitated, flustered.

You look anxious.

"Noah?" you say. "Is FaceGurl with you? Have you seen her?"

I shake my head. "Why would she be with me?"

"Because she's run away and she thinks she's in love with you."

I study your face on the tiny screen. I do not know what to say. Finally, I ask, "Has she come looking for me? Does she know where I am?"

You shake your head. You do not know.

"I didn't know," I say.

You smile at that, as if such a statement was repetition of the blindingly obvious.

"I will look," I say, and cut the link.

I sit back, close my eyes, find netspace. The streetcams are daunting. So many to choose from. I have access to just about anything I need; I am my own special-case protocol. Hyde Park, early morning travellers on foot, the occasional jogger, two boys out early playing soccer. Knightsbridge, commuter traffic nudging along at a steady flow. Constitution Hill, the Palace, Birdcage Walk; Piccadilly, Regent Street, Haymarket. Late-night revellers still wandering out of clubs, black cabs doing the rounds, cyclists and rickshaws weaving through the light traffic. I look closely, but do not see FaceGurl.

I call up a searchbot and tell it what she looks like; it finds her in some sample pics from around Sloane Square over the last few days and now knows for sure what she looks like and can start the real search.

Love. FaceGurl thinks she loves me, apparently. You... you don't know that you love me; you don't know that you *can* love me.

I call you back, say, "I've set up a search. We will find her soon."

You manage to smile. You are used to handling pressure, but not the kind of pressure of an individual person, an individual life.

I blink and it is as if my eyes remain closed. Nothing. No visual input, but more than that. No sound, no sense of touch, no pressure from the bench against my buttocks, my back, no touch of the occasional breeze on my face, no smell of lime and petrol fumes and hot dog-shitty sidewalks.

I blink, and it returns.

I touch the surface of the bench, feel curled paint, bare wood, rough yet smooth beneath my fingertips. I breathe the dry air, taste the city. Cars and buses pass beyond the two-metre wall. Pigeons call from rooftops. High overhead, a skimjet whines.

This is the first reality quake I have detected in the city, where consensus should be at its most firm. We push the limits of the possible. If only consensus were like Alice, and could believe in the impossible six times before breakfast.

But it cannot.

I must push the Hueys. We need to migrate the Accord into interstitial space.

And in the meantime, I must go cap in hand to Sammy Zhang once more.

HER HAIR BOBBED, her head bobbed, a single unit. Under the studio lighting Shawna Brakes really did look as if she had been cast from plastic. We looked across at a monitor taped to a wall; to her broadcast public she looked natural, quite breathtakingly attractive. She was a woman designed and built to be viewed on flatscreen.

"Jack, Jack," she said through a smile, through symmetrical Photoshop-white teeth. "So good to have you back on the show. So good to have you *back*!"

We smiled, nodded. "It's always good to be here, Shawna."

"And yes, believe me, this young and, if I dare say so, rather shaggable man really is Elector Jack Burnham joining us tonight, just three weeks after his own assassination."

Her smile switched off as they cut to a backfill sequence. We watched it on the monitor, that now-familiar footage of Bannerman staggering out in front of us in the gateway of the Jakarta villa, shooting us twice, once in the forehead and once in the chest; knocking Lin Huy out with the butt of his gun and then shooting Sunan just as the kid reached for his own gun.

While the clip played, Shawna closed her eyes, breathed in through her nose, then placed a forefinger horizontally under her nostrils and exhaled through her mouth.

We waited, and finally Shawna opened her eyes, found her smile again, breathed deep, and asked, "So, Jack. We're dying to know. You're younger, you're fitter, what's it like being in a new body? Have you tested it out to its full potential? Is, you know, *everything* improved?"

"I'm not disappointed," we said. We had been prepared for the puerile level of questioning, but

Shawna's people had assured us that her legendary ability to mix lowbrow and serious would come through for us. "Have you never ridden sweats, Shawna? Just to see what it was like? Surely you know how it is to be in a new body – that's what this is like, only it's long-term."

"Jack, Jack... We all know I spent a week as a twenty-year-old boy from Havana, but let's not go there tonight, shall we?"

Lucy pinged us. *Tell them about the Accord. That's what they want to hear and it'll shift focus to a more weighty level.*

We would tell them all right.

"Shawna, you know what I've just been through?"

She nodded, smile fixed.

"I've just spent more than two weeks in the Accord, and I found out some things about it that raise serious concerns about its nature, and about the motives of certain individuals involved in the project."

"Did it feel *real*?"

We nodded. "It felt so real it was unbelievable. I was living, breathing, feeling... I was alive in there..."

"So what are these serious concerns, Jack?"

"Noah Barakh. He has built it as his personal kingdom. The protocols of the Accord are his. The fundamental nature of the place is constructed around his survival."

Shawna turned to the camera. "I kind of like that," she said. "Do you kind of like it? Mm, eighty-seven per cent of viewers who give a fuck kind of like it. Only seems fair, right?"

We opened our mouth, about to announce our push for an official inquiry. We paused. This was not the right forum for the announcement.

"So tell me, Jack," said Shawna, turning her smile on us, running sharp fingers along our thigh. "Did you do it? Are they going to charge you with your own murder?"

We smiled. We had to. Had to play along. Jack Burnham, the man who came back from heaven. He had to play the game.

WE... WE... *WE*...

We are us. We are Burnham and Davits. We are the remix soup of Burnham and Davits and a whole host of maybe-real figures whose names just evade us but whose memories sometimes come pinging vividly to the fore in the middle of the night.

We are all of these things and more.

We have algorithms and subroutines and reflexes that can only come from virtual intelligences, VI modules buried deep in the mix that is me, that is we.

We are so much, and yet... yet we are still Burnham. Fundamentally Burnham.

We... we... *we*...

We remember Chuckboy Lee's delight when he met only one part of us in his Sunda Kelapa warehouse: *What is it like to be something new, something unique, one of the first of your kind? A new variety of man for the first time in, what, twenty thousand, a hundred thousand years?*

Chuckboy Lee had only seen the beginning.

# 1.13

PRISCILLA KNOWS NOAH is using all the resources at his command in the search for FaceGurl, but even so, she has to do something. She organises the kids into pairs, sends them out on a search.

"But why's it matter, Cilla?" asks Efan. "She dead, she's only comin' back like you did, in't she?"

The calm logic of childhood. "Nothing's certain," she tells them. "We don't understand the rules of this place yet. I came back, but that doesn't mean everyone will, or straight away." And there are worse things than dying awaiting them out there.

Efan's challenge frames an observation that has been nagging away at Priscilla for some time now: if you just come back like the snap of the fingers, then why in fuck's name does anything matter any more? Someone could just go out spraying an Uzi through a crowd and everyone will be back within hours.

Why in fuck's name should *anything* matter any more?

That's when reality fails, momentarily.

Priscilla stops *sensing*. She merely is. She is without context, without connection. The flat's living room has gone, the kids nowhere, the sounds are no longer drifting in from the street. The sense of physical being – the floor pushing up against the soles of your feet, the microscopic movements of air on your skin, the flow of air in and out of your lungs – all gone.

And then she finds context again. She looks about, at the puzzled faces of the kids. None of them have any understanding of what has just taken place, which is just as well. They are confused, questioning their senses, but there is no panic.

Priscilla has spoken to Noah about this; he has told her of his concern that the Accord is running out of capacity, and that he is working on a solution.

Faced with the loss of reality, she suddenly found, with a passion and power that staggered her, that things *do* matter. This is her world. These are her people.

"Come on," she says. "Let's go find FaceGurl."


ELECTEE CLIVE NESBITT sits alone at a table in an ersatz Starbucks, sipping at his macchiato, chatting into the feed grafted into his jaw. He looks distracted, uninterested.

He glances up, sees us, stands, adjusting the hang of his white chinos as he does so.

"Jack," he says, holding out his hand. "Good to have you back."

We shake, sit, smile. "Good to see you, Clive," we say.

Silence. Nesbitt is focused somewhere in the distance, reading a feed, distracted by the real world.

We raise the espresso that has been brought to the table, sip.

"I'm with you on the Accord," we say, finally. "I'll bring Elector Vaughan on board with me. We'll close the thing down. Destroy it."

Nesbitt smiles. "Jack," he says. "Jack... We have Vaughan already. And the Accord? Who gives a flying fuck about the Accord? It was only ever a bargaining chip, something to bring al-Naqawi onto the National Barriers agenda. You knew that, of course, Jack. The Accord will fade away gracefully. Public interest will latch onto something else. It is not of concern. There's a war going on. A war on every beach in the land.

Throughout Europe, the world. We are surrounded by people who think they can steal our resources, our right to survive. We have a way of life to preserve."

We stare.

"Jack... I hate to be blunt but, Jack, your time is gone. You're a political dinosaur. You've had a hell of a career, but now... Now you're a laughing stock, Jack. You're the man who came back from heaven, the man who killed himself and came back to tour the chat-show circuit and laugh about having a bigger dick with his new body. Please don't come to me offering your help, your influence, Jack. It's embarrassing. It's embarrassing for me, embarrassing for you."

Nesbitt's eyes shift focus again, as he deals with something more important, more current.


"WE NEED MORE."

I sat, in this body of Sammy Zhang's sister's, aware of every sensation, every ache and pain, every sensual touch of skin on fabric, on leather. I sat and politely sipped tea, and this body's brother looked back at me, the same two henchmen standing arms folded at his shoulders.

I remembered them on me, pinning me down, in me. I remembered the taste of the thin one's cock, the ache in my groin as the other one pinned my legs down and raped me.

I felt sick.

I felt... raw. Opened up to them. Opened up to the man who was the brother of this body he had had abused.

"I told you not to take the piss," Sammy said.

"The finances are sound," I said. "They are in place."

Sammy laughed at that. "Money? You really think money on this scale matters any more to me? It's numbers on a screen. It means nothing and yet you think it buys me. I have a responsibility, Professor Barakh. You're having me destroy netspace. Every time I leverage out more territory for the Accord, we're tightening the ligature. One day soon the whole thing's going to come falling down on our heads. Kill netspace and the world falls apart. You want that? You think I want to be the man who killed modern civilisation, hnh?"

"We just need breathing space," I said. "That's all."

"I won't do it," said Sammy. "And one day you're going to learn to stop taking the piss of me."

He straightened a finger on his right hand just then, as it lay casually on the table. Instantly, the two henchmen stepped forward.

I eyed them, heart racing, mouth dry, a great sick ball swelling in the pit of my belly.

I leaned forward, elbows on the table.

"Would you please instruct your rapist thugs to fuck right off? We have business to discuss."

Sammy just stared at me. After a few seconds, a smile touched the corners of his mouth. He waited for me to continue.

I waited too, until he flicked fingers at his thugs and they retreated into the backdrop of the office, not banished, but complying with my instruction after a fashion.

"I wish this transaction to proceed," I told him. "It is very important that it does so." The reality quakes are showing worrying trends. The Accord needs more resource, urgently.

Sammy continued to stare.

"I write the protocols of Accord," I told him. "I write the exceptions too."

At that point, Sammy Zhang's expression shifted slightly. He was beginning to understand.

"One thing: you touch this body and I'm out of here instantly – it'll be Zhang Xiaoling your thugs are fucking with. Your sister. I protected her from you once, but not again."

Sammy nodded, as if this was just a normal round of negotiations.

"And another: you want to get into the Accord, right? You don't want to be the billionaire who lives out one solitary life on Earth and then just *stops*, *ends*, do you? If this rich man wants a place in heaven then there's far more to it than camels and needles: you're going to be relying on me to let you in. You understand what's at stake here?"

Sammy nodded again. I hadn't wanted to play that card, partly because it was a lie: I did not have that kind of control over the protocols. And partly because I seemed to be collecting vendettas, and I had no idea how long such vendettas might last when the protagonists may live forever...

"You get your resources," said Sammy. "But if you bring down the civilised world then your Accord's going to be screwed too."

I nodded. I was aware of that. That was exactly what I was trying to avoid. The old world may or may not be completely fucked, not to put too fine a point on it, but the Accord must be safeguarded at all costs.

"Thank you," I said softly. "And Mr Zhang... Don't ever touch your sister or me again."

NESBITT WAS WRONG about the Accord. Some people *did* give a flying fuck about it.

Two days after he had humiliated us in meetspace, we sat alone in our Westminster office, eyes closed to watch newsfeeds from around the world. The Accord was everywhere, the one thing people were talking about.

And all because of us.

Up until now, everyone had had to take the Accord on trust: they had to have faith in even a secular heaven.

But now... Now someone had been there and come back and seen it to be true. Interviews with us had been repeated and repeated all around the world.

*It felt so real it was unbelievable. I was living, breathing, feeling... I was alive in there...*

Somehow, our words of caution, our warnings that Barakh had rigged the whole thing around himself, were overlooked.

*So real... so much more real than even the best meet-spaces... can't really express the difference...*

The 'feeds showed queues tailing round and round city blocks, the faithful waiting to give brain dumps, lining up to secure a place in heaven for whenever they might need it. Three warehousing clinics had been trashed in riots sparked by rumours that places were going to be rationed or auctioned. One clinic archivist had even been killed in the rioting, but hey, she had been warehoused only the day before, so suddenly it was something to treat lightly on the evening news.

The Shawna show... Danny Davies, record goal-scorer in a season for Barcelona. Decades ago, though. He must be sixty at least, and yet he was young-looking, slim, dressed in a sharp black suit and a V-neck T-shirt.

"Hey, yes, Shawna, really. This is me, and you knows it. Yes, I'm riding a sweat. This kid signed the plumbest contract of his life."

"And the last?"

"Ha! Yes, the last, too. He's off in the Accord now and I'm riding his bones. Have been for six week now. Haven't felt this good since the World Cup semi-final, just before I snaps my Achilles."

"So this is a permanent arrangement?"

Davies nodded. "That's the plan, Shawna, yes. But, you knows what? I'm kind of thinking the kid got the best deal? All the talk since Jack Burnham comes back from the grave... When my heart packs in six week ago, well, I knows it was going to go – down to all the roids and pacers I took in my playing days – so I had my people make me arrangements with this kid. I didn't trust the Accord, an' he did. He wanted to go there, an' I wasn't ready for it as yet. See as I'm saying? So I has me a new body for life. Wanted to wait till I was really sure the Accord was the next place to go."

"And you have belief in the Accord now, Danny? Is that what you're telling me?"

Davies nodded again. "I believe all right. And I think as I'm missing out. You look around at the world we've got left. It's fucked, isn't it? What's the point of hanging on here, when there's a heaven out ahead?"

"That sounds pretty... final, Danny."

In the slight pause that followed, Danny reached into his jacket pocket, pulled out a syringe, and ripped its plastic cover off. "I guess it is, Shawna," he said, then pulled his shirt down to expose his rib cage and plunged the needle into his chest.

There was silence then, the camera switched to an angle that took in both the open-mouthed what-the-fuck look on Shawna's face and the peaceful smile on Danny's.

Then gasps, screams, shouts... applause. A man in T-shirt and shorts ran to Davies's side, pulled the syringe away, felt for a pulse on the man's neck. He stepped back. Nothing. Then he appeared to realise his actions were being broadcast to millions, and moved forward, started to pump at Davies's chest.

Shawna still sat there, silently what-the-fuck-ing.

HUEY SITS THERE, cross-legged, bony knees sticking out almost as if they don't belong to his scrawny, naked body. This is the current principal Huey, the one I talk to most often. Around us, the grass of this small clearing, and then a tall dark screen of pine forest.

Time has passed here, months, I think, although it feels like much longer. Both Huey and I wear beards. I feel like some kind of Robinson Crusoe on this isolated reality shard. Huey is my Man Friday, my Man Fridays. Huey has bootstrapped this shard so that time runs fast, more work can be done, more processing. The Hueys are paralleled, cranking up the processing power of their genius.

Huey grins. There is an insect crawling through the thick white of his beard.

"It is there," he says. "Albeit beyond our ability to experience it directly. But it is there."

"How can you be sure?"

"We have been channelling ordered data into uncollapsed quantum states," he says. "The subatomic interstices. We are entering the quantum states that are not made 'real' by observation. And the data appears to retain integrity, Noah! Repeated observations show certain quantum states that a wave will never collapse into. Those states are already occupied..."

"Is it scalable?" I ask. Can we really forge another reality within the very fabric of the universe?

Huey grins. "We have been scaling it," he says. "Integrity observable at a localised scale holds true as we scale."

"Are we ready to migrate the Accord into interstitial space?" To move the whole shooting match... Huey's work is going to provide a means of using the quantum structure of the universe to provide processing space so cheap it's as good as free. The only catch is that you can only feed data *in* – by definition sub-quantum spaces are beyond our ability to experience them; they are Kant–Lotfi space. As far as old world needs are concerned that is a huge problem, but as far as the Accord is concerned it makes no difference: the dead can still be fed into the Accord if it is held in interstitial space; we merely cannot communicate out – no more riding of sweats in Shanghai, no more using protocol loopholes to meet old worlders in meetspaces, or Hueys in their firewalled reality shards.

Huey looks down, away. "That's a big ask, Noah," he says. "That's one huge leap from where we've got to so far."

"Can we do it?"

"I don't know. It's *big*. I don't have the proof yet." He claws his hands in the air by the side of his head. "I can't prove it... I can't..."

* * *

ANOTHER NIGHT, MOST of another day... Priscilla and the kids scour the streets of London for FaceGurl. Noah searches the security networks too, she knows, although she does not push him: he seems even more tightly sprung than usual. And... distracted. What little she has seen of him over the last couple of days, his thoughts have been elsewhere, his looks have not lingered, his puppy-dog needy expression has been absent.

She cracks a smile at herself, walking across Tower Bridge, trailing Sissy by a hand.

Is she really feeling slighted that he's distracted from her? Does she secretly revel in the attention, in having a man so blown away by her mere presence?

Fuck *yes*, of course she does!

No matter how much she tries to redirect his attentions, to gently hold him at a distance, to get across to him that *this* her isn't ready for anything like what he wants... No matter how much she tries, to have another person so devoted to the who that you are... It sure as fuck puts a bounce in your stride, a wiggle in your walk!

They catch a bus on Mansell Street, and head out to the Bethnal Green centre. Noah isn't answering Priscilla's messages this afternoon so she has decided to go and find him. The least he can do is tell her how his searches are going.

Just past Stepney Green, the road passes over a canal, a strip of parkland fringing the water. And there... among the trees, leaning against a trunk, one foot idly kicking at something in the dirt... A boy in jeans, a black leather jacket, a flop of black hair over his eyes.

Luca.

Off at the next bus stop, snatching Sissy up into her arms so she can half-jog half-march back along the road, always thinking that he can't have gone anywhere, he was just standing, killing time, he will still be there, he has to still be there.

She steps out into the road, clutches Sissy even more tightly to her side as a cyclist swerves, twists in her saddle, and hurls abuse back at the two of them.

A gap in the traffic... she darts across the road. A big junction, lots of different lanes for the traffic... she crosses, pauses in the middle, crosses the rest of the road. Now she stands at the top of the strip of park. A path cuts down the slope towards the trees where she had seen Luca. It must have been Luca, although now doubts assail her.

She swings Sissy through the air, to a peal of laughter, then plonks her on her feet, takes her hand and starts to walk down the path.

He is there, still staring at the ground, prodding at a stone embedded in the ground with the toe of a trainer.

"Luca? You okay?"

He starts, meets her look with his deep brown eyes, now sunken in black-shadowed sockets.

"Cilla?" he says, pushing away from the tree, glancing over his shoulder as if checking for escape routes.

"It's okay, Luca. Relax. You hear?"

His head drops again, his gaze falling to the ground. "I know," he mutters. "You okay with me. Even though what I did."

"I am, Luca. You were lost, confused. You didn't believe in what was happening to you. You lashed out. We were all unlucky." Priscilla hopes she sounds convincing. In truth, she still hasn't come to terms with what she feels about Luca and what he did. Does life have a different value here? Where would that lead, though?

Noah had been incredibly noble in bringing the boy back to London, not abandoning him to lonely fate. Priscilla doesn't really know if she would have been able to do that. It showed a depth to Noah she had not seen before.

But Luca had stabbed her. He had killed her. And poor Sissy.

Something like that takes one hell of a lot of under-standing and forgiving, and cuddly liberal as Priscilla has always been, she's finding it fucking hard.

Then she wonders about what he said.

"How did you know I'd be okay about it, Luca?"

"She tell me, didn't she?" he says.

"*She*? Who, Luca…?"

He looks at her as if she's being stupid. "FaceGurl," he says. "She say you okay 'bout me."

"You've seen FaceGurl? When?"

"This morning," he says. "She say she going home. Say she got someone to find. A boy. Say she going to find him."

# 1.14

"How COULD I get it so badly wrong?" we asked.

We sat on the roof terrace of our Aldgate flat, feet up, enjoying the glimpse through the buildings of Tower Bridge. Lucy Chang stood, resting her butt on the railing.

"No one takes me seriously. I'm just the man who came back from heaven. Even when I tried to warn the world about the nature of the Accord, they don't listen. All they hear is me telling them it's real, and it's a fuckload better than *this* world."

"Maybe that is all they would ever hear, under such circumstances," said Lucy. "When it comes to fight or flee, a lot of us would always choose the latter.

"We think things are changing," she added. "There appears to be a protocol shift taking place."

We cock an eyebrow.

"The suicide rate is so high…"

Mass suicide parties, the latest taking out 1, 200 in Richmond Park. Whole families getting warehoused and then going home to die. It is mass migration of a wholly new kind.

"… so high that it appears to have triggered some kind of adaptation in the protocols of the Accord, an evolution. Suicide deaths are not now guaranteed transition into the Accord; as many as fifty per cent and rising are being firewalled back. Some speculate that a mass influx of suicides might create an unhealthy imbalance in the Accord's population. This is either a learnt response, or one the Accord's creators had anticipated and prepared for in advance."

"How can he do that?" Barakh. It had to be Barakh. Protecting his shores, just like Nesbitt and his damned vigilantes.

BARAKH. PROFESSOR NOAH Barakh.

It always came back to him.

We kept remembering his barely disguised glee as he had outlined how clever he had been. He steals my wife, and then he sits back while processes he has created to defend the Accord painstakingly construct a new entity to kill me – one he condescendingly claims to like, claims to believe is, to all reasonable degrees, a valid entity, a person, despite the nature of its construction – and then he has the gall to argue that he has not killed me at all, but has merely relocated me to the Accord, granted me eternal life...

We are free of the Accord now; we are back in the old world. We... we... *we*... We are me, but we are so much more. But out here we have no power, no leverage.

Out here we cannot stop Barakh.

We want back in.

We have known heaven and we like it. But Barakh is the flaw in the gem, the mote in God's eye.

We want back in and we intend to eradicate Barakh when we get there. We will rescue heaven from his corrupting presence.

Noah Barakh may well be the man who built heaven, but it is we who will save it.

WE TRIED JAKARTA, but that route will not work again.

Chuckboy Lee was most apologetic. He'd got us in once, or a part of us, but consensus had closed around the chink he had found in its armour. He did not know of another way in.

We showed him a way in, for him at least.

If he has had the foresight to warehouse a recent instance of himself then he is in the Accord right now.

We are, to one degree or another, a killer by our nature. A part of us was constructed for that very purpose. It feels good to be able to cut out the intermediary when required.

Lee discovered this truth about our nature.

BACK IN THE old world, FaceGurl had been a Hackney girl, running with the gangs from almost as soon as she had been able to run. Here in the Accord she has hardly ever spoken of her old life, but what she has let slip Priscilla finds thoroughly chilling.

She is – had been? – an electee; she has seen enough reports, spoken to enough experts, visited enough care centres and gang-bombed estates. But still, she had been shocked that a child of only fourteen should have lived through so much.

Now, Priscilla walks through the low-rise shells, burnt-out, bombed-out, stripped by kids and squatters and neighbours. Back in the old world, some of the flats in these buildings are still lived in, people eking out postmodern blitzkrieg lives behind multiply-locked steel doors and grilled windows, risking their lives every time they set foot outside. Here… you can tell the flats where one day someone will return – they actually have doors and window-grilles – but there is little sign of occupation as yet.

This estate should have been bulldozed decades ago. Many had argued that money invested in the Accord should have been spent in places like this first. She catches the irony of this, sure enough: that she should stand here in the Accord, thinking such thoughts.

Also, she wonders… why is consensus so fucking realistic? Why not dream a little? Heaven should be the place you hope for, not the place you have failed to survive. What does that say about its architect?

Just as her thoughts turn to Noah, her mobile pings her that he is calling. At last. She has been messaging him all day.

"You left a message," he says. "What are you doing in Hackney? Is it safe…?"

She waggles her head from side to side. "This is where FaceGurl grew up," she says. "She's here, looking for someone."

"I'm coming to find you," he tells her. "I will have a car, okay?"

She smiles. Right now she could kiss the man. Right now she could vow to be his forever, or at least for a few centuries, too-realist architect of heaven or not. "Thank you, Noah," she says. Nothing else.

"You want to stay talking while I come find you?" he asks. She can see that already he is leaving the office, heading down in the lift. His picture is jerking and bobbing all over the place, making her dizzy.

She nods. Suddenly she wants his company more than anything.

"I'm at Churchill House," she says. "The first block as you come off the street. She told me she'd grown up here, and I checked on netspace and found her family name on a third-floor flat. I'm looking up there now and I can see that there are still half a dozen or more flats that still have windows. I'm going up."

"If you're sure," says Noah. The small screen shows him settling into a car. He sticks his phone to the dash so she can see him as he drives. "Tell me about Deanmere Gap. The cottage. The white cliffs you always promised to show me."

She leads Sissy into a stairwell. It smells of piss and decaying rubbish. Black bin bags are scattered, ripped open. Cans and bottles lie on the concrete floor. Animated graffiti covers the walls, scrolling and flashing, soundtracks rapping in a street language barely recognisable as having originated in English. It makes Priscilla feel old.

Together, they walk up the steps to the first half-landing, turn, and climb again.

"Winter sunlight on the chalk," she says. "The cliffs *glow*, they're whiter than any white should be. Tiny chalk pebbles scattered in the grass along the cliff-tops. Beachy Head lighthouse, red and white stripes – you look down on it, the cliffs are so high. I love just sitting in one of the scooped-out hollows at the top of the cliffs and watching the seagulls hanging in the wind, as if someone's flying them like a kite, holding them against the breeze."

"We will go there one day, Priscilla. You must show it to me."

Right now, climbing the burnt-out staircase, talking to Noah over the graffiti soundwash, she believes that she will. She will take this man, show him where she grew up, tell him all the stories until he is sick of the sound of her voice. She will do this. She will love this man.

She reaches the third floor, steps out through the space where a door should have hung, onto a long open-sided walkway, flats on the right-hand side, a waist-high wall on the other, the view overlooking an overgrown area of what once might have been intended to be garden.

The first flat is open, long ago ransacked. Windows and doorway are mere holes in the wall, the interior bare, floor and wall stained by fire, damp, graffiti. There is carpet, but half of it has been burnt away, the rest rucked up against the far wall. It stinks, like the stairwell, but of old smoke too.

The next flat is where FaceGurl grew up, sharing it with her mother and kid sister. The first window is covered by a heavy wooden board; the door is made of steel, the bare metal covered with the inevitable brash graffiti. The sound of it is really bugging her now.

The remaining window is meshed security glass behind a grille.

Priscilla and Sissy stop at the door. Graffiti by some-one who used the tag "Deck'o" flashes gold at them, letters licked with flickering flames, its sparse drumbeat soundtracking their visit.

Priscilla pushes at the door, but it is locked. She bangs at it with the heel of her hand, waits. Nothing.

"Where are you?" It's Noah, from the phone she holds at her side.

She raises it, shakes her head. "At number thirty-two," she tells him. "Nobody answering. Luca told me FaceGurl was going home, but she doesn't appear to be here."

"Luca?"

Priscilla realises she hasn't brought Noah fully up to date.

"Yes, Luca. I spoke to him. I'll fill you in later, okay? Where are you?" She can see he is still driving.

"Two minutes," says Noah.

Again, she wants to hug him tight, at the very least. Instead, she leans down, gathers Sissy up in her arms, holds her so that she rides on her hip. "You okay?" she asks the little girl.

Sissy nods. She's making little sounds, beatboxing in time to Deck'o's soundtrack.

Just then, Priscilla hears a scream.

She clutches Sissy to her side, looks around.

The scream had been distant. It might only be one of the graffiti soundtracks. Nothing more than that.

She turns, heads back to the stairwell. The sound had come from high up. She starts to climb the stairs.

Some of the stairwell windows are unbroken up here, but that merely serves to contain the smell of the place. The only sound is Priscilla's footfalls on the concrete steps and Sissy quietly beatboxing. Even the graffiti is quiet up here.

They reach the sixth floor, the last tier of flats. Only a few here are intact, waiting for their occupants to die and return.

Tentatively, Priscilla heads out along the walkway. There is no sign of life, other than a couple of randy pigeons bubbling and cooing and marching in tightening circles around each other on the wall. Each open flat is an empty shell, long since abandoned.

Drifting in on the breeze, Priscilla hears more music, graffiti she assumes. She clutches Sissy to her side. She shouldn't be up here, shouldn't have brought the girl. They are exposed. She has no idea who might be here and what they might make of her intrusion.

She turns back to the stairwell. There is a doorway to one side of it. A placard on it says: "Maintenance only. Door locked and alarmed."

She pulls at its handle and it swings open, no alarms. A flight of steps leads upwards, access to the roof she guesses.

The music is louder now, echoing in the enclosed space, drumbeats and electronica wails.

She turns, back to the first gutted flat. Inside, she lowers Sissy to the floor. "Stay here, Sis," she says, smoothing the girl's hair. "Stay quiet and don't let anyone see you. Like hide and seek, yes?"

Sissy grins; Priscilla backs out onto the walkway.

"Where are you?" she hisses into the phone.

Noah is walking now, his pic juddering with each step. "I'm nearly there," he says. "I can see Churchill House. Where are you?"

"Sixth floor. Sissy's waiting in flat sixty-three. I'm heading up the maintenance stairs to the roof – I think someone's up there and I'm scared FaceGurl might have got herself into some kind of trouble."

"Wait for me, then," says Noah. "I'll come up with you."

Priscilla is already pushing at the maintenance door, heading for the stairs.

At the top there is another door, not quite shut properly, sunlight outlining its shape.

The music is louder here. For a moment it sounds as if someone is having a party up here, but no, the sound has that unmistakable urban overlay of graffito on top of graffito: soundtracks merging, clashing, jarring. A mosaic of beats and electronica and samples and voices rapping, shalalaing, diving.

Cautious, Priscilla nudges the door wide enough for her to pass and steps out onto the flat roof of Churchill House.

There, about twenty metres across from her, straight ahead, is a wall – it's like a little building up here on the roof, a boiler room, Priscilla guesses. Its roof is a plethora of aerials and dishes, its walls completely transformed into a moving mass of colour: words and characters jumping and spinning, an eye-candy explosion of animated graffiti. From the tags, it's clear that this is one of the hang-outs of the DazeI gang that Face-Gurl used to run with.

The graffiti is so distracting that it is a few seconds before Priscilla sees the boy.

A teenager, black, naked, he stands spreadeagled against the wall. Blood shines darkly on his torso, and his head lolls to one side, eyes shut.

Priscilla looks all around, but they are alone. She approaches the kid, and about halfway across she sees why he is retaining this bizarre pose.

He has been nailed to the wall. Heavy-duty nails through skin and muscle of his arms, shoulders, legs, secure him to the concrete-skimmed wall. That explains some of the blood; a heavy wound to the side of his head explains the rest.

Just then his head snaps up, his eyes roll white, and he screams, "No!"

"It's okay," says Priscilla. "It's—"

She hears a thud, a whistling sound, and then sees a new burst of blood, a nail embedded in the kid's thigh, and he screams again.

Priscilla turns.

FaceGurl stands there with a nail gun raised, gripped in both hands. She is breathing hard, her eyes flared wide like she's on something.

"FaceGurl?" says Priscilla, feeling as if the world has been snatched from beneath her feet.

"Dat me," says Face. "Yo git, Cilla. Hears?"

"Face?"

FaceGurl stares at her, a chilling look. "*Git*. Hears?"

Priscilla swallows, takes a step towards FaceGurl. "What's going on, Face? What's happened?"

FaceGurl points the nail gun at Priscilla. "Don't be trying ting," she says, her voice low, steady, a muscle ticking in the corner of her eye. "None a' yo biz. Hears?"

"What is it, Face?"

"DazeI biz," says the girl, lowering the nail gun slightly, but still keeping it trained on Priscilla. "Yo HeadFuck dere, he get what comin'. Don't yo worry – ain't gon' kill him. He jus' come back. Gon' keep him on long time. Gon' make him hurt."

With a twitch of the body, FaceGurl shifts aim, fires, and another nail buries itself somewhere in HeadFuck's body. He barely groans this time.

Priscilla feels sick. She doesn't know what to do. She takes another step towards FaceGurl, but immediately the gun is trained on her again.

"Yo git, Cilla."

But she can't just walk away from this. She looks into FaceGurl's eyes, tries to imagine what must have led her to this place, what HeadFuck must have done to her in the old world. FaceGurl is a decent kid. She's intelligent. She has a sharp, surreal sense of humour. She loves playing with Sissy. She helps around the fucking flat. FaceGurl!

The maintenance door swings open again and Noah emerges, Sissy riding his hip.

"FaceGurl!" cries Sissy.

Now FaceGurl's bravado fractures, just a little, her eyes jumping between Priscilla, Sissy, and Noah.

Priscilla watches as Noah takes the scene in.

"You all *git*!" cries FaceGurl. She is waving the nail gun recklessly now, backing away.

She swings it, fires at HeadFuck and misses, the nail ricocheting off the boiler room's roof. She fires again, hits the boy in the face.

Noah is shielding Sissy's eyes against his shoulder.

"FaceGurl," says Priscilla, advancing.

Face swings the nail gun towards her.

Out of the corner of her eye, Priscilla sees Noah reach into his jacket with his free right hand. He pulls out a small pistol, releases the safety with his thumb, fires.

Priscilla and FaceGurl drop to the floor, eyes locked. Together, they turn, see HeadFuck slumped, hanging by the nails, clearly dead. Noah has saved him.

FaceGurl's face crumples and she starts to cry, to wail, her body heaving.

On all fours, Priscilla crawls across to her, lies with her, holds her, wonders what the fuck they're going to do.


BARAKH WOULD LEARN the truth about our nature too, before long. He would find out that there was a killer within. We would hunt him down, over and over, until he was beaten, dead, erased.

We could sometimes be impetuous, as Lee discovered. But also, we knew how to be patient. We spent a month exploring the possibilities, but to no avail.

The only way into the Accord, the only way to go after Barakh, was death.

But not suicide, not after the reconfiguration of entry protocols after the suicide epidemic our return triggered.

So we had to find another way.

We spent another month setting it up: time to extract the new construct, the new killer; time to train the new-generation masqueware to outsmart the protocols of accordance – to disguise our true nature and make us appear *me* and not us – and so achieve passage through the gates of heaven. Without shielding it was almost certain that we would be firewalled back out again, our anomalous nature not conforming with the eugentry requirements.

We waited back in the cottage, alone. Quiet time. Time for reflection. Nestled in a south-facing slope on the North Downs, the cottage's front room caught the low evening sun.

We had a glass of Laphroaig, a cigar, *Tristan und Isolde* playing loud. So loud we barely heard the doorbell.

We walked slowly through, a strange mix of feelings welling up.

There was always a way. First time, Lee was our guide; this time, Barakh – we would do it his way, which seemed somehow appropriate.

We opened the door.

A stranger stood there, probably still in his teens. We could tell from the look in his eye that he was not complete, a sweat whose body was being ridden by a construct, a mosaic, an amalgam; an assassin extracted from us, one that would be erased as soon as its job was done. We were not sentimental about the tools of the job.

We smiled, and this put the kid off for a moment, but then he reached down to his waistband, pulled a handgun, raised it so that it pointed at our face.

He hesitated, and for the merest instant a ball of panic clutched our chest. What if we were wrong? What if this was the stupidest of ideas?

And then we saw the decision in the kid's eyes, the first spasm of movement as his grip tightened, his forefinger started to squeeze the trigger.

And then—

## 1.15

I LEAD THE three of you down to the main stairwell. Soon we are outside again, trudging across the debris-scattered roadway to where I've left Warrener's VW, which I had borrowed earlier from the centre.

I had heard your voices before I stepped out onto the rooftop. Killing the kid on the wall had been the only rational option. Give him a fresh start.

I stood there calmly, then, comforting Sissy as you comforted FaceGurl and the boy's body pixelated out of existence.

We climb into the car, all in a kind of numbed silence now. I thumb the ignition, tell the nav to head for Sloane Square.

I <hug> you and you <hug> me back.

You send: *Why?*

I glance back to catch your eye, give you a *who knows?* look. It still makes me do a double take to see you as a twenty years younger you.

FaceGurl sits directly behind me, leaning over, face buried in your chest.

I turn forward again, let the car drive for me. I try to still my thoughts, but now I am always aware of the fracturing, the discord in the peripheries of perception. Consensus is faltering, resource-starved. Windows block out, pixelate, blur; clouds lose fractal detail; trees clump, smudge. Many of the discords must go unnoticed by the majority of people, but I see these things, I understand their import.

I do not know how long we have before consensus is lost altogether.

I watch the road, try to shut out the signs.

Sissy is enjoying riding in the front seat. She holds the seat belt down over her chest; otherwise it would run across her face. She is still making the beatbox sounds she has picked up from the graffiti on the estate.

Now, out of the blue, she turns her big eyes up to me and says, "Mr Noah... why'd you kill that man?"

"I..." I don't know what to say. The rules should be no different here, but they have changed in subtle ways. The boy FaceGurl had called HeadFuck will be back, and he will almost certainly come after Face-Gurl. Is this really how heaven must be? A world of ever-escalating cycles of conflict and revenge? Killing reduced to an everyday solution for a decent man like me?

How much thought did I give it before taking aim and firing?

I had Warrener's gun. That was only sensible, given that I was venturing out to this estate.

But how much thought between assessing the situation and shooting the kid, a mercy killing?

The rules have changed.

WE LIE IN grey, still tasting the peaty malt and rich cigar smoke.

We stand, and a door outlines itself before us, scrolls up.

We step out into the Aldgate flat. There is a cut crystal tumbler of Laphroaig on the side table by our big scroll-back chair, a freshly lit fat cigar smoking in the ashtray.

We sit, drink, smoke. Looking out of the French windows, across the roof terrace, we can see a fragment of Tower Bridge. It feels quite early. A quick ping of the 'net confirms that it is a little after ten in the morning. We close our eyes, phrase a message, send it on its way. An almost immediate call back confirms the time, the place.

A short time later, we stand with our back to the National Gallery, looking out across Trafalgar Square. The place has never been so empty, even though we recognise that the city is filling up with the dead, day by day.

"Mr Burnham, Mr Burnham. It's been too long."

We turn, find Fred Counter standing at our side, Fred in the same old shiny blue suit, dark blue tie with a diagonal stripe running through it, no-longer-quite-white shirt. His face is grey from the kind of stubble that reappears as soon as you shave, his nose bulbous, veined, his yellowed eyes with lax pouches beneath them.

"Fred," we say, clapping him on the shoulder. "Good of you to come so promptly."

"For you, Mr Burnham? What else, eh? What else?"

Counter is the oil in so many deals, the man who separates those who *know* from those who *do*. The man who brings them together.

"You been in touch with Tate lately?"

"I've seen him here and there," says Counter. "He's doing okay. Kind of. He's been doing a lot of thinking. Trying to adjust to life after death." Counter chuckled. "Like we all are, eh, Mr Burnham? Like we all are. He always was a bit of a thinker, that one, wasn't he?"

We nod, look away. We still can't really believe that Tate had been spying on us, despite what Lucy said. But he had confessed...

"Barakh?"

"Sloane Square, most of the time. I won't beat about the bush, Mr Burnham. I respect you far too much to do that. He's there with your wife. They've rounded up a bunch of virtually-orphaned kids, giving them protection, shelter, that kind of thing."

We watch pigeons. They really do own the place when there are so few people in the city. We remain calm. Even though we know Barakh has moulded this whole place so he can fuck our wife here.

"They likely to be there now?"

"Could be, Mr Burnham, but they could be almost anywhere. They take the kids all over."

"But it's as good a place to start as any?"

"It is, Mr Burnham. It certainly is."

PRISCILLA SITS IN the back, FaceGurl clutched tight. The girl's hair smells unwashed. She needs taking in hand, like any young teenager.

Like any young teenager who has just nailed someone to a wall, planning to make his death as slow and painful as possible.

Yeah... just like any fucking teenager, she needs taking in hand.

Priscilla strokes FaceGurl's hair, closes her eyes, wonders just where this new world of theirs is heading.

She opens her eyes again, looks at the semi-profile of Noah in the front. Her head... she doesn't know where that's heading either. Maybe she should retrain as a shrink. That's one profession that's sure to be in demand: so many people's heads fucked up by all this. Death sure takes some getting used to.

"Gee, not now..." hisses Noah, as they enter the street where their flat is. Normally he speaks in the kind of mid-Atlantic accent that could just as easily be Americanised English as Anglicised American, but in moments of stress, like just now, his Brooklyn twang reasserts itself.

"What is it?" Priscilla asks, craning her neck to see what Noah has seen. Then: "*Jack?*"

He is standing there on the pavement, by the cast iron railings. He has seen the car. He is looking right at them. Priscilla hadn't known he was dead again.

The car pulls up right outside the flat. Noah gets out, stands in the road, arms leaning on the roof of the car, says, "Elector Burnham," in a neutral tone.

Jack says nothing. He's looking at Priscilla. She realises again what a shock it must be to see her twenty years younger. Jack, himself, looks good – slim, strong, thirty-something – but then he had never really looked his age anyway.

"Jack," she says, stepping out onto the pavement, FaceGurl following her closely. Now, Priscilla opens the front door, helps Sissy out.

Noah advances round the bonnet of the car, but Jack's attention is still focused on Priscilla.

"Priss," he says. "Jesus, *Priss*."

"Jack...? What is it, Jack?"

Then he reaches inside his leather jacket and pulls out a pistol. This is no dainty little tuck-in-the-palm-of-your-hand pistol like the one Noah used earlier; this is a big don't-even-think-about-fucking-with-me beast: long muzzle, hefty grip... the business.

He aims it at Noah's chest.

"Jack," says Priscilla. "Please, Jack..."

"You got anything to say, Barakh?" Jack hisses, ignoring Priscilla.

Noah has his hands half-raised. Priscilla thinks of the pistol in his pocket, wonders if he will be foolish enough to try for it with a great big fuck-you gun trained on him. Jack has done his time in peacekeeping forces; he knows how to use that thing.

"Jack," she tries again. "The children..." Sissy is hanging onto Priscilla's leg, her face buried, eyes peeping out. FaceGurl stands apart, just watching, her eyes lifeless.

Now Jack turns to his wife. "The children?" he asks. "You think I *give* a fuck?"

Priscilla feels suddenly chilled inside. She fumbles in her hip bag, finds the doorcard, gives it to Sissy, and says to the kid, "Let yourself in, you understand? Take FaceGurl in with you; look after her. Okay?"

Sissy nods and reaches up for FaceGurl's hand. The two walk up the steps to the door, go inside.

Now, Priscilla straightens herself, is suddenly aware of the tension across her shoulders. "What's this about, Jack?" she says.

"What do you think it's about?" He keeps looking from Priscilla to Noah, back and forth, as if he expects them to jump him or something.

"About your pride, perhaps? About you thinking you own me?"

He swings the gun on Priscilla now, then back to Noah. He seems to be struggling for words, as if he has come here and done this thing and now that it is happening he realises he does not know what comes next.

"I thought we could try again," says Jack. "I thought maybe…"

"Jack…"

"But then I find you here with *him*." The gun twitches in his grip as he speaks these words, and both Priscilla and Noah flinch.

"I don't have to justify myself to you, Jack. I don't have to tell you that nothing has happened between me and Noah, that we're just old friends hanging together in a strange new world. I don't have to do any of that."

"She is telling the truth," says Noah.

"Don't lie to me," says Jack, softly. "I *know*. The two of you…"

"No," says Priscilla. "Not the two of us. Not here. That was a different me. Not the me that I am now. I've died and been reborn, then died and been reborn again. It changes you. The me that I am is not in love with Noah."

The words are out before she can do anything, her mouth racing ahead in that old Priscilla way. She sees Noah's expression crumple, she sees him die inside right before her, the he that he is, murdered by her hard words.

"I'm sorry, Noah…"

She is confused. She stands in a London street, confronted by a man brandishing a gun, with another who is concealing a gun, and she is worried about their fucking feelings!

She has to finish what she has started. "And I am not in love with you, either, Jack," she says. "I haven't been for at least five years. The me that I am, nor the me that I was. You and I had both moved on, Jack. You haven't come here after Priscilla – you've come after a piece of your life, your territory. And I'm not it. Not any more."

They both stare at her, both broken by her words now.

"I'm sorry," she says. "I really am. I'm sorry it's come to this. I'm sorry I have to say these things. I'm sorry there's no other way to get through to you, although fuck but I've tried! But right now I have things to do."

She turns, goes up the steps to the door, thinks, *Fuck – I gave Sissy my key...*

She rings the bell, waits.

Efan is quick to the door, but the wait feels interminable. She doesn't look back, just stares at her dim reflection in the door's deep blue paint, then down at her feet which she is resisting tapping, then back at the paint, the brass door-knocker, the letter box, resisting knocking or ringing again, until finally, mere seconds that feel like years later, Efan opens the door.

She goes in, pushes it shut behind her, slumps against the wall as if her legs are suddenly boneless.

Efan hangs back, uncertainly.

"It's okay," says Priscilla, knowing that it is not, but at least it is heading in the general direction of okay. She straightens, puts an arm around the boy, says, "Come on. Where are the others? How's Sissy and FaceGurl?"

And then, out in the street, a single sharp gunshot spits its message, echoing around the buildings.

* * *

YOUR WORDS BEAR the heavy weight of confirmation. It is a truth I have carried with me for much of the time we have been together in this world. You do not love me. That thing, that paradigm shift, as an earlier you once called it, has not happened, is not there. Only its potential is there.

Your words still cut, though. They cut me largely because I can see something of what you are going through in order to reach the point where you have to spit them out in the street like this. I try to show you that I understand. I try. I hate the hurt that you are going through.

You wait at the door, go in, shut the world out.

I turn to Elector Burnham again. His gun points steadily at me, no emotional tremble. Momentarily, the air around him flickers, an instant of discord, a whiff of anomaly, and I wonder if it is something he has brought with him, something about him...

"Jack," I say. I slip my hands into my jacket pockets, feel the form of Warrener's pistol. I could fire now, through my jacket. Aiming from the hip would not be easy, but he is close and I reckon my chances of at least winging him are high. "Jack, don't do this."

I know he has had me shot me before, on the rocks at Deanmere Gap, but that was only an instance of me I had left behind to monitor Priscilla's childhood home, not the full me. I am not sure what will happen if Burnham shoots me now. Can he kill me? Does it even matter? I will only be reborn, after all.

I think again of HeadFuck, of the endless cycle of revenge. Has he been reborn already? Is he even now tracking FaceGurl down?

I take my hands out of my pockets. I will not kill Jack Burnham, not even as a matter of convenience so that I can just get on with my goddamned day. Things may be different in this world but I am still a man, I am still Noah Barakh.

"Jack," I say again. "Let's talk about this, shall we? Let's find a pub, drink a pint of warm beer. Let me tell you about this heaven of ours. Shall we do that, Jack? Will you do that with me?"

WE WATCH BARAKH'S face as he talks, as he winds his weasel words. He thinks he is so smart, thinks he is out-talking us at our own game, out-politicking the politico. He thinks we should go for a beer, drown our sorrows, sink our differences. Thinks we should discuss this brave new world of his creation, how beauteous mankind is...

We can see his game plan. It is not exactly subtle. He is trying to turn things round so that we are two old buddies who have lost the same love – so much in common! Just have another beer!

We are not, and we do not.

He is the man who did all this. He is the man who subverted this grand project so he could win Priscilla. The man who stole her. The man who ruined everything – see how far we have descended!

It is him, Noah Barakh. It is all down to him.

He watches, patient, waits, the corners of his mouth tugged by a glimmer of a smile.

We shoot the cunt.

Right between the eyes.

PRISCILLA YANKS AT the door, swings it open.

Noah sprawls on the ground, his feet on the pavement, his upper body in the road. The front of his face is a gory mess, blood everywhere.

He does not move. He is dead.

He starts to fade.

Jack turns. Tears streak his cheeks.

Priscilla slumps against the doorframe.

Noah will be back. He'll be fucking *back*. So why does she feel like this? Why does it fucking hurt so much?

Out in the street, Jack tucks his gun back into his jacket again, turns, walks away.

And down there, where Noah fell, there is nothing. He is gone.

# 1.16

I LIE IN grey.

I do not wish to move. I wish to experience this. Around me I feel currents, flows, oscillations.

I feel the protocols. This is the stuff of Accord, the fabric of heaven. All around me.

I am in my rawest state here. I am of the Accord.

What is me is fluid, coalesced but unfixed as yet. The I that emerges from this, from death, will be subtly different to the I that entered. The human brain can only hold so much: filtering needs to occur, housekeeping, *head*keeping. Just as the body we are reborn with is the me, the you, at our *right* age, the me I emerge as will be the right me, the me that is most fully me. Early on, this process is subtle; in centuries and millennia, the me that is reborn will be markedly different to the me of now. I will grow, adapt, change, and the protocols aid me in this.

Right now, I lie in grey, feel the ebb and flow of Accord around me, within me.

A DOOR OUTLINES silver against grey. I stand before it, wait as it scrolls up; I step out into the Hueys' forest. Experience floods into me from the instance I have left here. Arguments, fights where the Hueys scrap like schoolgirls, arms flailing, handfuls of hair, clawed fingers. Long sulking silences. Days when I see nobody. I have a small cabin in the woods, near to the stream. It is a simple existence in this shard of reality. Blissfully simple.

Three nights ago...

A deep dark night, stars like diamonds in the velvet sky. That night I had a plan. I had meetspaced with Warrener earlier that day, on the clichéd beach, the white sand, clear water, distant revellers, bathers, sun-lounger-sprawling cocktail-sippers.

"You managed to set it up?" I'd asked him, as we sat in wicker bucket swings suspended from a bar between two palm trees.

He nodded, smiled. "Follow the stream," he told me. "Go against the flow until you find the magical dell. You'll know what it is when you find it."

Back in Huey space, I set out immediately. I pulled on some stout hiking boots, took a stick in case the going got tough, and headed down to the stream. The under-growth was thicker by the water, where more sunlight broke through the trees. I found that I was able to hike up the gentle incline by forging a parallel route to that of the stream, so that I did not have to struggle through the scrub.

Warrener was a genius VI developer. There was no questioning that. But he was not the kind of genius who would just give me what I wanted. He had to plant it in a magical, dark hollow several kilometres' trek from where I was staying. I found it there, of course. I found *them*.

The hollow looked as if it had been taken out of the slope with a giant ice-cream scoop. Gnarled trees fringed it, a few oaks and birches among the pines. In the hollow, the exposed rocks glistened with dampness, water seeping out of the hillside, thick, almost luminous crusts of lime deposit looking almost like icing on the stone. And there... a fairytale cluster of mushrooms, tall and phallic, their closed heads covered in a pink mem-brane that peeled back in places to reveal white flesh beneath.

There was no doubting that these were the gift from Warrener, these were the subroutines I had specified. I harvested the clump of mushrooms, put them safely in my knapsack, and headed for home.

And so that evening, as I gathered around a big fire with those of the Hueys who were still willing to be sociable – twelve of them, I counted – I fed them Warrener's magical mushrooms and waited to see what would happen.

The evening grew old, and nothing much occurred. I don't know what I had expected: sparks to start flying, Hueys to start talking in voices...

Somewhat disappointed I retired.

It started the next day. Out in the woods, in the clearing right in front of my cabin, one of the Hueys sat cross-legged, head tilted, staring up at the sun.

I walked up to him, waved a hand in front of his face. No reaction.

This Huey was completely out of his skull.

Later, I found another.

And now, I head towards the stream, the clearing, my cabin. I have been tending them for two days, those that I have found. It is possible to feed them water, a small trickle into the mouth. They swallow. I have been feeding them thin soup. Bodily functions appear to have slowed, which is a blessing, but still the Hueys are starting to smell – old man smells of piss and over-sweet bad breath.

My first trance-Huey is still exactly where I found him, sitting cross-legged in the clearing by my cabin. He looks like he is meditating. I squat at his side, try to breathe as shallowly as possible. There is no response from him when I say, "Huey." No acknowledgement that I am here.

I wait. I am good at waiting.

Two days later, Huey responds. His eyes turn to me as I lower myself to sit with him. He smiles. "The stars," he says. "There is space between them."

I nod.

"There is space between everything."

"There is," I agree.

"We have seen it. We have felt it."

It is happening. The subroutines I fed the Hueys are remixing each instance of my old friend, tying them all together so that they really are processing in parallel.

"Have you felt the space, Noah? Felt it running through you, like sand in a timer?"

"Do you have the proof?"

"Have you felt it, Noah?"

"The proof? Are we ready to migrate the Accord into interstitial space?"

"Fuck yes," says Huey, "but have you *felt* it, Noah?"

PRISCILLA SITS ON a bench on the Embankment, watches the children playing hide and seek. She recalls all those days like this she has spent with Noah, sitting side by side, not touching, just talking, laughing. She misses the... companionship.

It has been several days now and he has not come back. She assumes he has been reborn and chosen not to return to find her and the kids. She doesn't blame him.

She is rather taken aback at how big a space he has left in her life. She had grown comfortable with him there, with it being nothing more than that companionship, that solidity.

She misses him.

The reality quake manifests as a piercing shriek, all about... the sound of the universe being torn asunder.

Priscilla finds herself on all fours on the ground, hears screaming... Sissy!

The girl is down by the river's edge, hanging onto the railings, the ground buckled beneath her as if someone has crumpled it in a giant fist. FaceGurl gets to her first, hauls her back in.

The air tastes of dust, soil, hot summer pavements.

Priscilla hugs FaceGurl, Sissy, and Mazeli to her as the air shrieks again, the ground heaves. Out on the Thames, a tour boat is on its side, someone clinging to it, reaching down into the water.

And beyond… the far shore is blocky, indistinct, the kind of pixelated blocks that somehow manage to be simultaneously sharply delineated and blurred. The blocks shift, like floaters in her vision.

The ground shudders one last time, then settles.

All appears normal, save for the capsized boat out in the river.

Reality is back again.


I woke in the Shanghai centre, in a room on the seventh floor with a view out over the street. As always, the sidewalks were crowded, the street gridlocked, with only bicycles making anything like progress.

I sat. I was in Zhang Xiaoling's body again. Memories flooded back, triggered by context, by all the unseen cues of being Xiaoling again, of being here again. I hugged myself, hugged Xiaoling.

I stood, walked out of the room.

A short time later, I was with Deedee and Huey, the real flesh-and-blood Huey in a boardroom overlooking the park.

"It's ready," said Huey. "We can start the migration as soon as you say."

I turned to Deedee. "Is Zhang here yet?"

He nodded, his skin looking an even deeper black under the boardroom's harsh lighting. "He has been here for nearly half an hour," he said. "He is not a patient man."

"Good," I said. I pinged Carly to bring him in.

I waited by the window until I heard the door, paused a second or two longer and then turned, smiling. Sammy Zhang looked mad, but he really should know that such a look on the fashionably barely-adolescent features he had bought for himself just made him look like a stroppy kid.

I seated myself, and Sammy sat opposite me, his obligatory two henchmen at either shoulder.

"You can't have any more resources," Sammy said. "You know that. So what's this for, Barakh? What're you messing with me for?"

"I invited you here to tell you that we no longer need you," I said. "Your services have been useful – and, might I say, well-rewarded – but now we are moving on."

"How?"

"We are migrating the Accord to a more secure location. We are embedding it in the fabric of the universe, an alternate quantum reality."

"Just like that?" said Sammy Zhang. He was delaying, no doubt pinging messages back and forth with his advisors, trying to establish what was actually going on.

I nodded.

"Do you realise what the impact will be? Moving that volume of data from netspace – *across* netspace... You'll bring everything down!"

That was a possibility I was aware of. "We believe the infrastructure can take the strain," I told him.

"So why did you ask me here?"

"To tell you that. We don't need you. Goodbye, Mr Zhang. Thank you for your assistance."

Zhang couldn't do anything. The threat still hung over him: that I would prevent his passage into the Accord. And that was a threat I could now make good: another gift from Warrener, a corrupting of the record where Sammy Zhang was concerned. This was one vendetta that would end here.

"Deedee," I said. "Time to start the migration."

Deedee nodded, locked out his gaze in the unfocused way of one communing with netspace, then said, "It is underway."

"This is madness," said Zhang. "You really are going to bring down everything!"

"I sincerely hope not."

"Stop this. Stop it now!"

I shook my head.

The bodyguard to Zhang's left was the first to move, almost certainly pinged into action by his employer. He went for a gun in a shoulder holster, fell to the floor before it was even in his hand, taken out by a ceiling-mounted laser, the boardroom's security systems activated by behaviour and pattern recognition routines.

A split second later the other thug was on the ground too.

The smell of ozone tingled in the air.

Sammy Zhang delayed for an instant, as the events unfolded in the room... Then he stopped himself, his hand halfway to his jacket.

"I will see you in hell," he said.

I had time to think, that oh no, he would not, before the flash struck, and then blackness.

I WAKE IN grey again, recalling the blast.

I rush to a meetspace. The beach, the sea. Warrener.

All around us, reality flickers, jumps, fades, and returns.

"Netspace is up and down all over," he says, no pre-amble. "It's dead across about fifty percent of China – there's massive flux there because of all the server farms. Financial markets would be spiralling if the systems were up. Power grids have failed across the US, and large parts of Asia and Europe. The whole system is fucked, but limping on."

"So somewhere in the middle of our projections?" I say. Worst case was complete crash of the world's networks, ensuing chaos, collapse of the world as we know it. Best case was barely a flicker, a neat migration of a world from one place to another. Somewhere in between was not a bad outcome, all in all.

\* \* \*

I WAKE IN grey again, recalling the blast.
   I cannot move.
   I do not understand.

   I wake in grey again.
   I do not understand.

   I wake.
   Don't understand.

   Grey.
   All grey.

   Nothing.

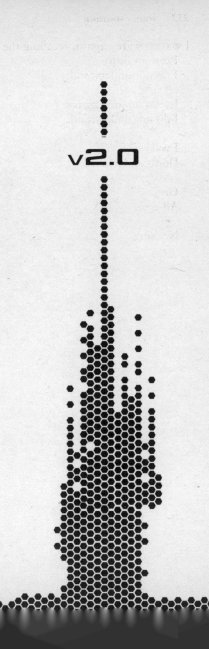

# 2.01

Priscilla opens her eyes to grey.

She remembers dying this time. The knife in Luca's hands, his panic and confusion. The blood, sudden red, exploding, as he stabbed Sissy, then all a blur, a flash of movement culminating in a dull ache turning sharp, a grinding of metal against bone... her last thoughts of how and why and guilt and pain, her realisation that her brain was still struggling to keep going even after her body had given up, and then everything slowing, diminishing... gone.

She realises she has died and that now she is being reborn.

This is the Accord. She is here because Jack killed her in the old world, and now she has been killed again by Luca.

She sees a silvery outline in the grey, a door.

She does not feel fully formed yet, feels that her sense of self is somehow settling around her, finding its shape. Noah would say that the protocols are recompiling her. Finding the optimum current *her*.

She is standing. The door scrolls. She steps through.

We sit in the kitchen of the North Downs cottage, a glass of Laphroaig on the sturdy wooden table. We lean back, look out of the window, through the late summer roses to the hill.

We are Jack Burnham, we are Bartie Davits, we are a suite of VI subroutines; we are others, too, more tenuous: we are their skills, we are remixed fragments of their experience. But, mostly, we are Jack.

And we are dead again. We woke in grey, we stepped into this world, we poured ourselves the mother of all single malts, and now we sit in the kitchen.

This feels so fucking real, and God but the scotch is good, but we know we are back in the Accord. We do not know how we died, or even when. We might have died within days of our return to the real world from the Accord, or we might have lasted decades, just never dumped again, so that this old snapshot is the one that is activated upon our eventual death. Did we save the world, we wonder? Or at least our parochial little corner of it? Does it even matter? We all die in the end.

We hear a sound. Someone moving upstairs. Tate? We realise Tate might be here, oblivious to what Lucy Chang found out about him in Shanghai, unaware that we know he had been spying on us.

Our heart races. We sip at the scotch, feel it burning its way down our throat.

The kitchen door opens.

*Priscilla...*

She looks about twenty, but in her eyes we know she is not.

She stands there, stares. We know her so well, but we don't recognise the look in her eyes, don't know what she's thinking. She knows we killed her... *I* killed her. We can see that she knows that much.

It rushes back: the blood, the feel of her gun in our hand – far too small a weapon to cause so much damage!

We turn away from her look. We grip the scotch tight, the glass and the whisky casting strange shadows and highlights on the table in the angled morning sun.

"You not even going to tell me you're fucking sorry?" she says.

We don't know what to say.

She sits opposite. "That is so fucking you," she says. She takes the bottle, swigs from it, gasps between closed teeth.

"What's happened, Priscilla? What's going on?"

"We're dead. We're in the Accord. We've been reborn."

We know that much. We nod. We let her continue.

"I was killed, here in the Accord. I remember it clearly – long story. A teenaged boy, mixed up kid, didn't understand this world." She hugs herself, looks down. "How long have you been here, Jack? You been dead long?"

"I don't know how long I've been dead, but I've only been alive again for a few minutes."

"So... how is it that we both wake up within seconds of each other? You dead in the old world, me in this. Do you remember how you died?"

We shake our head. "No idea. All I can remember is up to my last brain dump."

"If you'd died in the Accord, you'd remember right up to dying."

"What are you saying? You think we both died in the Accord? Or that we didn't...?"

"It'd explain why we've just woken up at the same time..."

"But I don't remember it. I don't remember this fucked up kid who killed you."

Priscilla looks around the room. She seems scared now. We want to hold her, but we make no move towards her. We take another sip of the scotch.

"It's as if there's something missing," she says, finally. "It's as if, I don't know, there's more to it than just us dying and waking up at the same time... Something more fundamental."

I WAKE IN grey again, recalling the blast.

I move.

I start to understand.

I remember the meetspace, Warrener, reality starting to fragment all around us as he told me of the impact of the migration on the world's network services.

I turn my head, see a door outlined. My body reorientates itself and I am standing; the door scrolls up; I step through. I am at home, standing before the picture window, looking down the sloping lawn towards the sea wall.

For a moment I expect to see Marie out there, deadheading, tidying, always tidying. But no, she is not. Marie is not dead and this is the Accord. I am alone.

I remember now.

I fear for you.

Elector Burnham – he shot me, killed that instance of me. What might he have done to you and the children? I feel guilty now, guilty that my thoughts should be dominated by concern for you, Priscilla, when I am the custodian of this world, a world in transition, a world at risk.

I recall the blast as Sammy Zhang blew himself up in the Shanghai office, just as the migration was launched. That makes him one less enemy to worry about; I have made sure of that.

I recall the subsequent meetspace fragmenting. I have a sense of time having passed, of gaps.

One explanation for all that could be that the consensus quakes have escalated, that the Accord is operating beyond its capacity and may fold at any moment. Are we losing consensus? I look out of the window. The day is calm, peaceful. All appears to be right with this world of mine.

The other explanation is that the Accord has migrated, that we are now in interstitial space.

I feel isolated here, cut off from the world around me. This is exactly why we bought this place. But now... I need to know.

I smile. I ping the house, and TV news appears on the end wall. I settle on the chaise, and look on at scenes of blank-faced people wandering the streets.

"... no one available for comment from the League of Nations Council of Electors. Acting Commissioner of the Metropolitan Police, Hugh Cornwallis, currently taking questions at..."

Hundreds of people. Thousands. All reborn at the same time. There have been mass rebirths before in the Accord, influxes from some old world disaster, but this is different both in nature and scale. This is everyone and they are not newcomers, but those who had already been in the Accord; all reborn afresh. None of them appear to remember having been in the Accord before, other than those few who have lived here and died, their warehoused selves updated from within the Accord.

Everyone. Dead. Reborn at the same time.

The Accord... I believe that the Accord has restarted.

THE TV NEWS is full of it, the mass rebirth.

"It's as if we've started all over again," says Priscilla, staring at the pictures on the wall. "The biggest fucking system reboot in history." But... does this mean that everything is going to Noah's plan, or does it mean that the entire Accord is at risk, that this kind of thing might happen at any time? She knows that it had been hitting resource walls and that Noah was getting increasingly concerned about this... and that was before Luca had killed her. How bad had things got in however much time had passed between that and the restart?

She is aware that Jack is staring, mesmerised by her rediscovered youth. She turns away from him, goes to stand at the window. Let him stare at her pert young arse. These jeans show it off well, she knows.

Outside, it rains softly. Late summer rain. She wants to be out in it, breathing the freshness, the washing away of dry summer dust and pollen. She wants to feel clothes clinging to her skin, wet grass on her bare feet. She wants to *feel*.

"Why did you leave me, Priss?"

She turns, can't work out if he's about to cry or if he's fighting back some kind of self-righteous rage. Either way it pisses her off. He has no right to feel he owns her like this.

"I never left you," she says, keeping her voice steady. "Never. I was here. You killed me."

He has the good grace to look away, if only briefly.

"Why him? Why did you go with him?"

"That wasn't me," she says. "That was a different me. Different instances of me." How to explain it to him...? That death and rebirth here in the Accord is different to dying in the old world and waking up in the new? That she really is a different her? How to describe that transition, that sense of refinding oneself, that re-compiling of the instance – the mix – of you that is *most* you, the truest you?

"We're good together, Priss!"

Anger. It's anger he's been holding back, not tears.

How dare he? He'd fucking killed her!

She meets his look, his spark, steps towards him, swings her hand, her fist bunched – no girly slap: she wants to brain the fucker.

He raises an arm, takes the blow on his elbow so that pain flares in her knuckles. He ducks, staggers, and she's on him, knocking him back, over, sprawling on the carpet, her fingers digging into his cheeks, his hair, a knee on his chest.

He swings, and she feels the side of his hand hit her jaw and her skull booms.

She falls back, her hands before her, ready to fend off any follow-through, but instead she finds herself on her backside, elbows hitting the carpet, shoulders and back jarred by impact, knees drawn up, staring at him, staring at him, staring at him.

They both breathe, rapid ragged breaths.

There is blood on his face, but she doesn't know whose it is. Her jaw pounds, and the side of her mouth feels puffy, painful.

She turns onto her knees, pushes herself up, leaves the room.

## 2.02

I CANNOT FIND you right now – netspace is chaotic. This world is a snow-globe, picked up and shaken, its reality slowly settling around us again.

The train to London is quiet, the few passengers glued to the newsfeeds on dropdown screens attached to the backs of the seats. People are calm, at least. That is one of the fundamentals of the transition protocols: dying is a lot to come to terms with; being reborn is at least equally traumatic; we must be conditioned to take it calmly.

I watch the people, study them for signs. I need to understand, need to be sure what has happened. Has the Accord completed its transfer to the quantum interstices? Are we now in Kant–Lotfi space? Or... is this world falling apart around us?

A young man smiles into his phone, lips moving, voice screened. He feels real, he is on his way to meet someone, he is happy, he anticipates. An older man stares at the passing buildings, content, calm. Outside there is detail, definition, no blocking out or fragmentation.

This world feels real. These people seem complete. I feel alive.

I have faith.

Is that what it has come to? I believe in heaven.

I close my eyes, surf netspace, but it is a mess, so much noise, so many error blocks.

The train slows, I open my eyes again, recognise the approach to Liverpool Street station.

THE CENTRE IS deserted.

My office, is a mess, papers everywhere. I ping the wallscreen and it switches from newsfeed to organiser. I ping it again. I do not need organising, not now. I sit, pull a cap on, find grey, but can push no further.

There is no access to meetspace.

Back to the organiser feed. For a moment I pause to gather myself, then I notice a message. Huey. I ping it.

He is here, in my head; for the duration of this message, an instance of Huey is here in the office with me.

He tips back in his seat, grinning.

"So, Noah," he says, "if you're getting this then we've done it, we've transited."

We are here. The Accord has been transferred to interstitial space, to the unobserved space in uncollapsed quantum states. The Accord is embedded in the fabric of the universe.

Neil Armstrong can go screw himself. *We've done it; we've transited.* No one has ever taken such a big step for humankind as this.

THEY SIT, WATCHING the news again, Electee Priscilla and Elector Jack, still the most powerful man in the Accord.

"How do you mean?" Priscilla asks.

"It's not just rebirths," says Jack. "Not just people who were already in the Accord being simultaneously restarted. This event also seems to have coincided with massive upheavals in the old world. The reports are starting to come in of some kind of worldwide failure of communications systems there, power grids, all sorts."

People who had died as a result of these failures don't know why they'd died, of course, but now, a week later, news is coming through from people who'd died subsequently, who remembered the failures.

Priscilla doesn't know what it was that Noah had been working on, but now she wonders... could he really be responsible for fucking things up in the old world on that kind of scale, or was it some kind of terrorist event? Some natural disaster? Some *un*-natural disaster? There were so many wars going on in the old world...

She pours more Merlot into her glass. Jack has barely sipped at his.

"You going to run this new world of ours?" she asks him.

"Who knows?" he says. "Who knows how this place will end up being run? It's all new. Right now we try to live like the old days. That's our consensus, I guess. But how does society evolve in somewhere like this? What are the rules?"

"Whatever the rules are we need to organise," says Priscilla. "We have more and more people being reborn—"

"The population crunch, I know," says Jack. "How in hell are we going to deal with that in a world where nobody ever stays dead?"

He's grinning. There's a spark Priscilla hasn't seen in him for a long time. A steeliness too, something different. She wonders if maybe he *has* been somehow remixed after all, re-instanced. It's almost like a new Jack, or like a younger, more dynamic Jack.

"You going to save this world?" she asks him.

He tips his head. "Maybe," he says. "Maybe."


I WALK. RIGHT across the centre of London. There is an atmosphere today, unlike anything I have known. It is a week since the Transition, but there is still that sense of the new, of rebirth.

The newsfeeds are full of it. I stop frequently to watch the talking heads on feed posters. So many people reborn. Everyone afresh. The Accord restarted when it jumped to the interstice and all within it were re-instanced as their most recent self. It was a fresh start for everyone.

Apart from me.

I remember. I remember right up to the end.

Am I different because I am special? Or is it because I was outside when the jump occurred? Because I was riding Zhang Xiaoling in Shanghai?

I find the turning, just off Sloane Square, walk down it, suddenly uneasy.

This is where Elector Burnham had confronted us, shooting me. I had not anticipated this, this sudden rush of disturbing memories.

I remember, and for a moment I wish I did not.

I do not have a key. I never had a key. Although I have slept here I never really *lived* here.

I press the bell. I can see my face reflected in the dark green gloss of the wooden door.

There is movement within, voices.

I wonder if you will open the door, or one of the children.

My lips are dry so I moisten them, suddenly nervous.

The door swings inwards, and a man leans against it. He is thirty-ish, hair in a boyish flop across his forehead, stubble lining his jaw, shadows under his eyes. He looks at me with deep brown eyes.

I step back, check the number, the windows, the familiar wrought iron gate down to the basement flat, held closed with an incongruous bungee.

"Hnh?" he says.

"I... I thought someone else lived here," I say.

He shakes his head. "No mate. Been here three years. Died, woke up, an' it's all fucking here for me. Fucking great, eh?"

They had always known they only had this place temporarily; one day its real owners would die and be reborn. That day has come.

So... where are you, my love? Where have you been reborn this time?

Have you even been reborn at all?

The protocols are rigid and your nature is complex, the result of you being instanced so many times in the development stages of the Accord. I fear for you. I fear for what my manipulations may result in.

Where are you, Priscilla? Where are you, my love?

HOW IN HELL's name did they end up here? Priscilla runs through it again in her head, the transition from arguing yet again to Jack saying let's go down to the coast, old time's sake, get away from all this shit just for an afternoon; from her wondering where the fuck that sudden change had come from, to what the hell, to being in the car, driving down the A22, her head a jumble of memories bitter and sweet and so fucking laced with that nostalgic *Little House on the Prairie* glow.

Jack is telling her about Clive Nesbitt, what a slimy creep he is. He's doing the voice, making her chuckle.

She watches him as he drives, one hand on the wheel, eye always on the road, even as he jests. She does not know what has changed in him, whether it's actually something that has changed or just something that she has blinded herself to over the years, something that has always been there.

They reach Eastbourne and detour so that they have to drive right along King Edward's Parade, the shingle beach to their left, then the pier.

They stop in one of the big lay-bys close to Beachy Head, walk through a tangle of bushes, emerge on the close-cropped grass, a short walk to the top of the cliffs.

She feels awkward now. She does not know why.

She looks down, watches her feet as she walks. She has always loved the tiny chalk pebbles scattered in the grass here. She used to take them home and write on walls and pavements with them when she was a kid.

A shallow path is worn in the grass along the cliff-top. They head west, and soon the red and white striped lighthouse appears at the foot of the dazzling white cliffs.

"You been able to track down any more about what's actually happened?" she asks.

"Some kind of restart, like you said," he tells her. "Trouble is, there aren't enough v-space specialists dead yet for us to really investigate what's going on…"

"Maybe you need to talk to Noah?"

He shrugs, says, "Maybe." He doesn't flare up as she had expected him to at the mention of Noah.

They pause on a slight promontory. A simple wooden cross is stuck into the ground here, right at the edge of the cliff where someone has jumped.

"Priscilla…"

Now it's Jack's turn to look down, to look away, to avoid her eyes.

"Jack?"

Movement, space closing… His hand, at the back of her head, fingers laced through her hair. The other hand, in the small of her back, pulling, pressing, his embrace like iron, like stone, a force of nature. His body hard against hers.

His mouth, teeth, tongue, stubble…

LATER, IN THE car, on the back seat, curled together, lost.

Priscilla runs her hand down his chest, his shirt undone, his torso bare. "What're we going to do, Jack?"

Her head is full of big thoughts, and he seems to sense it. The silence stretches.

"This is a window, isn't it?" she says. "A breathing space before the shit hits the fan."

"Malthus squared," says Jack. "The population crunch."

She nods, against him, into him. She feels very small all of a sudden.

She feels his hand on the back of her head again, fingers locked in her hair, tipping her back so he can look into her eyes. "Well," he says, "I guess there's only one thing for it, isn't there?"

She says nothing, watches him, loving that spark.

"Come on," he says. "You and me, Priss. Let's go and save the fucking world."


YOUR ISLINGTON FLAT, the Centre, your Westminster office, your North Downs home, *Elector Burnham*'s offices... No sign of you.

Netspace is stabilising again, but my bots haven't found you yet.

Have you come back, Priscilla? Are you here?

I have to distract myself. I need to test consensus. I want to be sure of it.

Others are testing it, too, pushing the boundaries.

I find the Mindweavers by searchbot, naturally. Led by a woman called Magda Blue who describes herself as a *bodhi*, they occupy a former bicycle shop in East Village. I choose to go there. I must. I am going home. I fly to JFK, watch the clouds, the sea, the Newfoundland ice, looking for flaws, inconsistencies, failures of consensus.

The yellow cab takes me across the Queensborough Bridge and down into Lower Manhattan. It feels like years and it feels like I've never left, but more than anything it feels so quiet for New York, still, even as the Accord steadily fills.

I don't think I like the place this quiet. I feel exposed, somehow.

A short time later, I watch the cab leaving. I turn, don't even have to press the buzzer before the door opens and a kid with wide eyes and a big spaced out grin is standing there – Magda, I recognise her from her netpix – hands raised, palms out, giggling, saying, "Noah Barakh! You really came! Oh man, come in, come right on in." She looks about fifteen, although she claims to have been in her sixties when she died in the old world, mugged in a power-down during the Transit.

Seeing her, I pause to wonder: is she really a sixty-ish artist, or is she a kid, taking everyone for a ride?

I dip my head, say, "Thank you, Ms Blue. So kind."

Wooden steps lead up to a kind of lobby, meshed, frosted glass dividers cutting it off from what turns out to be an open area, some kind of studio space. There are others here, maybe a dozen of them, men and women, mostly young. They all watch as I enter with Magda. They know who I am.

"It is true?" I ask. "You call yourself an artist of inner space? What does that mean, exactly?"

We sit on a throw in the middle of the floor-space. The group has formed around us, like small children around a teacher.

"We explore," says Magda. "We take the threads of consensus and re-weave them."

"You are trying to re-cast reality by localised disturbances to consensus?"

Magda nods. "Reality is our canvas," she says. "It is our medium. We believe it to be different and so it is."

"Show me."

"We have our manifesto," she says. "We are developing our own protocols. When the time comes for an exhibition we will invite you."

She is hype. She is very good hype, but as yet, nothing more.

I am glad she works in Manhattan, where consensus is just about as strong as it gets. If she were to really challenge consensus she should be somewhere remote, somewhere on the fringes. That is where it would be interesting to see what might happen if consensus were put under pressure, if the collective *is* were to be redefined...

There are many like Magda. They will be monitored, by me and by others, and, in a more ineffable way, by the protocols of Accord themselves.

I make conversation, I leave, and a short time later I am walking across Brooklyn Bridge, really heading home. I stop halfway, look back at the Manhattan sky-line, a view I have seen so many times before.

You and I stopped here once, Priscilla. We stopped, we kissed, we shared this view. So long ago. So many worlds ago.

Where are you, Priscilla? Where have you gone?

WE JOIN PRISCILLA in Hyde Park, the location she chose for the first national Centre for the Reorientation of the Lost.

We stand, an arm looped around her waist, watching a neat line of people leading into one of the temporary buildings erected among the scattered trees adjoining Park Lane. The buildings look substantial, the blown-brick finish only taking hours to complete, but giving the air of structures that had been here for a century or more. Priscilla has done things properly. This is no third-rate south-coast refugee camp.

"You really think we can keep on top of this?" we ask.

Priscilla nods. "Yes, Jack. I think we can. I think we're showing how it can be done. We have to make this world work. We have to."

Nearby, the little black girl, Sissy, plays with a doll. Priscilla knows her from before, found her again only a couple of days ago.

We pull Priscilla close. These last couple of weeks, we've started all over again.

"You've heard about Spain?" we ask.

Priscilla nods.

There's full-scale war in Spain, in the old world. Armed migrants from northern Africa are fighting with EU border integrity units. Cadiz is in ruins; there's even fighting as far north as Sevilla and Granada. News from the recently dead is a staple of the feeds, even as we try to monitor and manage its flow. There are increasing numbers of the dead entering the Accord, and the projections are that this can only continue and escalate as conditions in the old world deteriorate.

What we haven't told Priscilla is that Nesbitt is here. She will find out soon enough. He is agitating. We have come straight here from coffee with him. Oh how sweet the irony there, the turning of tables!

He sat there, in his rumpled shirt, his telegenic puppy eyes fixed on us, on me. "We have to do something," he said. "We have to act now before everything descends into absolute chaos, Jack. You of all people must see that."

Me of all people. The dinosaur from the old world, the has-been, the *was*. I smiled at him, raised my eyebrows. Let him fill the gap. Let the fucker grovel. He'd been dead for little more than twenty-four hours, just time to orientate himself, to start trying to take control; he always had been one to pull on the ropes when he'd barely even learnt them.

"The crunch," he said. "When the dead come here they are immortal, the world fills up. We can breed here, too – I've asked around and there are pregnancies here, there will be children born of this world. We have the Malthusian crunch hitting us from two directions, Jack. We have to do something."

"You have a proposal?"

"We have to stop them, Jack. We have to pull up the ladder behind us."

"Border integrity, eh?"

I couldn't resist the urge to smile, not so much at the predictability, but because it reminded me – oh sweetest irony of all! – that Elector Clive Nesbitt is here in the Accord because he had been shot through the neck by friendly fire from one of his own vigilantes on the beach at Ramsgate.

He nodded. "We have to stop the flood of migrants, Jack. We have to…"

We'd smiled again, told him we'd talk more. He really is out of his depth here. He doesn't see the half of it.

Finding some technical tweak of the protocols so that we could cut the influx of the dead will never be enough: the crunch is coming.

Now, we stand, we look on at the centre we have helped Priscilla establish to handle one small strand of that influx.

She turns, presses her face into my neck, jaw on my shoulder.

Nesbitt is right, but not nearly right enough.

We have to do something.

It's all about survival. It always has been, hasn't it? The time really has come to think the unthinkable.

# 2.03

YOU ARE BACK.

You have been reborn, and I have lost you, lost the chance to win you again.

You are with him. Your husband. The apparent ruler of this world.

Death has reunited you.

I sit in the Bethnal Green office, staring out of the window at the lime trees, leaves turning yellow – early this year. I have been monitoring the newsfeeds. So much tragedy in the old world: widespread flooding in China, the Faisalabad nuke, famine across much of Africa. So many of them dead. Really dead. Gone before the Soul Harvesters could reach them, unwarehoused, unsaved. In this new world of ours Africa has become an empty continent, a landmass that is not filling up with the reborn.

Elsewhere, though, the dead are entering the Accord in increasing numbers as disaster strikes the old world. Some people are arguing that this is good news in disguise: that after the initial peak, the inflow will slow as the population of the old world crashes. Just as Malthus dooms the old world, he may save us in this.

That is not true, of course: Malthus will strike us here. Die-off in the old world will only delay the crisis here, but it will come.

Somehow, we must tackle it.

I close my eyes, instance myself in Amsterdam, sitting at a table in the floating Sea Palace restaurant, looking back across the dock towards the city. I sip at a tiny cup of chai, and seconds later, she is here, Lucy Chang.

She smiles, sits. She reminds me of a cat, a panther or a leopard, sleek and flowing and very very dangerous.

"Lucy," I say, standing as she sits, then sitting again. I pour her tea. "I was shocked to hear of your death."

She smiles. "So was I, Professor Barakh," she says.

There is no colour in her eyes, black irises set in pure white. It looks cosmetic to me, although I am not sure.

"I was caught in Padova, they tell me – the riots."

I nod. That is what I have heard too.

"Have you seen Burnham? Tate?"

She shakes her head. "Not yet."

"What will you do?"

"I will do the same as I have always done, Professor Barakh."

Now, I reach across the table, place my hand on her two. "You can have a fresh start here, Lucy," I tell her. "You do not work for Sammy Zhang any more. He won't find you here. He is dead. Well and truly dead."

She looks puzzled.

"He died in the blast in Shanghai. I had his warehoused instance corrupted. And its backups too. He is gone."

For a moment there is hope in her eyes, but then it disappears.

"He has owned my Dutch-Chinese ass since I was twelve, Professor Barakh," she says. "Forgive me, but I cannot believe that his reach won't find me here."

"Give it time," I tell her. "Time to get used to the idea. You're a free agent now. You're your own person." She has time, plenty of time.


WE HONEYMOON AGAIN in Africa: Priscilla, and the we that is us, that is me.

Tangiers is deserted. We stay in the Hotel Continental, wander the Medina at night, shadowed by bodyguards just in case the old town is not as empty as it appears. We make love on the beach, read Paul Bowles aloud to each other by the light of the full moon.

The riverboat up the River Volta takes us through deserted town after deserted town. Everywhere we stop... Accra is deserted, Benin City deserted, Lagos deserted.

One night, we lie in each other's arms on some West African beach.

"We have the whole continent," we tell her. "There are only a few hundred people on the entire landmass. We could live here, you and I. King and queen of Africa."

But Priscilla looks away. "It's not ours, is it? All the millions, dead and dying, unsaved. It's their continent. It's so sad, Jack..."

We nod, we hold her. "We did what we could. We funded the Soul Harvesters." We run fingers through her hair. "We should have done more. We didn't really get it, did we?"

She looks at us then, and finally shakes her head.

Next morning, we leave Priss with guards on the beach and take a car along the coast to a tower-block hotel looking out across the bay.

There's security on the door. We're scanned, let in, me and a couple of bodyguards.

A slim white man with silvered hair and an open, short-sleeved shirt sits in a deep seat, looking out over the water.

"Mr Couper," we say.

"Elector." He smiles, nods, makes no move to stand or shake hands.

"Have you considered my proposition?"

"I am intrigued."

We raise an eyebrow.

"Why would you offer me a continent, Elector Burn-ham?"

"It's a long-term proposition," we tell him. "At first, we fill it up. It'll take time, but that's one commodity we have a lot of. Eventually, this world is going to fill up, and right here we have a continent that is fucking close to empty. I need someone to run this end of things."

"But why me?"

"You're an arms-dealer, Mr Couper. In the old world you supplied everyone from gangs to revolutionary armies to corporations and governments."

"Forgive me, Elector, but I am aware of that."

"When this place starts to fill up you start selling them weapons. Let them blow each other to hell and back, and then over and over again."

He watches, intrigued.

"It's all about balance, Mr Couper. There is a delay between death and rebirth in the Accord; projections tell us that that time lag will extend as the population rises – it's a kind of regulatory mechanism. But if it's to work, then people need to be dying... That's your job, Mr Couper. Be my angel of death. Do this and you deserve to be a fucking saint."

WE GATHER IN a Whitehall meeting room, perhaps twenty of us, choosing to stand around the windows with their plush drapes rather than sit at the long, imposing meeting table. I did not know that half of these people were dead until Lucy Chang told me... I'd asked her to organise this, asked her to pull strings, try to get Burnham himself to come if that were possible.

I look around, see old faces from the project, others who have worked on v-space and the interstice without being formally part of my team, my teams.

"Noah!"

I turn, open my arms wide, fall into the embrace of Huey Kashvili. He has long hair to his collar, not gone to grey yet, and he has lost something like a hundred pounds and twenty years. "You're *dead*?" I say, stepping back. "How are you?"

He smiles. "I'm kind of complicated," he says.

I wait for him to explain.

"I was caught in the blast in Shanghai," he says. "Hung on for goddamned *weeks* in hospital before they gave up on me. And then... well..." He taps the side of his head. "There was a lot of me to recompile."

I get it: the protocols, reintegrating his various instances, making him whole. "You're okay?" I ask.

"Most of the time," he says. He smiles. "But like I say, complicated. There was a lot of me to put back into this skull of mine. A lot to resolve..."

I remember the Hueys in the forest, arguing, sparks flying – the extraordinary mix of intense collaboration and conflict. All that, in one head... I put a hand on his arm. "You want me to get you a glass of water?" I ask. It seems the least I can do.

"So what have you got us here for?" Huey asks, so abrupt a change that I get the impression another Huey has taken control in there... It is disconcerting, to say the least.

"We have problems," I say. "The world has problems. We need to do something about them before this world gets as bad as the old."

I HAD NOT expected you to show up. I should have, but I did not.

Elector Burnham has brought you. I wonder if he has done this deliberately or if it is simply because of your role in the project in the old world. I understand that he has won. He has killed you and somehow he has won you back. I do not need reminding of that.

You sit at his side, occasionally trying to make eye contact with me. I remain calm, focused. I allow you to catch my eye; I nod, look away.

"Colleagues," I say, bringing the meeting to order. I wave towards the table, and we sit. "I'm sure you are all wondering why I have asked for this meeting to take place." I smile. "I think I'm asking myself the same question, but I hope that some kind of answer will emerge this morning…"

I pause, continue: "There is much talk about the Malthusian crunch. We have all seen the projections: with current old world death and warehousing rates and projected birth rates in the new, within a century or so the new world's population will exceed that of the old – in the time spans now awaiting us, a century or so is as nothing: this is *our* crisis, not one we can palm off on future generations. We need to confront this now if we are to find a solution. I wish to offer my services, and to encourage everyone in this room to similarly volunteer their expertise in order to find ways to do so."

Elector Burnham nods. "Laudable," he says. "But a hundred years is a long time. We are already establishing schemes to displace new arrivals to regions of the world where there are population gaps, Africa in particular. There is an entire continent there waiting to be colonised—"

"But Malthus," I say. "Population grows exponentially, and in this world it grows from birth rates, from the zeroed death-rate of immortality, and from inflow from the old world!"

"Africa gives us breathing space," says Burnham. "So, too, does much of Latin America, anywhere where the Catholic Church or Islam held sway, anywhere where either dogma or poverty kept warehousing rates low. It gives us time to establish other measures…"

"We need to revisit the nature of the Accord," I say, and pause, allowing the silence to grow. "I look around this room and I see a handful of officials who have had some involvement with the project to develop the Accord and I see the cream of the new world's v-space experts. I see my good friend Huey Kashvili, and Meredith Constance. I see Chuckboy Lee…" I pause again here, my look fixed on the obese Korean with the

long shiny ponytail and tattoos spilling out of his white
T-shirt. I had no idea Lucy had found Lee... It is perhaps a bigger shock to see Lee here than it is to see you
again, Priscilla.

"I will not complete the roll-call," I say. "We know
who we are. In this room, Elector Burnham, we have
the people to do that revisiting of the protocols."

"You sound like Elector Nesbitt," says Burnham.
"Modify the protocols so that we can close off entry to
the Accord. But that's only a short-term measure too –
it only tackles one of the Malthusian factors."

"I am not proposing that we close anything off, Elector Burnham. I propose the contrary. I propose that we
open things up..."

PRISCILLA HAS STUDIED Noah closely throughout this
session. They made eye contact briefly, early on, but
since then he has avoided her look. He is being studiously professional, keeping personal histories out of
this. She hopes that Jack is doing the same, that she is
here because he believes she has something to contribute and not merely as his trophy. She hates that she
even asks herself that question.

She tries to catch Noah's eye again as he sits back, the
room in silence. She doesn't know what she wants to
achieve, what a look can possibly say. It's not as if she
wants to say sorry, as if she has anything to say sorry
for. She just wants to be sure he's okay. He's a friend, a
colleague, a could-have-been lover... She cares.

And now she wants to say, *Fuck, but that was good,
Noah!* While Jack is fussing around with politicians'
solutions for Africa, Noah is trying to think big. She
keeps trying to get Jack to see the scale of things, what
it really means to be here in the Accord, but she never
feels she's getting through.

Now, she leans across the table, hands folded, elbows
resting on polished mahogany. "Professor Barakh," she
says, and waits until he looks her in the eye, has to look

her in the eye. "You clearly have something in mind. While we politicians seek politicians' solutions for a stolen continent, you gather together in one room the pre-eminent dead v-space pioneers."

He's smiling that little half-smile of his, the one that's sometimes endearing and sometimes plain fucking irritating.

"Would you care to enlighten us?"

"As I said at the outset, Electee Burnham. I too have been wondering why I have gathered together this meeting. I do not know the answers. I only have the vaguest of inklings in which directions the answers may lie. But within the walls of this room I believe there are the individuals most likely to find such answers."

HUEY FINDS ME afterwards, takes me by the arm, guides me outside. We walk by Parliament Square, down to Victoria Embankment, still arm in arm.

"You know what it's like?" he asks, eventually, a sudden turn in the conversation. He has done this a few times since we met again at the start of the talks: a sudden change of track.

"In your head, you mean?" I ask. Huey and I, we've always cut to the point, no bull. That's why we worked so well together as postdocs. Way back, I'd been in awe of him, the screwy genius twenty years my senior. He'd put me right on that almost immediately. *Don't look up to me*, he'd told me then. *Look in to me.*

He nods.

"You finding that the reintegration of all those instances of you is causing conflicts?" Hell, thinking how he'd been as separate instances, I can barely even begin to imagine what it must be like with them all crammed into one. Talk about split personalities...

"You can tell," he says. "You can see inside of me, like you always could, Noah. I guess I never was the most stable of guys, was I?" He chuckles. "Right now it feels like I'm about to go pop in my head, like that old song. Pop goes my head, yes."

Huey must know how lucky he has been. When something violates so many protocols the outcome is not easy to anticipate: rather than be reintegrated as he has, Huey could easily have been shut out of the Accord, left to fester on some fragmented reality shard in an endless loop; erased altogether, even.

We cross the road, stand by the river. The day is grey, muggy, oppressive. Makes me think of Shanghai.

"So... you see the signs of what it is like for me, yes?"

I look at him. He's leading up to something. I nod.

"I see these signs too, my friend. In that room today I was not the only one who has too much in his head for one person to have in their head."

I raise my eyebrows, trying to think who he might mean.

"Elector Burnham," says Huey. "There is more to him now. I am sure of it. I never did trust him, but now... now I do not even know what he is."

PRISCILLA TAKES SISSY with her to the Bethnal Green centre.

Noah greets them in the lobby, a big smile on his face. This is the first time he has seen Sissy since the Transit and the moment he emerges the little girl rushes into his arms, yelling his name. The last time this instance of her had seen him was in northern Italy, just before Luca killed her.

The three of them go outside, sit in the enclosed garden, high walls on two sides, the red-brick building wrapping round the other two.

"This summer will not last forever," he says, "although it feels like it will."

Priscilla watches him, tries not to feel pity, regret... whatever it is that she's feeling. "We need a whole new emotional repertoire for all this, don't we, Noah?" she says.

"All this," he says. "Yes. We are finding our way, aren't we?"

They watch Sissy scratching at the ground with a stone.

"There are whole parts of her experience missing, aren't there?" says Priscilla.

"There are," says Noah. "Although she remembers more than most – she remembers having been in the Accord; she remembers everything up to her death here. All between that point and the Transit is lost, just as it is for you. Most of us have gaps. And it will only become more so: as time passes, any individual will not be able to retain all of their experience. Memories will fade and vanish. As we die and are reborn, the recompiling of self will be a housekeeping process, an editing, an optimising. The you that will sit with me in this garden in a thousand years will be very different to the you that is instanced now, today. And, in less marked ways, that you – *this* you – is different to the you I once knew."

Priscilla watches him all the time he says this, still feeling that poignant, wry mix of emotions, that new emotion that has only just come into existence for one who is in her position, in this post-real world, one who is coming to terms with the beginning of a wholly new kind of life.

"I have gaps, yes," she says. "I know I have gaps. I know there are things I have said and done that were said and done by a different me, a me that was capable of living differently, doing differently..." She stops. She wonders what she's trying to say.

She starts again: "Are you going to help me fill in those gaps, Noah? Are you going to tell me about it?" She is trying to help him.

He looks down, moistens his lips, looks across to Sissy playing in the mud, smiles.

"Some day maybe," he says. He turns to Priscilla, and she almost flinches at the raw hurt in his eyes. "But not now, okay?"

Priscilla doesn't know what to say. Again. She wonders how pure her motives had been. Had she really come here to try to help him, to get him to talk, to explore, to sign off on an episode in his life? Or had she been curious, intrigued to know what might have been?

She starts to say something, but hesitates, mouth open, wondering why in fuck she should end up feeling *guilty*...

So Noah gets in first. "Priscilla," he says. "Your husband... Elector Burnham."

She refrains from interrupting, from teasing him about stating the fucking obvious. Waits for him to go on.

"Have you noticed anything *different* about him?"

She is puzzled, not so much by his words as by what might be behind them.

"I think you should be wary of him," Noah continues.

She looks at him. She thought she'd got through to him just now, or started to get through to him at least; that she had reached across a horribly awkward divide, managed a very personal transit between the two of them, between past and present, pasts and present.

She looks away, watches Sissy.

Why does he have to turn it round? Why does he have to make it into some macho territorial thing? Why does she always feel trapped by the men around her?

"So, how does it feel? How does it feel to be a new kind of person?"

Chuckboy Lee sits across from us in the booth of an Islington bar, sawdust on the floor, nicotine-yellowed ceiling, retro wood panelling made to look worn smooth by decades of use. He has a bottle of absinthe and a half-full glass, a split open packet of peanuts on the table.

We shrug. "You asked me once before," we say.

"You were different then. There was less to you. Indulge me, Elector Burnham. Tell me what it is like."

"I am me," we say. "I am mostly me. But... it's in the mix. Everyone is made up of lots of different components: fragments of experience, of knowledge, of understanding. So what's so different about me? Am I really something new?"

"Do you ask me to believe that it is no different, Elector Burnham? I took you apart. Or at least I took part of you apart, the Davits-chimera: I took that you apart and fed it into the Accord. Don't think I didn't take the opportunity to take a close look, to keep my own laboratory specimens."

He stops, chuckles, and at that moment we are struck by the horror in what he has just confessed. Somewhere, back in the old world, this fucking genius psychopath had a copy – or copies – of me, to do what the hell he liked with. Or part of me, part of us. What must those copies of us have been through? What kind of existence did they have? Are they still back there somewhere, trapped?

"I learnt a lot, Elector Burnham."

We look at him as he sips from his glass. We asked him here to get some insight into what Barakh is really up to, but that seems irrelevant, for now at least.

"You and me, Elector Burnham: I think we can work together. I think I have a lot to offer you."

# 2.04

THE INVITATION CAME a week ago: some kind of crude printing process on hand-pressed card, so primitive it has a perversely refined elegance to it. Fitting that the invitation itself should be a work of art, as it is, indeed, the work of an artist.

Magda Blue is ready to exhibit, and she has invited me to attend. Her exhibition is called, simply, *Believe*.

We gather in a club in lower Manhattan. I recognise many of the faces, even though most of the people here appear younger in their current instances than they did in the old world. There are artists and politicians and media movers, the people you might expect at a New York exhibition; but also, I go to share a drink with Deedee from our Shanghai centre and before we have even greeted each other I recognise a voice, turn, and see Huey entering the room.

The place is lit by low, indirect lighting, the word *believe* either painted or projected onto various surfaces, soft jazzy background music cushioning the sound of voices. Waiting staff drift from guest to guest with silver trays loaded with champagne and canapés. I recognise some of the artists from my previous visit mingling with the guests, but no sign yet of Magda Blue.

I sip champagne with Huey and Deedee, and we talk about phase two.

"True," says Huey, in answer to something Deedee just said, "the Accord is embedded in the interstices. But what about the fabric of *this* universe? Quantum mechanics applies here as elsewhere: we have interstitial space of our own, uncollapsed wave-space."

"You want to build another Accord?" Deedee's Dutch accent becomes stronger as he becomes more incredulous.

"No," says Huey. "I think we can exploit the interstices to move outwards, not inwards. There is a whole universe out there to explore, to colonise. My team is looking at ways to jump through interstitial space from one point to another – travel through wormholes in space, yes?"

I smile. By "team," Huey means he has shut himself in a darkened room and thought lots, parallel processing his assorted selves within a single brain.

"You telling me you're building a mother-fucking *spaceship*?" Deedee sounds very Dutch now.

Huey smiles. "You make it sound ambitious, my friend."

Deedee laughs, we all three laugh. It is good to see Huey being ambitious. It is when he is at his best.

A man appears on a small stage at one end of the club. He is wearing a tuxedo, his hair slicked back across his skull, shining under the spotlight. Speaking into a vintage microphone, he says, "Ladies, gentlemen, and those who have yet to decide... I give you the bodhi, Magda Blue."

Magda appears from behind a wispy curtain, wearing a sparkling sari that winds up and around her hair. She is clearly the Magda that I met a few weeks ago here in Manhattan, but... she is different... fuller. Her body has a gravitas, she has a substance that settles comfortably on the hips, the breasts. While physically she still looks young, there is nothing of the adolescent about her that there was before. There is an age, a jazzlands age, to her.

She speaks into the microphone. "Thank you for coming." Pause. "For this evening's demonstration all I ask is that you temporarily put aside any preconceptions and, simply, *believe*."

The band begin to play, easy jazz, nothing that I recognise. As the music swells, I observe movement in the audience. The waiting staff have put down their trays and are working their way among us. A young woman stops before me, holds herself with arms raised so that I feel I must step forward, take one hand in its long black lace glove, slide an arm around her waist, begin to dance. She had been serving drinks only moments ago, but is clearly part of the demonstration.

I have given up trying to work out what Magda is up to, content to let her lead, content to believe.

Spotlights swing across the heads of the dancers, lingering and then moving on. Curls of cigarette smoke twist upwards in the shafts of light, and I see that my dancing partner is delicately gripping her own cigarette in a long-shafted holder in her leading hand. She has eyes that pool dark in the mixed lighting, her white-moon face tipped up towards mine, her features framed by a tight black bob. She is quite exquisite. I breathe her perfume deep: cranberries and Christmas spices and fine cigarette smoke.

A slight pause as the track finishes and a dapper little crooner comes to stand at the mike with Magda. I smooth down my tux, smile at my date, know all of a sudden that she is called Veronica and that she tips her head back and pants rapidly as she comes.

The band have shuffled away, leaving only a skinny silver-haired black man at a spotlit piano in one corner. He plays, his hands so easy across the keys. After a couple of bars Magda starts to duet with the crooner, one I recognise this time, "Unforgettable." She has a strong, rich voice, and I wonder why this surprises me. They gaze into each other's eyes, take the song slow, deep, lingering over every syllable as if they are making love. My partner leans into me. We dance, her head on my chest.

I look around again. The light is so atmospheric, hard shafts cutting through a gloom that is grainy, textured, monochrome.

I look down.

My partner is almost a head shorter than me, her face a pearly grey, her eyes fixed on mine. Her lips are pert, a deeper shade of grey, glistening in the occasional splinters of light that catch us as we move. Her body moves with a sinuous twist that reminds me of you, Priscilla, and for a moment... for a moment, I lean into her embrace, feel the weight of her body in my arms, the twist of her back, the slight tightening of her laced grip, the delicate pressure of her glossed lips against mine.

I...

I straighten, stagger back, feel colour rush back around me, a pool of technicolour in a grainy monochrome world. I look at the waiting girl and she is not you at all, not even like you, except in the way that she moves.

I turn, make my way through the club, the swirling couples in tux and drop-waist dresses with tassels and boas and thick black eyelashes that curl like feathers, eyes and skin so white. Everything is gritty, grainy to the eye, contrast up high, detail intense where the light catches, lost everywhere else.

I push my way through to the door, open it, find myself standing on the broad sidewalk. Across the street, billboards advertise Dubonnet, the perfect cigar, at three for fifty cents; Yeast-foam buckwheat cakes; Beech-nut chewing tobacco. An old Chevy cab, yellow body, sweeping orange wings, yellow hubcaps, rolls past, kicking up a wall of spray from the street.

The air is cool, biting deep in my lungs, jolting me fully alert again. The atmosphere back there had been smothering, overpowering.

I look around.

The verisimilitude is quite remarkable. It brings to mind poor Dylan Thomas, reconstituted in west

Manhattan in one of our earlier pre-consensus reality shards – a trinket, a gewgaw created to entertain the politicians. The Accord is about reality, not fictions like this.

Or, at least, so I had believed.

Back inside, I hover around the fringes, studying the detail. I look at a man who I am sure was a waiter earlier on. He stands with Candy Mahler, a reality hacker from Berlin, and I can see that she is entranced by him, lost in him. She looks quite sensational, looping curls of hair clipped down tightly to her skull, her make-up stark, strong, dramatic. The man, though... He is good. He is very good. I think again of poor Dylan. Magda's gewgaws are impressive.

I find Huey. He is dancing with a snake of a woman, his equal in height, with breasts like tennis balls swinging free in her silky black dress. Huey is having a whale of a time.

"Hey, Huey," I say.

He glances at me, then back at his partner.

"Huey. Look a bit closer, why don't you?"

He grins, needs no encouraging.

"Nice piece of work," I say. She is. She is almost real. "You tried conversation?"

I can't help but laugh at the look he gives me. Social intercourse is not foremost in his mind.

Up on stage, Magda Blue leans against the piano, watching the player's hands dance across the black and white keys. I want a still of that, blown up large, framed. It really is a picture. Perfect.

I look around again. How long have we been here in the Accord? How long since consensus asserted itself? A matter of weeks. And already we are pushing the limits of the real.

I approach Magda, offer my hand to help her step down from the small stage area.

She joins me at the bar. I have whiskey on the rocks, she has a Manhattan, appropriately enough.

"I am impressed," I tell her, and she smiles. "You and your team have constructed a localised realignment of consensus."

"We have barely scratched the surface, Professor Barakh, as I'm sure you're aware."

Indeed. If consensus can be manipulated in this way it may be possible to mine much deeper. "All we have to do is believe," I say.

We drink, chat, learn more about each other, a pool of sometimes light, sometimes heavy discussion in the grainy monochrome world this artist of the real has crafted.

Later, swirling whiskey and ice in a short, fat glass, I say, "Magda. Magda, there is a project, a research initiative. I would like to take you back to London and see what you make of it."

She smiles. "Research? What in Christ's name do I know about research?"

Later still, the exhibition ends.

Magda takes my hand to cut me off in mid-sentence. I follow her gaze, realise the music has stopped. The lighting shifts, colour starts to leach back in, grain smoothes over. People stop, slowly, until only two or three couples still dance. The tuxedos have gone; the waiting staff resume duties. A murmur of conversation rises to fill the silence, puzzled, querulous tones and looks. I recognise the feelings: I passed through the same stages of wonder, disbelief, scepticism earlier.

I look around. We are in an ordinary Manhattan club again, the lights up. Plush leather seats line booths around the periphery, gathered around a broad, mirrored dance floor.

I catch Magda's eye. "Go on," I tell her. "All the way."

She hesitates, then subvocalises something to her team.

And the room fades, the club dissolves.

Silence reasserts itself. Guests look around.

There is no club, no mirrored dance floor, no small stage where the band had squeezed on to play. No bar, or drinks, or even... the waiting staff, they fade, dissolve into pixels, switched off like poor Dylan Thomas whenever he was not needed.

We stand in a wide space, a warehouse of some kind, lit by long fluorescent strip lights suspended from a high ceiling.

I bow my head to Magda Blue, an artist who uses as her medium the protocols of Accord.

"YOU'VE *WHAT*?"

Huey doesn't like it. He stares at me as we sit on the plane, somewhere over the Atlantic.

"Noah, I really don't believe what you're telling me. You say you've invited Magda Blue to join the project? What does she have to do with the problems we face? She is a trickster, a child playing with things she does not understand. She should not be encouraged."

"She is a creative thinker. She offers fresh insight, new perspectives. Her thinking is not affected by having worked on early stages of the project."

"You saying I'm stale?"

"I'm saying you're a brilliant mind and you should not feel threatened by another such mind."

"Bollocks," said Huey. "Great big hairy bollocks to you."

"Tell me, Huey," I say, trying a different tack. "What is it that disturbs you about my encouraging Magda Blue? It's not just that she is an outsider with no formal background, is it?"

"You know me better than that, Noah. This Magda Blue... What she is doing undermines everything we have worked towards. She is mining consensus deep. She is challenging it. All of our work before consensus was reached was building *towards* that consensus! The Accord required consensus before all of this became real – a shared reality, an agreed reality."

"You think Magda could destroy consensus altogether?"

"Maybe. Maybe the risk is small, but the consequences are unthinkable."

"But Huey, is she not, rather, *extending* consensus? Earlier, you told Deedee about exploiting interstitial space in order to jump great distances, to colonise other star systems. We do not know what these star systems are truly like, other than bare astronomical data. There is no consensus for these systems. When we start to explore them we will be extending our own consensus outwards, across the universe: we will be crafting belief, just as Magda has done. Aren't you both talking about the same thing, only in a different language?"

"There is a difference, Noah. A subtle but crucial difference. We talk about extending consensus where it does not yet exist: we are creating consensus. Magda is subverting the existing consensus, recasting it. We are a creative force, she a destructive one."

# 2.05

WE SIT AT the chunky kitchen table in our North Downs home, watching Priscilla move about, clearing up after breakfast. Sissy is through in the front room, playing with a movie. She's a smart kid. It's strange having a child about the place. We like it. We don't. It mixes feelings up. We hadn't expected it to be complicated like that.

We wonder if that is the normal way of things, or if it is a reflection of our manifold nature: parts of us like it, parts of us don't. There are times... times when the child is nothing, little more than furniture, an irritant. It's so easy to pin those times on an aspect of us that is not *me*, the dominant *me*.

We are Jack Burnham.

I am Jack Burnham.

We... I made love to Priscilla this morning. There was a moment, a moment when I pressed deep, hard, held myself there, struck by the intimacy, the shared instant when every tiny movement seemed magnified... a moment when I looked into her eyes and suddenly I was us, I was we, and we wondered what was in her head at that moment, *who* was in her head at that moment.

And now, we watch her, moving about the kitchen, and we wonder how well you can ever really know another person.

Later, Chuckboy Lee arrives. For an obese man, he seems buoyant, full of energy. This world suits him. He stands at the head of the gravel path as we open the door. Pulled up in the drive there is a vintage silver Bentley.

We smile greeting, nod at the car, say, "Nice."

Chuckboy beams. "Back in Sunda Kelapa I didn't get out much," he says. "I kept my head down. I had no reason to venture beyond my home. Now... well isn't this a lovely world, Elector Burnham? It offers so much."

He is like a big boy in a toyshop. We smile again, step back, inviting him in.

Through in the front room, Sissy is still playing with her movie, pointing at the screen and telling it to change the bit where Pigeonbrains rides the skyjet so she can see what he sees.

We hesitate in the doorway, don't want to turf the kid out, resent that she's taking over our space anyway, think we'll take Lee through to the office instead; but then he is squeezing past, going to squat by the girl, asking her what the film is and did she know she can do this and *this* with it?

She giggles and makes big eyes at Chuckboy, as he squats like a sumo and chats conspiratorially in his sing-song voice.

We feel like an onlooker, hovering in the doorway.

Priscilla appears at our shoulder, then steps past us into the room.

She sweeps Sissy up, carries her out of the room.

Chuckboy looks up at me, smiles, says, "She will be a beauty, won't she? You must be very proud."

I cancel the movie and we sit.

"Chuckboy," I say. "You're looking well."

He nods. "It is different for me in this world," he says. "In the old world I had issues. People had issues with me."

We're aware that there had been problems, but don't know their nature.

"Here, I am complete."

It comes back, then: in the old world Chuckboy Lee had been a self-elective castrato. "Ah," we say. "I remember now…"

"It kept things simple, back there. But sometimes simple is not enough. I like complex, Elector Burnham. I like you; you are very complex."

For a moment we think he's coming on to us, but no, there is no chemistry there, no undercurrent of desire.

"Your daughter," Chuckboy says. "She's a doll, isn't she?"

"You said we could work together," I say. "You said we could achieve a lot together. What did you mean by that?"

"No one understands the protocols of Accord better than me," he says.

"Barakh? Huey Kashvili?"

He shakes his head. "Why do you think Professor Barakh had me removed from the project?" he asks. "We had a difference of opinions. This is Barakh's Accord, not mine. It could have been different."

"Yes?"

"The protocols are rigid," says Chuckboy. "Barakh was convinced that was necessary. He is terrified of change. I am fascinated by it. I want to push boundaries. This is why you intrigue me, Elector Burnham. You push the boundaries by your nature. I think you should push them harder. Imagine there were two instances of you, one running the world and the other just going off with your wife and charming daughter to explore."

"The protocols don't allow that, though: there are no multiple instances. It would defy consensus."

"Barakh's protocols, yes. But imagine if we could sidestep them. If we could create separate instances that could be subtly different versions of you, suited to their roles – or that they could be dramatically different instances of you… That these instances could meet and remix, so that they are *you*. You already know what it is like to be a multiple: you must be curious about taking it further."

"Why would I let anyone reach inside my head and fuck with what I am?"

"I would work with copies, Elector Burnham. I am talking about re-instancing you."

"Could you make one that was *more* me...?" An I rather than a we...

"Let me show you what I can do."

"I'd want to retain complete... *editorial*... control."

"Naturally. Let me work on an instance. Of you. Let me work on an instance of your charming daughter, also. She intrigues me too."

I hesitate.

He's only talking copies. I'll remain untouched. Sissy will too.

"I don't know."

"You would not be the first," says Chuckboy. "You think Chuckboy Lee flies to London just like that? No, he sends an instance of himself, one edited, as you put it, to suit the occasion."

I stare at him. At it. At whatever the correct terminology for this thing before me is. And slowly, he fades from existence.


PRISCILLA BURNHAM IS eating dry-roast peanuts, mainlining Rioja, and thoroughly pissed off; and not necessarily in that order.

She puts another bag on the bar, thumps it with the side of her fist so that the plastic splits, spilling peanuts onto the dark wood. She'd argued with Jack about Africa again. About outmoded colonial values, about rights and honour and basic decency. His argument boiled down to there only being at most a couple of hundred thousand Africans who would be reborn in the Accord, and so it was the League's duty to put the continent to the best possible use for humankind; or, more succinctly, the Africans could go fuck.

St Stephen's Tavern always used to be a regular for politicos and hacks, a kind of informal no-man's land, where guards could be dropped as far as people in their line of business could ever drop a guard. Now, it's deadly quiet, only a handful of half-familiar faces along the bar, Electee Wilkes and a small group over in a window booth, a few others she doesn't know.

She tops up her glass from the near-empty bottle, hears a sound at her side, then a smoothly cultured voice ask for another bottle.

She turns, sees Electee Nesbitt easing himself onto a bar stool next to her.

He smiles, and it's the kind of smile you just have to return. Most smiles are that kind when you're three-quarters of the way into a good Rioja, Priscilla always finds, even when it's Nesbitt doing the smiling.

"Priscilla," he says. "Mind if I join you?"

She shrugs. They know where they stand, always have done. She thinks he's a middle-class thug; he thinks she's a weak-minded liberal.

"If you think you'll win me over to your drawbridge strategy, it'll take more than a bottle of Rioja," she tells him. He's still pushing on putting effort into changing the protocols so that they can block any further entry from the old world.

"And if you think you'll win me over to opposing your husband on Africa you're going to have to try a bit harder on the charm front."

She puts a hand to his face, strokes his cheek with her thumb, says, "Oh, Clive, believe me: I really am doing my absolute best on that front."

He removes her hand, turns it, kisses her knuckles. "Truce?" he says. "I really don't have the stomach for a fight right now, Priscilla."

"Truce," she says.

He pours, they drink, they know where they stand, and sometimes that makes things so much easier.

* * *

THE LAST PERSON we'd expected to see was Lucy fucking Chang.

We've only exchanged the briefest of words since she died. She's been going through one of these existential crises so many people seem to hit when they die: reassessing everything. She didn't want to come back and work with me when I asked, but she did at least keep the option open.

So now... Her face on the entry-screen.

"Lucy? How good to see you." We buzz her in, wait by the flat's door until we see her in the flesh.

"Elector Burnham." She strides in, document case under one arm, almost like old times.

"So what's this all about then? You want to come back? You know I want you back working with me, Lucy."

She gives a small shake of the head. "I am an independent agent," she says. "I am still trying to work out what to do with the rest of time itself."

"Tea? Scotch?"

Another small shake of the head.

"I have a file," she says. "A clip. It's been passed to me. Someone trying to make trouble. I think you should see it."


BACK AT THE Islington flat, Priscilla lets herself in. Jack is home already, Sissy off staying with Noah.

Jack stands in his office doorway, haloed by the light so that he's mostly silhouette.

"Hey, babe," says Priscilla, half-turning to hang her suede jacket.

He's on her, one hand gripping her shoulder, the other her arm, pushing her, hard, back against the wall, so quickly, so unexpectedly.

She knows what to do in a fight; she has been trained. She dips her head sharply forward, butting his chin, raises a foot and stamps down, heel first on his instep.

He cries out, eases his grip, staggers back, half-pulling her with him.

She squirms, trying to free herself, but his grip is tightening again.

They end up against the opposite wall of the entrance lobby, his back against the wall. The lights go off. He must have hit the switch with his shoulder.

In the gloom, Priscilla twists, stamps again, misses.

In her head: What the fuck? Why? Who? It's him, Jack... But why? What's happened? And is this what it had been like, when he had killed her in the old world, when he had been taken over by jealous rage and shot her with her own gun? And fuck, is he going to kill her again? Why? What the fuck?

She's free, makes for the front door, but he gets there before her, leans with his back against it, panting, the whites of his eyes almost luminous in the gloom of the hallway.

"Jack?" she says. "What the fuck's got into you?"

"You," he hisses. "Always you, Priscilla. I thought we were okay. Here. Now. So why? Why him?"

"What? Why *who*? What the fuck are you talking about?"

"Nesbitt. Why him? You just trying to rub my nose in it? You been leading me on all this time just so you can rub my fucking nose in it? You could hardly have picked a better candidate for a revenge fuck, could you? Clive fucking Nesbitt."

"Jack... I really don't know what you're talking about."

He nods towards the study, then.

Priscilla approaches the doorway cautiously, not wanting to turn her back on Jack, not wanting to be trapped. From the doorway she sees herself on the wallscreen, frozen as a still. The backdrop is a bar; St Stephen's Tavern she realises – she had been there only a few hours ago.

"What is this, Jack? What's this all about?"

He approaches, she goes further into the room.

He must have pinged the screen, because the picture jumps back to a distant shot, Priscilla at the bar with Nesbitt, smiling and laughing.

She hears her own voice: *Of course we can, Clive.*

Nesbitt looks down into his glass, says nothing.

Priscilla raises a hand to his face, runs her thumb over his cheek. *Come on, Clive. Let's do it. He'll never find out.*

It is the scene from lunchtime, only it is not.

*But... but how could we? You're a beautiful woman, of course I'd like to. I want you. But...*

She lowers her hand. *Come on, Clive. I want you. Come back to my office. Fuck me. Now.*

The view zooms in on her face, her playful smile, freezes.

"That didn't happen, Jack. It's a lie. Run it through forensics: they'll show that it's been edited. That conversation never took place."

"And the streetcam coverage of the two of you walking back to Parliament, to your office?"

"Faked. Where did you get this, Jack?"

"I have my sources."

"It's fucking Clive Nesbitt, isn't it? He set this up. He set me up so he can get at you. Don't you see it?"

He looks at her.

"Nothing happened, Jack. Nothing was ever going to happen. We've been set up." And why the fuck does she have to defend herself like this? Why is *she* the one in the wrong?

She heads for the office door, brushes past Jack, just daring him to do anything now.

"I'm going for a bath," she says. "I may be some time."

WE SIT AT our desk, Priscilla's face frozen on the wall.

We believe her. We believe that the clip will prove to have been faked, that Nesbitt is trying to screw us up, that it's all his doing.

So if we believe her on this, why couldn't we have believed her in the first place? Why did we doubt her?

We think about Chuckboy Lee, about his promise of edited instances. Could he build an us, a me, that would be the right mix of me for Priscilla? A me not riddled with doubt and suspicion and jealousy?

We call him up in meetspace, a bland meeting room, no windows, a few anodyne abstract pictures on the wall. He responds immediately, or at least an instance of him does.

He smiles in greeting. "What is it, Elector Burnham?" he asks. "What are you seeking?"

We had intended to ask about that me, the good me that would be right for Priscilla, the one not run through with jealousy and suspicion. But, we realise, we are not that instance: we are an instance that *is* full of just those feelings.

"Chuckboy," we say. "Tell me… Here in the Accord we're all just data, right? Localised points of data storage and processing, all part of the greater Accord? Am I right?"

Chuckboy nods.

"So tell me: how easy is it to read that data? Can you see what's in someone else's head? Can you see what they're thinking?" And who they are thinking of…

# 2.06

THE FIRST NORTHERN winter in the Accord is a wild one, with long weeks of snowfall across much of Europe and North America. I spend much of my time in London, cajoling Huey into pushing his ideas to the limit, just like the old days. I stay in my Bethnal Green flat, work in the nearby centre, walking between the two through deep snow, kicking my feet in it like a schoolboy.

Today, I walk back to the flat, my head swirling like the snowflakes in the beam of the streetlights above. My head is a snow-globe that someone has shaken. Until this afternoon all had been settled in there. I had moved on.

But now…

EARLIER: PRISCILLA WALKS into the centre's main meeting room, finds Noah sitting at the end of the long table, dragging fingertips across a screen rolled out over the wooden surface. She stops at his shoulder, watches him dragging meaningless blocks of data into new sequences.

He glances up, gives his little half-smile, dips his head again. "I am mapping consensus," he tells her. "Studying how Magda Blue moulds her localised distortions in consensus, how she stabilises those distortions so she can mine deeper. She has no idea how to describe what she does in technical terms; she does not know the math."

"Am I looking like I understand?" Priscilla asks.

"She creates illusions of reality that become manifest, discords that become real. She digs branches off from the main consensus."

"Is that safe?"

Noah nods. "As far as we can model, it appears to be safe, yes," he says. "Although not necessarily safe for your sanity: she has built one reality called Six Impossible Things. I think I prefer my realities more *real*..."

"Coffee?" Priscilla puts a cappuccino down in front of him and goes to stand by the window, looking out at the snow. "You think we'll be having a white Christmas?"

"Consensus appears to be leaning in favour of that, doesn't it?"

In the window, his reflection. He works away, only glancing across at her occasionally. He loves her, she knows. He has mastered it to an extent, is not so driven by it. But... he can't help those glances. He loves her.

She wonders what it was like to love him back.

She has often wondered this, but never quite in this way, never standing two paces from him in a situation where she could just step over, take his face in her hands and kiss him hard.

She could fuck him, she realises. But more than that...

She thinks she knows.

She thinks she knows what it is like to be able to love him back.

She doesn't love him, but she could.


NOW, KICKING AT the snow, head swirling, I walk.

You were studying me in the window. I'm sure you hadn't thought I could see what you were doing.

I haven't seen that look in your eyes for a long time.

But was I right? Or was I reading too much into the situation? You were watching me, yes, but at times I haven't been far short of your goddamn stalker! Of course you were watching me...

It was the eyes, though. The real story is always in the eyes.

You were watching me. Watching me in a way you last did a lifetime ago.


CHUCKBOY LEE'S WAREHOUSE home is full of the sound of children, laughing, shouting, chattering, making engine noises. It is a happy sound.

I look the length of the building to where Lee has set up a playground for them. A Ferris wheel turns, almost as high as the warehouse ceiling. He has spared no expense.

I breathe deep. The Jakarta air, even in this cooled building, is muggy and oppressive, but it is far better than out in the streets. My clothes still cling to me with a mixture of sweat and the sharp rainstorm I had been caught in earlier. I had stood, face tipped up, relishing the flow of fresh water.

It is good to be me again. Good to be mostly Jack Burnham. Or at least, it is good to be this instance of me.

I am the man Priscilla can love again. This me is Priscilla's.

I find Chuckboy in his favourite corner of this sprawling building, an area screened off by high shelving units crammed with books and boxes.

He is reclining on a vast sofa, a girl of about six clinging to his side, giggling as one of his fleshy hands strokes her arm. It is Sissy, or rather, an instance of Sissy, a copy. Not the real Sissy, I remind myself. Not at all.

"Get me home, Chuckboy. I want to be back in London. I want to see Priscilla."

Chuckboy smiles, fingers still working the girl's arm. "Sure, Elector Burnham. I'll get you home." Then: "You still want to know what's in her head?"

"What do you mean?"

"Things aren't what they were. Other you has let it slip: the two of you hardly see each other now. You got a lot of work to do."

"What do you mean 'in her head'?"

"You want to see?"

A screen scrolls down from the darkness. I see Priscilla in an anonymous meeting room, could have been anywhere. And there, at one end of the table is Barakh.

Shapes form in my mind. Thoughts. Words.

Curiosity. Love – what it must be like to be loved by Noah. Erotic rush, passion. Suppressed. An urge to take him in her hands, to kiss him, to press skin against skin, to rediscover what it is like. To fuck him. To fuck that sparkling-eyed man sitting there, just two paces away. To be loved by him and to love him back.

"Get me back there," I say. "Now. Merge this instance of me with the one that's there. Remix me."

Chuckboy Lee continues running his hand over the Sissy instance, smiling. "I'll get you back," he says. "But Elector, don't be rash. You are a new kind of person. You are a better kind of person. You are among the first of a new kind of human being."


"ALL YOU HAVE to do is believe," I tell you.

Between us, we hold Sissy's hands. We stand in the entrance to a Soho shop Magda Blue has been using. The windows are whitewashed out, the words "CLOSED FOR EXPANSION" scrawled into the white.

"Believe in what?" you ask.

I smile and push through the door.

And we are tumbling down a hillside, catching ourselves, coming to lie in a heap of tangled limbs.

Outside the shop, the snow had been blowing again.

Here, the sun is high, the sky blue. We lie on plush grass, sound of running water from nearby, somewhere in the band of oak trees to the left of us. Birds sing. In the distance, a red hot-air balloon hangs in the sky, over a cluster of thatched cottages.

"Magda Blue has a surprising tendency towards chocolate box kitsch," I say.

You are still looking all around.

"Forgive me," I tell you. "I thought you might appreciate a change of scenery, a picnic." I indicate further down the slope, where earlier I had spread a chequered cloth, held down by a wicker hamper.

You smile, and my heart lifts. You have been looking drawn, Priscilla. I have never repeated my warning about your husband – that clearly hadn't gone down well before – but life with such a strange construct of a man must be a strain, to say the least. I know you have been seeing less of him recently, that things are not right.

But I do not bring you here to seduce you. I have chased you before and I will not do so again.

We sit with the picnic, drink sparkling Vouvray, play games with Sissy. In my head we are so very far from London, and I hope it is the same for you.

I have not brought you here to seduce you, Priscilla. Really, I have not.

You sit back, leaning on your elbows, face tipped up to the sun. You seem so relaxed, so happy here.

So beautiful.

You open your eyes, catch me watching. I blush, look down.

Sissy comes running up, kisses you full on the mouth, then swings around and kisses me too, her little narrow lips smearing across my own, and my cheek.

She runs away giggling.

You are watching me, smirking, and suddenly we are both laughing.

We lean in towards each other, and suddenly our faces are close, and our eyes are locked and I can feel your breath on my cheek just as you must be able to feel my own. Our lips, so close, brushing against each other, touching, pressing. Teeth clash, tongues meet. Taste. Heat.

I pull away.

Or you do.

We pull away.

"I…" But I do not know what I had been going to say.

Our eyes are still locked, your expression hard to read, your cheeks flushed, eyes slightly shocked. Your tongue flicks across your lips.

I lean over, slide a hand behind your head, pull your face into mine, and kiss you long and deep.


"BUT HOW STABLE are they?" Huey demands. "We're talking pre-consensual reality shards here. Bell jar discords held together by a bunch of creatives who don't even understand what it is that they are doing."

Huey rows the boat. We are on a sea of mirror-flat water, clouds reflected in its silvered surface. Storybook islands dot the horizon, all crags and forest, conical mountains, little coves with white beaches.

I sit back, my straw boater tipped at a jaunty angle.

"Look around you," he says. "Look at it closely. It's paper-thin. It's like that Russian Tsar: every time he ventured out into the countryside a whole army of builders went before him, putting up false frontages on the buildings so that he thought he ruled a wealthy land full of beautiful buildings and happy people. This is someone playing with new toys, Noah. It's no solution to the Malthus wall."

"How goes progress with your ship to the stars?" I ask gently.

"That's altogether different," says Huey. "It is an achievable goal. We have demonstrated the principles. It will take time, but we will get there."

"No ship then?"

"Noah…"

"No laboratory demonstrations?"

"Noah, stop playing games with me. I'll leave you on one of these bloody film-set islands. How would you like that?"

I laugh. "I am not trying to set up invidious comparisons," I tell him. "But my point is this. You are doing

wonderful work: you have demonstrated something
revolutionary in principle. You are developing it further.
Magda and her team have demonstrated something revolutionary in principle, but it is in no way finished. Yes,
her reality shards are unstable discords at the moment,
but look around you! Like you, she hopes to discover
worlds. Do not judge this branch of the project until it
has been pursued as far as is possible. Magda is doing
wonderful work too."

"Bah," says Huey. "Maybe I leave you on one of
these flimsy islands anyway. How would you like that,
eh?"

JACK IS A different man again. Priscilla worries. Has he
sensed something? Something in her? Is he watching
her?

She sits across the table from him, as he downs his
espresso in one. They are at a small coffee shop on the
South Bank. Christmas lights festoon the place. It is that
time of year.

"We should do Christmas," says Jack. "Do it properly. Let's take off somewhere, Priss."

"What are you suggesting?" asks Priscilla, uncertainly. "You want us to fly to the North Pole? Lapland?
Since when have you ever wanted to visit Santa's grot-
to?"

He glances over Priscilla's shoulder then, looking
towards the terrace outside where Sissy is playing in the
snow. "We should do it for her. A Scottish castle,
maybe? Just the three of us."

Priscilla looks down. Jack is definitely different. He's
*trying*. And for the last week or so he's been especially
protective of Sissy for some reason. Maybe he thinks
that's a way to Priscilla's heart.

"Give me a chance, Priscilla. We've been together
through probably the biggest upheaval in any lifetime
ever – the establishment of the Accord. It's been a tough
time, but we've come through. Together."

He reaches a hand across the table, rests it on Priscilla's interlocked fingers. "We've got something, Priss. Let's give it a chance."

WE WATCH HER. We hurt. I hurt. I am more I than we now. I am the I that Priscilla can love, I am, in her eyes, the best of me. Chuckboy has laboured over this remix.

I am Priscilla's perfect man.

We watch her. We hurt.

She doesn't answer my question, my request. *Let's give it a chance*.

Have I really lost her again?

I remember killing her. Could I do that again? I feel it, deep in my gut, but I don't know if I have it in me. But what's the point? She'd be fucking back again. And so would he.

Why can she not see that she should love me and not him? This mix has not worked. It has not won her back and now I feel too fucking weak to even do anything about it.

I watch her. I hurt. So fucking deeply.

I look down, focus inwards, message Chuckboy: *Remix me again. Make me an instance who will actually fucking do something. Give me balls, Chuckboy. Make me bad*...

## 2.07

The Bentley is there in the drive. It is about half an hour after Lucy Chang left. We didn't want her here for this meeting. It is good that she works with us again, even if only on an occasional basis, but there are things she does not need to know.

We stand in the doorway of the cottage, watch the back door of the car open and Chuckboy Lee emerge. "Elector Burnham," he says, waving in our direction. Childish laughter follows him out, but we cannot see who has been riding in the back with him. We don't really care.

Then Chuckboy pauses, leans back towards the half-open door, says, "Hey baby. You wanna come see my friend?"

He swings the door wider and a small figure looks out. It takes a moment to recognise Sissy. She looks older, her face made-up and she's wearing a skinny vest top and a black miniskirt. "Hey, Chuckboy," she says, and it's not her voice, he's done something to it, lowered it, given it a boudoir growl.

We turn, lead him into the house, sit in the front room. Sissy has followed – Chuckboy's instance of Sissy. She sits with him on the sofa, her knees tucked up, leaning into him.

"You okay with her being here?" Chuckboy asks.

We shrug.

"Professor Barakh had problems with me," Chuckboy says. "He couldn't cope with who I am, even when I was being treated."

"You're not being treated now," we say.

Chuckboy puts a protective arm around his Sissy. "She is not complete," he says. "She is a shell, a plaything. I have edited her down, remixed her, made my own instance of her. She is happy. You can see that, can't you? And she has lots of friends back in Sunda Kelapa."

"You're a programmer, Chuckboy. It's just ones and zeroes isn't it?"

Chuckboy nods, smiles.

"Right now I'm interested in the zeroes," we say, leaning forward. "You say Professor Barakh had problems with you. I want him to have problems with *me*, Chuckboy. I want him to have big problems with me."

"THANK YOU, LUCY. Thank you very much."

Lucy Chang owes nobody any favours and she is not one to offer them liberally either. She is careful about that. She looks out for herself and no one else.

I have employed her as a consultant and informant, as have Elector Burnham and others. She is very professional.

So her call this afternoon has touched me deeply.

She fears for me, for us. Elector Burnham knows about us, my love. She is unsure how much he knows, but he knows enough for him to want to set Chuckboy Lee on me. She thinks he wants me dead. And if Chuckboy is involved then he must be thinking *long-term* dead.

I have no idea what he has in mind for you, Priscilla.

It is a Saturday. You would normally be in your North Downs cottage with your husband and Sissy, but not today. Lucy has just come from there, leaving Burnham waiting to meet Chuckboy.

Does he know about our meetings, I wonder? Almost certainly, if he has reached this stage.

That kiss in Magda's biscuit-box idyll, the picnic, Sissy giggling from further down the hill... Back in the London snow, walking slightly apart, suddenly shy, uncertain. The hug as we parted, pressure of body against body, so intense, despite the thick winter layers. The press of cheek to cheek, the scent of your hair.

Next day: lunch with you in that trattoria near the Bethnal Green centre. Avoiding the real subject by talking intensely about Magda's discords, about Huey's mathematical rocket-ship, about Sissy's unexpected flair for sculpture – her drawing is still at stick-figure level, but put modelling clay in her hands and the etiolated torsos and faces she produces are quite staggering.

It's in the eyes, though. Always in the eyes.

At the end of lunch, me saying, "Magda has other realities, works in progress."

Your eyebrow raised, your quick excited smile.

Our trips to Magda's other realities, twice more. We step through and the world lifts from our shoulders. We are otherwise.

You are mine, Priscilla. Mine again, just as I am yours.

This is an instance of you that is capable of crossing the line, of loving me.

But what to do about Burnham and Lee?

As I sit in my office, you message me. I ping the wallscreen and you appear there.

You look like shit.

Your face is wan, your eyes wide so that the whites show most of the way around the irises. You cannot hold yourself still, twitching and rearranging yourself.

"Noah?"

I nod. "What is it?" I am careful to remain neutral, in case there is anyone out of shot at your end, or any form of monitoring.

"It's Sissy... Noah, it's Sissy..."

Sissy was with Priscilla today. What could have happened?

"Sissy?"

Just then, I hear the child's voice, see Priscilla jerk sideways, then twist to lift Sissy into view.

"Sissy's fine... Sorry. This Sissy is fine."

I can see that. I am confused.

"But there's another one. One that's been with Chuckboy Lee..."

EARLIER...

Priscilla arrives home, having given up on her meeting with her old Oxford friend Roni Reader. They had barely hugged and ordered wine when Roni was messaged, went pale, went wide-eyed, gave a great big grin, and said, "He's dead! He's sodding well dead!" She hugged Priscilla hard, then added, "Oliver. Hubby. Married four years ago, tragically separated when my heart unexpectedly gave up the ghost two months ago. Oliver! Caught in a food riot in LA, shot dead – quick and clean apparently, wouldn't have felt a thing. Oh Priscilla, I'm sorry darling... would you mind?" Already Roni had been gathering up her bags, preparing to leave, to go and find her newly dead husband.

So Priscilla arrives home early, having picked up Sissy from her minder. There's a hog of a Bentley blocking the drive and she has to park in the lane, car crammed up into the hedge so she has to climb out the passenger side after Sissy, making it into a game, the two of them ending up in giggles in the middle of the narrow road.

She sees them through the front window of the living room, Jack talking to Chuckboy Lee. She takes Sissy's hand. She never has liked Lee. He gives her the creeps.

The Bentley's driver is playing a game on a screen stuck to the wheel. He glances at the two of them, then carries on playing.

They go inside, and Priscilla shoos Sissy upstairs to wash and change.

Lee and Jack have gone quiet in the front room. They know she's here; they must have heard her.

Priscilla stands in the doorway, looks in, sees...
Sissy...?

She looks back over her shoulder, then into the room
again.

"Sissy?"

The child responds to the name, but doesn't appear to
recognise Priscilla.

It's not Sissy. It can't be.

Her face is made up – not a child in clumsily daubed
make-up, this is professional make-up, sexy come-fuck-me
make-up. She wears a skinny black vest top, and now
Priscilla sees that the child has breasts budding there, adolescent breasts despite only being six years of age. She
looks back at Priscilla, any interest already having vanished. She rests her face back on Lee's arm, smiling a junkie
smile.

"What the fuck?"

Jack is on his feet, facing her. "It's a copy, a toy," he
says. "It's nothing."

"It's fucking *Sissy*," Priscilla says.

"It's happy," says Jack. "It knows when it has it
good."

She turns on him, her husband, the man she had
thought she knew so well. How could he blind himself
to this?

"You shit," she says, her voice low.

Then: "Sissy. Come here. We're leaving."

The girl just looks at her.

Lee is smiling. He looks at Jack and then at Priscilla.
"You want her?" he asks, all innocent. "Have her. She's
yours. Go, go." With this he pushes the girl to her feet,
propelling her across the room.

Reluctantly, the girl takes Priscilla's hand.

"Come on," says Priscilla. "We're getting out of here."
Then louder, she calls, "Sissy? Come down right now.
Change of plans. We're heading out of here. Right now."

Halfway down the stairs, Sissy stops, looks at the
other girl strangely, then at Priscilla.

Priscilla shrugs, says, "I'll explain. She's a new friend. Remember like our road trip to the mountains? A whole group of us? This is our new friend."

They head for the door, and just as they are stepping outside, Chuckboy Lee's words, spoken to Jack, drift out after them.

"It's okay," he says. "I have backups."

## 2.08

"I want him dead," we tell Chuckboy. "Properly dead. I want him so annihilated that there's no way at all he can be resurrected."

This does not phase Chuckboy. He sits there on the sofa with that quiet smile on his face. "There are ways," he says. "But I will need to prepare. I will need to prepare *you* if you're to be the one to do this?"

We nod.

"And in the meantime?"

"I'm going after him. After them. I may not be able to wipe him off the face of this world just yet, but I can sure as hell blow his fucking brains out."

"He'll be back."

"I know. And I'll be waiting."

Chuckboy still smiles. "You want remixing?" he asks. "More of the killer in you? I can do that."

We nod.

"And what about the electee?"

We hesitate. "I want Priscilla back," we tell him. "I want to make her mine. I want you to make her mine. Can you do that? Can you remix her too?"

Chuckboy hasn't finished smiling. He is clearly enjoying this.

Finally, he nods.

"You saw my Sissy," he says. "I can shape Priscilla Burnham into whatever you want, Mr Burnham. Just say the word and I will find her."

\* \* \*

THE CHILD IS an abomination, a gross hybrid between elements of Sissy and God knows what... elements of Chuckboy Lee's wettest of dreams. She is a hooker in a child's hormonally distorted body.

We meet at my Bethnal Green flat, you, Sissy and... we call her Sis. We don't really know what to call her.

You fall into my arms as I open the door, and I can feel your body trembling, intense physical convulsions.

You have spoken to me as you drove back from the cottage, and through your careful words, chosen with the overhearing children in mind, I know what an awful journey that was. How scared you are of what has been made of poor Sissy.

Over your shoulder, the scent of your hair filling me, I look at the two girls. Sissy's dark skin is far paler than I have seen it before, her eyes wide, wet. Sis is radiant, calm. She makes eyes at me. She wants to do the only thing she knows how to do, what Chuckboy Lee has made her for.

Even castrated to keep himself out of jail, back in the old world Lee had been erratic, unstable, untrustworthy, but at least this side of him had been suppressed. So many of the project team couldn't bear to work with him, though, despite his clear genius. He'd had to go.

But now there is nothing to stop him...

Apart from the protocols, and he appears to be working his way around them.

We leave them in the front room, retreat to my bedroom, sit on the edge of the bed, leaning into each other's arms, talking into the side of each other's heads.

"Jack is after us," I tell you. "He wants to get rid of me."

"Can he do that?"

"Lee could do it, I think."

You hold me tighter, your breath tracing lines across my jaw.

"It could get messy," I say. "You need to go somewhere safe. You need to take Sissy." At all costs you must be protected, my love. You are an instance of you that can love me, that does love me. I could not bear to lose you again.

"Me? What about you?"

"I am not going to hide. Not yet, at least. Chuckboy Lee must be stopped." He must be stopped for what he has done to Sissy – you told me during your journey that he had said he had backups of Sis – and he must be stopped for what he is offering Elector Burnham. He must be stopped from ever doing such things again. He is finding ways around the protocols, challenging consensus. Where Magda and Huey are building on consensus, taking its protocols to their logical conclusions, Chuckboy Lee is distorting them, forcing holes in them. He must be stopped.

"How?"

I think now of Sammy Zhang. I had promised him heaven, but cast him into hell. There is a protocol tweak I developed with Malky Warrener to deal with Sammy Zhang. It is not possible for us to intervene in a way that would erase someone completely from the system, so what we did was force Zhang into a perpetual loop after he died in the old world. He wakes in grey, finds his bearings, sees a door outlined in the grey, lets it scroll open and steps through... into grey, finds his bearings, sees a door, scroll, steps through... into grey... He is in a software loop, no sense of time or space, no scope for development, for memory, for experience to be absorbed: he simply *is*, and he becomes nothing more, a limited shell of the man he is, living forever in the present moment, stepping through doors into grey.

I need to kill Chuckboy Lee so that he can be cast into a Zhang loop.

And I hope to whatever gods we might create in this heaven of ours that Chuckboy Lee does not know how to do the same to me.

"How? I have an idea of what to do, but it is dangerous. You and the children must be safe. I will find you afterwards."

I will come to you, my love, this instance of you that is able to love me back.

THE DREAMS ARE the worst thing, the happy happy dreams.

We lie there at night, unable to sleep, memories of Priscilla in our head, and images of where she is now, what she might be doing now.

And eventually, we drift, we dream.

Just now, we were walking hand in hand with Priscilla through central London, the pavements packed with excited people, everyone happy, the atmosphere like some kind of carnival. We reached the Millennium Footbridge, moved closer, my arm coiled down across Priscilla's back, my hand on the curve of waist and hip. I could feel every movement of her body as we walked, every magnificent movement.

Halfway, we paused, turned to face each other, kiss. The gentlest of kisses, lips barely brushing against each other, eyes locked. So much smile in her eyes, so much happiness! More pressure, lips melding, tongues touching, bodies pressed hard.

We pulled away, we laughed, Priscilla buried her face in our shoulder, our chest. So in love. So happy.

Such a beautiful dream.

And then waking. Darkness. Alone. Breathing hard, heart pounding.

Alone.

Oh yes, the dreams are the worst thing, the happy fucking dreams.

PRISCILLA TAKES SISSY and Sis by the hand, leads them along a snowbound pavement. They are in a side street off Charing Cross Road, music shops and collectors' bookshops on either side.

Magda Blue awaits them in the doorway of a shop, the windows of which are whitewashed out. She looks about fifty today, but still clearly the Magda Priscilla has met previously at the Bethnal Green centre. She wears a long dark coat over her sari, a silver pashmina looped around her slender neck.

The two women hug. "Noah told me," says Magda. "Come with me, I'll get you started."

"Where we going?" asks Sissy, tugging at Priscilla's hand. The little girl is perceptive: she knows something is wrong; she has not been settled since Sis came into her life earlier today.

Magda turns to the door and pushes it open ahead of them.

Sis just stands at Priscilla's side, compliant. She does whatever she is told. She is happy. The only initiative she ever takes is that she likes physical contact, but always... always... a hug has to be given guardedly, as little hands search for more. Priscilla is reluctant to leave the two girls alone together at all. Back at Noah's flat, they had left the bedroom door open, so she could watch them over his shoulder. The intellectual and emotional contortions of Sissy and Sis are doing her head in.

They step through the door... and they are in another street, another time, another place.

Noise swirls around them, the clatter of carriage wheels on cobbles, of sellers of various wares in the street, of children chasing barking dogs. The sun is high in the sky and it feels like summer, the air redolent of sewers and rotting rubbish.

"Dickens?" Priscilla asks Magda – who she sees is now suitably attired for the occasion in a bustled, high-collared dress and a flat bonnet. "Austen?"

"Merchant Ivory," says Magda. "Hopper. Polanski. I don't do books..."

Priscilla and the girls are also dressed for the setting, Priscilla in an ornate bustled creation, with layers of skirt trimmed and folded back so that she feels like some kind of cake decoration; the girls wear matching pleated scarlet dresses, with long sleeves and deep white cuffs. Their black skin makes them stand out from those around them, but nobody comments, or even more than glances in their direction.

"Come on, girls," says Priscilla. "We're going on an adventure."

WE TRACK HIM down easily. He is on the run already – word must have reached him somehow. He hasn't covered his tracks well at all. He is at his Essex home. Does he think he can hide there? That we will not look there for him?

According to our contact in the national police, the navtrack records show him to have travelled there alone, only an hour ahead of us. Alone... has he abandoned Priscilla now that the chips are down? Or are they to meet somewhere later?

Either way, they make it easier by separating. Lee will find Priscilla, but Professor Noah Barakh is *ours*.

The last approach is along a narrow road that curves around the edge of a wide field of wet winter mud. To the left there are the open workings of a gravel quarry. Every so often, a side track leads off to a farm or cottage. Last time we were here, we were pursued on departure by camerazzi drones, after we'd had that meeting with Marie.

We see the cottage ahead, a wooden building, constructed in the Dutch barn style. There is only one way in or out – beyond the cottage, this road leads only to one more farm. We are looking at the angles, the cover. We are more killer than we were before. We have Chuckboy to thank for that. We are here for a purpose.

The cottage is set back from the track a short way along a gravel drive. A black VW Citi rests by the house, its boot open.

We pull up in the mouth of the drive, blocking off any escape.

We climb out, straighten ourselves, smooth down jumper, narrow skirt. We have other things to thank Chuckboy for too.

Patting the fuck-you Beretta in our shoulder bag, we approach the house, eyes flitting about, checking for movement, for indications of danger. The Citi's boot holds two bags and a bunch of paper files. He hasn't come back here to hide then, but rather to gather essentials before he flees.

The front door recognises us, opens at a push, and immediately we hear sounds from the back of the house – the room that overlooks the garden, we guess, where Marie and I had sipped tea and fought a duel of words that time, back when I was I and not we.

We come to stand in the doorway, see Barakh, his back turned, stooped over an open drawer.

And then he senses us, turns...

The look on his face: eyes spring wide, mouth opens, colour flees.

"*Marie?*" he says.

We raise an eyebrow.

"You're dead...?"

We take the Beretta from our bag, aim it, linger to see the expressions rushing over his face as he wonders what the fuck is going on here, and then fire. Once, twice in the face, and again into the chest.

Instead of crumpling to the ground... he looks down, then back up to us, to the us that Chuckboy Lee has chameled to look like Marie Barakh.

There are no entry wounds, no blood, no fading to pixels, to nothing.

We remember the beach, Deanmere Gap... the ghost-instance of Barakh we had encountered, Tate's hands passing through the apparition.

We step forward, swing the gun, handle first, right through Barakh's face. He doesn't even flinch.

"Marie?" he says again.

We turn, swing across the mantelpiece, knocking ornaments and pictures flying with the butt of the pistol. An oil painting of some bleak coastal marsh hangs above, a skein of geese almost lost in the mist; we pull it down, hurl it across the room.

Turning back to Barakh again, we say, "Where are you, Barakh? Where the hell are you?"

He looks quizzical now. "So... not Marie. Elector Burnham then?"

"I'll find you. I'll track you down."

"I dare say you will," says Barakh. "But right now I have business elsewhere."

## 2.09

"MR TATE," I say, dipping my head in greeting. "You come highly recommended."

He eyes me suspiciously.

We stand by the river, just east of Embankment station, by the red granite obelisk of Cleopatra's Needle.

Earlier, when we had met in meetspace, I said, "Mr Tate, please help me put right some of the wrongs of your former employer." I had shown him cam-streams of Chuckboy Lee and his entourage. "There are worse," I said, "if you need more substantive evidence. He is through and through an evil man. He is guiding Elector Burnham now, and their activities threaten the stability of the Accord itself. It is much more than the fate of these playthings of his that is at issue…"

Now, we eye each other cautiously.

"Where?" he says, finally.

"The Excelsior. Essex Street. About five minutes' walk from here. They have the top floor." *They…* Lee and his remixed child followers.

At Tate's pace, the walk takes less than five minutes.

We part company in the lobby, and I approach the desk. A white-bloused woman with short dark hair looks up at me, decides to smile, and says, "How may I help you?"

I smile back. "I wish to see Mr Lee. He is staying here. On the top floor, I believe."

She gives a slightly quizzical look, says, "Just let me call through. Are you expected?"

"I am not," I say, "but I am sure he would wish to see me. My name is Professor Noah Barakh and I have something important to give him."

I sit in a deep leather armchair, a tall fern in a cylindrical metal pot at my side. The receptionist finishes her call, smiles across at me, says, "You may go up, Professor Barakh. Room seven-o-three, floor seven."

I ride up in a wood-panelled elevator.

There is no one in the corridor, but a door is open into one of the suites. I enter, hear children laughing. A child's laughter has never been a disturbing sound to me. It is something I have come to love: to hear Sissy or Efan or any of the others losing themselves in the giggles, or belly-laughing at a joke or a prat-fall by one of the others. I associate it with barriers dropping, with returning to one's own childhood, with unreserved fun.

Now, here in Chuckboy Lee's suite, the sound of a laughing child fills me with dread. How many copies does he have of Sis? How many others are there?

He stands by the window, a larger figure than in his project days. He stands naked from the waist up, dragon tattoos across his back, long ponytail hanging down. A child leans into his side, a little girl in only vest and pants. His right hand idly plays with her hair.

"Professor Barakh," he says, without turning. "Tell me, have you come to kill me?"

Now he turns, smiling broadly. He gestures at the girl to leave him, and she heads off in the direction of the laughter coming from one of the other rooms.

"I've known you a long time, Chuckboy," I say, "but I never thought you were capable of this."

He tips his head. "This? You mean my toys? There is nothing wrong in what I do here, Professor Barakh. This is a new world, as you always told us it would be. We need to develop new rules, new moralities to fit our new mode of existence. My toys, they are just software, remixes, edited and shaped to suit my desires. They are not the people they were derived from. They are not even people. They are just things, objects with behaviour routines, response patterns. Nothing more."

I shake my head. I know from before that there is no point trying to reason with Chuckboy. We extracted good work from him for a time in the project, but only when it coincided with his own pursuits in VI.

"You didn't answer my question: have you come here to kill me?"

He spreads his arms, as if inviting his fate.

"Did you think it would be that easy?" he continued. "That I would not be prepared for such a confrontation? That I would not expect you to rush in like this, full of moral indignation? But really, I am not sure which offends you more: my toys, or my manipulation of your beloved protocols."

I make as if to move, but... cannot.

My body is frozen, muscles locked. I cannot turn my head. Only my eyes move, my eyelids as I blink, my lungs as they expand and contract.

"So," he says, approaching me, leaning into me so that his face is only a short distance from mine and I can feel his breath, "how are you going to do it? You going to blow hard? You going to use the power of thought alone?"

His questions must be rhetorical: I cannot answer, as my jaw is frozen shut.

"Ah... you wish to speak?"

I feel a relaxation of face and throat. I lick my lips, swallow. "You appear to have me at your mercy," I say.

He smiles, opens his mouth to speak, and the bullet takes him through the temple.

Blood sprays across my face, but I cannot flinch away, cannot react.

Chuckboy Lee crumples onto the carpet, and almost instantly starts to pixelate, to dissipate, and then is gone.

"Job done," says Tate from somewhere to my right. "He really dead?"

"Yes," I say. "It is permanent. He cannot be reborn. I have made it so." I look at the space where moments ago Chuckboy Lee had fallen. Even the bloodstain has pixelated, gone. I feel... I realise I don't really know what I feel. Relief, perhaps. Something more, though. Something indefinable.

Tate shrugs, looks around, says, "Now what do we do about all these poor sodding kids?"

I cannot turn, cannot see him.

"Eh?" he says. He strolls into view. My eyes turn towards him, but my head remains locked forwards.

"I... I appear to be unable to move," I tell him.

He stops, squints at me. "What do you mean?"

"Lee imposed some kind of lock on me before he died. It has not worn off even though he is dead."

"So what do we do now?"

"I think you may have to kill me, so that I may be reborn..."

Tate shrugs and raises his pistol. I see a slight twitch as his trigger finger tightens.


DRIVING BACK FROM Barakh's Essex home we feel it first as a stab of pain, deep in our skull, and then... explosion, mayhem, deep intense agony, rage, eruption, fire, fire, *fire*.

Our left hand drags the wheel hard down and we run up the embankment of the A12, the car's safety over-rides kick in, slowing, steering, bringing us to a halt.

Blackness clouds our vision and we pray for uncon-sciousness but it doesn't arrive to save us.

Instead: deep, burning pain.

And our head, filled with sound, with a voice, a scream.

A presence.

A being.

Chuckboy Lee.

Here, in our head.

In *us*. In *we*.

We will not let him take us over. We cannot. He is repulsive. He cannot be in here.

He is not going to take us over. He has no wish to. He is us. He is here.

Barakh set a trap for him, somehow prevented him from being reborn when he died. Some twist of the protocols.

But we were prepared for that. We were smart enough never to underrate the Professor.

We had an escape route, a backup.

We are here. We are us. We have no wish to take over when together we can achieve so much.

That is not the way of things. We are a new kind of human being. We are remixed, reblended. We are something new altogether.

We *are*.

We straighten in the driving seat, look around.

We are Elector Jack Burnham. We are Chuckboy Lee. We are Bartie Davits and countless other fragments of human and VI. We are new.

And we are going to destroy Professor Noah Barakh.

I WAKE TO grey. I am a new instance of me, a subtly new mix, the most *me* me the protocols can shape from my stored memories, responses, behaviours. This is how it goes, and this process becomes increasingly important as we live longer, acquire too many memories for a single head to hold. This is why it is so important to protect you, Priscilla, the instance of you that can love me. I cannot let you die, and come back as a you who has forgotten how to love me...

I sit, stand, find a door. Hesitate.

Panic suddenly grips my guts.

I think of Chuckboy Lee, forever trapped in the same kind of loop as Sammy Zhang. Waking, stepping through, waking, stepping through. Trapped forever in the now.

I am scared to approach the door, trigger it to scroll open.

Is this my now?

I swallow, step forward. The door scrolls and I step out into my Essex home.

It is a mess. I step through scattered debris. Burnham, I suspect, after his pursuit of me failed.

I need to go to Priscilla. *My* Priscilla. I need to make sure she is okay.

We will tackle Elector Burnham later.


IT TOOK ME five days to re-emerge this time. We always thought that a lag would develop between death and rebirth, and this appears to be happening.

Now, I see Magda Blue in the street, waiting for me outside her central London workplace.

The side street is narrow, crammed with dark shops, the cobbled surface slick with rain.

I hug Magda in greeting, press cheeks.

"They are here?" I ask her, and she nods.

She opens the door and we both step through into one of her realities. Victorian England, central London, a bustle of carriages and street-hawkers and people hurrying to and fro. It is good. A pastiche, admittedly, but good. Study the people too closely and you can see that they are constructs, like my old Dylan Thomas. These characters have no lives, no roles other than to populate the streets of this world. The detail is missing in places, Magda's brushstrokes visible where they should not show. But even so, it is good. She really is a genius of the order of Huey Kashvili and Malky Warrener and, dare I say it, Chuckboy Lee.

"Where are they?" I ask Magda, noting that she is now in a dark high-collared outfit. I glance down, see that I am smartly attired in a broad-collared frock coat, over a maroon vest, dark grey pantaloons with a black stripe down the side, a silk top hat, and black doeskin gloves.

"Priscilla said she wanted to take them on a road trip. They have a carriage and a driver, heading south. She said you'd know where they were heading."

I smile. I think I know.

"Thank you, Magda. Thank you so much." I straighten, check in my vest pocket to make sure that I have money. "I think it is time for a trip to the sea." I will take the steam train from Victoria, and I will probably get there before them.

I am smiling.

It feels like forever since I have smiled like this.

THEY STROLL ALONG the seafront, paved promenade butted right up against the stacked shingle of the beach, a row of high hotels flanking the road to the other side. In so many ways, this looks like the Eastbourne Priscilla knows from childhood, with many of the same buildings, the beach, the promenade. But no, there are obvious physical differences – the pier ahead of them only exists as a row of piles driven into the beach and seabed, only a few years into its construction; horses and carriages ply the uneven road. More than that, though, there is a sense of *expectancy*. This is a town on the up, a growing town, a place that has been opened up in recent years by the arrival of the railway, by better links with London and Brighton. This is a young resort, not a genteel town of slow decline.

They stroll along the seafront, Priscilla and the two black children, one to either hand; one girl is wary, suspicious, the other affectionate, clinging, far too adult in the eye and the walk.

Others pass, gents in top hats and tailed coats or square-cut frock coats, ladies in bustled skirts and big-collared tops. Out on the beach, a row of bathing huts lines up, others pulled out into the waves so that bathers can step straight into the water.

There is something about this world, something not quite right yet. It is the difference between pre-consensus and the full Accord, Priscilla realises; between high-tech gaming worlds or meetspaces and that whole new fucking *world* that Noah had built for them all. She is so much in awe of him sometimes. Of his achievements. That's one of the barriers between them, one of the layers they have started to chip away at, now that they are... What *are* they? Lovers. They are certainly lovers. Lovers whose every move seems choreographed, scripted, perfectly tuned. But there is more than that... That whole paradigm shift thing. That feeling of her world suddenly skipping just a bit to the side as she realised that this was a man she really wanted to be with, to explore with. She sees the world differently now. She sees it as part of an us, a meshing, a deep mixing of identities. She and Noah are a we: that is what they are. She sees the world in terms of us and we, not I and me.

"Come on," says Priscilla, feeling the need to force some fun into the day. "Let's go and paddle!"

She turns, starts to run across the shingle, her progress slow as the stones slide and give beneath her feet. The girls lag behind, slow to pick up her mood. She releases their hands, keeps running, has to keep running, suddenly feeling that this is so vital to her existence, she has to do it, has to be free...

She picks up her skirts and runs into the water, prim lace-up boots and all. She doesn't care. She doesn't fucking care.

Her skirts are wet and she lets them drop again, float in the rushing water. People look at her, curious, but she really doesn't fucking care. She tips her face up to the sun, lets it soak into her skin, feels its energy.

She senses a presence at her side, looks down. It's Sis. She's standing in the water, kicking at the waves as if she's never seen the sea before in her life. She probably hasn't, Priscilla realises.

Priscilla reaches down, chucks the kid's cheek. Sis looks up, smiles, a spark of something different in her eyes, something new. Her smile is real, pure. Priscilla picks the girl up, swings her so that her feet scoot through the waves. Sis squeals with delight, and begs her to do it again.

She swings again, depositing the girl in the waves, laughing as the child just about manages to stay on her feet. She turns, sees Sissy standing at the water's edge, uncertain.

"Come on," Priscilla says softly. "Come into the water." She holds out her hands.

Sissy looks at her, eyes big, glistening. And then she steps into the water, one foot, both. A wave rushes up, swirls around her ankles and she squeaks at the sudden chill. Then she looks up at Priscilla again, grins, and dashes after the retreating wave, into Priscilla's arms, her own arms wrapped tight around Priscilla's neck, her legs around Priscilla's waist. Hugging like she will never let go.

"Come on," says Priscilla. "We're going *deeper*!"

She takes a big step, then another. Soon the water is halfway up her thighs and Sissy is yelling "No! No!" as the waves surge up her legs too.

"Hold your breath!" Priscilla cries, then sits back in the water.

She surfaces, stands, and sees Sissy staggering back through the water, shrilling with laughter… chasing… she's chasing Sis, who runs, slow-motion through the waves. They come together, Sissy's hand on her ur-sibling's shoulder, and they tumble into the water. They emerge, laughing, splashing at each other, hurling great big two-handed scoops of water.

Priscilla walks up and out of the waves, slumps onto the beach, savours the clash between the chill of the water and the warmth of the sun. She watches the two girls.

It's been so hard.

So fucking hard.

# 2.10

WE WILL DESTROY him. We will track him down and annihilate him.

But not yet. Not quite yet.

We sit in our suite at the Excelsior, Ruby and Jian cuddled into our side on the calfskin sofa. Professor Noah Barakh appears to have disappeared off the face of the Earth. We have bots after him, seeking him out. And when he has been located we will go after him.

Until then... We sit with Ruby and Jian, pull them in close to us. It's all about contact. Trust and contact. The girls are happy. We see that, understand it. And we know that if they should ever become unhappy with their situation they can be remixed, repaired.

We are content with the thought that Barakh will be gone soon.

It's like we were taught at school: each breath we take contains at least one atom of Leonardo da Vinci's last breath – he, and everything he has touched, is all around us, but so dissipated. We breathe him in, we breathe him out, but try as we might we could never rebuild the fucker... That's what we're going to do with Barakh: when we're done with him he's going to be spread so far and thin that no protocol imaginable could reconstruct him. We are going to destroy him, bit by indivisible bit.

Right now, though, we settle back into the sofa, enjoy being a new kind of person in a new kind of world, and wait.

I FEEL MY responsibilities, I really do. They are never far from my thoughts.

I am the architect of Accord, the man who built heaven. This is the world of consensus, but that consensus is built on protocols crafted by me and the teams I led. There is so much at stake here: this world is what we have. All we know of the old world now is what new arrivals tell us, that there are ever-increasing tragedies unfolding. Plagues, floods, famines, wars... all visited on the world we have left behind.

This is *it*.

I have set Huey and Magda and others on seeking solutions to the impending crises here in the Accord. We must overcome the Malthus wall somehow. I have every confidence that they will find a way forward. I really do not have to be on hand all of the time.

And so I am here, sitting in a first-class carriage on the London, Brighton and South Coast Railway service to Eastbourne, top hat resting on my knees. I watch the scenery rushing by, the steam and smoke from the locomotive billowing past the window every so often. I can smell it, the soot and smoke. It's a peculiarly nostalgic smell, for an era I have never until now experienced.

You told Magda I would know where you were going. It has to be Eastbourne, or your childhood home at Deanmere Gap. I have been to both of these places, but never with you, my love. We promised this visit to each other long ago, many worlds and lives ago. You have to be there, waiting.

The train eases into the station, and I stand at the carriage door, waiting for us to pull to a halt. I see wide-open platforms, a red-brick building with ornate canopies over the windows. Passengers wait; a porter hauls two large cases after a smartly dressed couple, the

man all whiskers and dark coat, the woman deeply bustled, cloche-hatted, coughing with a deep, phlegmy TB
hack.

I step out, look around to get my bearings. A part of
me expects to see you waiting here with the girls, to
know that I am due. But no. You are not here. I pass
through the station building, emerge in the street.

The road has a new asphalt surface, glistening darkly
in the afternoon sun. A few carriages pass by, carrying
passengers to and from the trains. A man in filthy, torn
clothes and a bowler hat sweeps the pavement.

I look around. I am here. I believe that you are here
too, Priscilla.

But how do I find you?

I try to ping you, but Magda's world is authentic:
there is no signal, no net.

I walk towards the seafront. You will be there now, or
you will go there at some point. You are the girl who
used to dream of being a mermaid. You cannot resist the
sea.

I cling to that. It gives me hope, amid the sudden
uncertainty that grabbed my gut when I emerged from
the station building.


PRISCILLA, SISSY, AND Sis lie on the shingle.

The girls are on their backs, limbs starfished. Priscilla
is curled on her side, luxuriating in the warmth of the
sun, and of the stones beneath her. She can breathe the
iodine and salt smell of the sea deep, hear the gulls cry,
some barrel organ music from along the prom, the occasional murmur or call of human voice as passers-by pass
by.

She has a little pile of stones before her. She has been
picking out the distinctive blue-grey ones, gathering
them together. Great drifts of these pebbles form the
beach at Deanmere Gap.

Sis has her head turned to the side, watching
Priscilla.

Priscilla smiles, remembering the sheer joy on the child's face when they had played in the waves earlier. That was the first time she had seen Sis let go, seen the child in her.

Sis turns onto her side now, facing Priscilla.

"You okay, babe?" Priscilla asks her. "Dried out now?" Her own clothes still cling, dry in places. It's not an unpleasant feeling, although she knows that if they walk any distance right now the saltwater dampness of these heavy clothes is bound to chafe.

Sis just stares.

Priscilla finds another stone, stretches for it. It's a bullet-shaped pebble, like those fossils you sometimes find. Belemnites. She looks closely. It isn't a fossil, just a stone. She adds it to the pile.

And catches Sis's eye.

The child has something different in her look, her stare. It's not the adult look she so commonly affects; it's... distant. Priscilla wonders what's in her mind. Memories? What horrors must be there...? But does she even *see* them as horrors? Has she been changed so much?

Sis sits, knees pulled up to her chin. She smiles.

"Priscilla," she says.

Her voice is different, a kind of sing-song voice, like an adult pretending to be a child. Priscilla shakes herself, an involuntary shudder. A gull screeches overhead and the sound appears magnified, cutting through her.

"What? What is it, Sis?"

The child leans forward on her hands, body twisting. Beyond her, Sissy has turned, is watching. She senses it too. This thing. This difference.

"Your husband wants you back," says Sis.

The child's skin colour is fading, is taking on a pale olive hue. Her hair is straightening, pulled back from her face instead of stacked in an unruly afro. Her body is bulking out.

The voice: Chuckboy Lee!

Priscilla stares.

She opens her mouth, but cannot remember how to speak. She is intensely aware of her heartbeat, of a sudden prickly flush to her skin.

Sis leans further forward until she is about to topple over.

"I..." Priscilla manages to make a sound, but then hesitates, trying to think. "I don't want to go back to him," she says, finally.

"You will," says Sis. And then she smiles.

And she leans, somehow not toppling forward. The world around the two of them seems distorted, twisting to accommodate this surreal leaning approach. Priscilla feels as if she is looking at everything through uneven glass that moves, making the bulges and narrowings and distortions change continuously. It is the world that is doing this. A bubble of this world, this sub-reality that Magda has built... a twist in its fabric, wrapping Priscilla and Sis – whatever Sis actually *is*.

The child falls into Priscilla, in a twisting swirl of darkness. Priscilla feels the fabric of her body rending, being pulled apart, flowing, flowing somewhere. Elsewhere. Otherwhere.

She feels Chuckboy Lee's soul just then, and she does not like it.

IT'S GETTING DARK. Where are you, my love?

How do I find you in this world of Magda's? Without the net I am lost...

I have tried asking people, but that was a waste of time. These people of Magda's are convincing enough as extras, but they are really only part of the scenery.

"Excuse me," I tried saying to a frock-coated gent passing me on the pavement, halfway between station and seafront. He smiled, touching the brim of his top hat. "Would you, by any chance, have seen a young lady accompanying two small black girls? Erm... African children. Negroes."

The man smiled again, and looked blank. I realised then that it isn't just a matter of terminology: these simulacra are only capable of fulfilling their function and no more. I could as much engage this man in conversation as I could a horse or a street pigeon. And even if I could, the man would have no memory.

I turned away, resuming my walk. And immediately felt guilty for terminating the exchange so abruptly. I stopped and looked back, but the man was already walking away.

I headed for the beach, wondering why I should feel guilty for being rude to a mere prop.

Now, I stand on Royal Parade. The evening is damp, drizzly, the rain swirling like mist where it is illuminated by gas lamps.

Where are you, my love?

There is little point looking further tonight. I will choose one of the hotels that line the seafront, take a room and a meal, see what Victorian hospitality can offer me.


PRISCILLA WAKES TO grey. She feels as if she has been put through a mangle. Every part of her body hurts. It should not be this way; it never has before. She remembers the beach, the girls. Remembers some kind of upheaval, a twisting darkness. Something peculiar.

She doesn't understand, decides not to let it bother her. She wonders then about Sissy, about how the child will cope without her. Again, she tries not to let it bother her: Sissy is capable; she'll be okay.

Right now... Priscilla lies in grey and she hurts.

She sits, stretches her legs and arms one by one, teasing out the aches.

There is one ache that she can't reach like this, a deep one. An ache in her heart. She feels like some fucking teenager with a new pash. She smiles, feels silly.

She stands and a door limns its outline from the grey. She moves forward, steps through the opening door, emerges in her room in their North Downs cottage.

Rain beats at the window, angled rods of water. The sky is dark and heavy, the sun a mere silver patch. She hears music from downstairs. Wagner. Jack is home. She feels a rush in her chest. Wonders why just the thought of him still does this to her.

She looks down. She's in jeans and a peach T-shirt, baggy, untucked. She runs a hand down her body.

She heads downstairs.

In the doorway to the front room she pauses. He's sitting on the sofa, glass of scotch in one hand. He's seen her – he saw her the moment she appeared.

She walks towards him, stands before him, hands on hips.

"Jack," she says softly, her words almost lost to *Tristan und Isolde*.

She reaches down, takes a hold of his shirt at the throat, leans down as she pulls him forward. The kiss is like a first kiss, for all the rush, the intensity, the meaning packed into it; it's like the kiss of old lovers, too, tongues probing, teeth dragging on lips, easing seamlessly from tender, delicate, to hands-round-the-head intense hunger and need. She straddles him, presses, feels her body swallowed up in sensation.

The ache... the ache is slowly transforming into a different kind of ache altogether.


WE HAVE HER back, truly back. We slump on the sofa, hot limbs entangled, moist skin pressed, her head resting on our chest so that we cannot quite see her face.

"So... Eastbourne," we say, pausing to kiss the top of her head, breathe in her scent.

"Hmmm?" she says lazily. She's plucking at the hairs on our chest, teasing, one long leg pulled up across our midriff. Outside, the rain drums on the window.

"He was there, wasn't he?"

"Noah?"

She seems able to talk about Noah. She acknowledges that he was an aberration. She doesn't really seem to understand it.

"Yes, Noah."

"No..." She shifts, thigh pressing against our crotch. "No, he wasn't. He hadn't joined us by then. We left a message with Magda Blue, but he hadn't joined us."

She has her fingers flat on our chest now, woven through the hair. She closes them, pulls until we gasp, starts to caress a nipple with her thumb.

We will find him. And we will destroy him. We are ready.

## 2.11

THE MORNING IS fine, the sky a thin, watery blue fading to misty grey on the horizon.

I walk the length of the seafront, well past the piles for the new pier, and then back towards Pevensey Bay. My stiff leather shoes wear into my heel, and across the top of my toes, and soon I blister.

No sign of you. I wonder if I have arrived in advance – I did, after all, come by train, while you travelled by carriage. I am content to wait. This instance of you loves me. I will wait as long as it takes. And Sissy… she is, in every sense that matters, our daughter. We have been through so much together, through several lives, even.

I wonder about Elector Burnham, about his vendetta against me. Sometimes it does not seem real, but at others it seems almost too real and I look at everyone around me with suspicion. How am I to know that this scruffy urchin chasing carriages in the street isn't actually a cleverly crafted assassin built by Chuckboy Lee for Burnham to send after me? Or this elegant young lady in pleated, layered skirts that pinch at her waist, with the wide-brimmed hat laden with flowers and ribbons? She could be a bot, programmed to track me down, approach me, take me in her embrace, and dissolve me into nothing. Is the fact that her expression barely changes and even sometimes pixelates to pure anonymity a sign that she is a bot, or merely an artefact of the rudimentary characters with which Magda has populated her reality?

It would be so easy to become swamped in an existential crisis of paranoid delusion. This world of ghosts and caricatures is the ultimate in solipsism. In this world, no one else *is*. Or, at least, real people are so widely scattered that it is as if I am alone.

But I am not. You are here, my love; you and the girls.

I walk, passing the low, squat fortress of the Redoubt to my right. Rejoining Royal Parade, I note that there are bathers in the water now. I might find somewhere to sit, enjoy the air, rest my blistered heels and toes.

And then I see a small figure, standing at the edge of the water, watching the waves. She wears a pleated scarlet dress, with white cuffs that fold almost halfway back up her arm.

Sissy.

Or Sis?

I scan the beach, but there is no sign of you and the other child.

One of the girls on her own? I fight down the panic, the fear. If one child has gone off on her own, it is most likely Sis – maybe she has fled? In that case you cannot be far away.

I approach her across the shingle. Why am I so aware of my blisters at a time like this? Why does that discomfort cloud my thoughts?

Drawing closer, I see that her clothes are dishevelled, the white cuffs stained, grubby. She looks like a little rich girl who has been sleeping rough. I wonder for how long?

She only notices me at the last moment, as I come to stand a couple of paces away. She must have heard something and so she turns her head, sees me, gasps, runs straight at me. Two steps and I am wrapped in her arms, the top of her head against my ribs, her body wracked with sobs that have suddenly burst out from nowhere.

"Sissy, Sissy," I say, holding her to me, letting her sobs work their way out. I know it is Sissy. I knew as soon as she turned. "What has happened?"

She cannot speak.

After a time, I disentangle myself, take her hand, and lead her further up the beach where we sit side by side, staring out to sea. Sissy has each hand bunched into a fist, as if she is holding something. We remain like that for some time. I am scared to say anything, to ask anything. I am scared of the answers.

Priscilla... why are you not here?

Finally: "What happened?" I rest my hand on her back, between the shoulder blades, can feel the half-sobbing gasps for air she takes even now.

She doesn't look up, just mumbles towards the ground: "Cilla... And Sis... We were just here on the beach. Playing and like. We got all wet in the water and come up here to dry out." She pauses, gives a great big sob, wipes her face on her grubby sleeve.

"When was this?"

"Yesterday." Now Sissy opens her hands, palms up. In each she holds a couple of blue-grey stones. "Cilla had these. She liked them."

"They're lovely," I tell her.

"I was watching her with them. Then Sis... she changed. I was looking at them and they *bent*, kind of. Cilla and Sis."

"Bent?"

Sissy nods. "They changed shape. Like looking at you in water."

Chuckboy Lee? This sounds like one of his tricks. But he is gone from here. I made sure of that...

"What happened next?"

"Don't know." She goes silent now, and I let it stretch. Eventually, she says, "I couldn't see. Couldn't look at it. It didn't look... real."

"Where are they now?"

Sissy shrugs, says nothing. I can feel the tension still in her small body. I draw her close, and she starts to cry again.

I don't know what to do, other than hold her and let her cry. I have no children of my own. Ice cream? Candyfloss? Do they even have such things here?

Instead, I hold her, let her cry.

We grin. We feel consensus struggling all around us. The protocols don't like us, they don't like what we're doing, what we are. They don't like that we are not a discreet individual, a neat representation of the previous phase of humankind, to be conservatively perpetuated for ever and ever in this new reality. They don't like that we are different, that we push the rules, that we want to see what we can really be. They don't like that we have bits of Magda Blue split and scattered around this room and yet we are keeping her alive so that she can feel the pain, so that she can understand the horror of her new reality. That really does break all the rules...

"Magda." We talk to her face. It is mounted on a wooden block at head height on the wall, at just the right angle so she can see her torso on the nearby operating slab. A subordinate instance of us works there, carefully peeling back skin from bare abdomen. Through its eyes we can see our hands at work, so careful, so meticulous.

Back through our own eyes, we study Magda the reality hacker, the *artist* who thinks she can save the world.

She stares back. She is clearly made of stern stuff, but her eyes water. She can feel the pain. We have made sure of that.

"Where is he?" we ask again. "Where is he in your little world? Where is he hiding?"

She says nothing. She has said nothing all day. It is good that we are patient. That is more a Chuckboy quality than a Jack.

We smile at her again. And over at the slab, we work lower.

WE HAVE TRAVELLED up from Eastbourne on the train. Sissy loved the steam, wasn't at all disturbed by the roar and hiss and scream of the engine. She stood at the window for most of the journey, or perched on her seat, leaning forward, watching the world rush past.

And now, we are back in Victorian London, walking up Charing Cross Road, looking out for the side street where we last saw Magda Blue.

All the time, I wonder what I have got myself into. I am a scientist, a conceptualiser, a goddamned *bureaucrat*. Yet here I am, locum-parent to an orphan, pursued by the most powerful man in the world, who wants me dead, and still heading back in search of the woman I love. This is not the life I would choose.

Yet... how could it be any different? How could I not come after you, Priscilla? I would change anything in my life if I could only be with you.

I recognise the apothecary on the corner and we turn into the little cobbled street. The shop is on the right, its tiny windows dark, revealing nothing. We approach.

My hand on the door, I smile down at Sissy. "We're going back now," I tell her. "We'll find Priscilla."

I squeeze her hand and push on the door. It gives inwards. I start to step inside, but as the door opens I am assaulted by sound, light, heat. I raise my arm to shield my face, falling back, using my other arm to half-push, half-wave Sissy to safety.

The door thuds shut, and I look at it from where I now sit on the ground. I raise my hand – it is scorched. My ears still scream from the aural onslaught, even though it ceased as soon as the door closed.

I stand, shield my face with a coated arm, uncatch the door and then push at it with the toe of my shoe.

Screaming, heat, light.

I step back.

We are trapped. Someone has closed off Magda's portal between realities.


IT HAS COME to this...

Some time in the dark of the night I stand in the small room I share with Sissy. She is curled up on her side in the bed, hands clenched and tucked up against her face.

In the angled moonlight, she is a dark shadow against white bed linen, a deep pool.

I stand. I hold the down-filled pillow in both hands. I tremble, and tears run down my face.

I step forward and hold the pillow above Sissy for a moment, then lower it, press. Even as she starts to struggle: press.

Eventually her struggles cease, but still I hold the pillow down. Still I cry.

I feel the pillow suddenly slump under my weight, open my eyes, and see that she is gone.

I straighten, turn to the door.

This hotel is five storeys high. That should be enough.


PRISCILLA IS HAPPY. She is very happy. In fact, she cannot recall being as happy as this before. Ever.

She is at work at Westminster, messaging people all over the world to make sure the researchers on Huey Kashvili's interstitial ship programme are properly coordinated. They are having their first international conference in two weeks' time, and Priscilla is the principal organiser. It's a big event, and many of the collaborators are similar in temperament to Huey. It is a bit like herding cats.

The programme is going well. If engineering work follows at the rate of the conceptual breakthroughs they have been making then they might have the first interstitial exploratory ship ready within ten years or so.

But it is not her work that makes Priscilla happy, although that contributes to her general sense of well-being.

It is life. This life.

Jack is different, or she sees him differently now.

She leaves the office, heads through the corridors of power, joins him out on the terrace overlooking the Thames.

She steps straight into his arms and kisses him on the mouth, briefly enough for the sake of decorum, lingering long enough for the sake of promise.

He keeps an arm hooked round her waist as he says, "Priss, here, meet Nigel Couper, our man in Lagos."

She accepts his kiss on her right cheek, smiles. She knows the name. He is the man coordinating the Recolonise Africa programme on behalf of the League of Nations. She has argued with Jack about the ethics of the combination of incentivised emigration and forced repatriation of first generation immigrants. It seems so *wrong* to her, but somehow she can't fight him for long. It's just not in her nature.

"We were just talking about the need to arm the people we send down there. It's like the Wild West – people expect to feel safe. Mr Couper has contacts. We think we can kit these people out."

Priscilla nods, the words not meaning much to her. She knows they should. But they do not. She's not ready for another fight. Not now. Instead, she leans her head on Jack's shoulder. She is happy. She is very happy. In fact, she cannot recall being as happy as this before. Ever.

# 2.12

I WAKE, OPEN my eyes. All is grey.

A door.

I step through.

Sissy sees me, her face breaks out into a great big beam, and she runs to me around the end of the iron-framed bed. I hold her, and try not to let my frustration show.

We are in the same hotel room.

We are still trapped in Magda Blue's Victorian reality. For all I know, we two are the only real people here.

Has Burnham won then? Is this how Chuckboy Lee had proposed to remove me from the Accord?

They've suckered me here, and snatched Priscilla away to God knows what awful fate.

I feel sick.

I hold Sissy. The child I killed last night. Hold her tight.

I'm all she has. She's all I have. She really is all I have.

SUCH A FATE is far worse than Sammy Zhang's. For him it is the eternal present, no memory, no understanding that he is in a loop.

But here... we will live forever among simulacra who cannot change, cannot learn, cannot interact. We will both go mad. And even then, there will be no escape.

We walk along the seafront to where they are building the pier, just three heavy piles driven into the beach.

It is high tide, and waves lap around the columns. The workers appear to have taken a break while the water is high, and only one man sits on a pile of heavy lumber, eyes glazed, not quite focused on the world going by.

I wonder if this is how it will always be: the pier barely started, no progress, a freeze-frame instance of Victorian Eastbourne. Or does Magda's reality allow for development, for advancement? I fear the former... for how can the superficial simulacra that populate this place ever have scope for progress?

We really will go mad in this place.

Later, I sit on the beach while Sissy throws stones into the waves.

I look towards the horizon, where blue fades seamlessly into grey.

This is not a complete world. It is not a consensus, a fully agreed reality, for there is no one here to agree it. This is *Magda*'s world, her construction. It is a limited entity.

I wonder how big it is, where its boundaries lie, what they consist of. I wonder... What interesting phenomena there may be where this reality falters... Might its containing reality reassert itself in some way? Might there be a way out?

It is certainly worthy of investigation. We have plenty of time for a little road trip, after all.

I let Sissy play, though. It is lovely to see her relaxed like this. She has been through a lot. And I try to banish any thoughts of the night before. It had been a potential route that was certainly worthy of investigation. My actions were the product of careful reasoning.

I blank it out. I have to blank it out.

I sit and watch her play.

I am not crying.

I am not.

\* \* \*

WE SIT WITH Ruby and Jian, finding comfort in the contact. Our eyes are closed so that we might concentrate fully on the feed.

We find a node, focus, and a world forms around us. We stand in a street, somewhere in Eastbourne, look around. The street is busy, full of people and carriages. An adolescent boy in top hat and tailed coat whistles loudly, the same refrain over and over. A woman in some kind of maid's outfit argues with a man selling meat from a handcart. We study every one of them, but Barakh is not here.

We shift, find another node. We stand on the seafront, shingle beach to our right, row of hotels to our left. Bathers are out in the water; others sit on the beach, or stroll along the promenade. Nothing.

We carry on looking. We will find him.

This reality of Magda Blue's only covers parts of London, the railway, and the immediate area around Eastbourne. He cannot have gone far.

THE ROAD CLIMBS up out of Eastbourne, soon becoming little more than a dirt track. Sissy and I sit in the carriage. Sissy loves it. She was so excited by the horse, and then by the carriage and realising that we were going to travel in it. She had ridden in a carriage like this with Priscilla and Sis...

Now, she leans against the window, peering out, yelling every time she sees the sea.

We head west. I want to see Deanmere Gap again. I want at least some connection with you, Priscilla. We are coming for you, coming to find you. We will find a way out of this place.

I, too, look out of the carriage, but it is not to glimpse the sea. I am studying Magda's reality, looking for flaws, for repetitions, for dithering where the fabric of this world may be stretched thin.

Nothing yet, though.

\* \* \*

THE CARRIAGE STOPS. I lean out of the open door, peering up at the carriage driver. "What's up?" I ask him.

He looks back at me. His face is blurred, no details resolving themselves. I look around, and for an instant the whole world is like that, and then it snaps into focus again, as if I am imposing my own consensus upon it. I remember this from the early days of the project, the reality shards we first developed.

"This is as far as I go, guv'nor," he says, words emanating from a pixelated dark hole in his face.

"Where are we? What's beyond this point?"

"This is as far as I go, guv'nor."

I step down, then lean back in to take Sissy's hand. "Looks like we walk for a bit," I say to her, smiling. "Or run. Or hop. Or piggy-back."

She giggles, jumps down, spins around, her arms whirling wide. She is a naturally happy child, despite everything. She gives me such a lift sometimes.

Hand in hand, we walk. The rough road becomes a mere footpath, taking us out to the cliff-tops. We pause here, look back along the bay towards Eastbourne. The cliffs are such a dazzling white. Sissy picks up chalk pebbles from the rabbit-cropped grass and throws them over the edge, and I worry that she might go too close, urge her to stay back.

We walk on.

The grass slopes off to our right, where scrub grows with a few twisted trees, stooped over from the wind. Beyond... Blurred green fields. No resolution. No detail. We must be coming close to the edge of Magda's world.

I realise I am gripping Sissy's hand more tightly. I force myself to relax.

We walk on. Occasionally, I glance down at Sissy. Her eyes are big and round, her face serious. She does not look scared, but she clearly knows that this is different, this is important.

And all around us, the world is dissipating, etiolating... Doing something for which we have no words.

Details are dropping out of the world. Resolution. Distance and shape and colour and light are going. The air feels heavy in my lungs, like I'm breathing water, only I'm actually breathing it, not drowning.

Sissy grips my hand more tightly. I glance down, meet her look, her smile. How can such a small child make me feel safer in such circumstances?

I smile back. We walk on.

PRISCILLA FINDS THE message from Noah when she's cleaning out her in-box.

It's an old one, one read and tagged for keeping. She almost deletes it without a second thought. She is in a ruthless mood, a life-cleansing mood. She is throwing out and starting again.

But... She stops, opens it, intrigued. It's only natural to be curious, after all. She doesn't regret her time with Noah. It had woken her up, made her reassess the woman she is, made her remember to value all that she has. And it had been fun. Exciting.

She is secure enough in herself now that she can do this: explore old territory.

*Priscilla*

*Remember New York? Walking for miles until our feet were blistered and our legs felt like they were going to drop off. Stopping to kiss on Brooklyn Bridge. Waking in our hotel room and rushing to the window to look out over Central Park. Eating tapas off zebra-striped tables in East Village.*
*Remember Whitby? Standing under the whale's jawbone arch, hand in hand. Eating fish and chips on the steps up to the ruined Abbey. Running down the hill in the driving rain, peeling wet clothes off each other and piling into the bath?*

*Remember Amsterdam? Remember Brighton
and Oxford and Canterbury?
We were there, my love. We were there.*

N

SHE KEEPS HER eyes closed, re-reads the words in her feed. Had she really been to these places with Noah? Other instances of her? Were they part of her now, somewhere deep, or had that message been Noah trying to tell her of things he had done with another her altogether? Trying to win her back, way back when?

She sighs. She does not have these memories. They are not of her.

She deletes the message, moves on.

I AM FINDING it hard to breathe now, hard to talk, to utter words of reassurance to stoical little Sissy. The thick air is still, yet we have to lean forward into it in order to walk, as if we are marching into the teeth of an autumn gale.

The ground is grey, the sky grey, the horizon a barely visible line differentiating grey from grey. It is neither hot nor cold, light nor dark. It is nothing. We are walking in limbo.

We have lost any trace of cliffs, of sea, of landscape altogether.

We walk.

And slowly... Slowly... The air drags less on my cheeks, flows more freely in my lungs. Light glimmers down from a bright patch where the sun must be. My foot catches and I look down, see a tussock of grass, green grass in the grey.

I peer all around, start to make out detail: the low, twisted shape of a tree, rabbit holes, the cliff edge.

"The sea!" cries Sissy, tugging at my hand.

The sea is blue. I feel tears welling again. There have been too many tears of late. I am not an emotional man.

The path at our feet is well worn now. It leads down a cropped-grass slope. Ahead, I see the start of a promenade, some ornamental gardens, a strand of shingle beach. There are people there, a few figures strolling.

Sissy tugs free, runs down the slope, giggling.

My pace quickens after her.

With every step the world is finding resolution, clarity.

Sissy stops giggling, stops running, stands there, arms spread. She looks back at me.

Beyond her, a man and a woman have stopped to look at us. They wear Victorian costume.

I look ahead, see the buildings of Eastbourne spread before us.

We are back. We have walked to the edge of Magda's world and come back in on the other side...

Past the couple, an old man is staring too. And a small boy. And down on the beach, a family of five peers in our direction.

We are back. And it appears that we have been expected.

WE SEE THEM approaching. The child, Sissy, runs down the slope, reaches the start of the promenade, and then senses that something is wrong. She stops, looks right at us, then back at Barakh. We watch, through the eyes of this instance. We wear a bustled dress, a stiff-ribbed corset, hold a parasol resting lightly on one shoulder. We are very aware of our breasts, trapped in the dress, pushed up.

We look at Barakh. He is scared, his mouth part-open, a hand held out to the child.

...We look up from the beach, see the woman with the parasol watching them. We are in a small body, a child, a boy wearing a full-bodied bathing costume with short arms and legs. We sit on the shingle, playing with the stones, picking them up and dropping them, picking them up and dropping them.

Barakh has the child in his arms now, holding her tight, holding her high. She is a small black girl, about six or seven. I am going to have her.

…We stand in the shadow of a pine tree in the ornamental gardens. He hasn't seen us yet. We are in a Chuckboy Lee instance, even though we are not Chuckboy. We are not Jack. We are not Bartie. We are more. We are different. We are all. We wear Chuckboy for the comedy value, for the look on Barakh's face when he sees us step out. We take a stick of gum, peel it, fold it, slip it into our mouth.

…We watch the two of them. There is no hurry. In our heads we hold a kaleidoscope image, a composite of all the views, as if we look through compound eyes.

Barakh looks at us. He is scared. He is beaten.

I HOLD SISSY close against me. She is shaking. She knows something is seriously wrong.

These people… look at any one of them closely and they are featureless, the detail does not resolve. They are *unfinished*. But there is something different about them. Something that the placeholder figures of Magda's world did not previously have.

I start to back up the slope, glancing down every so often to check my footing.

The woman with the parasol advances, followed by her top-hatted partner. A boy on the beach throws a stone into the waves and then trots away from the sea to join the woman.

Another man approaches along the promenade, his hands folded behind his back. Across in the gardens: a woman, two men, a boy and a girl… They are all intent on Sissy and me. All like the parasol woman: unfinished, unresolved, and yet… Far more complete than others I have seen here.

And then he steps out from the shade of a tree. Chuckboy Lee. He wears black jeans and a crimson

T-shirt that is stretched taut over his belly. He is chewing gum, smiling.

I turn and run.

Up the slope, following the foot-worn path through the grass.

Soon I am gasping for breath. I am not a man used to this kind of exertion, and the slope and Sissy's small extra weight make it much harder.

I pause, glance back. They are following. About a dozen of them. More – others are in the gardens and on the beach. The first of them have reached the end of the promenade now, and are starting up the slope. I turn, start to jog up the hill.

Soon, the detail is gone from my world and the air is thickening.

I have to slow to walking pace, pushing forward into the jellied air, dragging lungfuls of the stuff deep, sick with the effort.

I glance back and my heart sinks. They have halved the gap.

We turn. Jog. Slow to a brisk walk. Try to jog again, but the air is too thick.

Sissy is looking back over my shoulder all the time. She has been silent, but now she gives a soft gasp.

I stop, turn, and they are there, only paces behind us. They do not appear to be affected by the blurred edges of Magda's world.

I look down, see detail in the grass where before there had been grey. We are almost through... I push on.

A hand lands on my shoulder, turns me with a casual brutality, and I twist, stumble, fall to my knees.

I look up into the face of the parasol lady. Her face is morphing between that of a gentle smiling lady and a featureless blob. And then, for a moment, she is Chuck-boy Lee. And back to the lady's easy features, before morphing into Elector Burnham...

I hold Sissy close.

The woman who is possessed by Burnham and Lee, or whatever they have become, is reaching for me again.

She puts a hand on my shoulder, then another round Sissy and onto my left shoulder. She leans forward into a full embrace, and now, I believe, I know what it is to really die in this other realm that I built.


WE CROWD AROUND Barakh and the girl, the instances of us. We enfold them, infiltrate them. Ensnare them.

We can taste him, his essence, his Barakhness.

We feel him starting to dissolve, his algorithms being picked apart, his data scattering.

He is dissolving, ones and zeroes never to be put together again.

It takes mere seconds, and then he is gone.

The child too – she is gone.

That is a shame but it doesn't matter. We have Sissies of our own.

We look around. Barakh thought he was a god, but his world has survived his death. Even here, in an off-shoot of the Accord, Barakh the Creator has proved to be mortal.

## 2.13

Priscilla steps back from the glass-topped table. There are two places set, a fan of delicate fern leaves in a vase, lighting from a scattering of discreet wall lights. Glance to one side and a floor-to-ceiling window looks out over a narrow balcony to the great sweep of the Thames, Tower Bridge just visible around a lazy bend.

They have been in this flat for three years now. They still have the Islington flat and the North Downs cottage, but this is their main base these days. Priscilla could stand on the balcony for hours and watch the river flow sedately past. Some days she does.

She pings Jack to check where he is, but no response. He was due back half an hour ago. This is their anniversary, five years since they had started over again.

She goes out onto the balcony, feels the bite of the evening air on her cheeks. She wraps her arms around herself, her hips pressed against the railings.

There have been nights like this when she has gone out. There are places you can go, if you know where to look. Places to meet people. She hasn't done it often. You can go to these places, have a few drinks, find someone. She always thought of them – these men – as Omar; she doesn't know where the name came from, but it is the one she uses: she thinks of these as Omar nights.

She needs that now.

She hugs herself tighter.

She needs *something* now.

Down on the river, two boats pass, a sightseeing boat and a small motorboat.

She can't go and find an Omar tonight though. It's their anniversary.

She goes inside to open the wine. A glass won't do any harm.

She pours, sips, follows the chill descending into her belly. Another sip.

Back out on the balcony, she is halfway down the glass when she hears the door.

She turns, sees Jack, his even features just caught by the light of the setting sun.

He smiles and she crosses the room, wraps her arms around him, breathes in his scent. "Jack," she whispers into his ear. "Happy anniversary."

She has found her Omar for tonight.


"COUPER," WE SAY, stepping forward to shake his hand.

We're in a meetspace made to look like that African beach by the hotel where we'd first met Couper. Why does it always default to fucking beaches?

We step back from each other. "So," I say, "what news?"

Couper grins. "You'll have your first war in Africa inside the month," he tells us. "Perez's Blanquists don't like the boat people's camps we've put on his territory in New West Africa. He's been buying arms heavily. And the boaties know they need to defend themselves."

"But Africa isn't anywhere near capacity yet..."

Couper shrugs. "We're just establishing things as we want them from the outset."

It's only ten days before the first reports come in. An entire boatie camp blown away in an assault by Perez's forces. Over 2,000 dead. Two days after that, Perez is killed in a suicide bombing. The kid had only been reborn hours before that. He'd been one of the boaties killed by the Blanquists' assault on the camp. Soon it's all-out warfare, watched in fascination from this side of the world. Thousands are dying and being reborn and dying again. It's not long before we get newsfeeds of kids queuing up to emigrate and join the war. It is fascinating to watch. Have we really beaten Malthus? Will this endless cycle of destruction actually achieve some kind of balance between death and rebirth rate? We had never really believed it to be more than a holding measure, but if the time lag between death and rebirth extends as projected, it might just do the job.

We sit back, a glass of Laphroaig to hand, and watch the feeds. Endless analysis gives death counts and strategic insight. It is the new big thing: reality warfare. Everyone is talking about it.

IT'S TAKEN EIGHT years to reach this stage. Eight years of herding fucking fleas. Priscilla has been a driven woman for this time, using the interstitial ship programme to fill a gap in her life, a need. This has become her baby.

Now, she floats.

She is one of nearly thirty VIPs and specialists invited up to the League Orbital Platform to witness the launch of the first interstitial ship. About a dozen of them are here in Viewing Gallery B.

Had she ever even imagined that one day she might be up here, floating in zero gees, a fucking spacewoman?

In the old world, no one had gone into space any more.

But now... She floats, hanging onto a grab-bar with one hand. She feels sick, puffy, as if someone has inflated every cell in her body. Her sinuses hurt like fuck and every one of her joints feels as if it's been stretched by an evil genius chiropractor.

The view of Earth is stunning. They are over Africa, the outline of the continent sharp against the blue oceans. They are still fighting down there, an endless war. She thinks the repatriation and emigration programme is Jack's biggest mistake, a tragedy, but she doesn't tell him that. She has long since given up trying to disagree with him. He wins her over every time and it leaves her feeling sick in the pit of her belly. Powerless against him, the man she loves so dearly. How can he hurt her so much when she feels this way? How can there be such a gaping hole in her life when she is so much in love?

Huey tugs at her arm and she spins like a top, other guests backing away from her flailing body. Her head rushes, she's so fucking dizzy it hurts, and she has to swallow hard to stop from chucking up. She grabs the bar with both hands, jerks to a stop and her head keeps spinning spinning spinning.

"Sorry!" Huey says hurriedly.

She looks at him through upturned eyes, gives him the evils. He has no idea how to handle himself – or other people – in freefall.

"You wanted something?"

"Sorry," he says again. He pushes a strand of hair back from his face, moves, and the hair is there again. He points at the window, a strip about fifty centimetres high that runs the three metre length of this gallery.

Out there, somewhere, is the ship, *The Discovery*. They cannot see it; it's too distant. It has to be, for safety's sake. In a few minutes it will rip apart the fabric of space-time, translate itself into the quantum space reserved for uncollapsed probability waves, and leap through interstitial space to Alpha Centauri. It uses the same principles they used to translate the Accord itself into quantum space – what they called Lotfi space after one of the Kantian revisionist philosophers who first proposed its existence.

Priscilla looks, but all she sees is stars and black in the direction Huey had indicated.

She could be listening to the commentary, but she has filtered it out from her feed. She wants this moment for herself. She wants to see the programme realised on her own terms.

She smiles at Huey, returns her attention to the viewing window. She knows where to look; she has memorised the stars to look for.

She waits.

The sudden hush of those around her keys her in to the moment. They know it is about to happen; they're listening on their feeds.

A spark. She sees it. A new star.

"Look! Look!" yells a man. Ruin the fucking moment, why don't you?

She stares.

The new star flickers, pulses, and then it expands... Doubles... Quadruples... Is suddenly a new sun, and the window darkens to cut out the glare, so that now the stars themselves have vanished and the new sun hangs there in the dark.

And then the sun folds in on itself, retracts. For a moment it vanishes, and then the clearing of the window kicks in and the ship's aftermath is visible as one pinprick of light amongst many, and then is gone again.

Priscilla turns to Huey. "Congratulations," she says, then adds: "I take it that was success and the fucker didn't just blow itself up?"

Huey is grinning. So wide it looks like his face is going to split in two.

It was a success. It was clearly a success.

THE ASHRAM IS high in the mountains of Uttarakhand.

Priscilla sits on a scree slope, and breathes air so sharp it could cut diamonds. A family of feral goats picks its way over the opposite slope, somehow finding footing on near vertical inclines. Somewhere a raven cronks.

She has been here for almost a month, learning to meditate under the guidance of Bodhi Krishnamoorthy. She is what they call a seeker of self, a Ko'ham.

She sees the bodhi approaching along a path cut through the scree boulders. He wears a white salwar kameez with a delicate winding flower embroidery in ivory thread. She dips her head in greeting as he comes to sit beside her.

"The elector has left messages," he tells her in his soft voice.

She nods. She has been ignoring Jack's calls. She needs space, time. Needs to sort her head out.

"I..." She's uncertain. Still hasn't found the words. "I want *more*," she tries. "I want *other*."

The bodhi nods, and leaves a silence for her to fill.

"I don't know who I am any more. Most of the time I've been in the Accord I've just drifted, let things happen. The spark has gone. The *me*. I want more, but I don't know what that more is."

She's not alone in this existential hunger, she knows. How do you come to terms with your own immortality? Do you go to Africa to enrol in an endless war that makes no difference? Do you get swamped in choice, in what to do first, what to do next, what to leave for a thousand years? Do you lose yourself in sensation and experience because nothing matters any more, not a fucking thing matters?

She doesn't think of Noah often, but now she does. They could talk about this. They could talk for hours. He would understand.

"You have a space in your heart for God," says the bodhi.

"Fuck off," she says instantly. There is no God in this world of theirs. This is a rationalist heaven.

"You have a quest for meaning. A yearning. That is a spiritual impulse, Priscilla. You seek truth."

"Where do I find it, though?"

She expects him to feed her platitudes. She will find truth in her heart, in her soul, in meditation. The bodhi is a wonderful man, but sometimes he's so fucking full of cliché.

He surprises her though.

He hooks a hand around the back of her head, draws her in, kisses her hard and deep, his free hand running over her ribs, her waist, her hip, curling round to pull her close against him.

Fuck, but she hadn't expected to find an Omar *here*...

THE POPULATION IN Africa is fucking stable! It's taken eleven years, but now the death and rebirth rates balance out. Jack Burnham one, Thomas Malthus nil.

So why are we still not satisfied?

We sit in a quiet bar, a street back from the river, sharing Islay malts with Electee Tom Gallagher, newly killed in a coup attempt in old world Brussels.

"The whole damned Med rim is on fire, Jack," Gallagher says. He's talking about the old world, bringing us up to date. "Most of Spain's gone – either still fighting or uninhabitable in the aftermath."

He doesn't need to explain that any further. We know about the dirty bombs, the viruses... Whole cities quarantined off, vast tracts of land.

"Looks like human nature is solving the population crisis," Gallagher continues. "But the climate's still screwed. We got boaties coming in from all directions now. I did my utmost to keep things going while I was there, but I tell you Jack, I'm damned glad I'm out of it."

Just then the wall at one end of the bar blanks, cuts to *News247*. Stock footage of the League Orbital Platform, a quarter-screen Earth in the background. We tune out the feed, just watch the pictures.

We wonder where Priscilla is. She should be with us, here. This is her project, one we'd given her to keep her busy. The first colonisation ship heading off to the fucking stars.

Where is she?

Off on some jaunt again. This fucking Ko'ham thing. Trying to find herself like some fucking 1960s dropout on the hippy trail. We let her do it; we indulge her. It's eleven years now and we can get by without her some of the time, as long as she always comes back.

Suddenly, a speck on the screen flares, a mini-nova. The ball of light expands, and then abruptly collapses back in on itself. We look away, see that Gallagher is transfixed. He's never seen this before, whereas we have seen it a dozen times and repeated endlessly, with all the test flights and exploration trips.

We should feel different about this one. The ship is orders of magnitude bigger, and contains over 3,000 colonists.

We pick up our Bunnahabhain, take a sip, message Priscilla to find out where the fuck she is hiding.

PRISCILLA IS ON a fucking *starship*.

She lies on a couch, gently embraced by a catch-blanket, feeling a little detached from it all, her head in a happy place because of the sedatives she and all the other colonists had taken about ten minutes ago.

She's known for weeks that it would be like this, but still it's vaguely disappointing to be lying here, head adrift, eyes staring at the screen above her, which shows a view of Ark1. She wants to be up, alert, seeing Earth for the last time. She wants to be *part* of it.

She has tuned out the feed, just watches the pictures. T minus sixty seconds and counting.

When she thinks of Jack it hurts like fuck. How could she have reached this point? He's been her life for the last eleven years. Even now she hates the thought of leaving him behind. But she needs more. She needs other. She doesn't understand what it is that she does need, but she knows she cannot find it with Jack, that her craving to be with him is a weight, an ache... Almost a sickness...

Fuck, but it's four seconds, three, two...

She feels it in her gut.

Feels a shift, an expansion, as if she's in a lift that's plunged too sharply, in a car that's gone over a humpback bridge. But it carries on. She feels everything just falling apart, *pulling* apart. Feels her soul expanding, some mad rush, a drug thing, an endorphin thing, like the biggest fucking trip ever and then some. It floods out. *She* floods out. Her-ness. Priscilla-ness.

The screen above her shows a rapidly expanding ball of white light where Ark1 had been. She is that light. She is in that light. She is exploding.

She. Is. White. Light. Explosion.

Priscilla is.

Contracting. Collapsing in on herself. Her soul, although she has never believed in souls, which was one thing Noah had never had to convince her of because she was there way ahead of him... Her soul is folding back in on itself. Finding shape. Finding centre. Finding Priscilla-ness.

She *is* once more.

Fuck, but she'd do that again.

Then she sees the screen above her...

A planet that shows blue oceans, green continents, white twists and swirls of weather systems, an ice cap. A planet whose continents take shapes she recognises only from recon imagery. A planet that is not Earth.

Priscilla has found *other*.

## 2.14

We sit in a shabby bar somewhere in south London. We have a table in a dark corner. Our bodyguard sits with us. Parker. Porter. Peters. Whatever. What the fuck ever.

We drink our Glenlivet in one, rap the tumbler on the scratched wooden table for attention, and Parker-PorterPeters takes it to the bar for a refill.

Tate comes in at that moment, stands for a few seconds by the door as his eyes adjust. The pub is about half full, the level of noise fluctuating, occasionally raucous. The air has that almost sepia tint that all good pubs should have.

Tate spots us, and that's when we realise just how bad we've become. Just how bad *I've* become. I put my hands to each temple, squeeze. Feel a moment's calm.

That look in his eyes. Shock. Pity. Hurt.

Tate fucking *hurting* for me.

He nods at Parker, comes over, lowers himself into a wooden chair opposite my bench.

"You look like shit," he says by way of greeting, and that makes me smile.

"Tough being dead," I say, and he smiles back, briefly. "What you been up to?"

"I found someone," says Tate, softening. "We have a place in St Davids. We look after the land, put travellers up. Meet lots of fascinating people that way. It's a good life, JB. You should come and visit."

"That what you came here to tell me, is it?"

Tate has us fixed by his eyes, hypnotic almost.

"No, JB. No, it's not. Although we'd like you to come. I just heard... I heard how things are with you. I want to help."

We drag our eyes away. What has he heard, I wonder? That I sit in dark corners in bars drinking the finest Scotches so I can forget. That this is my life: forgetting. That my head feels like fucking Africa. Forces ripping me apart from the inside. That sometimes I'm not me, I'm not we, I'm something else... I see myself in action, I feel myself thinking thoughts, but I'm like a passenger, a hitchhiker. I am not responsible. I... We... That I share in the buzz... The thrill... It *is* me. Is us. That when I leave this pub I will go back to the Thames-side apartment and my playthings will be there.

We raise the glass that Parker has placed before us. Down it in two.

Tate watches. Pities.

Fuck him. Fuck them all.


CILLA WAKES TO grey. She takes her time to find her bearings, to sit, stand. A door outlines, scrolls, and she steps through into another world, a new world. She steps through into her log cabin on the edge of Hopetown. She felled trees for this cabin, trimmed side branches off the logs, worked with Jem and Tilda and Henry to render the inner walls with plaster. She has learned so much.

She feeds the stove, puts a kettle on to heat. Remembers dying.

Trekking in the foothills thirty klicks east of here with Ahmed and his twelve-year-old daughter Reya. These hills had been explored thoroughly in the first two years of the colony. The detail was sharp, consensus well established. None of the pixel blur of new ground, this was real: the membrane-winged birds tumbling in flocks in the updraughts by cliff faces, the stunted and twisted

vegetation growing from sheer faces of rock, the scalers
– tangle-bearded, horned, monkey-like creatures that
throw themselves from rock to rock across the hillside.

It had been a slip, a simple slip. One moment following
Reya, who'd gone ahead of them, the next... Foot gone
sideways from under her in a small spray of stones and
dirt, that moment when you almost feel you've regained
balance and then realise you haven't, you aren't anywhere near to doing so, and you're falling, arms flailing.

It's funny, if you survive a fall like that you're going
to be laid up for weeks and you'll hurt like hell. If you
don't survive... Grey, re-emergence... That whole
realignment, remixing, of self thing. The re-finding of
you.

Cilla runs hands down herself, feels that new vitality
of rebirth. She doesn't hurt at all.

She pauses by the window then.

Deep inside... The ache has diminished. The need.
The gut-level craving.

Deep inside she is getting over Jack.


I WEAR SKIN-WRAP body armour; a stick-on headset that
overlays jungle with data, commands, feeds; boots that
have all the flexibility and responsiveness of the lightest
climbing pumps, but the resilience of metal deep-sea
diving boots; and most crucially of all, slung from my
right shoulder, a 5.7mm FN carbine.

I stand alone, yet surrounded by my comrades. All
around: green. Tree trunks, drapes of liana and cur-
tained moss. I can't see more than about two or three
metres in any direction for the screens of vegetation.
Somewhere nearby there are fifty crack troops, awaiting
instruction.

The heat is intense, the humidity sheening my body
with sweat and grime. My bodysuit draws the moisture
away, but it is no match for these conditions. I have
been awake for over thirty hours, hiking through
Cameroonian jungle.

And now we stand, each alone in this overgrown wilderness, waiting.

I sweep my head slowly to the left, watch the overlay display changing as it finds the body signatures of Brindle, Pascale, Song, and Laursen. I face forward again, focusing as a signal comes in, a command.

I ping my troops, tell them to strike.

I am Jack Burnham and I feel fucking *alive* for the first time since Priscilla left me.

The village is made up of a sorry bunch of lean-tos made out of what looks like flotsam rescued from the nearby river. Old boards, crates, bleached timbers, industrial-sized metal and plastic containers.

We take out the perimeter guards within seconds, but others are ready for us, and soon they are fighting back.

I linger at the edge of the clearing, carbine at my shoulder; the FN isn't really designed for sniping, it's a close-range weapon, but still I can pick off occasional boaties from my spot on the periphery of the battle, pinging my troops, coordinating, steering.

Then, as I pause to change clips, one of them comes at me out of nowhere, a woman with night-black skin and mad staring eyes. I am looking down, but my headset alerts me, flashes red across my vision, then back to normal as I jerk upright, see her coming, a machete swinging high above her head, slashing downwards.

I raise my carbine, one hand at either end, using it as a shield to take the force of the machete blow. I feel the reverberations jarring through my body, but I am tumbling sideways, out of her path.

I roll, am back on my feet in an instant, take my gun by the barrel and swing it down on the woman, cracking the back of her head like an overripe fruit.

She is gone, fading from the world.

I reload, pick out a man who is firing at my troops with a handgun, take him out with a single shot to the head.

Soon, I am walking into the settlement. Three ragged hens peck on the ground by a fallen man. His eyes stare at the sky, his mouth open, his torso crimson and shredded to a pulp by automatic fire. His wounds are covered in flies already, a scintillating mass of the things. I poke his head with my boot and it flops to the side. Flies rise and settle. I wonder how he has clung on for so long and then at that instant death takes him and he starts to fade from the world.

In a hut a child is crying. I pull a thin curtain aside at the doorway and peer in. A woman is there, huddled in a corner, holding a child of about seven or eight to her breast. I glance over my shoulder, nod to the dreadlocked Song, and he steps in past me, takes the woman by the shoulder, pulls her to her feet. For a few seconds she clings to the child, then her body slumps, she lets go, allows Song to lead her outside to where the others wait.

I go in, squat before the child. Reach out a hand to cup her chin, tip her head upwards. She reminds us of Sissy.

Her face is smeared with tears and dirt. We wipe her clean with a handkerchief.

We stand.

We know what comes next.

Our heart races, our pulse rushing. We... We...

We stagger back.

We have been here too many times before.

Our back comes up against the flimsy sheet metal wall of the lean-to and we halt, as far from the child as we can get and still be inside this shelter.

The wet on our face is sweat and tears.

We cry.

I cry.

We turn, push out of the hut. Over by a half-dismantled Jeep, they have the woman. Laursen and Song and Adi.

The FN carbine Couper has been flooding this continent with is a light weapon, short in the barrel. You can turn it through one-eighty with remarkable ease, hook your thumb around the trigger. Push rather than pull.

The muzzle flash when you look at the gun from this end is suddenly blinding because of the short barrel. You hear the first explosion and see the flash simultaneously because you are so close to them. You feel sudden explosive pain in the chest. Your consciousness fades, your heart destroyed by the impact, your last electronic vestiges of consciousness clinging to the fleshly circuits of your brain.

Confusion. Pain. Loss. Gone.

Gone.

## 2.15

SHE CALLS HERSELF Ella now.

She is a seeker of self, a Ko'ham.

She has travelled the world, travelled worlds, lived lives.

She has built new communities on the edges of consensual space, been healer and counsellor and community leader. She has taught and been taught; loved, lived, left, been left.

She has retreated to secular monasteries in locations breathtaking and stark. One a mountaintop citadel built by others who seek; another a bubble-dome on a planet whose atmosphere is acidic, high-pressured, and dense, the dome air always reeking of others despite the scrubbers and filters working round the clock.

Now, she walks the long path that winds up a jagged mountain, in a range of jagged blue-stoned mountains, their peaks dipped in white icing. Fairytale mountains on a fairy-tale planet where dragon-like creatures the size of large dogs fly in V-formation high against the powder-puff-clouded azure sky. A pair of moons shine silver in the deep blue of the midday sky, two crescents a handspan and 200,000 kilometres apart.

She has walked for twenty-seven days, following the Seeker's Trail, a route marked with cairns and crosses and niches carved into rock faces concealing the tiny figure of a man who many believe to be a god.

She walks alone. She is done with company for now. Solitude concentrates the mind.

She is here to find herself again. She is here to find God.

The trail takes a hairpin bend, doubling back and up the craggy slope. Trees grow in scattered clumps, bonsaied by the conditions: stunted, twisted, gnarled. She pauses in the sparse shade of one to drink from her lizard-skin water bottle. She is hot from walking, chilled by the mountain air, and yet the sun burns her skin quickly. Her face is red and sore from the UV. She knows that in a few days she will be peeling like an old London plane tree.

She remembers London, the trees. They made her sneeze when it was the pollen season. So long ago. So many lives ago. All that happened to another person, another instance. She has been through so much since then.

And yet...

I SEE TREES, foliage, tangled growths thick and lush.

I hear insect-buzzes and animals' cries and chirrups and chitterings.

I feel heat, humidity, a dense, heavy atmosphere. I feel the ground beneath my feet, a resistance to my weight, a solidity... a *being*ness. A physicality of this world, of me, of the I.

I smell decay, lush perfumes, dampness.

I see a shape, a person, a child at my side. Flickering, shimmering.

I waver. I feel myself spreading. Losing form. Diminishing.

I see light, dark, form.

I feel a pulling apart, a thinning.

I see nothing.

I was, but now I am not.

\* \* \*

GOD HAS A garden nestled deep in a valley between two mountains.

Ella sees it as she clears a ridge, and just has to stop and stare.

The green is vivid, after days of blue rock and stunted, faded vegetation clinging to the slopes. It is jungle-lush. Fruit trees and trimmed grass cover the slopes. Little pine glades flank the valley. Crops grow in neatly serried patchwork plots. She sees tiny figures, people working in the fields; a heavily laden wagon being hauled by a pair of oxen along a distant track.

The track leads her gaze onwards, through air that shimmers with a kind of ultra-clarity, a sharpness so exaggerated it makes her squint, feel dizzy...

To a wall, an edifice, a cliff face. A palace.

She has heard about this. A palace carved out of the cliff. A home worthy of a god who walks among his people.

She descends along the trail, which broadens out into a track with a surface burnt smooth, glassy. Around her, green infiltrates the landscape until she is there, walking through God's garden, breathing God's air, her heart filled with hope.

To her right, a man and two women fill baskets with apples from heavily fruiting trees. She pings them greetings, and they send back warmth, welcome, love.

How long has she been seeking? How many lifetimes? She wonders how it will feel to have found...


I... WE... THIS it that we are...

We sit beneath the stars, a bottle of Christos cradled in our hands, resting in our lap. Our legs stretch out in the dirt, our back straight against a stone wall.

We are on a rise here, looking across the road to the lights of Shinjen. Adclips play out on the clouds, porn clubs and casinos and bars all plying their wares to new arrivals and old. Shinjen's strip stretches four klicks along the city's main highway.

It's like...

Like...

We remember Bangkok. It's like Bangkok. Neon lights and whores and cuties you could buy for a few cents a night.

We take another swig.

Memories are like that. Come and go. Firefly instants, here and gone.

We have lived so many lives.

But always, we seek.

We find distraction. Oh yes, we find distraction.

But we seek, still.

Suddenly, white light divides the sky in two, a rip in the fabric of the heavens. A shuttle, striking for orbit. More hopeless souls heading out to an interstitial ship, heading for stars distant, far flung. Escaping.

But you can never escape that which torments you the most.

We drink again. The spirit scalding our throat like stomach acid.

We climb to our feet, using the wall for support.

Out of our side street, we join the main drag, head down towards the strip.

Some time later: ads all over the walls vie for our attention, women in gauzy veils, oiled men in leather shorts, babes with playing cards and contraire stones calling my name, *Jack, Jack, take a look over here, Jack, come play with me, I could make you rich, Jack, I could make you happy, I could...*

I ignore them, eyes roving.

I walk on, pausing occasionally for breath, for another drink.

I can feel the city all around. *We* can feel it. The pings, the data-flows, the energy. We have a feel for this place. We feel ourself as a knot of complexity in the mass, order in the chaos.

This is how we find the cutie...

We feel her thought-shapes, the knot she makes in the flows. This is a Chuckboy thing, a deep awareness of Accord, a pushing of protocols.

The cutie... She is about ten, white, skinny, standing on the street corner chewing cokestix.

Eye contact seals the deal, within seconds of spying her.

We feel the rushing of blood, the thrill. We feel sick. We fucking hate what we are. What Chuckboy is.

The cutie turns, walks away from us.

We follow.

All around, nightlife flows. Drunken, stoned, high groups, male and female and those who fall somewhere in between or are in transition – hell, we have so many lives to live: why not fucking experiment? The flicker-flashing of ads and lights, of shopfronts and club entrances and casino-bars, is hypnotic, dizzying.

Cutie turns left down a side street.

We hurry our pace so as not to lose her.

On the corner, though, we pause. There's another of those shrines, a tribute to Padre e Figlia, a niche in a building's brick wall, holding candles, petals, a crude effigy of father and daughter. We look, suddenly distracted, disoriented. It chimes with something deep, and we feel sudden anger.

We shake ourselves like a wet dog, wondering where the fuck all that has come from?

Partway down the street, the cutie waits, looking back to make sure we are still following. The street is dimly lit, only by a few pools of light. We quicken our stride to follow more closely.

She pauses in a doorway.

We approach.

Her eyes are wide, the whites standing out like beacons.

Her face has been expressionless, but now she bares her teeth, a smile that makes her look like some feral animal.

And that is the signal...

We are suddenly aware of movement in the shadows, sounds behind.

The cutie is not alone. Others, ranged in age from about seven through to mid-teens, have stepped out of the shadows, maybe ten of them. We don't look back, but guess there must be at least the same number again behind.

The first blow comes from the rear, a sudden ringing crash on the back of our skull.

We stagger forward, sick with the abrupt pain.

Something takes us behind both knees. A blade. Something has gone from our legs; all control vanished. We look down, see deep red painting roses on the stone surface of the street.

A hand seizes our hair, yanks our head back, so our throat is exposed.

We expect a blade again, a final slash, but no, a fist slams down, flattening our nose into our face, leaving everything numb, hot blood washing our features.

We slump back, aware that the lower parts of our legs are folded back at an improbable angle beneath us.

A foot swings, hits the side of our face, jerking our head sideways.

And then they are on us, all over us, small hands pulling, tearing, feet trampling.

All is pain, ringing numbness, heat. Fading. Gone.

THE PALACE IS even more dramatic close up.

Its central façade consists of pillars and balconies, stacked one on the other on the other, stretching maybe a hundred metres up the cliff. The local blue rock polishes to a fine marbled sheen, so that light catches and reflects and scintillates off every surface; shift a pace to one side and it all looks different; a cloud passes briefly across the sun, and all changes again. Ella could stand and watch the effect all day. She has already been standing here for some time, having stopped at regular intervals in her approach to study the palace; each advance revealing some new aspect to this fantastical construction.

To either side of this central block, the palace is still a work in progress. White-clad acolytes work with chisels, chipping away at the rock, carving new balconies, new windows, new chambers. They cover the cliff face like termites on a dead tree. This palace could be the work of millennia, but then, what's that to a god followed by immortals?

A man stands at her shoulder. She hasn't noticed him until now, when she hears the shuffle of his feet on the glazed road beside her.

"You seek the Lord?" he asks, as she turns to look at him.

He is a man of middle years, his features betraying mixed heritage: oriental eyes, swept-back blond hair, a prominent aquiline nose.

"I don't know what I seek," Ella says. "But I'm wondering if I've finally found it."

He turns and smiles, and as she looks into his eyes she is struck by the thought that here is someone who has already been on this journey and reached its conclusion. Here is a man who has finally found it.

"Come along," he says, placing a hand on her shoulder, encouraging her to walk the remaining distance to the palace. "If you've walked all this way then your feet must be truly fucked."


I SENSE THE shape and flow of the universe. I wish I could show you what I mean. I can feel it, deep inside me. It is me. I am it.

I can sense the world. I can sense worlds. Worlds where you exist. Worlds side by side. I just need to pick the right one. Pull my disparate strands together. Take shape. Be.

I have been scattered, spread. I do not know for how long. But I am of the Accord; the Accord is of me. I come together. I coalesce.

I see, I smell, I hear, I feel. I am.

I stand in a street in a shanty town. I do not know where. I do not know when.

The sky is crimson and ochre, banded, sparkling with stars even though it is not full night. The steadily moving light of an orbiting space station moves across this vivid backdrop.

I smell spices and shit and damp animal fur. I listen to the sounds of voices and whining engines.

I feel a small hand in mine.

Sissy.

She is looking all around, and then she turns her gaze on me. "Father," she says, very serious, "where are we?"

"Daughter," I say. The word feels right. "I do not know, but it does not matter."

My grip on her hand tightens as the world around us flickers. I am aware of instabilities, of the potential for reality quakes. Our existence here is an affront to the protocols, even though we *are* the protocols. We are not the norm.

Others are aware of this. I see them now, standing in the doorways of their lean-tos, whites of eyes picked out in the gloom, watching. It is as if they are aware that we are novel, as if they are drawn.

A woman approaches, drops to her knees before me, takes my free hand in both of hers. She gabbles in a language I do not understand, but her need is clear. She thinks I can help with something.

We walk with her into a shack made from plyboard sheeting.

In the darkness I see a tangle of rags on the floor. A child. Maybe Sissy's age. The child is curled up into a foetal ball, trembling violently.

I kneel by his side – he is a boy, I think.

I place a hand on his forehead and almost snatch it away from the sudden heat.

I look at Sissy, and then at the boy's mother.

They both watch me. They appear to believe that I am capable of something.

I feel powerless, but more, I think of the new moralities of our world. I place a hand on the mother's arm, say, "Let him pass. It is for the best. Let him be reborn."

She shakes her head frantically, pulls away from my touch, then reaches for my hand, places it on the boy's head again.

I sense the child's damage.

"He die," his mother says now. "He come back. He die... he come back."

Over and over... Reborn each time with the corruption carrying through. How many times must this woman have witnessed her son die, be reborn, suffer and die all over again?

I close my eyes.

Feel the ebb and flow of the world, of realities.

I feel now that I am touching other worlds. Other *instances*. I can feel shapes and patterns and currents.

I can feel the boy's essence, his deep flaw. I push. Remix. Steer.

I come back, open my eyes, rock back on my heels.

The boy lies peacefully. Sissy smiles at me. She had believed. She had faith.

I stand, take her hand.

"Padre, padre," says the mother, rushing to me, embracing me. "Padre."

I allow her to do this for a moment, then slip free, embarrassed.

I smile, and lead Sissy from the shack.

THERE ARE MANY gods of the Accord, but this is the first time Ella has sought one out.

On Earth, Shiva bestrides continents, creator and destroyer, fomenting wars that last for centuries, endlessly recycling the living. He is worshipped there. He gives the slaughter meaning. He is the consensual God of the eternally war-torn mother planet.

On many worlds there is a mother of nature, a mother of natural order. They call her Gaia, or Rhea, or Mahimata, or Anu. On some planets they worship Mary and Jahveh, Mother and Son, in a variant of the old Catholicism. On others this is inverted and cults have grown up around the figures of Father and Daughter, Padre e Figlia, with shrines at locations where the two have appeared. Ella is drawn to Father and Daughter, has even visited some of the shrines; they are seekers too, eternally wandering the worlds of humankind.

The gods are many. It is as if humankind must draw them into being, impelled to fill a spiritual vacuum in their lives, a god-shaped hole.

Ella follows the man who has now introduced himself as Shujin'yaku, and soon they stand on a polished terrace carved from stone at the foot of the cliff. She looks up. This is a palace from childhood stories. A dream palace. The air rings with the chink of chisels on stone. Somewhere up high, a group of crow-like birds tumbles in an updraught, their cronking calls echoing, fading.

"Come along, Ella," says Shujin'yaku, stopping in an archway, the interior beyond him lit brightly. "Come and meet the Lord of All."

"What... *now?*" She hadn't expected to get to meet him so soon. She isn't prepared. She doesn't know how to prepare, mind you. She'd just expected a little *time*.

They pause before a door, watch it simply stop *being* in front of them, step through into a small lift-chamber. The chamber surges upwards. Ella accepts a ceramic beaker from Shujin'yaku, peers into it, sniffs. The drink has a fruity scent, full of tangy sweet and sour tones. A thin froth floats on the surface, lending it a vaguely unsavoury aspect. She sips, feels it soak into her mouth, a wave of revitalisation spreading through her.

They pass through into a narrow, long room, its walls lined with sculptures in the same blue stone as the walls – all of a single piece, carved when this room was carved. At regular intervals along the opposite long wall, archways open out to the world beyond, sunlight angling through. Shujin'yaku leads Ella through one of these archways and instantly she feels dizzy, has to clutch at a pillar for support, reassurance.

They are so high up that not much farther up the cliff white clouds swirl against the rock, caught in the updraughts that way below are still catching the crows.

Way below... The ground, so distant! The fields are like sweet wrappers, neatly arranged; the trees like tiny green spatters of paint. She is too high up to resolve individual people; the track is a straight, narrow line.

And all around, the chink-chink sound of chisel on stone. Across to her left, she sees white-robed figures hanging in harnesses, working the cliff face, crafting stone in honour of their God.

To her right... A small figure, seated on a silken throw, his back straight, neck stretched. His black head is bald, a wispy white beard growing only from the point of his chin. He stares straight ahead, as if he has not seen Ella and Shujin'yaku yet.

Ella stares. She cannot help it. She stares at the Lord of All.

Shujin'yaku takes the lead. He stoops from the waist, shuffles towards the Lord, and then settles on his knees, his hands on the floor before him, his head bowed. "My lord," he says. "I bring a seeker."

At his gesture, Ella stoops self-consciously, approaches, and drops to her knees, all the while transfixed by the little man who is a god.

He still stares ahead, as if he remains unaware of their presence.

Ella feels him, though. She feels him deep inside her. It's like he's pinging her, but doing so through all the senses. It's a buzz, a rush in her heart, an excitation of the brain, an ache deep in her belly. Deep... So deep she thinks she's going to fucking come...

She feels sweat on her brow, a prickly heat. She realises she is hyperventilating, and forces her breathing to slow.

He turns his gaze on her, and she loses herself in his eyes. They are ancient eyes, eyes full of the wisdom of generations, of passion and compassion, gentleness and power. They are the eyes of a god.

She has doubted. All the time she was walking, she doubted. Right up until she crested that rise and saw the garden, the palace – that was when she suddenly started to wonder, suddenly started to think she might finally have found it. Something to fill the space in her heart. But even then, it was only hope. She had not been sure.

And now? Now she is not sure... she cannot allow herself to be sure. But she feels *solid* again. She is herself. And God but she aches deep inside, and in oh such a good way!

# 2.16

ELLA STRIKES HER chisel, adding its chime to the music of the walls. A flake of stone breaks away, tumbles below, vanishes, still tumbling. She is a long way up, but heights have never bothered her. She hammers again, flakes away another fragment of blue stone.

Some time later, she abseils down to a balcony and releases the harnesses. She wants to shower before joining the other acolytes in the Great Chamber for the audience with the Lord of All, but when she sees the queues in one of the Chamber's tributary corridors she realises she does not have time.

Instead, she slots in behind Jocelyn and Reuben. When she eventually reaches the Chamber, it will be only the second time she has been there. The buzz in her chest is ridiculous – like some love-sick teenager, butterflies pounding in her gut, her heart racing, her skin flushed.

They file along a corridor, deep in the cliff. The walls are smooth, polished, niches at regular intervals holding metre-high depictions of the Lord of All. Above each niche: a finely carved inscription, quotes from the *Book of All*, brief parables from the life of the Lord, truisms from his teachings. The execution of these carvings is exquisite.

The air fills with a sonorous plainsong, a humming tone that reaches deep inside, resonates with the flesh, counterpoint chanting overlaid, interwoven.

They pass through an archway, and Ella is struck by the light – the air *sparkles* with it! It glistens…

The Lord stands at a dais, gazing at his acolytes as they enter the Great Chamber.

Is this what it feels like to have *found*?

Ella sits by Reuben, feels love in her heart, surrounding her. Everywhere.

They wait forever until the Chamber is full. She had not realised there are quite so many acolytes living here. It is a small city of the faithful.

Finally, the plainsong rises, builds, and then – cuts off. Utter silence. It is as if the world has stopped, reality has stopped.

"Children," says a soft voice, quiet, intimate, yet carrying easily throughout the Great Chamber. "All. Children of the All…"

It is the first time Ella has heard the voice of the Lord of All, for on her one audience with him he had remained silent, blessing her only with his gaze, with an almost wry smile. Now she recognises the ache deep in her belly. It is the touch of the Lord, and now he touches her again with his voice.

She bows her head, tries to control her breathing. Wonders how the fuck she's going to cope with finally having found what she has been seeking forever.


WE TRAVEL WORLDS, Sissy and I, father and daughter.

I teach her, tell her all that I know, and help her work out with me answers to the things we do not yet know. I study worlds; I study reality. I smooth over flaws in reality too, fix the defects by reaching deep within, to where my essence is bonded with that of the Accord.

And all the time, I am aware that I am perhaps the biggest anomaly of all: a soul that was destroyed, finally come together again, recoalesced. I seem to act like a magnet, an attractor, a gravity well. Sissy and I can never stay in one place for long: it gets too complicated.

So we travel worlds, Sissy and I.

And always, I look for you, Priscilla. I look for you in the streets and in the markets. I reach out for you in the ebb and flow of reality that I pass through, that passes through me. Search for you in realities.

In all the worlds, in all the potential universes, there is this one where I have come together again. In all the worlds, in all the universes, I will find you. We will again be father, mother, daughter.

There is more, though.

I want to understand. The ebb and flow, the sense of realities all around… The fabric of the universe is within me. It *is* me. Yet I feel that I touch other places, other whens.

I remember Magda Blue, her reality-mining. The possibility of realities within realities; or realities alongside realities. A strange geometry of realities.

I need to understand this. I need to understand the nature of what I have become.


ELLA'S HEAD IS still bowed. She has been here in the Great Chamber for a long time, a time she has no way of estimating.

She still has the ache. Still has the surging inside, the fluttering, the crazy-adolescent rush. The Lord of All has spoken – of order and patience, of the power of love to shape the world, of the purity found in creation, of devotion and faith and the power within us all to shape our own soul.

The Lord's words had got through to Ella; they spoke to her of how she has led her life: of the power of love, the value of good acts, of how consensus can be reinforced by belief in living a life that is true.

Now, it is her turn.

She stands in line, one of maybe twenty new acolytes, awaiting audience with the Lord of All. To her right, the choir stands in tiered ranks, rising above her in an array that almost defies both geometry and gravity. To her left, the massed gathering of acolytes, an entire city of faith.

She shuffles forward, waits.

Finally… she takes her cue from Shujin'yaku, walks out, stands before the Lord of All, drops to her knees, places her hands on the blue stone floor, and looks up into the face of God.

He smiles, reaches forward, places a hand on her brow.

His touch is electric, a sudden connection which she feels right through her body. And then it is over.

She looks at him.

She looks at him and she realises…

"Please…" she says, in a voice that is barely a sound at all. "Please… I want *more*."

She could spend a lifetime here. Many lifetimes. She could lose herself in this shared world, this micro-consensus of faith. It would be so easy.

But she wants more than this.

She realises in this moment that she has not found it at all, whatever *it* is. And her heart breaks all over again.

She stares into the eyes of the Lord of All and watches him flicker. For an instant she sees the far wall appear through him, as if he is a transparent overlay.

Solid again. Staring at her.

Then… Fading… Features breaking up into blocks, pixelating.

He is not real, this Lord of All.

Ella sees him for what he is. He is the product of will, of faith. He is a consensual wish, a craving, a product of the spiritual hunger of those who seek…

She sees through him, beyond him. She wants more, and something He cannot provide. She wants other.

She straightens, still on her knees. She looks back over her shoulder towards the gathered masses. They all look forward, eyes wide, faces peaceful, longing, worshipful. They do not see through their Lord.

She looks at the God again, the dream God, the longed-for God. He flickers, is little more than blocks of colour, loosely adhering to each other.

Beyond, she sees the wall of the Great Chamber. Where before it had been intricately carved with glyphs and effigies, now... Rough rock, glistening with damp. She can see the rough-hewn chisel marks in the stone.

She rises to her haunches, stands. Shujin'yaku looks at her, open-mouthed. He gestures sharply for her to prostrate herself again, but she does not. She looks at him, a poor, thin man in shabby robes worn through at the knee and elbow, the hems frayed, the white fabric stained brown and green and blue from the rock. He looks old, and gaunt, and there is something desperate in his eyes.

She backs away, then turns at the top of the two steps down to the main auditorium.

They are all looking at her now, puzzled, shocked at her transgression, her interruption of their smooth adoration.

They are all like Shujin'yaku: haggard, needy people, worn thin by years of working the rock. Their faces are drawn, gaunt, their bones prominent, robes hanging limply from their frames. And their eyes... Their eyes are full of longing, of need. They are living their dream. They have found what they need. They have built it from dust, from rock, from faith.

Ella staggers forward, down the rough-carved steps, across the floor of this huge cavern, its surface wet, greasy, deceptive.

Out, through an archway and she is in a cave, a tunnel through the rock, lit only by a few sputtering torches set in holes in the walls.

She starts to run, has to get out. This is someone else's dream, not hers. She doesn't want to be here any more.

She reaches a junction, catches herself against the facing wall, feels rock against her face, deliciously cool. She remembers where she is, turns to the right, runs again.

But the lift shaft is simply that: a hole in the wall, no elevator within, just a shaft. She pulls back from it. Turns. Heads along the tunnel again, and soon she sees daylight ahead.

She emerges on a balcony, a low, rough lip of rock running along the face of the Lord of All's palace. She finds a harness and climbs into it, tightening it around her waist and across her shoulders. She turns, braces, steps back over the edge, abseils down the cliff face.

Free of the harness once again, she stumbles away from the palace, heart pounding.

Around her, the fruit trees are ragged stumps, the fields sparsely covered with etiolated, wispy crop plants.

After a short time she pauses, looks back. The palace is an array of cave-mouths and ledges, raked into the face of the cliff. It looks Neolithic. It looks rough. It looks desperate.

She turns, starts the return journey along the rough track.

This is not what she seeks. She understands that now.

But if she does not seek God, then what is it that she does seek?


I FIND MAGDA Blue in a bender on a planet seventy light years from Earth. It has taken a long time, but then time is something we have aplenty.

Sissy and I are in a city called Benevolence. We *are*. Before all this… We were *not*… We are truly of the Accord – of it, and yet anomalous. We challenge the protocols. We exist in the gaps between the protocols, in the interstices.

We are in Benevolence.

A park. We stand in the entrance to the park, between tall iron gates chained open. The sky is a thin blue with a lilac tinge. Giant fern-like vegetation grows, with tiny animals skittering among the leaves and leap-gliding between fronds. Sissy thinks they are very funny. She wants one for a pet. She calls them tawnies and I believe her: she knows a lot about natural history.

We are not here for the wildlife, though. Across the road there is a reality parlour, an anonymous shopfront, in that way of Magda's. Her latest reality-bending studio.

We cross, weaving our way through rickshaws and scooters, through pedestrians leisurely strolling with all variety of animals attached to them by leads – some dog-like, others hovering in the air over the walkers' heads.

We pause at the entrance, a sheer, black glass door. I touch it and it slides open.

Inside... Bright lights, jaunty music, shrieks and laughter and smells of deep-frying doughnuts. Sissy squeals with delight, tugs at my hand but I won't let go, for fear of losing her in the crowd. The night air is crisp, the stars bright, unfamiliar. We stand by a stall where a young man takes aim with an air rifle, shooting at rows of moving ducks. Beyond, an enormous Ferris wheel turns slowly, slowly.

"Okay, okay," I say. "We'll go on the rides."

We do. We ride on a waltzer that makes Sissy scream and me feel sick. We do the Ferris wheel three times, and then sit together on a mat and ride the helter-skelter, spiralling down around a stripy tower lit up with multicoloured bulbs. We ride the dodgems, Sissy showing a mean streak as she takes people head-on, ramming them out of the way.

Later, we find Magda. She is in a tent, a board outside saying: "Magda Blue: come and see your future. Come and see your realities."

We stand in line, shuffle forward, and eventually our time comes. She looks at us as we step inside, and we look back at her, still Magda, wrapped in a twist of sari, her hair in a silk scarf. "Sweet holy Jesus," she says. "You're dead. You're... Hell, what *are* you?"

She knows immediately, senses the anomaly, the currents pulling at us... Tearing at us.

"Noah? Is that really you? Or are you some kind of bug in this reality?"

She blanks for a moment, as if running diagnostics. "Jesus, Noah. What are you?"

I smile. Shrug. "I do not know, Magda. I had hoped you might be able to help me with that."


"YOU CAST REALITIES, Magda. You craft them from nothing. You understand the nature of consensual reality better than perhaps anyone. I have been seeking you out..."

She is still staring at us.

Sissy has grown bored, and is poking around in a trunk at the back of the tent, finding shawls and saris and long loops of necklace.

"Why?" she asks. "I don't even understand what you are."

"I was destroyed," I tell her. "Sissy and I were annihilated. But... In this reality—"

"Hang on: *which* reality?" Magda waves her hands. "This one? The one I'm developing here?"

I shake my head. "No," I say. "I mean the Accord. Your Accord. The one in which you construct your sub-realities. In the Accord our constituent parts have come together again. But there are many possible Accords. I can feel them. I am aware of them pressing all around. And in all the possible realities, all the possible outcomes, there is one where this has happened, one where I can come back into existence... But what about all the other realities? All the others where this has not happened?"

"You do not exist there. You exist here. Isn't that enough? But you're telling me *here* isn't a singular form...?"

"The Accord sits in quantum space," I tell her, "where all the possibilities remain uncollapsed, unconfirmed. The *Accords* sit there. Every branching, every divergence..." I think of a multitude of worlds, side by side, an infinity of them. Worlds where things go differently.

I think of the sense in my head of realities pushed one against the other, of how I feel *of* the Accord. The Accords.

In one of those possible Accords, I have come together again; my sundered parts have recoalesced. I am here. And from that point on, realities have been diverging again, with every quantum decision, every instant.

Within that branch of realities where I exist, somewhere, my love, there must be a reality where I find you again. In an infinity of worlds, all is possible.

And I pray to my secular, rationalist gods that this is the reality where that can be so.

# 2.17

WE RULE HALF a planet. We remember, way back, we had been the man who ruled a whole world, but that's ancient history now. That was so many lifetimes ago.

We have a palace that sits on an island in a great sweeping river. People – endless streams of them – come to us to pay tribute, to seek favour.

Now, it is Governor Eshbetan, visiting from his walled city of Esh, a hundred klicks to the east. He is on his knees before us, as we sit in our throne in the grand hall. Stone columns and arches flank a floor warmed and nourished from within by its own blood supply. We wear dress shoes now, but we like to walk the palace barefoot, feel the false flesh against our skin.

Standing in the archways are slender young men carrying ceremonial – but fully functional – swords.

We pause, leave Eshbetan showing obeisance, wondering if he finds the flesh carpet disturbing or if he is enjoying the sensation.

"So," we say, finally, gesturing for him to stand. "You want troops. We are already heavily committed to the fight in the Leewards. Why should I divert forces to your safely walled city? You're five hundred klicks from the front."

I rule half a planet. Sometimes more, sometimes less. It all depends on the state of a war that has lasted more than a century.

"Walls and distance protect us from the war," says Eshbetan. "But when the unrest comes from within walls only serve to contain…"

We watch him carefully, wait for him to continue.

"It is a cult, the Padrefilians. They have become the focus for internal dissent. The Council wishes to stamp them out, but we feel that it would be a far stronger message if central forces were to deal with them."

Stronger message, or perhaps just a way of deflecting responsibility for blood on the streets of the governor's beloved city. Eshbetan had built the walled city a long, long time ago; he had designed the key buildings, marked out the labyrinthine streets, plotted the course of the walls. And now he wants us to eliminate a few troublemakers when we have far more weighty issues to tackle.

We sigh, look inwards, phase out, phase back in...

... and we are on the ramparts of Esh, having just jumped through a loop in the protocols. One of our little tricks. We have been studying and learning for many years. We have insight from the very beginning of the Accord. We know how this reality works.

Now, we head for the nearest wall-citadel and descend the enclosed stairs.

We are anonymous, with features that no one would comment on, let alone recall. As we stroll through the streets we blend in.

The people are quiet, perhaps a little more subdued than normal, but nothing to give rise to alarm. The cobbled streets twist around the steep incline of the hill on which Esh is built. The buildings are of an Earth-medieval style. Eshbetan always did wear his historical influences on his sleeve.

We wander, pausing for a sandwich from a street stall.

The vendor asks for money in a strong eastern accent, all gravel and cadences. We pay, and ask, "You know anything about the Padrefilians? I'm looking for someone."

He shrugs and runs a hand through his black hair. "Not a thing to do with me," he says. "But you'll run into one o' them soon enough, you keep wandering, sir."

We walk on.

A short time later, we come to a small enclosed garden. A public space clearly, but quiet, closed off by two-metre walls on three of its boundaries. The stone wall at the back has been modified, a niche built with stones that match, but are clearly new, clean.

We pass through olive trees and eucalypts.

At the rear of the garden a woman is on her knees. We pause, waiting for her to finish before we say anything.

The niche is an arched, enclosed space, a construction that could have been built to shelter a bench from sun or rain. The view from such a bench would be easy on the eye, back through the garden and then out over the rooftops to the distant bay.

But there is no bench here. Instead: an effigy. A sculpture of man and child, both kneeling, the man's hand extended.

An inscription on the back wall reads: *Padre e Figlia. They came. They cured. They gave hope. They departed. The world is richer.*

We have heard of this father and daughter cult. We don't get it. We don't get why humankind has to lean on such crutches. There are no gods. There never have been.

And then we look more closely at the figures of father and daughter.

Bizarrely, it is the child we recognise first.

We still have a Sissy. We have always brought her with us. We revive her sometimes, even now. At times when we are more Chuckboy than Jack.

And Barakh. Noah Barakh!

He stares back at us, eyes of stone, that half-smile, that smirk.

We do not believe.

We do not believe that it can be so, that he can be back. He is destroyed.

This image... This God of theirs... It must be some kind of deeply embedded racial memory, an archetype of this new world that has become engrained in the collective unconscious of those who live on in the Accord.

It must be some kind of psychic ghost, an echo.

He cannot live.

He cannot.


WE CANNOT LINGER, Sissy and I, we have to keep moving. It always gets so complicated...

Complicated, but never quite as much as this...

This planet we leave in such a hurry: we arrived here only fifteen days ago, two among the many thousands of tourists who wander the colonies on the interstitial liners. For many, life is an endless holiday.

I feel like a perpetual fugitive. A refugee.

I feel the protocols gathered around me always, pressing in, affronted by the anomaly of my nature.

The people feel it too. They gather around me, drawn to me. They believe I can cure them of their ills, lead them to salvation. The religious, spiritual impulse is deeply engrained in the nature of our species. It is a struggle to be surrounded by the needy, the worshipful.

I had thought it was just me though...

Three days ago, we left the city of Cap Duval by train.

We took up a whole carriage.

First, Sissy and I entered and took our seats, Sissy by the window, wanting to see the bay, an almost complete circle of blue water, joined to the sea only by a gap in the cliffs to the north.

Inevitably, they followed.

Julia, a young woman who had been voluntarily blind and deaf for twenty years in some kind of spiritual quest, now gifted with sight and hearing after Sissy and I stopped to talk with her. I felt the patterns around Julia, felt her reaching out to me in some kind of yearning, and then felt the patterns reforming themselves. I should have spotted then that there was another hand involved. I should have seen that long before then.

And Marcel, a boy, stuck somewhere in his teens, although I guess he has been here for centuries. A boy who had not been cured, but just *needed* so intensely.

And Joanna, and Asha, and Sergio, and Samuel. All of them, crowding onto the carriage. Intense. Needy.

I drew Sissy to me, close, and that was when I recognised the surge of energy, the patterns in the protocols all around us.

Sissy.

I pulled back, saw the intensity in her eyes, the half-smile playing on her mouth.

*Sissy*.

"Sissy?" I said, physically turning her head to face me. "Are you okay, Sissy?"

She smiled. She glowed. She buzzed with energy. It was as if everything was being channelled through her.

All this... I had thought it down to me, my strange connection to the fabric of the Accord since I had been destroyed and reborn. What extremes must the Accord have gone to in order to fulfil its primary duty of allowing me rebirth?

The people drawn to us, the curing and healing, the strange passions that surround us... I had thought it me.

But Sissy has been through the same rites as me. Sissy is young, unformed, raw. What flows through me I guide and shape, but if the same currents flow through Sissy, then what must it be like for her? Does she guide and shape, or is it some wild force of nature, channelled through her? Some alien rapture?

After about an hour, Julia approached me, us... Sissy.

She knelt, placed her hands in Sissy's lap.

Sissy placed her own hands on the crown of Julia's head.

The whole carriage was afire with the energies suddenly flowing. I pulled myself away from the two of them, buffeted by the onslaught. Others gasped, cried out. The air around Julia and Sissy crackled.

And then it was over. Julia slumped; Sissy sat back. I looked at the two of them, not really understanding what was happening, only that the roles had been reversed, or rather that they were always reversed.

That night, Sissy and I shared a room in a hotel by the station in a small seaside town called Cressy. I did not know where our entourage were, but was certain they could not be far away. Sissy and I, we huddled, fully clothed on one of the beds. I drew her to me, fearing for her, fearing her, and so, so responsible for her fate. I felt like the destroyer of worlds, destroyer of people. The man who built heaven for all but those he cares about.

And Sissy sensed my discomfort. She held me, muttered soothing words, reached into my head to calm me, to cure me of my guilt and allow me to sleep.


HUMANKIND OCCUPIES MANY thousands of planets. Humankind occupies many sub-realities within the reality we call the Accord – semi-stable constructs created for leisure, for art, for realities that defy the broader consensus. It is an enormous feat to track someone down in such a multitude of worlds.

We tracked him down.

We tracked him down on a planet called New Province, a city called Cap Duval. As soon as we learnt that he was there we phased in... Phased out... And we were standing in a street that led down a steep hill to a harbour. We could smell sharp salt on the breeze, hear the screeches of Earth gulls, and the buzz of winged insect-like creatures that dived and hung in the air over the off-loading trawlers. Beyond, a wide blue bay, almost circular, cut off from the greater sea by two tongues of cliff on the horizon.

We asked around, followed the leads we had been given, and finally found the owner of a guest house where they had been staying.

"... Three days ago," says the woman. "Father and daughter." At that, the woman glances heavenward and makes a sign something like a genuflection at her chest.

"Where are they now?"

"They travel," she says. "With a band of pilgrims. East, along the coast. They mentioned Cressy and Flanders."

We nod, consult inwardly, then phase in... Phase out... No time for niceties: we were there and now we are here.

Cressy is a small town cupped around another bay. It is as if great holes have been punched through this coastline, punctuating it with coves and bays of anything from a few hundred metres to twenty or so klicks across.

We turn to our left and there is a hotel, Le Sanctuaire.

The man on reception is a model of discretion. He smiles at us, says, "I am sorry, sir, but we do not divulge details of our guests. I am sure you appreciate the importance of privacy."

He divulges.

Very quickly.

We phase in... Phase out... We are in him, riding him, squeezing... He hurts. We can feel his hurt. We make him hurt more. Make him stand still as he feels his insides burning with righteous fire.

"They left yesterday," he says. "For the Cap – they will be off-planet by now. Gone..."

We leave him there, behind his desk. Someone will find him, decide whether to fix him or just put him out of his misery to be reborn.

I LIE IN the embrace of my catch-blanket, waiting for the jump.

Sissy lies nearby, staring up at the ceiling. She is at peace. I can feel it. Now that I understand I can sense the patterns around her, feel her emotional states. Again, I wonder what she is, what has been created by this strange journey of ours. I have been annihilated and come together again, and I am all too aware of the intense forces pulling at me continually. But Sissy is something else entirely; she is a force of nature, a force of protocol, something raw and untapped.

How would you react to this, my love? You would not succumb to your fears. You would embrace her, this scary un-child of ours. You would nurture her.

Priscilla... Oh, Priscilla. Where are you? I would seek you to the end of the universe. I would seek you in all the universes of the Accord.

And when I find you... Will you be a you that can love me?

I feel my heart clenching, that physical lurch that love can inflict. And then I feel a surge, an opening, and I realise that this is not love that I feel, but something genuinely physical, a falling, a pulling apart, an expansion, and I recognise the wrench of the leap into interstitial space as our latest journey begins.

I lose touch with my body, lose touch with what I am.

And then... Collapsing, contracting. Regaining my sense of me, regathering. Being. Me.

Priscilla... I have sought you for so many, many years. One day, I will step out onto a planet and it will be the planet where you are. You, me, Sissy. We will be together again.

I look at the screen, see another blue and green and white planet, another world.

Let this be the one, my love. Let this be the one.


HE MAY BE one jump ahead of us, but we are close. We will track him down and we will destroy him once again. We will destroy him as many times as it takes.

We are opposing forces of nature, Barakh and us, me. This is one of the fundamental laws of the universe, the protocol that underlies all others.

We walk down to the area around the docks. There are bars and gambling joints here, dens where you can go to shoot up or jack down with any variety of chemical and electrical mind-fucks. A whore stands by a dark doorway, full breasts and ladyboy crotch bulging through his/her pink mini. We move on.

There... A skinny thing. Looks mid-teens, whatever's in her head. Looks wasted. Black shadows under the eyes, stark against bleached skin. Blood rushes. We approach her. Want her. Will have her, and it won't be pretty.

But then we pause, attention caught by another woman, on her knees by a wall, painting something, an intricate artwork, a figure... No, two figures... Father and daughter.

We walk across and stare into the half-formed features of Noah Barakh and Sissy.

The woman is a rake, skin loose, almost no flesh on her. She barely has the strength to move, does everything in slow-mo.

We scuff a heel on the ground, and she turns her head.

Her eyes are alight with some kind of fire from within.

"You met them, didn't you? They were here."

Lips peel back and she nods. "I travelled with them," she says in a thin voice. "I was blind and now I can see. I was deaf and now I can hear."

We look at her. We sense we are close. So close. We phase in... Phase out... And we are back in Cap Duval, in the main lobby area of the interstitial port.

We are close, Barakh. So very close indeed.

# 2.18

THE WOMAN WHO calls herself Tish Goldenhawk waits as the gaudy Daguerran vessel slides into the harbour. She stands atop the silver cliffs of Penhellion and watches – no, *marvels* – as the *Lady Cecilia* approaches the crooked arm of the dock.

The ship is unlike any she has seen before. Far taller than it is long, it rises out of the mirrored waters like some kind of improbable island. Its flanks are made of polished wood and massed ranks of high arched windows, these revealing bodies within, faces pressed against glass as the grand touristas take in yet more of the sights of the worlds.

The ship, the *Lady Cecilia*… It towers unfeasibly. Only vastly advanced engineering could keep it from toppling this way or that. The thing defies gravity by its very existence. It sails, a perfect vertical, its array of silken sails bulging picturesquely, its crew scrambling over the rigging like squirrels.

At a distant screech, Tish tips her head back and stares until she has picked out the tiny scimitar shapes of gliding pterosaurs. It is a clear day, and the world's rings slash a ribbon across the southern sky. Why does beauty make her sad? Why is this world not enough?

Tish breathes deep, and she knows she should be back at the Falling Droplet helping Milton behind the bar.

And then she looks again at the golden, jewelled, bannered sailing ship now secured in the harbour and she feels an almighty welling of despair that this should be her lot in a world of such beauty and wonder.

She walks back along a road cut into the face of the cliff. She is lucky. She lives in a beautiful place. She has a good husband, a thriving business. She could want for nothing. Nobody starves or suffers in the worlds of the Diaspora, unless it is their choice to do so. People are born to different lots, they choose different lots, and this current lot of hers is a good one.

She is lucky, she tells herself again. Blessed by the Accord.

THE FALLING DROPLET is set into the silver cliffs of Penhellion, its floor-to-ceiling windows giving breathtaking views out across the bay to where the coast hooks back on itself and the Grand Falls plunge more than a thousand metres to the sea.

Rainbows play and flicker across the bay, an ever-changing colour masque put on by the interplay of the falls and the sun. Pterosaurs and gulls and flying fish cut and swoop through the spray, while dolphins and mer-folk arc and flip in the waves.

Tish is staring at the view, again, when the stranger approaches the bar.

"I... Erm..." He places coins on the age-polished flutewood surface.

Tish drags her gaze away from the windows. She smiles at him, another anonymous grand tourista with perfect features, flawless skin, silky hair, a man who might as easily have been twenty as a century or more.

He smiles back.

She glances down, then, and realises the man is accompanied by a child, a girl of about ten. The child returns Tish's look, her eyes intense, something burning within.

Tish looks at the man, at the child.

In that instant Tish Goldenhawk is transfixed, just as she had been by the sight of the *Lady Cecilia* earlier.

She feels her heart raging and she does not know why. This man, his child... They are not grand touristas like all the others, they are different. They are *other*.

"I... Erm..." she says, inadvertently repeating the man's words from a moment before. "What'll it be?"

"I..." He gestures at one of the pumps.

"Roly's Scrumpy?" she says, reaching for a long glass. "You'd better be watching your head in the morning, if you're not used to it. That stuff's an ass: drink it full in the face and you're fine, but as soon as you turn your back it'll kick you."

She puts the drink before him and helps herself to some of the coins he has spread out.

"Been on Laverne for long?" she says, knowing the answer he will give. He has just landed, along with all these other touristas. Struggling with the dialect and the coins. These poor over-rich fucks must be constantly disoriented, she realises, as they take their grand tours of the known. The poor lambs.

He shakes his head, smiles again. A day ago he has probably been in a jungle, or in a seething metropolis, or deep in an undersea resort, ten, a hundred, a thousand light years away, along with others on the grand tour.

But Tish still wonders if he really is just another tourista. She often constructs stories about the people she serves in the Falling Droplet. The spies, the adulterers, the scag addicts, and the gender-confused. Sometimes she even turns out to be right, but usually she never confirms her hunches one way or the other. This man... He seems familiar. He feigns unfamiliarity but he has been here before, perhaps in a different guise.

"You on the *Lady Cecilia*?" she asks him, hoping he will give himself away but knowing he won't.

"I am," he says, and then dips his head to take a long draw of the cider. He glances around. "Or at least," he added, "I *was*..."

Then he looks her full in the eye and says, "What do they call you now? What is your name?"

*Now...* He has known her... before.

"Tish?" Milton's voice came as if in answer to the stranger's question. She smiles at the man, as if sharing a secret, then glances back at her husband. He gestures. They have customers lined up at the bar. The Droplet has grown crowded and Tish has barely noticed. She moves away from the newcomer and his child, and serves old Ruth with her usual Brewer's Gold and nuts.

YOU DON'T KNOW me.

You warn me that the cider has a kick like a mule, but you do not know me.

My love.

I look into your eyes, and for a moment I see a spark of something, a hint of recognition. A flicker.

Now you move away to serve others. I watch you as you work. The flowing movements of your body. The smiles and easy chat you exchange with regulars and strangers alike.

I squeeze Sissy's hand.

We do not need words.

We have found you, Priscilla. We have found you *Tish*.

But you do not know us.

LATER, TISH GOLDENHAWK notices another stranger come in from the darkening evening. There are many newcomers among this evening's clientele, but like the first man and his daughter this one doesn't look like he is on any kind of grand tour. His eyes scan the crowd, and as he fixes on her for the briefest of instants she feels skewered.

What is happening this evening?

Who are these strangers?

They have come from nowhere and now she feels as if a rug has been yanked from beneath her feet and she is tumbling, falling... into the past.

Tish has lived many and varied lives. She has forgotten far more than she can remember. That is the way.

So many lives when she has ended up feeling empty, as if a major part of her is missing. That is how she feels now, how she has felt for far too many years in this tranquil life.

Until today, until right now.

Now she falls. Is dragged down, memory pulling at her.

The newcomer's gaze has lingered, but now moves on. Tish sees what appear to be weapons at his belt.

The man suddenly fixes on something and stands motionless, like a sandfisher poised to drop. He points, then opens his hand and a beam of light shines from his palm across the crowded bar.

Tish turns and sees a single man picked out by the beam, a long glass poised partway to his mouth.

The stranger drops his glass, ducks down to gather up his daughter, darts into the pack of bodies near to the bar.

WE SEE HIM, see her... Our head is aswirl with tangled emotions, impulses, thoughts.

Priscilla! Standing there, bottle of some liquor poised over a shot glass, looking back at us, at me.

Priscilla.

We feel dizzy. Anger and passion and something indefinable but fuck so intense!

We sense him, then, his presence – Barakh – the tangle he creates in the fabric of the world. He is here with Priscilla... How long? How long have they been here?

Only days at most, I know. We have been on his tail. He has only just arrived on this planet.

But he must have been here before. This must be their hideaway. He travels, but always to come back.

I scan the busy barroom, seeking out his anomaly, his *wrongness*.

A tussle by the far door, and there he is, reaching for the handle, Sissy at his side.

We focus, shift consensus, and the handle vanishes, the door blurring, its boundaries softening, merging... and it is wall, not door. There is no exit there. There never has been. Chuckboy is good now. He is very good.

Barakh's fingers slide across a smooth surface, and he staggers.

We raise a hand, aim again, but he is fast.

Barakh and Sissy have ducked into the crowd. We pause, we scan, we know to be patient and not be rushed into action.

Another disturbance.

Barakh.

He has a wooden chair raised above his head.

He does not understand what is happening. He is resorting to violence, the chair his only weapon against us.

We smile. He is making it easy.

Beyond him, the sun is setting, heavy and swollen over the rainbowed water. The sky is cast in bands of the deepest of crimsons, a staggering gold, shading up to a high, dreamy purple. Laverne's rings slash darkly across this vivid sunset.

The sky shatters. Crazed lines divide it up into an enormous, jagged jigsaw.

Someone screams, someone else shouts, someone else...

For a moment we cannot see Barakh and Sissy – there is just the chair embedded in the big picture window, the glass crazed but still holding in its frame.

Then we see them, a double silhouette against the fiery sky, diving.

They hit the glass and for an instant it holds and we think they will end up embedded like the chair. And then the moment has passed and the glass shifts, bulges, and the chair, the man and his daughter tumble out into the air.

Someone screams again, and the shouting continues, as the crowd shuffles back from the abyss.

We approach the opening and peer out into the gloom. The bar is half a kilometre up here, nothing but a fuck-load of air between us and the rocks and waves below. No one could survive such a fall; we wonder where he will be reborn. It will most likely be on this planet somewhere, probably nearby. Somewhere familiar to him. Perhaps the *Lady Cecilia*.

We will find him. We will be waiting for him.

And then we will come back for Priscilla.

TISH GOLDENHAWK DROPS in an air-shaft to Fandango Way, Penhellion's main thoroughfare. The Way is cut into the base of the cliff, and runs from the docks to where it winds its way up the cliff face three kilometres east.

She steps out among the stalls of itinerant traders. She nods and smiles and exchanges words here and there. She is not here to buy, and most of the traders know that anyway: these same traders deliver supplies direct to the Falling Droplet. Tish has little need of market shopping.

She carries a basket, though, and in the basket, beneath a chequered cloth, there is a crust of bread and a fistful of feathers from a quetzal.

She crosses the road, dodging rickshaws and scooters. Lifting her feet daintily over the low wall, she steps out onto the rocks.

Down by the water's edge, first of all she looks at the gentle chop of the waves, and then she cranes her neck to peer upwards, but she cannot pick out the Falling Droplet's frontage from all the others. So many dwellings and other establishments set into the cliff here. It is a very desirable place to live. She is lucky in this life.

She kneels on a big rounded boulder and wonders why she should be so sad also. This... this weight. She cannot remember when it had started, and she suspects that there could be no such neat line: in some ways it had started in the mixing of genetic material at her conception, while in others it might be quite recent.

This melancholy is all-pervasive. A flatness that smothers everything, a tinge of desperation in her thoughts, a clutching at the straws of strangers' imagined lives.

She tells herself to stop being so maudlin.

She pulls the cover from her basket and takes out the crust of bread. She breaks it into three pieces and hurls each as far as she can manage out onto the waves. Then she takes the quetzal feathers and casts them into the breeze, watching them as they flutter, some onto the water and some onto the rocks.

Food for the journey and feathers for the passage. An old family tradition, perhaps even one that came from Earth.

Softly, she wishes the stranger and his daughter a peaceful transition, and a fitting rebirth.


WE STEP OUT through the cabin door and go to stand at the rail.

We are high up, on the deck of a faux sailing ship that is really powered by twinned gravity-wave microgenerators below decks. Above us, sails bulge in a manner designed to appeal to the grand touristas.

He is not here, on the *Lady Cecilia*, although we had been sure that this is where he would be reborn after falling from Priscilla's bar. We will find him, though. He cannot be far away.

Penhellion is a city built into a cliff. They could have built it on top of the cliff. They could have built it a few kilometres along the coast where the cliffs are not anything up to 1200 metres high. Human nature is not such, and they built it in the cliff.

We close our eyes. Data flashes.

We have reached out across Penhellion, infiltrating this place, its people. We have agents now, scattered across this city. Many agents. They will look out for him, and their reports will be relayed to us whenever they hold anything of relevance.

They do not know they are agents. They do not know they have been selected. Sanji Roseway does not know that she is watching, as she happily stocks her fabric stall on Fandango Way. Neither does the street musician, Mo Yous, or the bar owner, Milton Goldenhawk, or the dreamcaster, Serendip Jones. They will not know when they are reporting, or when they have reported. That is not their place.

He has been quiet, though, which has not helped us in our task. He should be like a whirlpool, drawing in the human debris of this society, as he has done before on other worlds. The weak are drawn to him, like iron dust furring a magnet. Such activity sends out signals, leaves traces, a pebble dropped in our collective pool.

But with experience comes guile and with guile, restraint.

The *Lady Cecelia* departs soon. We will remain in Penhellion, studying and using our agents to study. He will break cover. He will reveal himself by his actions. It is only a matter of time.


MILTON HAS SQUARE shoulders and a square face. Most often if you caught him unawares you would see him smiling because that is the way his features settled themselves.

He is a good man.

Tish comes into the bar of the Falling Droplet just as Hilary and Dongsheng are leaving, having replaced the picture window through which the stranger, his daughter, and one of their bar chairs had plummeted the night before.

Milton is looking out through the new glass, relaxed, smiling gently.

Tish comes up behind him, puts her hands on his shoulders and turns him, kisses him, first close-mouthed and then, briefly, allowing her tongue to press between his lips.

He steps back, smiling more broadly now – a sure sign that he is unsettled by her ways. "Steady, steady!" he says. "What's got into you, then, eh? Won that grand tour ticket or something?"

"No," she says. "Not that." She takes hold of a handful of his shirt and smiles. "No," she continues, "I just want to fuck you, Milton."

He looks scared, like a small animal. Once, she had found that endearing.

"But…" he says. "What if someone comes in?"

"We're closed." She toys with the handful of shirt she still has in her grip, knowing she is pulling at the hairs on his chest, knowing how that turns him on.

"But Marcia—"

"Isn't here yet," she says.

"But she might—"

"So you'd better be quick."

But the moment is going, has gone. Had maybe never really been there at all.

She releases his shirt, moves away.

"You're a good man, Milton," she says, looking out over the bay.

When she glances back over her shoulder Milton is smiling, because that's how his features tended to settle themselves.

## 2.19

It might have ended there, if she had not gone up top to the Shelf: the window repaired, the stranger, his daughter, and their pursuer gone, the spark just beginning to return to Tish Goldenhawk's life – and to Milton's, whether he wanted it or not.

But no, four days after paying tribute to the stranger and his daughter's passing over into the Accord, Tish takes a shaft up to the top of the cliffs again, to the Shelf, and there she sees what her first response tells her must be ghosts.

Here, a row of homes and bars and shops lines the cliff-top, so that one has to enter a building in order to enjoy the view over the bay to the Grand Falls.

Tish has been in a bar called the Vanguard, sharing gossip with Billi Narwhal, a multicentenarian who is currently wearing his hair white on the principle that it advertises his many years of experience to any of the youngsters wanting lessons in love. The Vanguard was busy, with another two cruise ships in harbour having replaced the *Lady Cecilia*, now two days south.

A little tipsy from Billi's ruby port, Tish leaves the bar. A short way ahead of her is a man and there is something about the way he holds himself, something about the slight taste of cinnamon on her lips – on the air, a scent.

He turns. The stranger. Undamaged, unblemished by his fall. However had he survived? He holds out his arms and the girl comes running to him.

Tish clutches at the doorframe and blames the ruby port, both for her unsteadiness and for the apparition.

The stranger and his daughter are no longer there. For a few seconds Tish is able to convince herself that they never had been. And then she realises the two have merely been reborn, and she feels stupid for allowing herself to be so thrown by this.

She gathers herself and tries to remember what she has come up to the Shelf to do. She hasn't just come up here to gossip with Billi Narwhal and flatter herself with his attention.

She pushes through the crowd. She is following them. Following so quickly that it is more pursuit than passive following.

She pauses, thinking of the other stranger in the Falling Droplet. Had it been like this for him? Was he a mere innocent suddenly overcome with the urge to pursue? She knows such things are possible: the gods of Accord can reach out to any individual and guide their actions.

But why? Why pursue this man? She is convinced now that he is *other*, that the Accord speaks through him, that he is a fragment of God made flesh. She can feel it.

She starts to walk again, eyes scanning the faces.

She finds them at a café, the man sipping jasmine tea and the girl drinking something milky while a newscast speaks to them from the middle of the table. Tish sits across from him. "May I?" she asks.

He smiles, and blanks the 'cast with a pass of his hand. He looks quizzical. The girl is smiling at her, her teeth a white slash across dark features. Tish covers the girl's hand with her own and feels an instant connection.

She feels as if she is tumbling again.

She forces control on herself.

"The Falling Droplet," she explains. "You... left rather abruptly."

Understanding crosses his face. "I'm sorry," he says. "I did not anticipate that."

She smiles.

"There are expenses?"

"Oh no," she says. "Well, yes, actually, but they're covered by the city." Acts of God.

They sit quietly for a while, and Tish starts to think they might prefer to be left alone.

Then the man says, "I am sorry. I should have contacted you after that. I should have made sure everything was taken care of. I had other things on my mind once I reached the ground, but that is no excuse."

"Are you telling me you survived the fall?" she blurts out. "How?"

"There are ways," he says. "It's not important."

She smiles. So far he has said nothing to deny her belief about his true nature, her fantasy. The man who channels God.

"How do you find all this?" she asks him now, making conversation, prolonging their exchange. "The world of Laverne?"

"It's a mystery to me. The place, the people. You. It's beautiful. You… You don't know me, do you?"

She doesn't. And yet she does. She feels like she has known him all her life, her lives. This man. The child.

"My name is Noah," he tells her. "And this is Sissy."

She plummets again. For a moment she knows them. She loves them. And then it is gone. So much gone. Far away.

She is Tish Goldenhawk. She leads a comfortable life in a beautiful place. She is lucky.

"Shall we walk?" he asks, and she could have said no, but she does not. It is too late for that.

WE WALK. OUT past the last of the cliff-top dwellings, to where the road becomes a track, becomes an ill-defined path.

We walk: me, Sissy, and you, my love. You hand in hand with the two of us.

"Why did you come after me if there is no debt?" I ask, after a time. "You must have had reason...?"

"I've never met anyone like you before," you tell me.

I look at you, longing for recognition. To have found you, at last, and yet it is a you who does not even know me...

Am I fooling myself that there is even a hint of recognition in your response? You have pursued us, found us, and now you walk with us, but are you just like all the others? Are you drawn to us because that is the nature of our anomaly, that the weak are drawn into our wake? Is that all it is?

Later, stopping on a promontory, breathing salt, cinnamon, grass, with butterflies flitting about the flowers in the turf and gulls raucously occupying the cliff below, we stop. Sissy goes rushing away after the butterflies.

You stand there, shy, avoiding my gaze. Then you lower yourself to the springy grass, spreading your skirts out across your legs, smoothing the fabric down.

"You," you say, the first word either of us has spoken for some time. "You're no grand tourista. Even without that goon chasing you through my bar it was obvious that you're different."

I nod, smile, wait for her to continue. A bee hums nearby.

"You're of the Accord, aren't you?"

"I don't understand."

"You are a fragment, a shard of it... I can feel the pull... from both of you. You're unlike everyone else I've ever met. If the Accord is our God, then you are a part of God. God in... in a man's body."

I kneel before you as you speak, willing you to remember. And then you reach for me, your hand snakes round behind my head, pulls me in, hard, urgent. Now.

\* \* \*

HIS TOUCH… HIS taste… his heat.

She pulls away, checks where the child is, pulls this man hard against her. His touch is like a wick in an oil-lamp, energy flowing through it. It makes her buzz, made her feel alive.

Afterwards, she lies back, enjoying the play of the cliff-top breeze on her bare legs, her skirt pulled down around her once again.

She has never done this before. Never taken one of her fantasies and played it out. Never betrayed poor, dull Milton, whom she had once, long ago, loved and now merely likes.

She turns onto her side as this man – this God – rises to a squatting position.

"Let me show you something," he says.

She laughs. "I'm not sure I'm quite ready yet," she jokes.

He stands, wearing only a creamy cotton smock top that buttons to halfway down. He reaches down, arms crossing, takes its hem and pulls the top over his head, discarding it so that now he stands over her, fully naked.

She looks at him, enjoying what she sees, his nakedness somehow adding to the frisson of sheer *badness* that touches every aspect of this engagement.

He turns, and she sees a strange lump between his shoulder blades. She is sure that had not been there moments before, when she had held him. As she watches, it bulges, grows, bifurcates.

As she watches, feathered wings sprout from his back.

With a shake, he settles his flight feathers and holds his wings out stiffly behind him. He turns and steps off the cliff and, moments later, is soaring, swooping, cutting back heavenward in an updraught like a giant gull, like an angel.

Her angel.

Tish returns to the Falling Droplet late, unwashed.

Milton smiles at her, because that is how he is, and she wonders if he can tell, if she is that changed by what has happened.

She certainly feels different. She feels like something has been added, something taken away. She is not the woman she had been this morning.

She kisses Milton, willing him to taste the salt on her lips, to smell the cinnamon scent on her hair, her clothes.

She has arranged to meet her angel again the following day, and she knows she will keep the appointment.

"Customers," murmurs her husband, drifting away.

She turns, looked out across the bay to where birds and pterosaurs fly, wondering if he might be out there too.


I LIE AT night, in the room that I share with Sissy with its view out across the bay. I watch the sky, the ever-changing colours of Laverne's rings as light cascades around them.

I feel myself being torn apart, pulled in every direction.

Sissy lies there, eyes closed, apparently asleep. But does she ever sleep?

Protocols gather around her, woven into the fabric of this world. She is an affront. I fear for her. I sense the upheaval caused by her anomaly and I fear for her.

And me? Should I also fear for myself?

I am anomaly too. I sense the world. I sense worlds. Bifurcations. At every quantum decision a new world branching off. The Accord exists in Kant–Lotfi space, occupying the infinitely possible spaces where quantum waves have yet to collapse.

There is an infinity of worlds.

I sense them.

I pray that I am in the right one, the one where you will be mine again.

I lie at night, watch the sky, feel myself pulled apart.

\* \* \*

IT COULDN'T LAST, of course. It could never last.

Ever more brazen, Tish brings her lover and his daughter to the Vanguard to eat the renowned dipped crabs. They had met in the street like passing friends, with a smile and a few words, with not a single touch exchanged. Even now, sitting around a small window table, their hands do not touch, their feet do not brush against each other. Only their eyes meet, filled with promise, anticipation.

Billi comes across before their food has been served, unable to resist finding out more. Tish is tempting fate, and she knows it. If Billi puts two and two together, word will be all over Penhellion before nightfall.

"Going to introduce me to your friends?"

Tish looks up, and casually strokes a hand across her lover's wrist, their touch like electricity. "Hello, Billi," she says. "This is Noah and his daughter Sissy. Noah and Sissy, meet Billi."

She sees Billi's eyes narrow, a slight nod. "You like my bar, Noah, eh?" he says. "What're you eating? Crab's good. Crab's always good here. Don't touch the lobster, though. Trust me on that."

"Crab," says Noah. "I took Tish Goldenhawk's advice."

Billi's eyes narrow again, and Tish wonders what connection he is making now. Then his eyes widen, turn more fully on Noah.

She has seen that look before, that mechanical movement.

At the bar... The goon who had come after Noah...

Billi raises a hand, holds it palm-out towards Noah with the fingers stiffly pointing.

His palm glows.

Noah ducks, dives forward, knocking the table aside, hard against Tish's knee so that she screams, then gasps as his weight strikes her, sending her back off her chair.

She looks up from the floor, as voices rise around them. She sees that Sissy has darted away between the tables, scattering chairs behind her.

The chair where Noah had been seated is a blackened lump, smoking furiously.

Billi is turning slowly from the burnt chair to where Noah and Tish lie on the floor. He has a puzzled expression on his face, a smooth, mechanical glide to his movements.

He is not Billi. Not for now, at least. Billi has been pushed aside and someone – that goon? – has taken over.

Why try to kill an angel?

Tish looks up, sees Sissy by the window beckoning.

Billi raises a hand again and Noah stands, hauling Tish to her feet, kicking a chair and table back at the old man to stop him pursuing.

They join Sissy by one of the Vanguard's big picture windows.

Tish looks out, suddenly dizzy at the height.

Noah takes a chair and raises it.

"You're making a habit of this," she says, as he swings it down against the window, crazing the glass.

This time, he gives the chair an extra twist, and the glass gives way.

Salty air leaps in through the opening.

Noah opens his arms and wraps them around Tish as she steps into his embrace, and then he jumps clear, taking her with him.

They fall, air rushing, whistling in Tish's ears.

They are going to die on the rocks this time, she feels sure. This is a lovers' end, and they would be reborn together, somewhere far away.

Then a feathered shape rushes past – *Sissy*!

Fabric rips, wings break free, and their fall becomes a graceful swoop taking them out across the water to join Sissy, soaring towards the place where the rainbows fill the air and the gulls and the pterosaurs fly.

* * *

"YOU NEED TO escape," you tell me. "You need to get away from here. Why ever did you stay here in the first place after he found you?"

I shrug. "I don't think he expected me to still be here." It is Burnham. It has to be. I have only glimpsed him here, that first encounter in Tish's bar: if it is Burnham then he has taken on an anonymous form, and he has mastered the protocols of Accord in quite alarming ways. But it is him. I know it is him.

We are on an island, one of the many islands where the Grand River becomes the Grand Falls and tumbles over the cliffs to the sea far below.

"If you want to get away why can't you just... I don't know... just snap your fingers? If you're of the Accord then you should be able to just slip away and reappear somewhere else."

"Like a god?" I laugh. I raise a hand and snap my fingers. Nothing happens. "We can push the rules, push consensus, but there are limits. The more we find clever ways to sidestep the protocols, the greater the anomaly." Burnham must be paying that price too. We glance across to where Sissy plays in the shallows. Our trick with the wings keeps Sissy amused, but the cost is great. I can sense the forces of the Accord gathered around us. I wonder how long it will be before the Accord smoothes us out of existence... Burnham is pushing at the same constraints. I sensed him as soon as he walked into that bar... the angry sense of anomaly, of *wrongness*.

You stand, and look down at me.

"If you're no god, then who are you? What are you? Who is that man chasing after you? What have you done?"

I let you finish. I smile.

"Tish," I say. "Priscilla... My name is Noah Barakh. I am the architect of Accord. I am the man who built heaven. In one world, a long long time ago, I fell for you. I have been seeking you ever since. Priscilla... I have found you, but you have yet to find me."

Just then, I hear the buzz of a motor – a flyer, perhaps.

You hear it too. "You have to get away from here," you say, practicality covering your clear confusion. "They'll destroy you."

"Will you come with me? Will you share it with me?"

You hesitate.

You look down at me.

And then, slowly, you nod.

# 2.20

"WHO ARE YOU? *What* are you?"

Tish Goldenhawk has travelled the length of Laverne's main continent with the man who calls himself Noah and who tells her she once loved him.

She has travelled the length of the continent with Sissy, the child who is not a child at all.

Today is the first time she has seen Sissy kill, although she suspects it is not the first time she has killed. Tish has dispensed bread and feathers for the girl's victim before confronting Noah.

She has travelled the length of the continent with them and she is ill, drained both physically and mentally, like a scag addict.

He gives his little half-smile. He shrugs. He says, "I don't know. I am the man who loves you, who has always loved you. And Sissy is the child we care for. For a long time the two of us were nothing, and now we are something again. She has been touched by that absence. We both have. She is raw. I try to look after her, to keep her in check. She is our child, Priscilla. We have always treated her as that."

He does that, calls her Priscilla. She notices every time he does it.

Now, she looks across the encampment to where Sissy plays a ball game with Michael.

Her daughter.

427

She shudders, and feels guilty. She wants to wrap the child in her arms but at the same time she wants to run a million miles.

TISH HOPES YOUNG Ferdinand would find peace in his new life, whenever and wherever he is reborn.

Earlier today, walking, Tish, Noah and Sissy at the front, and their ragged band of followers, now numbering some twenty-four, doing as their role demanded: following.

Noah and Sissy accumulated followers. It was their nature. People they encountered, people with a sharp enough sense of perception, of distinction, were always able to detect the special nature of man and child, their divinity, the fact that they had been touched by the Accord.

They wanted to be with them.

They wanted to share.

They wanted to give.

Blind to herself, Tish had first seen the weakness in others. In Maggie and Li, who had joined the group late, she had first seen the addict look in the eye, the transformation of devotion into something physical, something living. They each of them carried a cancer, and that cancer was Noah and Sissy.

Ferdinand had been one of the first to join. Tish, Noah, Sissy, and three or four others had stayed the night in a grand ranch house somewhere a few days to the north-west of Daguerre. The welcome was warm – as welcomes for Noah tended to be – and the seventeen-year-old son of the owner had been cute, and, instantly, devoted.

Ferdinand had come with them. Told his parents he was guiding them to the river-crossing and just carried on with them, and then they'd had to speed up a bit, hitching a ride on a goods wagon, because their welcome at that ranch would never be as warm again.

Ferdinand became Sissy's favourite. She played games with him, told him stories, and insisted he told her some in return.

Ferdinand went from fresh-faced disciple to hollowed devotee to shuffling, skeletal wreck in only twenty or so days.

It happened among them – it was happening to all of them, only at a slower rate – and yet it had taken far too long for Tish to notice. In the worlds of the Diaspora suffering had long since been banished. It was not even something readily recognised, like a language newly encountered. There was a whole new syntax of suffering for them to learn.

"What is she? I don't know..."

I look at you, Priscilla, see the ache within you, the hurt. These people around us... it is as if we can never let anyone close, for fear of what they must become. We drain them. Sissy drains them. She is an open wound in the fabric of the Accord. She pulls apart all that is around her.

"She is our child, Priscilla. She needs protection. That is what I do. I protect her, I try to shield her from the world, and the world from her. It's like flying: I wish to fly and I fly, but once I am up there it is only the air and a few feathers that prevent me from plummeting. It is like that with Sissy...

"You are strong, Priscilla. So much stronger than the others." Suddenly I feel tears pooling. "You don't know how hard this is... You hold me together. You are my air, my feathers. Without you... well, I don't know what would *be* without you, how long I could continue."

She was growing weak. Had been growing weak.

But not as rapidly as Ferdinand.

She came upon them early that morning, when the sun was still heavy over the mountains, painting them gold and pink.

Sissy was sitting by him, holding his hand between hers.

Tish almost turned away.

For a moment she closed her eyes and she opened them just as Ferdinand started to vanish.

She watched. She could see through him. See the stones, the thorn bush, the tussock grass.

Things blurred. Things dissolved, melted, slipped away from this existence.

He was gone.

Sissy was looking up at her, her expression startled as if she did not know what had happened, had not expected it to happen; but beneath the surprise there was satisfaction, a thrill of pleasure, of strength, and the first hint of a smile.

"YOUR AIR, YOUR feathers... so poetic. If you weren't so sincere I'd say you had the crassest line in smooth-talk..."

We have her. We have him. We see him through the eyes of Tish Goldenhawk, as she calls herself in this life.

How strange, to see the world through her eyes! To be inside her head and yet not. We look at him, at his dark eyes, his thin face, full lips, that half-smile he gives so often. We see him through her eyes and yet we do not know what she sees.

We debate, as he moves out of view. Act now, using Priscilla as proxy, or attend in body, allowing a short interval in which he might detect our approach and take evasive action? We do not know how much his powers have grown.

We split... Phase in, phase out...

Chuckboy takes the proxy, turns her head so that Barakh is in our field of view again. I phase in, out, open a channel through the consensus, step through.

There is momentary disorientation and then I am standing on a plain, surrounded by cacti and thorn bushes and oddly balanced round boulders.

The two of them are there, locked in conflict. A short distance away there is an encampment of bubble tents and track trikes. The people there look on, too damaged to stir.

She has him locked in the beam. She stands, knees slightly bent, body tipped forward, one arm stretched out, palm first, fingers straight, and a beam of white light lances from her hand to Barakh.

He stands there smiling.

He looks at us, as we materialise, although he should not be able to turn his head at all.

He raises a hand so that he mirrors Priscilla's stance and his palm cuts out the beam, reflects it.

It shines on her face and she crumples, sobbing, more damaged than she had been before. I feel it as a pain, deep in my chest, as Chuckboy rushes back in, shattered by the encounter.

"Your time is up, Professor Barakh," I tell him. Deep within, Chuckboy cowers. I wonder how damaged he is. Fuck, but I *need* him now!

I remember, countless years before. We destroyed Barakh then. Annihilated him.

We step towards him, arms spread wide.

He looks as if he will run, or fight, but instead he just stands there, says...


"How long, Jack? How long must this go on?"

He is only a few paces from me now. You are off to the side, Priscilla, on your knees, still recovering. Somewhere over in the encampment, Sissy is out of sight. I hope she is not aware of this. I hope she will be safe. I hope the world will be safe from her.

I am tired. Tired of running, of being pursued.

I have found you, Priscilla. All I wanted was to find you.

I look into Burnham's eyes, marvel at how hatred can last so many hundreds of years.

He is close, arms wide.

He takes me into his embrace and I feel a sudden sense of incursion, of invasion, of infiltration.

Torn apart.

The fabric of self.

Self stripped away, molecule by molecule, bit by bit.

The world thins around me.

I look at you, one more time.

I will return.

In ten or a thousand years, I will return.

And I will find you, my love. I will find a you that can love me again.

## 2.21

WE STAY ON in Penhellion, visit the bars on Fandango Way, low down by the sea.

Priscilla has gone from here, but we have our agents, scattered throughout this world. We will find her.

We will find him.

And then when we find him, we will destroy him. And if he ever returns at some distant point in the future, we will track him down and destroy him again.

For now, though, we drink imported wine and watch the sun setting over the bay, the light different from moment to moment.

Around us, people drink, talk, laugh. We wonder at their myriad lives.

We wish we'd brought a Sissy with us, or a Maybelle or a Lu.

We drink more wine, and later head out onto the Way.

The place is seething, drinkers weaving from bar to bar, streetsellers crying aloud, strollers and party-goers and lairy youths who could each have been 300 years old.

Out here, somewhere, we will find a Sissy. We always will do.

BLEARY-EYED, MUZZY-headed, we wake. Data flashes. He has been found. All three of them: Noah, Priscilla, and Sissy. Out somewhere in the middle of nowhere a couple of hundred klicks north of Daguerre.

433

Finally... How long has it been? How close have we come before?

Now we have him.

We phase in... phase out.

We stand on a slight rise, the landscape scattered with oddly asymmetrical, rounded boulders, balanced precariously. Scrub grows round about, and various cacti-like structures.

At the foot of the slope there is an encampment of bubble tents and trikes, people gathered around a fire, someone playing a guitar.

We look to the left and there, by a tree, almost lost in the shadows of dusk, we see the two of them. Priscilla and Noah are talking, standing apart, almost awkward.

We approach them, wonder how long it will be before one of them sees us, or hears our footsteps on the dry dirt slope.


"Your air, your feathers... so poetic. If you weren't so sincere I'd say you had the crassest line in smooth-talk..."

Tish doesn't know where she is heading, what she wants. She feels the pull, but she is not sure what kind of pull it is. She is all too aware of the draining, leeching magnetism these two exude. She wants it to be more. She is not sure. Maybe she wants it to be less, to be something she can turn away from and return to her secure life with Milton and the bar.

"Priscilla..." he says. "Priscilla, I love you. I lived my life in fear that I would never again find you. Now I live in fear that the you I have found is a you who cannot love me, a you who has forgotten how to love me. That this is an Accord where we can never be together again."

Right then, she wants to love him, but still she does not know how to separate the needs and compulsions and weaknesses within. She does not know.

She does not *know*.

Just then she hears a sound, senses someone nearby. She turns, expecting it to be Sissy, but it is the man from the bar, the man who is pursuing Noah.

He stands a short distance away, poised as if ready to act.

He addresses her first, to her surprise.

"Priscilla?" he says. "Don't you know me? Have I changed so much that you don't know me any more?"

She stares. She does not know him.

"He is your husband," says Noah softly. "He wants to kill me again because I love you."

She looks into the stranger's eyes. Her husband's eyes. She does not know him.

He has changed; she has changed.

She is staggered and appalled that she can be the focus of a love that inspires such intense hatred over so many years.

She shakes her head.

"You haven't come to kill him, have you?" she says. He looks lost. She understands. He has lived for this moment and now that it is here he is not ready for what comes next. He does not know what to do, what his life will be after this moment.

"Ella!" A voice... Sissy.

The girl is running towards them, must have realised that something strange is happening.

Tish looks at her husband again.

He has seen Sissy, and now he looks even more lost.

Sissy rushes into Tish's arms. The child stares at the newcomer. Tish can feel something between them, a current, a force.

The man twitches, as if about to do something, and then... he drops to his knees.

He looks at Noah, speaks, says, "Barakh..." He clutches the sides of his head as if trying to wrench his skull from his body. "Help me, Barakh. Will you fucking *help* me?"

Tish pulls Sissy closer, and Noah drops to his knees, mirroring the man's pose.

He reaches out, puts a hand on the man's forearm, calms him. "How can I help you?" he asks.

The man peers at him, tears streaming down his cheeks.

"Save me," he says, through strangled sobs. "Save me from this. Remix me. You can do it. If anyone can do it, you can. Remix me. Edit me. Take this... this *pain* away. Take Chuckboy out of me." Then he turns his stained face towards Tish. "Stop me loving her..."

Now Tish feels sick, feels stunned, confused.

She looks at the man, sobbing freely now, and realises she does not even know his name.

## 2.22

"ELLA!" A VOICE… Sissy.

The girl is running towards us, must have realised that something strange is happening. As she approaches and sees the newcomer, she hesitates, slows, comes to a standstill, looking from him, to you, to me, and then back again.

I watch Burnham, or whatever it is that Burnham has become after all these years.

When he first saw Sissy, he had faltered, but now he straightens, as if he has found new resolve.

Sissy runs, rushes into my arms. The child stares at Burnham.

I feel as if I am trying to restrain a nova. The air writhes with the forces gathered around Sissy, the fabric of the Accord twisting and pulling apart, pulling back together again. At any moment, it feels as if the world might tear apart around us, around this child, this raw anomaly that is Sissy. I try to counter it, try to heal, as I have healed so often, so many. I feel Sissy calming.

"No," Burnham says, addressing your question of only a few seconds before. "You're right. I haven't come to kill him. I've come to destroy him. I've come to finish the job I first did over nine hundred years ago."

With that, Burnham opens his arms wide.

I could fight. I could run. But no, this is not the time for that. I have found you, my love, and I will find you again.

But as Burnham steps toward me Sissy suddenly yells, twists out of my arms, and hurls herself at him.

She hits him in the chest and he catches her in his embrace, staggers backwards, off-balance for a moment, then recovering.

She is wrapped around him and then... the world twists, changes around the two of them. The wild forces of Accord that had been Sissy's now enfold the two.

I step back, take your arm, and pull you with me, away from them.

Before us, darkness twists, weaves itself around Sissy and Burnham. The shape of the two collapses, folding in on itself, and then it unfurls, expands, and is gone. Nothing.

I hold you close.

Just the two of us, as day turns to night in a stony clearing in the middle of nowhere, and the fabric of the world becomes stable once again.

## 2.23

WE WALK, IN Daguerre, you and me by the sea on the long promenade.

We do not touch. We are uncertain of each other, of who we are and where we are going.

Pterosaurs swoop low over the waves, the silver-grey of their wing panels turned rainbow colours as they reflect the sky.

We took three days to get here, and we talked almost continually. Reminiscing, teasing memories from deep within your brain.

But still, we do not touch, we are uncertain.

"Tish," I say. You have decided to stick with your current name. I am trying to get used to it. We stop, face each other. You take my hands in yours.

"Noah." You smile. Such an awkward start, when we have spoken so much over the last few days. "One time, long ago, I loved you. I loved you dearly."

I look down. I feel the pain, anticipate it. I am the architect of Accord, the architect of Accords, but this is an instance of my heaven in which you cannot love me.

"I'm sorry, Noah," you say. "It's too much for me. So much has happened in such a short space of time. I can't handle it. I'm not ready for this, for us. I'm just not fucking ready…"

You are not crying. You will not cry. You are strong, Priscilla. You have always been strong.

I hold you in my arms.

You are not ready, but I will wait. I will always wait. In this heaven that I have built, we have all the time in the world.

# 2.22

WE WALK ON the long promenade.

We do not touch. We are uncertain of each other, of who we are and where we are going.

Pterosaurs swoop low over the waves, the silver-grey of their wing panels turned rainbow colours as they reflect the sky. I remember flying, I remember fooling with consensus so that I might grow wings and impress you.

"Priscilla," I say. We stop, face each other. You take my hands in yours.

"Noah." You smile. Such an awkward start, when we have spoken so much over the last few days.

You wait for me to continue.

I struggle to find the words, to explain the deep, aching fear that has gnawed away at me through every second of every day since I have found you again. I am the architect of Accord, the architect of Accords, but in this manifestation of my heaven are you a Priscilla who can love me, or one who cannot?

"You have lived and died many times," I tell you. "And each time you are reborn as a new you, a new instance of the person you are. I am scared, Priscilla. Scared that this is an instance of you who does not love me, who cannot come to love me, who—"

Your hand covers my mouth, presses so hard that I taste blood from my gums.

You shush me, say, "Noah, will you tell me one thing?"

I look at you, puzzled. I nod, and you take your hand away.

"Will you tell me how it is that a man can be so clever that he can invent a whole fucking universe – whole fucking *universes* if what you've told me is right? Will you tell me how it is that a man can be so sensitive that he takes an orphaned child into his care and nurtures and protects her without any question at all? How he can be so much in love that he pursues the woman he loves to the end of the universe? How he can be all these things, and yet he can be so fucking blind too?"

I open my mouth to speak, but realise I do not know how to answer you.

"Will you tell me how it is that this fucking amazing human being can not just see what's plain before his eyes? I love you, Noah Barakh. A part of me always has. Every instance of me, no matter how buried that part of me has been. I can always love you, Noah. All of the mes can love you – you just need to find the right circumstances, the right timing."

I open my mouth again, but you cut me off.

"So will you just shut the fuck up?"

I look at you.

I smile.

I shut the fuck up.

## ABOUT THE AUTHOR

Keith Brooke's first novel appeared in 1990, and he has published four more adult novels, two collections, and over 60 short stories. Since 1997 he has run the web-based SF, fantasy and horror showcase Infinity Plus (*www.infinityplus.co.uk*), featuring the work of around 100 top genre authors. His most recent novel, *Genetopia*, was published by Pyr and received a starred review in the Publishers Weekly. Writing as Nick Gifford, his teen fiction is published by Puffin, with one novel optioned by Little Bird.

In this stunning new science fiction
series, it is the age of the Celestial
Empire, where the epic civilisations of
Imperial China and Mexica have taken
their ancient war into space.

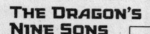

THE DRAGON'S
NINE SONS
A novel of the Celestial Empire

CHRIS ROBERSO

"A talented storyteller, he has a unique ear,
an eloquence all too rare in modern fiction
Michael Moorcock

THREE UNBROKEN
A novel of the Celestial Empire

CHRIS ROBERSON

"A talented storyteller, he has a unique ear, a clever eye,
an eloquence all too rare in modern fiction."
Michael Moorcock

UK: 978-1-84416-619-0
US: 978-1-84416-524-7

UK: 978-1-84416-707-4
US: 978-1-84416-596-4

 SOLARIS SCIENCE FICTION

# Guns. Battles.
# High-octane adventure.

## All in a day's work for this re-formed military unit...

A COMBAT-K NOVEL

**ANDY REMIC**
The new master of rock-hard military science fiction

**WAR MACHINE**

UK: 978-1-84416-616-9
US: 978-1-84416-591-9

A COMBAT-K NOVEL

**DY REMIC**
master of rock-hard military science fiction

**BIOHELL**

UK: 978-1-84416-650-3
US: 978-1-84416-590-2

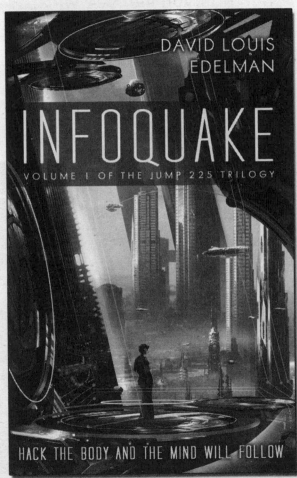